# Imogen's Quest

## John Campbell Rees

The TIMELESS Press

First published in the United Kingdom in 2018 by
The TIMELESS Press,
15, Stuart Street,
Treherbert,
Treorchy,
Rhondda Cynon Taff,
United Kingdom
CF42 5PR.

Also by John Campbell Rees
Winter Squad
Summertime Blue

For Rhian

**H**er parents looked so peaceful, as if they were in a deep sleep. They were dead, not slumbering, aboard their crashed spaceship. The extreme cold and absence of atmosphere on the frozen moon of a giant gas planet had preserved them perfectly for an unknown number of years.

'How the hell did it get in here, Dad?' asked one of the cosmonauts who had discovered the wreck. They had spent hours crawling through crevices, searching for the underground source of an electromagnetic anomaly playing havoc with radio transmissions.

'On this dirty snowball or in this cave, only the Angels know, son,' said the other cosmonaut. 'I doubt this was meant to be their final destination. The blessed Angels told our ancestors they would be isolated from other Human colony worlds because their ship had drifted so far from Human space.'

An alien race called the Aggelii had given an airless, frozen, rocky planet an atmosphere they could breathe. Then they had spotted a crippled Human ship approaching it. The Aggelii abandoned the planet and the solar system it belonged to, in favour of the Humans.

Aggelii had visited and taken samples from the Earth during its Stone Age. They had been the source of Angel myths on Earth. It was unsurprising the Humans believed they had been rescued not by winged aliens but by the Angels.

'Dragonshead, Sir. Your suit telemetry shows you have three and a half hours of air in your tanks,' said their mission controller, Jenny Hunter, using the Archduke's radio call sign. 'You should be commencing your return to Pendragon Central.'

'I think we will be back long before that, Control. Now we have the route mapped, we'll be back at the surface in forty minutes,'

Dragonshead replied. He and his son Earl Arturo, call sign Caliburn, had volunteered for this mission.

'I'll send a craft to rendezvous with you at the surface,' said Miss Hunter.

'Thank you, Control,' said the Archduke. 'We've found something that needs to be extracted with extreme care...'

Nobody heard the second sentence. It was drowned out by static. Which was odd, as that burst was early and had not originated here. Was his suit on the blink?

'Roger that, Dragonshead. I've switched to a secure channel. Please repeat the last statement,' she said.

Which explained the static, thought Dragonshead. No need to worry about my suit.

'I'm also dispatching a security drone for twenty-four-hour surveillance of that location,' Control said, continuing her message.

'Good idea,' said the Archduke, who had not given a thought to securing the site.

Jenny Hunter had been an undocumented eleven year old runaway serf when the Archduke's men raided the unlicenced space habitat she called home. She had been given a DNA scan to identify showed Jenny had an aristocratic father, but no clue of which great family he belonged to. Archduchess Doreen took Jenny under her wing, changing her life completely. On the Homeworld, Anseris, she would have been trained in courtly skills ready for marriage. Out on the High Frontier, she was sent to school, then college, in preparation for a successful career on Pendragon Central Station. Now Lady Jennifer and Earl Arturo were inseparable, which delighted Archduchess Doreen.

'Dragonshead, Sir,' said Jenny. 'In answer to Caliburn's question, it is likely that the ship you just discovered was buried in snow when it crashed. Its failed attempts to take off melted that snow, which instantly refroze forming an ice shell around the ship. Over the years it has become buried deeper and deeper.'

'How do you know it's a ship, Control?' he asked after a burst of genuine static that would have drowned out the voice as well as deafening an unprepared cosmonaut.

'From Caliburn's suit telemetry,' Jenny replied. 'His heart rate, adrenalin levels and breathing indicate he has won a lottery. Or in this case, discovered a starship with working hyperspace engines.'

'For centuries we turned our backs on technology,' said Caliburn, 'but Anserians remember we came from beyond the stars. By the grace of the Angels, soon we will be able to return to them.'

The first ruler of Anseris, Queen Kathyren Ellisford-Castle, had encouraged the amnesia about their arrival. Angels, the supernatural messengers of the Unknowable God, were worshipped on Anseris. Nearly every door frame was decorated with an angel plaque resting against a top corner. Everyone wore an avatar, an octagonal object mounted in a pendant with filigree wings. Even the two cosmonauts who discovered the crashed spaceship wore their avatars beneath their spacesuits.

'It's like nothing I've ever seen,' said Caliburn. 'Where in the twenty levels of hell are all the control panels? There's not a lever or a button on this ship. I switched off the distress signal causing the interference with an axe. Unfortunately, I also found the crew. They are both dead. Their life support systems failed.'

'So, two bodies for recovery and burial, Caliburn.'

'Angels preserve us. There's a baby in a suspension crib and it's still working. I can only see the face; don't know if it's a boy or a girl. The single display is registering five percent plus a battery icon. It's the only survivor.'

'Angel's wings!' said Jenny. 'Or rather, roger that, Caliburn.'

'That's OK, Jen, er, Control,' said Caliburn. 'The child's system obviously needed less power than an adult's unit.'

'There's no rush with the child,' said Dragonshead. 'The parents were awake before they died. The suspension field failed, then instant asphyxiation followed. It is unlikely we will be able to switch that crib off without its instruction book. We'll just have to wait until the battery drains and she wakes up. Five percent power. It could be years.'

N obody had known what to do with the baby and its life support crib. There were no dials, buttons or switches on the device. No panels that might gain access to the system's mechanics. Although, this was beyond Anseris's mostly Twenty First Century technology, nobody could have operated the thing anyway. The only display visible was the slowly falling battery level.

The crib had been taken to Eliphaz Castle, the centre of power on Anseris and its solar system. At the time, Eliphaz Castle was preparing for the coronation of a new queen. So the second most powerful woman on the planet, Archduchess Sophie Rushton-Browne, took the crib to her home at Arlesdorf Castle. She was the first person to hear the child cry in an unknown number of years.

'Page, bring Doctor Gethin to the chamber immediately,' she said to a passing young man in royal livery.

'Yes, Your Grace,' he replied, bowing and running from the room. He and the other four pages at Arlesdorf Castle had been waiting for this moment for months. As had everyone else in Arlesdorf ever since the display had reached zero and begun flashing.

The old lady spotted another page. 'You, boy. Go and phone Eliphaz Castle. Use this number and inform Her Majesty that the child has awoken.'

'Shall I fetch the wet nurse, Your Grace, when I return?' the boy asked.

'Yes, Marion is fetching me a book from the library. Bring her to me before you phone the Queen.'

**You've not seen it from the air, have you, Marion?'** the old man asked the teenager sitting next to him. He was Archduke Balthazar Gregory Rushton-Browne of Arlesdorf, sixty-eighth Archduke of Castlegate and Prime Minister of the Kingdom of Anseris. She was Marion, his wife's Lady's Maid. Both were afraid of flying.

'No, Your Grace,' said the young woman, sitting by the window of the airship's gondola. She was trying to hide her terror. 'It doesn't look real. Like a toy.'

'Oh, it's the real Eliphaz Castle,' said the older woman next to Marion. 'Built close to the last resting place of prison ship KHM#89. A medieval castle, built to be the capital of a world returned to the Middle Ages.'

'Queen Kathyren didn't want to adapt the ship we all arrived aboard into a space station, to rule from orbit,' said Marion.

'Well, she could hardly run a world devoid of technology from a technological castle in the air,' said Archduchess Sophie. 'The spaceship was broken up, its structure and contents recycled. She would not be happy with this airship, or any of the gadgets you find on Anseris these days.'

The Archduke laughed and his belly shook. He was a short fat man with a bald head surrounded by a ring of grey hair, and a grey goatee beard.

'Queen Kathyren was overthrown eventually, by my ancestor Andrew Rushton-Browne,' said the Archduke.

'So that was his name,' said Marion. 'He is only ever called the Boatbuilder.'

'Because he built a boat to escape from his exile on the Lonely Islands of the Northern Ocean. Then built ships to carry his army.'

'Thank the Angels he overthrew the Immortal Empress, but Anseris remained unchanged for three hundred years after the revolution because so much knowledge had been lost,' said his matronly wife, Archduchess Sophie Yuliana Rushton-Browne. 'One day the Kingdom might have a ruler brave enough to abolish all the legally enforced anachronisms.'

The passengers and crew of the airship looked like they did not belong there. The women were in floor-length dresses, fitted kirtles, beneath looser surcotes. The men wore thick stockings and tunics of various lengths and styles. To signify her rank, Archduchess Sophie's surcote was trimmed with sable, as was her husband's tunic.

The Archduchess was pointing towards the impossibly tall and thin stone tower. It was a metal cylinder clad in stone. 'She cheated. The hull of her private quarters aboard KHM#89 was used to construct the Queen's Tower. It's said if anyone could get into it before the Queen killed them, or worse experimented on them first, they would find it chock-a-block with working technology, which is how she unnaturally extended her life.'

'Wow, Aunt Sophie, I can see the entire length of the Pass,' said Marion. On superstitious Anseris, nobody ever lingered on the subject of Queen Kathyren.

At the narrowest point of what Humans called the Rushton Mountains, the Aggelii had bulldozed a path straight through, taking the millions of tonnes of stone for use all over the planet. The Humans called it Angel's Pass, a major trade route, connecting the productive farmland of the north to the pastures of the south.

'Well, Ellisford Castle was also built to guard the southern entrance to Angel's Pass. Sitting on that pimple of rock.' Then, changing the subject, the Archduke said, 'Oh, don't look so horrified. I'm not going to punish you. I know Sophie lets you call us aunt and uncle. She treats you more like a daughter than a maid. You've got aristocratic blood, haven't you?'

'Yes, Your Grace,' said Marion, 'and thank you. Aunt Sophie says my life is about to change.'

'Don't you mean Uncle Balthazar? Although, we had better maintain the secrecy until your family finds out about you.'

The airship landed at an airfield two miles from the Castle. The passengers transferred to a carriage pulled by four black stallions. Motor vehicles were barred from the Castle Precincts.

Marion was carrying the child, who slept as the carriage clattered across one of the covered bridges over the moat and between concentric curtain walls into the Outer Bailey, five square miles of the most secure real estate on the planet, surrounding the knoll with the Inner Bailey on top. The Middle Bailey, a fortified stockade, sat at the western side of the knoll. Anseris had initially been a prison planet, the Middle Bailey its high-security wing. Now it was home to the lowest level of Anserian society, the serfs. It was where Marion had been born and hoped she would never return.

What shall we do with her?' asked Queen Gertrude III, ruler of the planet Anseris, its space habitats and lunar settlements. The Queen, a tall, willowy woman had rich strawberry-blonde hair which was the same colour as her crown. She was sitting in Archduchess Sophie's drawing room in the Royal Apartments, watching as the older woman rocked the infant to sleep.

'Poor little mite. All alone in the galaxy,' said Aunt Sophie. The matronly Archduchess was the Queen's aunt. Only ten years separated the two women, but it looked more like forty.

'According to the documents aboard the ship, her parents were Fenzrian Defectors, looking for a place to live and bring up this child somewhere in the Confederation of Human Worlds.'

'A confederation of worlds inhabited by Humans,' said the Archduchess. 'What a wonderful idea, dear.'

Queen Gertrude knew her aunt found it hard to be formal at all times, especially in private, as protocol demanded.

'Aunt, you know you are supposed to address me as Your Majesty or Ma'am.'

'Oh, for goodness' sake, girl. We are in private,' the Archduchess replied, with emphasis on the word private.

'Even in private,' said Queen Gertrude snappily.

'In private we can let our hair down. Who would know?'

'I would, Archduchess Sophie Yuliana Rushton-Browne of Arlesdorf, Consort of Castlegate,' said the Queen.

'More fool you, then. You sound like my idiot nephew. He insists on using his full name and title. I just answer to Lady Sophie. Anyway, her parents seem to have named her Anira. What a funny name. We shall call her Anita,' the Archduchess said, unaware "Anira" was the Fenzrian word for child. 'It looks as if they were not ready for her either. They had none of the equipment needed so they popped her into suspension as soon as she was born.'

'How sad,' said the Queen. 'It's been suggested they were hiding from their former compatriots when their poky little ship crashed. They put themselves in cryogenic suspension, hoping for a rescue that never came.'

The baby began crying. Loud inconsolable sobs that only a baby can make.

'Hush there, dear,' the Archduchess said to the child, then turned to her niece. 'Babies can understand more than we give them credit for.'

'Oh, nonsense, Aunt Sophie,' replied Queen Gertrude. 'She has probably done something disgusting.'

'No, I don't think she's made a friend in her nappy.' Aunt Sophie rang a bell, and the wet nurse came running.

'It's still making a noise. Has it done something disgusting, or is it just hungry?' asked the Queen.

'She's merely hungry. I shall go and feed her,' said the wet nurse as she picked the baby up. Then she said to the Archduchess, 'You haven't told her yet, have you?'

'Don't worry, Marion, I'm about to.'

'Aunt Sophie!' said the exasperated girl in barely a whisper before she hurried out.

'You never had children. How are you so good with babies?'

'I don't know, I just am,' her aunt replied. 'Practising for the child that never came.'

'Oh, I'm so sorry, Aunt Sophie.' Queen Gertrude instantly regretted what she had said. She had suffered two miscarriages since the death of her first child. She knew the pain her aunt sustained before giving up attempts to start a family.

'Not to worry, dear, I'll take care of this problem child. You have a Kingdom to run,' said the older woman. It had always been a

Kingdom, not a Queendom, despite never having a king. 'But take my advice. If you don't take a regular break from all that Majesty rubbish, you'll end up as mad as all your predecessors.'

'True, I'm very busy. But without what you call the Majesty rubbish there would be anarchy. And my mother was not mad.'

'My Granmama was as mad as a box of weasels, by the end. As was your dear Mamma.' A broad grin crossed Aunt Sophie's face. 'Anyway, I know a family on the Pendragon Station that'll take her.'

'One of the space habitats, Aunt?'

'Well, she was born in space, she will be more at home on the High Frontier. Thanks to the Archduke it's civilised again. Fortunately, they are still a lot less hidebound out there.'

'The Archduke and his son have been busy during the extra decade Anita slumbered. They employed the finest minds working flat out to reverse engineer her ship's hyperspace engines,' said Queen Gertrude. 'A recent successful flight went beyond the Anserian system. Soon the Kingdom will have ships capable of visiting other Human worlds.'

'In the meantime, I play Bridge with Archduke Penry's wife, Doreen. Their son Earl Arturo and wife Jennifer are taking young Anita. They already have a girl, one boy, with another one on its way. This child will have plenty of siblings.'

'Would that be Texas Hold 'Em or Five Card Stud Bridge, Aunt?' asked the Queen.

'Don't do sarcasm, dear,' replied her aunt. 'It doesn't suit you.'

Marion was reading a book Aunt Sophie had given her. '"Under Queen Kathyren, the Immortal Empress, everything on Anseris had reverted to the European Middle Ages."' Her hushed tones soothed baby Anita while she rocked her to sleep in the cradle. The Angels knew the book was dull enough to send anyone to sleep.

'"Society was stratified with no social mobility. The twenty operational departments aboard KHM#89 became Great Houses, each controlling sections of the planet. The head of a Great House became an Archduke, his eldest son became an Earl the others became Viscounts.

'"After the fall of the Immortal Empress and the establishment of the rule of the Free Queens, the Archdukes formed a body called the Witan to advise their new rulers. Its chairman, the Archduke of Castlegate, has regular meetings with the Queen, informing her of the Witan's decisions. The Archduchy of Castlegate belongs to House Rushton-Browne, making the sitting Archduke hereditary Prime Minister."'

This made Marion laugh out loud, which disturbed the baby. Fortunately, it only gurgled to itself before returning to its well-fed slumber.

'And Uncle Balthazar is the only Archduke with any influence with the Queen. The Witan is a toothless wonder, which she and all her predecessors ignore,' Marion said to the sleeping child, who neither agreed nor disagreed.

'"The aristocracy expanded into a second tier when the owners of nine colonies on the moons of gas giants and four major space habitats were given the aristocrats' rank of Baron by Queen Agatha III. The four Space Baronies have recently merged into the Jovian Grand Duchy. Everything else belonged to Space Archduchy of Pendragon, under the recently established House Thompson-Uther."

'Why hasn't Aunt Sophie summoned me back?' Marion asked herself. It had been a good twenty-five minutes now. Perhaps she should just walk in there. 'No, Aunt Sophie knows what she is doing. She'll summon me when the moment is right.' Marion picked up the book and continued reading.

'"The next layer of Anserian society is the gentry. They are descended from prison officers who had maintained order whilst the planet remained a penal colony. Counts controlled large estates for the Archdukes. Lords controlled districts for the Counts. Knights controlled manors for the Lords."'

Marion stopped reading and looked at the clock. More minutes had passed, and she was no closer to being called back into the room. The baby was stirring as if it knew the reading had stopped.

'"The third and largest layer of Anserian society are plebeians and peasants,"' said Marion as she stifled a yawn. '"Aboard the KHM#89, the Convict Settlers were prepared for their new lives while in cryogenic suspension; taught the skills they would require to survive, as they slept. The less severe the crime they had been convicted of, the higher their status would be. Minor male criminals were trained to be craftsmen like builders, carpenters, blacksmiths, brewers and all the other vital trades. Major male criminals were trained to be farm labourers. All the female convicts were trained in domestic skills fit for Women's Work."'

Marion would have cursed if the baby had not been in the room. 'Women's work. They mean subservience.' Marion had always resented the ingrained sexism of Anseris, but had been unable to say or do anything about it. 'They became subservient to men who were too stupid to realise their family income was automatically cut in half, creating poverty that kept their family dependent on the charity of the gentry.' She picked the book up and continued reading.

'"Upon arrival on Anseris, they were assigned to a stockade where they would serve their sentence. A group of stockades made a manor. Several manors made a district. Likewise several districts made a county, which was in turn part of an Archduchy.

'"The stockades became the villages, and as some male convicts finished their sentences they were granted parole or probation.

'"Well-behaved and successful skilled convicts received paroles, allowing them to move, with prison office approval, to any manor within their district. Their descendants became plebeian."'

'"Badly behaved and unskilled convicts received probation, tying him to either village or manor, under the authority of that manor's prison officer. The convicts' descendants became the peasants.

'"In either case, this was not true freedom, as they could not leave the Archduchy they served their sentence in and needed permission for any major changes to their life."

'Yes, the prison guards who became the gentry – who bully anyone beneath them and crawl for anyone above them.'

This book was annoying Marion. Why had Aunt Sophie, who had some pretty radical ideas for an aristocrat, given it to her and insist she read it?

'"The lowest level of society are the Serfs, in perpetual penal servitude. They are descended from the worse category of prisoners. The mass murderers, multiple rapists and the generally depraved. They were not sent out to colonise the wilderness. With no power tools or heavy-lifting machinery, they constructed Ellisford Castle. Their fortified barracks became the Middle Bailey at the foot of the knoll. Everything in their lives was grey, including their clothes.'

Don't I know it, thought Marion. Her green and yellow outfit, like all her gowns, was decorated with her mistress' seal, a special dispensation. Without it, Marion would be flogged for wearing colours. But she would not need the dispensation for her colourful wardrobe much longer. Marion decided to finish the chapter and go back into the room. Aunt Sophie had obviously forgotten.

'"Under the Free Queens, social mobility became possible. They had encouraged the growth of towns by issuing them with charters, releasing the inhabitants from feudal obligations. Towns were supposed to be classless, inhabited by urban plebeians. Sadly, in a world addicted to hierarchies, an unofficial three-tier system soon emerged. The Guildsmen, the Craftsmen and the Labourers."'

'**J** hoped that the presence of a child might make you broody; and try to produce an heir again,' said the Archduchess, turning the conversation to the topic of children.

Part drunk cups of tea were cooling on the table. Crumbs that had once been sandwiches sat on dainty china plates. The temperature in room also cooled.

'Aunt, you know as well as I do, David is far too ill to father a child,' said the Queen.

Prince Regent David had broken his back jousting. Paralysed from the waist down and had lost the will to live.

'And you, my dear Gertrude, don't need him for this royal duty,' said her aunt. 'All you have to do is get in the mood, and nine months later, a beautiful baby girl will pop out.'

Queen Gertrude and all the preceding queens of Anseris were identical. All cloned copies of Captain Catherine Wellingford, aka Queen Kathyren Ellisford-Castle, the first ruler of Anseris; or as the people called her, the Immortal Empress. During her unnaturally extended lives, these clones were raised in isolation by machines. Fed on a diet of plankton bread and bacterial broth prepared within the Tower. Nine months before these empty shell bodies became the next host of Queen Kathyren's mind, they would become pregnant with a cloned daughter who would replace them in the machine.

Five centuries earlier, the Boatbuilder's Revolution overthrew the Immortal Empress. Her next body was freed from the machines in the Queen's Tower. The shock of liberation and childbirth was too much for the unamed replacement. Her daughter was named Elizabeta who grew up into a fully formed individual who had been surrounded by people and other stimuli all her life. She was believed to be free of the malignant influence of Kathyren Ellisford-Castle, and so she was crowned as the first Free Queen of Anseris. She ruled an ignorant and superstitious world, one with no way of knowing Queen Elizabeta had a genetically engineered third ovary. It was no coincidence that her daughter, Queen Elienor was identical to her mother, as was her granddaughter Queen Charlotte I. No-one saw it as odd over the course of the next five centuries that the Queen's first child was always a girl who looked just like her mother even if her siblings did not, and then becoming Queen after her mother's death.

'I wish Mamma had never allowed that autopsy of Granmama. Then we would never have known about the third ovary. I hate the fact I'm not a normal woman,' said the Queen, without a trace of irony. 'People still get touchy about things connected to the Immortal Empress.'

'If we hadn't completely demonised the Immortal Empress, it wouldn't be such an embarrassment. The most secret of all State secrets,' said her aunt.

'Poor Amelia, she would be four now,' the Queen said. 'If my first daughter had lived, I would not have had two miscarriages while recovering from the same illness that took her. Maybe I would have had normal children to provide her with a siblings. Maybe two by now.'

'More than likely, dear,' said her aunt.

'Oh, my poor David. I told him he was too old for the lists. Since the jousting accident he no longer has the vigour necessary. 'A well-balanced child needs a father as well as a mother.' Producing an heir has to look natural even when it's not. As you said, people still get touchy about things connected to the Immortal Empress.'

'That is true,' said her aunt in agreement.

'Anyway, I am not ready to go through all that rigmarole just yet, even if he does recover.'

'Well do hurry up, I'm next in line should anything happen to you. Despite being suitably gifted or cursed, I am now too old to carry a child to term.'

'And that would look terribly unnatural, Aunt.'

'It would indeed, dear,' replied the Archduchess. 'Fortunately, I have finally found your illegitimate half-sister.'

'She is also cursed?' asked the Queen.

'Yes dear. We have no idea how it works, but as soon as she comes into daily contact with you, the heat will be off me.'

'So who and where is my mysterious half-sister?'

'All in good time, dear, all in good time.'

'Oh, Aunt Sophie, you nearly had me fooled. You're no closer to finding the mythical missing sister as you ever were.'

'If you say so, dear.'

'Perhaps we should roast some of those blessed royal geese at a Jubilee banquet?' asked the Queen. 'They were Kathyren Ellisford-Castle's earliest creation. They reproduce without the need of a gander, so they would soon make up their numbers. I believe the Royal Goose Maiden's original purpose was to stop anyone seeing the inside of those eggs.'

'There would be uproar, dear. The goose is the symbol of Anseris. Its name comes from an ancient word for goose,' said her Aunt. 'And knowing Queen Kathyren's psychopathic quirks, they are probably completely poisonous.'

'Don't worry, that is not how I plan on celebrating my Jubilee, Aunt Sophie.'

'So, what do you plan to do to celebrate your upcoming Jubilee? Baby Anita arrived in her icebox just before your coronation. Ten years as Queen. That must be worth a party.'

Lady Sophie was ready for her big revelation, but Marion was taking longer with Anita than she had expected. She would have to be here so she could witness her half-sister discovering the truth.

'Clothes!' said the Queen.

'What about them?' her Aunt asked.

'They're so tedious,' said the Queen as she stood up. 'I'm wearing an outfit that would not be out of place on my granmama or her grandmama, all the way back to the building of Ellisford Castle.'

'You want to abolish the Clothing Regulations?'

'Yes, Aunt Sophie. Pendragon with its zero and low-gravity environments has always been exempt. So we start with the Jovian Baronies and the Guild Towns and Cities here on Anseris. We will keep all the definitions of traditional garb as it is part of our heritage, but leave the choice of whether to wear it up to the individual.'

'And the Sumptuary Laws as well?' asked Aunt Sophie. 'Who can wear what fabric and when?'

'Yes. Why should who your father is be used to regulate what fabrics you can wear?'

'My nephew and his cronies won't like that.'

'Well, tough. I'm an absolute feudal monarch who wants to dump the feudal. Of course the feudal lords will object.'

'Although, not the absolute part?' asked her aunt. 'That will annoy the radicals.'

'One step at a time. There has to be a grass root demand for democracy, with the mechanics of democracy to support it. Neither currently exist. I'm becoming more liberal as I grow older, but not that liberal. Maybe my daughter, can start that ball rolling.'

The Queen could not help but notice that her aunt was pacing between her chair and the door. 'So you approve of my changes? It's just you look a bit distracted.'

'Where's Marie-Ann? She wanted me to tell you. She should be here.'

'I really didn't like that girl,' said the Queen. 'As she left the room with the infant, she didn't bow or show any deference to me, and she was rude to you. You spoil her. She might not look it, but she is a serf. I shall punish her on her return if you cannot.'

'You won't, you know. Marion is a remarkable girl. Quite unlike anyone I have ever encountered. Widowed by fifteen'

'Well yes, that is sad, but she is still a serf,' said the Queen, who was growing concerned at how slowly her aunt was now shuffling as she walked.

'Gertrude, she is so much more than just a serf. She is your...'

Archduchess Sophie never got to finish that sentence. To Queen Gertrude's horror, the old woman collapsed onto her chair. A massive stroke hit her as she was drawing breath.

'Aunt Sophie, Aunt Sophie, can you hear me?' cried Queen Gertrude as she tried to administer first aid. But there was little she could do, apart from making the old lady comfortable.

arion walked into the room, hearing her aunt start to say something about her to the Queen, She watched in horror as the old lady slumped forwards.

'Ah, you girl. Go and fetch a doctor immediately,' the Queen said abruptly.

'Aunt Sophie. Don't die. Please don't die,' Marion mumbled. she asked, 'She didn't tell you, did she?' Marion asked the Queen.

'Didn't you hear me, girl? I ordered you to go fetch a doctor. Do not dare question me.'

'Yes, Your Majesty. Sorry,' Marion replied. 'But I fear she is dead, and there is nothing a doctor can do for her.'

Three days had past since Aunt Sophie's funeral. The old lady's grand plan had ground to a halt. Marion returned to the ranks of the serfs of Ellisford Castle. Dressed in a grey outfit, her fine clothes a thing of the past, she became invisible.

'Master Pheileydale, I really must speak to my master, the Archduke Rushton-Browne,' Marion said to the Castle's Chamberlain, her new day-to-day boss.

'It is important, Master Pheileydale. It is about my last orders from my late mistress.'

'All serfs within the walls of Ellisford Castle, regardless of owner, are answerable to me. It's a good job for him that I do not believe you. I will stop you wasting the Archduke's time.'

'But it is about the child,' said Marion, pleading.

'I told you to get back to work, you lying hussy. Your brat is in the nursery for other scum children.' The Chamberlain was an urban plebeian, a number of rungs above the serfs on the social ladder. He never let the serfs forget that.

'But I must see him, I must,' said Marion, in a desperate tone.

'Do as I say, or I'll have you flogged.'

'I'm following orders from someone higher than a jumped-up popping-jay like you.'

Marion didn't see the punch coming, but she felt it. She knew she would have a black eye for days after it. Pheileydale believed assaulting serfs was a perk of his job.

'I don't know what sort of cushy little holiday job you had with the Archduchess, but that is over now. You work, and you work hard. You are scum, descended from scum, and that brat of yours is also scum. You will never speak to me like that again.'

'You's a raving loony,' said a female serf after Marion had finished explaining how she came by the black eye.

'I am neither raving nor a lunatic,' replied Marion.

'Only a right nutter would call Pheileydale a popinjay; yous be just askin' for trouble, yous were,' the other serf continued.

'But I must see the Archduke, I must,' said Marion.

'He's legged it to a place named Arlesdorf, over in Castlegate, being his Archduchy and all. That's nearly two thousand miles from these parts, innit?'

'My home, one thousand, six hundred and eighty miles away. Arlesdorf. I wish I was back there, away from this dump,' said Marion. 'I'll have to write to him.'

'Eh, so you can write now? Yous be just a serf, like I? Ain't no reading or writing for us lot, that's for sure. If yous is caught, Pheileydale'll be a-givin' yous ten whacks with his cane. Whoever showed you how to read and write is gonna get in a right old mess.'

'She's already received her divine rewards,' Marion said, but her workmate had gone into the next room. At the age of twelve, Marion had been sold to the Archduke's castle in Arlesdorf and married to a local serf. At thirteen she had been widowed and miscarried. That was when she thought the Archduchess had chosen her as her personal slave. Marion knew older aristocratic ladies, usually the childless ones, sometimes took serf girls and treated them like pets. It would be good while it lasted but then, the other serfs had said, the girl would disappear, sent to a new home far away, returning to a life of drudgery. It was apparent that the lessons in how to read letters and count with numbers were part of this. Marion remembered confronting the old lady.

'You'll have I whipped, Ma'am,' said Marion, 'but I don't fancy being yous pet. I'd sooner never know the taste o' life 'yond the Grey than be a-given a taste and have it all took away from I.'

'Accent and grammar, my dear,' said the old lady calmly. 'No, I'm not going to have you whipped, Marion my dear. You are more than a pet.' Then came the bombshell. 'You'll have to speak properly at Court when I introduce you as my niece.'

'I'm a serf. I can't be of royal blood, so I can't be your niece.'

'No, but you're an aristocrat. Your DNA proves it. When I first saw you, it struck me how much you looked like my mother, your grandmother. I obtained your genetic profile and I noticed it had been defaced. Another girl's results had been inelegantly cut and pasted into your records. Data and results didn't match,' said the old lady, obviously angry. 'It fooled my Chamberlain who has no knowledge of Genetics, but I could see it was wrong. So I had the data re-analysed and compared to my DNA profile. There is no doubt, my brother Prince-Consort Ruben was your father.'

'That makes us family, can I call you Aunt Sophie?' Marion asked politely in an aristocratic accent.

'Of course, I am your Aunt. Although, as your Aristocratic Patroness you would call me aunt even if we weren't related. That would be my legal status.'

'But Aunt Sophie, if Prince Ruben was my father then the Queen is my sister,' said Marion, still getting used to the familiarity.

'Well, half-sister, Princess Marion,' said the older woman. This was one revelation too many, and Marion burst into tears.

'Don't cry, Marion dear, it's only the shock. Soon your old life will be over.' The old lady had sat her down and showed her the evidence.

'And you shall be Princess Marion.'

'So, the Queen is my half-sister,' said the still shocked girl, 'and I shall be Princess Marie-Anne, double-barrelled. I have a new life that deserves a new name.'

At fifteen everything changed again. Baby Anita had arrived and had been weaved into the grand design. After injection of Angels only knew what, Marion had started lactating, becoming the child's wet nurse.

'So, Marie-Anne my dear,' said Aunt Sophie, 'you shall take her out to her new home on Pendragon Central Station.'

'What then, Aunt?' Marie-Anne asked the older woman.

'After you've left, I'll tell your half-sister the truth. You'll be summoned back to Eliphaz Castle, to start your new life as in the Royal Family. For you, things have taken a turn for the better.'

'That's all very well, but why can't you just tell her now?'

'Oh don't worry, Marie-Anne, I'm as tough as old boots. And if anything does happen to me, your Uncle Balthazar will carry out my plans.'

'Too much risk, Aunt Sophie, and too much complication.'

'Oh very well, Marie-Anne, dear. I'm due to take tea with Gertrude this afternoon. She wants to see the child. You will come with me. I'll introduce you to your half-sister after she has seen the child. Now don't worry, everything is going to be all right.'

Except everything had not been all right. Aunt Sophie had died and her office sealed. Everyone thought Anita was Marion's baby. Things had taken a turn, but for the worse.


'Oi! Nutter! If yous not a-wantin' I to give yous other eye a smack, yew'd best quit yous dawdlin' and daydreamin',' said her colleague. 'An' 'nother thing, me hansome. You wanna stop a-tryin' ter gab like a Ristoze. It might be all the rage in that Arlesdorf spot, but not here, see? Best get on with it, 'fore Master Pheileydale wallops it out o' yous'

Marion should have realised the aristocratic twang had become her default way of speaking. She would have to change that quickly, now she was back in the grey gutter. Aunt Sophie had told her the accents of Anseris were the result of languages naturally evolving over time. The final generation crewmembers who arrived on Anseris spoke a different language from the thousands of passengers in cryogenic suspension when they awoke. The old lady had said, like the invading Saxon overlords speaking French when the Norman peasantry retained English; or was it the other way around? The gentry developed a third language, an amalgam of the two. Marion pointed out everyone spoke the same language now. This, she was told, was a product of the revolution. Angerlish, or English from the angry twentieth century, was introduced. However, each social group continued to use the accent of their old languages. This suited the Free Queens, who liked the variety of dialects making class and status instantly apparent.

Marion, had a good ear for music, quickly picked up not just the aristocratic accent, but all the others as well. Her ability to switch had entertained the old lady.

here was no privacy in the Middle Bailey. Soon everyone knew the stories Marion told her child. Serfs are conditioned from birth to never lie, so she must be crazy. The started calling her Mad Marion.

The completely sane Marion had watched her half-sister's descent into madness from the Middle Bailey. Nobody dared question the increasingly unstable Queen, an absolute ruler.

Marion gave up hope that Aunt Sophie's private rooms, locked and barred under the Queen's Seal, would ever be re-opened. Her hard work and good behaviour saw her rise to the rank of Junior Housekeeper, a position which serfs rarely attained. It meant that she had her own hovel in the Middle Bailey, which she shared with Anita.

When Queen Gertrude became pregnant, there had been uproar at Court. Her husband, Prince-Consort David, was not cold in his grave when Queen Gertrude gave birth to a baby girl two weeks before Anita's second birthday. Her sanity restored, the Queen named the girl Louise Imogen. Marion knew that Queen Gertrude did not need a husband or a virile young lover to do the deed. Her Aunt Sophie had told her the secret of the Queens of Anseris. Like the secret of the seven magpies of Ancient Earth, it was one never to be told.

At ten, Princess Louise was tall for her age. A classically pretty girl. Wavy strawberry-blonde hair framed her long face and narrow features perfectly. She shared her classroom with Lady Anita. She was just under two years older than the Princess, but she was shorter and her black hair in lanky braids made her look much younger. The two girls were dressed like wealthy children of a wealthy fourteenth-century Florentine merchant. This classroom was not in Florence, Italy, nor on Earth. This was 16th February, 5768, fifteen hundred and twenty-seven years since the planet Anseris was first settled.

'"Roughly two hundred thousand years ago,"' intoned the teacher, '"Anatomically Modern Humans, the sub-species Homo Sapiens Sapiens, emerged on the planet Earth then it spread into every inhabitable and uninhabitable nook and cranny on the surface of its Home-world."'

Princess Louise and her companion Lady Anita had heard the start of this lecture many times. For one reason or another, Tutor Altdorf never got further than the opening paragraph of his notes.

'"One planet was never going to be enough for a species of creatures so voracious and capricious as Humans,"' continued the teacher. '"It burned through the resources of the Earth with a frightening speed, not realising the biosphere of the planet had been sequestering these noxious compounds away for aeons. With equally frightening arrogance, Humankind dumped their waste anywhere they could. They believed the Earth was a bottomless cesspit."' Then turning directly to his pupils, 'So, Princess Louise, can you continue?'

A knock on the door interrupted the lesson. A vinegary looking woman dressed in serf's grey walked in.

'Her Majesty wants to see the Princess,' she told the teacher. 'The other one has jobs to do.'

That was it, classes were over for the day. For the Princess, it would be an evening of luxury and play. For Anita, it was back to reality with a bump. The fine clothes would be hung up, along with her mock title. She would change into the same grey garments as the messenger and go back to being Anita the serf again.

'Hurry up, girl, you haven't got all day,' said Master Pheileydale, he was still the Castle Chamberlain.

He knew everyone hated him, which was only fair as he hated everyone without fear or favour. He should have retired years ago, from a post handed down to son or grandson. But his wife had produced six daughters, who in turn had provided forty-two granddaughters. Thankfully, one of the granddaughters had just given birth to a healthy boy. Great-grandson was stretching a point, but the child would in time become Octavius Pheileydale, the new Chamberlain. Age had not mellowed Septimus Pheileydale. As far as the vinegary old man was concerned, the little brat was not growing fast enough. He was still a babe in arms.

'I'm going as fast as I can, Master Pheileydale,' said Anita as she tied a fillet around her forehead, and then pinned the long linen veil in place.

'I see no benefit in you receiving this schooling, girl. You'll never use it, and you have ideas above your station already. It's a good thing it is soon to end,' he said, casually slapping Anita's cheek as he did so. 'There is nothing like a pile of greasy pots to cure dreams of grandeur. Go report to Master Snakewood. He'll no doubt have enough crockery to keep you in your place until your twelfth birthday.'

'Good afternoon, Your Majesty,' said Princess Louise as she curtseyed to her mother.

'Imogen, dearest. Why on Anseris are you doing that here?' the Monarch asked her daughter. 'For your entire life you've known here in the Royal Apartments we can relax,' said Queen Gertrude, who had taken her late aunt's advice.

'Tutor Altdorf, said I must always show Dude References to the Queen, even if she is my Mamma. But what's a dude?'

'Yes, dear, I think you mean "Due. Deference",' said Queen Gertrude, emphasising where the split between the words should be. 'Other people must show us that, in public and in private. You should show it to me in public. When relaxing with our family here, to hell with protocol.' Then changing the subject, she asked, 'So what did you study today?'

'The usual. Maths, Angerlish and Music,' said Princess Louise as she started to smile, 'and he tried to give the lecture about the abandonment of Earth and the punishment by the Angels again. He never gets to finish it.'

'Yes, when the rest of the Human Race spread like a plague across this sector of the galaxy, overtaking the slow generation ship our ancestor was piloting with its cargo of convicts in cryogenic suspension.'

'Lady Anita says we must know the opening line of that lecture by heart, we have heard it so many times.'

'Yes, you're definitely getting too old for Tutor Altdorf. It is fortunate I have commissioned a new schoolroom and employed a band of teachers to take over your education.'

'Yes, Mamma, I'm looking forward to it. But it's such a shame Lady Anita Royal-Ward will not be able to join me after her birthday,' said the Princess. 'Nobody knows her real birthday, so everyone uses the date she came out of her cryo-crib.'

'But, Imogen, she's not really the Lady Anita Royal-Ward. I had the Foreign Girl fostered on one of Pendragon's habitats when she was a babe, somewhere she would feel at home. You're too old now to continue that little game. That girl is the daughter of one of the Castle serfs. Her forename is a coincidence. When she reaches her next birthday she'll be twelve, an adult amongst the serfs. She would not have time to divert from her duties.'

'But it's not a game, Mamma, she really is the Lady Anita, who never left the Castle. The only time she has been in space was when she arrived on Anseris.'

'Oh, don't be ridiculous, Imogen,' said Queen Gertrude.

'It's not. Lady Anita doesn't look like any of the other serfs.

They're all so skinny; Lady Anita is fat.'

'If you continue to defy me, Princess Louise Imogen, you shall go to your room until you decide to listen.'

'But, Mamma, I'm not defying you. I would never do that.' The child was close to tears.

No, thought Queen Gertrude. She is an unnaturally well-behaved child. Always willing to please, and do as she is told. Only once had Imogen been wilfully disobedient, and she had been in the right that day. Was she right again? The girl Anita was so unlike any other serf. With the seed of doubt planted, Queen Gertrude had to act.

'Very well, I'll check. If I'm wrong, then the Lady Anita will join us here in the Royal Apartments as our honoured guest. If I find you are lying, then I'll cancel your upcoming birthday party and send the girl far away.'

'Thank you, Your Majesty,' said Princess Louise as she curtseyed to her mother.

The Queen turned to her videophone. 'I wish to speak to Archduke Arturo Thompson-Uther on the Pendragon Station.'

'Yes, Your Majesty,' replied the operator.

A few minutes later, the Archduke appeared on the video screen.

'You wished to speak with me, Your Majesty?' he asked after bowing. 'Is it about the delegation from the Lambour? Their shuttle left for the Home-world an hour ago.'

'No, Archduke Thompson-Uther. I've been remiss in my duty towards our very first guest from beyond the stars. My aunt and uncle arranged for her to be cared for by yourself and your wife. How is she? I should have visited when I attended your father's funeral. She will be celebrating her twelfth birthday in a few weeks' time, won't she?'

The Archduke looked surprised. 'But, Your Majesty, the Foreign Girl never arrived.'

'Ma'am, after the death of your aunt, we assumed you had other plans for the girl.' The Queen noted that the new speaker, Archduchess Jennifer, like here husband, still wearing the traditional outfits from the recent diplomatic reception. The couple looked decidedly uncomfortable in the clothes rarely worn on Pendragon Station.

'It's probably for the best,' said the Archduke. 'Despite being raised to the aristocracy, we're still a bunch of space-rats out here. We've sent our oldest two kids down to Ellisford Castle to get some genteel polish.'

'I'm sorry to have disturbed you,' said the Queen. 'I'll have to have a word with my uncle.'

'Not at all, Your Majesty. It has been an honour to help you,' said a curtseying Archduchess.

'Good day, Archduke Arturo, Archduchess Jennifer,' said the Queen as she hung up and the faces faded from the screen. Queen Gertrude considered this information. Was Princess Louise right, again?

'Imogen, dearest, you have presented me with a prickly puzzle to solve. Go and play, while I try to solve it.'

'Yes, Mamma. Thank you, Mamma,' said the overjoyed Princess Louise as she headed to her room. She knew that soon she would have a friend to play with all day, not just in the hours they shared a classroom.

'Uncle Balthazar, what happened to the Foreign Girl?' asked Queen Gertrude. The two aristocrats were sitting in a large modern office like a pair of medieval ghosts. Her uncle was a busy man. As Archduke of Castlegate, he controlled the largest and most prosperous of the twenty planetary archduchies, in addition to being the hereditary Prime Minister.

'Foreign girl, Gertrude?' he asked with a note of confusion. 'Since making contact with the wider galactic community, many foreign girls from other worlds have visited Anseris.'

'The original. The baby found in the wreckage of her ship, Uncle. The one that gave us interstellar travel?'

Understanding dawned. 'That Foreign Girl. I've no idea. You know I delegated that problem to your aunt.'

'The trail goes cold with Aunt Sophie.' This was a conversation Queen Gertrude had hoped to avoid. Too many sad memories.

'It can't be that difficult to find the child?'

'So you would think, Uncle Balthazar, so you would think. She appears to have vanished completely and utterly.'

'Does it really matter, Gertrude?' asked the old man. 'You never cared what happened to the child all those years ago.'

'During my madness, Uncle. Grief drove my actions back then, not common sense.'

'Indeed it did. But that all ended with the birth of Princess Louise,' said the old man.

Having discovered her ancestor's method for moving from one host body to another, Queen Gertrude planned to steal the body of the clone-sister/daughter growing inside her. As the pregnancy progressed, Queen Gertrude began to doubt herself – was she really capable of being that evil?

'Once my beautiful baby girl was placed in my arms, all the wicked schemes I dreamt up returned to the dark places from whence they came.' For a second Queen Gertrude seemed distracted. She would never admit the digital ghost of Queen Kathyren had emerged from its hiding place and tried to trick her. 'It's Imogen who has caused this concern. She says that one of the Castle serfs is really the Foreign Girl.'

'If this serf girl turns out to be the Foreign Girl, what do we do then?'

'We owe her a huge debt of gratitude. She will move into the Royal Apartments, becoming my second daughter,' said Queen Gertrude.

'But, Gertrude, the fact is she has no real status here, or anywhere else in the galaxy.'

'No, that child and her late parents brought us a great gift. That gives her the status.'

'Not in the eyes of many aristocrats. Men like my nephew who regard interstellar travel as more of a curse than a blessing. I fear the day he becomes Archduke in my place.'

'True, but that will not be for years, Uncle Balthazar. Today our problem is finding the Foreign Girl.'

'Are you sure you want to do this, Uncle Balthazar?' the Queen asked. After days of searching for the Foreign Girl. The private rooms of Archduchess Sophie were the last places left to look.

'Yes, dear. I had Sophie's rooms locked and sealed after she died, then hared off to Arlesdorf. We had been so happy there.'

'Nobody has set foot in these rooms since. I placed them under the Royal Seal as a mark of respect to Aunt Sophie.'

'Then if there is any new information, it will be here. I have spoken to the serf girl, Anita, at length. She only remembers life here in the Castle and the stories her guardian told her.'

'Stories about her exotic birth, Uncle?'

'Yes.'

The key turned slowly, then the door creaked open. The seals had kept the environment stable. The rooms were almost pristine. Only the musty air gave away the time they had been unvisited.

'She always kept the most meticulous records,' said Queen Gertrude.

'Someone so absent-minded would have to,' Archduke Balthazar replied.

They spent hours searching in silence through the Archduchess's records. Seeing this place had triggered many memories, including her last conversation with Aunt Sophie. Something about an insolent servant.

'Here we go,' said the Archduke, snapping the Queen back to the present. 'Arrangements for the Foreign Girl to be fostered on Pendragon Central with Archduke Thompson-Uther's family. His son Earl Arturo and his daughter-in-law Countess Jennifer would have been her foster parents.' He handed the file to his niece. 'Thompson-Uther. Why is that name ringing a bell?'

'It's the surname of Arnold, the recently arrived page,' said the Queen, but it triggered no sparks of recognition. 'You must know him. Lady Marina's brother,' said the Queen.

'Oh him. Nice lad, wants to join the Space Corps when he is old enough, travel beyond this system into the wider galaxy. The boy must be cursing his dad for sending him here amongst all those cavalry cadets. He can't be getting many hours of flying time down here,' said the Archduke. 'His sister pretends to be just another vacuous aristocratic bimbo, but she is smarter than all her friends added together and multiplied by ten. Sophie played Poker with their grandmother.

'I know the Foreign Girl never arrived there,' said Queen Gertrude, amazed by the rush of information from her uncle once he'd remembered who Arnold was. 'His parents had no knowledge of what happened to the Foreign Girl when I spoke to them.'

'I sometimes wish I was that age again and could travel beyond the stars,' said the Archduke absent-mindedly.

'Hello, what's this?' asked Queen Gertrude as she read the label on a box-file. '"Gertrude's Sister". I don't have a sister. Aunt Sophie thought I might have one. She never found any proof either way. Oh, it's locked with Aunt Sophie's personal seal. Only you can open it now.'

'Here, let me.' The old man took a key from his belt and inserted it into the lock on the box-file. 'I remember Sophie was taking an unregistered aristocratic bastard she found amongst our serfs to meet her real family. I wonder what happened to her.'

'Oh my, I think I have just found out her fate,' said Queen Gertrude as she read the pages of evidence relating to her father's illegitimate child. 'Aunt Sophie, why didn't you tell me?'

'Oh Angels. You are the girl's real family. I agree, why didn't Sophie tell us?' asked her uncle.

'I believe she was trying to. I remember now. Her last words were "Gertrude, she is so much more than just a serf. She is your..." It all makes sense now. The girl Marion. The serf is indeed my sister. Oh, Uncle, I thought I only had one wrong to right. It now seems I have two.'

**P**rofessor Margo Giambattista, the temporary teacher, was giving the same lecture on Galactic History her sick friend had failed to complete so many times.

'"Humans used up the resources of our Home-world. Humanity spread out into the rest of the Solar System making a mess of Mars and the moons of Jupiter and Saturn as we went.

'"The rule of the Draconic League coincided with the coming of faster than light travel. Humanity found new homes amongst the nearby stars, promising it would not make the same mistakes again." Fat chance with the Dragons and their "use it up, wear it out and move it on" philosophy in charge. Soon our new worlds were as messed up as Ancient Earth.' Professor Giambattista's style was different from Tutor Altdorf's style. She had taught Economics at Baaden-Spitz University. She had recently joined the fledgeling Anserian Diplomatic Corps and she was currently covering for a sick friend before heading out into the galaxy.

'Yes, Lady Anita?'

'Ma'am, wasn't Anseris settled by a generation ship?'

'A hybrid sleeper/generation ship, but that is the subject of another lesson. Now, if I may continue.' Professor Giambattista would normally have let the lesson follow this new subject path for a few minutes before returning to her lesson plan. If the two girls had been older, she might have done the same. Today she was sticking rigidly to her old friend's notes.

'"A thousand years after our ancestors left Earth, the Human sphere of interest reached out to that of an alien race who possessed a civilisation older than Humanity. "'The Aggelii looked upon our species with growing horror. They had never expected us to survive long enough to venture beyond Earth. Humans were everything the aliens were not. The Aggelii lived in harmony with each other. War for them was abhorrent; they had not fought one for one hundred thousand years.

"'Yet no matter how much the alien cultures disapproved of Humans, they could not destroy them. Alien scholars studied Human history and decided the fall of the Zhou Dynasty in China and the end of the Etruscan Civilisation in Europe had been turning points. All that had followed started with the best of intentions but became steadily more destructive. So a congress of alien races decided to isolate the Human colony worlds from each other and then return them to the economic, social and technological level of the Iron Age, with the aliens acting as distant mentors.

"'A fleet of powerful alien crafts surrounded each Human colony world. In a day, all were cleansed of advanced technology. Their inhabitants were told to begin the rise back to interstellar civilisation again, without repeating the mistakes of their predecessors.

"'We now know it took two thousand years for Humankind to recover from this harsh punishment; that beyond Anseris there is the Confederation of Human Worlds, which we have applied to join.'"

There was a knock on the door. Instead of an impatient serf woman, a young royal page was waiting to collect Anita.

'I have been told to bring that one to the Archduke Rushton-Browne,' he informed the tutor.

'Oh very well, lad, off she goes. Your Highness, that is the end of the lesson for today.'

It might have been a new tutor, but it seemed the same old rules applied.


'𝕯o that again, Owen Snakewood, and you'll have more than a bloody nose!' shouted Anita, after striking the boy. For the past week, the obnoxious scullion had been becoming more and more insufferable. She should have been in the Royal Apartments, not washing dishes in the Keep's Grand Kitchen. Chamberlain Pheileydale insisted she catch up lost time from the previous week.

'You won't be able to complain when we're wed,' he said as he put a handkerchief to his nose. 'For 'tis a wife's duty to do whatever, whenever, her husband wants.'

'Us wed? I'd rather die.'

'Well, that is something else you have no choice on. It'll happen when you be twelve an' I be fifteen, whatever your mum says.'

'My guardian would never allow it,' said a horrified Anita. 'She has enough status to block such a union.'

A voice behind her said, 'I would not allow it, neither would the law. Her mother – and Marion is her mother regardless of the stories Marion tells – has no status.' Anita turned to see the old man standing in a doorway. 'Snakewood, you're a peasant, and Anita is a serf. The law prevents serfs from marrying non-serfs.' He casually clipped Owen around the ear for his stupidity. 'Anyway, enough of the idiot boy's fantasies. You've struck someone of a superior class. As Chamberlain, it is my job to discipline you.'

'I don't see any superior to me, even you!' Anita was struggling to control her temper.

'Even if you weren't a serf, as a female you are inferior to any man on this planet,' hissed the old misogynist. 'Now go to your quarters, while I decide upon your punishment.'

'I was on my way there anyway, to change into my finest dress. I have the rest of the day off, and I am invited to the Princess's birthday party.'

'You are not going anywhere. I will send a note to Her Majesty apologising for your absence, explaining you are ill. Now, do as I say.'

'I shall not be confined to my quarters. That oaf made an unwanted approach, I hate him!' screamed the serf girl, who then burst into tears.

The young man rapped sharply on the door, then he pushed it open when he heard the sound of a girl in obvious distress.

'Yes, what do you want?' asked the Chamberlain.

The boy Arnold Thompson-Uther had been on the wrong side of that old man since day one and doubted that today would improve the situation.

'That girl is wanted instantly by Her Majesty,' Arnold said, emboldened by his royal page's uniform.

'She's busy,' snapped the old man.

'Well, make her unbusy,' ordered Arnold. 'She was due at the Royal Apartments hours ago. How dare you defy the Queen by delaying Lady Anita.'

'Don't you speak to me like that, boy.'

'I shall speak to you however I like,' he said. 'Didn't you hear? The Queen herself demands the girl's presence. I carry the Queen's voice, which outranks a mere servant like you. As does the voice of Lady Anita here.'

'You'll learn to regret that, young Thompson-Uther,' said the Chamberlain as he headed for the door with Owen Snakewood scurrying after him.

'Lady Anita Royal-Ward, I am instructed to take you to Her Majesty, post haste.'

'Oh don't, only the Princess and Tutor Altdorf call me that, pretending I'm Ristoze,' said the girl, close to tears again.

'It's at the request of Her Royal Highness, Princess Louise Imogen, that Her Majesty Queen Gertrude summons you,' Arnold replied with a flourishing bow.

She curtseyed to the boy. 'Do I have time to change into my party outfit?'

'No, you are to come as you are, Lady Anita. I believe a new wardrobe of clothes has been acquired for you, as befits a lady of your status.' Arnold realised he had said too much. 'Please milady, try and act surprised.'

'Surprised about what?' she asked with a giggle.

'Thank you, milady.'

Their enforced isolation from the general gene pool had shaped the serfs. They were nearly all lanky, with light brown hair, grey eyes and buck teeth. Arnold knew they had always been treated as severely as rats. It struck him they were starting to look like them as well. He also knew every so often freaks were born. Freaks who did not fit the mould. So nobody thought there was anything unusual about this girl being a freak brunette daughter of a freak red-head mother. It was easier to accept than her actually being the Foreign Girl.

'You don't like being a royal page, do you?' asked the girl.

'You always have a face like thunder when you think no-one is looking. Not like the others, who always seem jovial and stupid.'

'I'm from a space habitat. Back home people would laugh at me. Girls wear this sort of thing,' said Arnold. The knee length tunic was narrow to the waist, then flared out to the hem around his thighs. Arnold could not believe how much he missed trousers. Beneath the tunic he wore braies, baggy one-size-fits-all drawstring underpants. Colourful leggings called hose were attached to the braies.

'And also, I resent my father for sending me here to be a page. I don't plan to be a Cavalry Officer until I inherit the Archduchy. I want to be a pilot. I'm not getting any flight hours down here.'

'Why did he do it then?' she asked.

'It's like my granddad used to say, aristocrats don't understand the making of money. They only understand the management of wealth inherited from their ancestors. He was born a peasant in a rural backwater. The aristocracy respected him as the policeman who had restored order to the High Frontier. When the upper class saw how well he managed old money, the wealth and property Granny inherited from her Archduke father, with none of the flash excesses of the nouveau riche, they accepted him into the Aristocratic Club. That is also why they accept my dad. He inherited the wealth of his parents. The fact that half of it came from Granddad's hard work in space means nothing.'

'So?' asked Anita, almost sorry she asked.

'So, if myself, my brother and sister go through the same social training as the other Archdukes' children, the last link to money from trade will be broken. The thing is, I don't want to break the link. Trade is in our family's blood.'

'I was born in space, but I can't remember anything about it,' the girl said.

'So I have heard.' He looked at her. 'Everyone in Court thought you had horns and a tail.'

'I'd hardly be missing if I did.' The girl laughed a pretty laugh. 'In the Middle Bailey nobody believed us. Serfs are patholagically truthful, so they said my "mother" is mad. Telling me crazy stories. I even started to believe the other serfs. Then yesterday and the day before, the Prime Minister himself wanted to see me. I had to tell him all the stories about myself on the first day and my guardian the next. Seems all her stories are true.'

Moving from one connected sub-basement to another they had left the Keep. The pair climbed the stone stairs into the boiler room of the Castle bath-house, where large copper boilers of heated water and laundry maids toiled away their days keeping the towels clean.

'Her Majesty was in a right state when she found out what had happened to you. Everyone will believe you from now on.' He bowed. 'So, you have an appointment with Bath-house Mistress Elsa, her bath-maids and a blue ribbon tub of hot water upstairs.'

'Oh, I know Mistress Elsa, I have been one of her bath-maids, changing the towels. She usually scolds me for being too slow.'

'I don't think she'll scold you any more. But don't be too long in the bath, you also have an appointment with the Queen.'

After a soak in a yellow ribbon tub, Arnold returned to his barracks to get ready for the birthday party. He also had to pick up a small and poorly wrapped package from his locker.

'What are you doing back here?' asked the duty Sergeant at Arms, a short fellow with bad breath.

'Getting ready for the birthday bash, Sarge.' He saluted. 'I'm representing my dad and the Archduchy at the event.'

Normally, as a royal page, he was expected to be always identifiable in his livery, even on his own time. All the clothes he had brought with him had been returned home. Today, the Royal Wardrobe had supplied a trad outfit in his family colours.

'Well, snap to it, lad,' said the Sergeant at Arms, who was wearing a similar uniform to the pages, except for his stripy hose. 'Pull the tunic down, then straighten the tabard.'

Arnold did as he was told, with a little too much force, pulling a golden button from the tunic. At home, he would have used a machine for this sort of simple repair. Here he had to do it by hand, which included threading a needle.

'It's nice to hear one of you lot complaining as you're doing something,' said the sergeant.

'Sorry, Sarge. I know I'm supposed to suffer in silence, stoically accepting every humiliation, to show that as an aristocrat I am above complaints.'

'What's that, lad?' asked the older man.

'It is what my colleagues have told me. I think that's a stupid attitude.' Arnold knew the Sergeant at Arms, a plebeian, rarely talked with the pages if he didn't have to.

'Well, Arnold, lad. It shows that they have completely missed the point and you haven't. You're supposed to moan and grumble like everyone else. This year is supposed to show them what life is like for plebeians and how to handle the unfairness of life that ordinary people encounter every day. Only a handful of them gets it. They are the Toffs as well as Ristoze. The ones who understand how the system really works grow up to be good bosses and fair-minded officers. You're the first boy, in the fifteen years I have been doing this job, to get it straight away. Which is why you're a Toff, lad.'

'Thank you, Sarge,' said Arnold, saluting as he left the barracks room. He knew ordinary people never used the word aristocrat and had never heard anyone use the word Toff. He liked it and decided that whatever happened, he would always act like a Toff.

Had Mistress Elsa really curtseyed when Anita entered the bath-house? Had she shown Anita to the biggest bathtub, filled with hot soapy water smelling of lavender, rosewater and almonds? One where Anita luxuriated for a full twenty minutes? Yes, yes and yes. This was so different from the communal shower all female Castle serfs took on a Monday evening. Here she had her own soft cake of soap and shampoo which smelt of lavender. When she had finished, she had dried herself in the luxurious towels she usually carried to and from the laundry in the basement. Now she was sitting in one of the fluffy bathrobes while Mistress Elsa herself prepared her hair.

'You have such lovely hair, Lady Anita,' said the older woman, 'straight and strong.'

'What a difference proper shampoo makes, Ma'am,' she replied politely. At least Mistress Elsa was speaking to her. Carys and

Esther, the two serf girls who had topped up the bath and brought her towels ignored her attempts at conversation. Only yesterday they had gossiped for hours and been scolded for wasting time. Now the scolding woman was plaiting Anita's hair. No curses were streaming from her mouth today.

'You're on your way up in the world, milady. Fine clothes and fine living. I've seen you only pulling a fine top layer over your grey kirtle for your lessons with the Princess. Then back to the grey,' Mistress Elsa said. 'Not anymore. It's fine clothes and good food for you now.'

There was no envy in the older woman's voice. Anita had to agree. Her new kirtle was in bright orange with a silky peach coloured surcote and a blue cotehardie. The most luxurious thing she had ever worn. Finally, to a silver circlet was pinned a chiffon oval veil over her clean and freshly plaited hair.

She studied her reflection in the mirror. Had she grown a few inches? No, she was standing up straight for the first time in years.

'You mustn't keep Her Majesty waiting, milady,' said Mistress Elsa, curtseying again at the mention of the Queen. 'There will be plenty of time to admire yourself in all your new fancy clothes in your new home in the Royal Apartments.'

Everyone knew more about her future than she did. After years of being treated like dirt she was now being treated like gold.

'Why is everyone suddenly being so nice to me, Mistress Elsa?' Anita asked.

'I really don't know, milady. Her Majesty will explain all.' She bobbed again. 'Now don't you go calling me "Ma'am" any more, nor that old fool Septimus Pheileydale "Sir", neither. You're not a serf nor never were one. You are going back up to where you always should have been.'

'But you're still mistress of this bath-house, and you have used your time and skills making me look so pretty. How am I supposed to show my appreciation?'

'There are ways the Toffs use. You will soon learn them if you don't become another Ristoze.'

'Oh, I'm under no illusions. I might get called Lady Anita, but I will still be a servant. Instead of "you, girl! Do this" or "you are ordered to do that", it will be "Anita dear, be a darling and do such and such" or "would you like to do this or that?"'

'Yes, polite requests you have no option to refuse,' said Mistress Elsa, nodding in agreement. 'Put up with the rubbish and enjoy the benefits.'

'Oh, I intend to,' she replied.

Mistress Elsa opened the door. 'Now, that handsome young gentleman page is here to take you to Her Majesty,' she continued, curtseying again. 'Watch and learn from him. He's a real Toff.'

My word, doesn't she scrub up well, thought Arnold, as Anita emerged into the corridor.

'M'lady, the Queen's Chambers are this way,' he said, bowing.

'It's all right, I have lived here all my life,' she replied, a grin spreading from ear to ear.

'So you know nothing about space, the galaxy beyond Anseris?' he asked.

'I'm afraid all I know about space is what I have learnt from other people.'

'I would love to travel amongst the stars,' said Arnold, 'but our merchant fleet is so small. We have little to offer.'

'I suppose that is why my parents were desperate to get here. To hide out in a backwater, but one so close to the Fenzrians they would never think to look here. Right under their noses.'

'Why were they afraid of their own people?' Arnold asked.

'They were dissidents and defectors,' replied the girl. 'We now know how the Fenzrians treat dissidents like my parents. I would suffer the same fate if I were captured by them, even though I have never seen the Fenzrian Asteroids.'

They had entered the Queen's sitting room, a comfortable affair, somewhere Her Majesty could relax. A trumpet sounded in the corridor, so Arnold and the girl stood then bowed respectfully as Queen Gertrude Ellisford-Castle entered the room.

'Anita, Anita, my dear child,' said Queen Gertrude, 'I badly wronged you.'

Yes you really have, thought Arnold, watching as the girl curtseyed to the Monarch.

'Oh do get up, my dear. Within the Royal Apartments we do not stand on ceremony,' continued Queen Gertrude.

Only with aristocrats, thought Arnold. All the lower orders still have to bow and scrape.

'Thank you, Arnold. And do sit, you are making the place look untidy.'

Arnold knew better than to sit down until Queen Gertrude sat in one of the comfortable chairs in the room. Her attention turned back to Anita. 'I assumed you had been happily fostered, as my late aunt had arranged, out on the Pendragon Central Station. With young Arnold's family, actually. I never dreamt you would be trapped here in my Castle, mistaken for a serf. The untimely death of my dear aunt had so many unforeseen consequences.' The Queen stopped when she realised the girl was still standing, like an obediant serf.'Do sit, my dear, next to me.'

He watched as Anita nervously sat next to Queen Gertrude. Fostered with his family? This girl should be another sister. One was bad enough.

'I'm not going to eat you, child,' said the Queen with her narrow-lipped smile.

'I'm sorry, Your Majesty. But I am still overwhelmed by the events of this morning.'

'As I said, we are relaxed in the Royal Apartments, as a Royal Ward you may call me Aunt Trudy.'

'Yes, Aunt Trudy.'

'So, you will be Princess Louise's Official Companion. She has requested one closer to her own age when Lady Marina goes home.'

Arnold had overheard Anita's conversation with the senior bath-maid. He noticed the wry smile that crossed the girl's face. Despite appearances, Anita was still a servant.

'And here she comes now,' added Queen Gertrude as her pretty daughter entered the room.

This is going to be interesting, Arnold thought. It's all very well having fun with a drab, watching her sitting uncomfortably in borrowed clothes, struggling with lessons. But how would the spoilt brat cope when she came face to face with the same girl, cleaned up and in her own finery?

'Oh Anita, my dear, you look so lovely.' The Princess embraced Anita like a genuine friend. 'We are going to have so much fun together.' Then realising who Anita was sitting with, she stopped and curtseyed. 'Your Majesty.'

Queen Gertrude smiled, and the girl continued.

'Mamma, can I show Anita her new rooms, all her new clothes and then go and play with her? We have so much to plan together.'

'Yes, Imogen dear. But remember, don't get too involved, you both have a party at 3pm,' said Queen Gertrude. 'Lady Anita, Imogen, you are dismissed. Go and have fun.'

'**I**mogen?' Anita asked as they left the room.

'It's what Mamma calls me, dear cousin.'

'But why? I know your full name is Louise-Imogen. Why doesn't she call you Louise, or rather Princess Louise, like everyone else?'

'Exactly. Everyone else does because it's my official name. Only family and close friends call me Imogen.'

'So do I call you Imogen now?'

'Of course. You're family now.'

**P**rincess Louise looked at the small and poorly wrapped box the boy was giving her. She had received so many large presents today, she really didn't know what to make of this tiny scrap.

'My sister, Lady Marina, told me to get you a gift,' said the boy.

The party was drawing to a close. Only Mother, dear Anita, who was struggling to come to terms with the opulence of her new life, and this boy Arnold were left in the room. Him giving her this little trinket was unexpected.

'I know Lady Marina. Is my companion who's about to return home,' Princess Louise said.

'Your Highness, she is seventeen years old, three years older than me. She is to attend Pendragon University.'

'She can be such a silly creature, only talking about boys and getting married with her silly friends. When she's alone with me she's a different person, so clever and entertaining. I shall miss her.' Then with the tactless wisdom of a child, she said, 'I can't imagine her recommending something this small.'

'You know my sister too well, Your Highness,' he said, 'this isn't the piece of large tasteless jewellery Marina recommended. I was carrying your mother's bags on a shopping trip. Her Majesty made a point of saying how much you'd like this.'

Princess Louise opened the box. It contained an avatar. This one had a dull metallic grey gem with three red inclusions. The dullness of the stone clouded the golden frame and feathery silver filigree in the wings. She put it on, and it appeared to disappear into the finery of her dress.

'Excuse me, Your Royal Highness,' said Arnold, as he lifted the avatar and removed a paper cover from the back of the stone.

Almost immediately, the stone began to clear, then sparkle different shades of blue, green and purple within the translucent white body. Finally, it developed a shiller, an internal glow.

'Pure Moonglow becomes attuned to something called the electrochemical field of its owner, Your Highness,' said the boy. 'Soon the only person for whom it will glow and sparkle will be you.'

Princess Louise considered this for a second, and against all protocol spread her arms around Arnold and gave him a big hug.

'Oh, Arnold, it's lovely. Thank you so much. I'll always wear it and treasure it above any diamond.'

'That's pretty,' said Queen Gertrude. 'Legend has it that Moonglow protects the wearer from evil spirits if it has little red flecks in it. The flecks are called "Drops of Loved One's Blood".'

'Look, Mamma, there are three drops of your blood in the gem.'

'Yes, dear,' said the Queen. 'Scientists call it aventurisation. Microscopic particles of metal looks like of drops of liquid in the crystal. May they hold my unceasing prayer to the Angels for your protection whenever you wear this avatar.'

A nita woke with a start. Had it all been a dream, she wondered. Am I back in the poky little room I share with my guardian? No, it was all true. She was in a luxurious bed with silky sheets and electric lighting, her belly still painfully full.

After the party, a carriage had taken them to Elizaburg for a night at the circus. Imogen had been disappointed that there were no clowns, trapeze artists or lion tamers at Gänsehals Circus. Her mother found this amusing, saying circus originally meant a round space. However, on her next birthday, the Queen had ordered a proper circus to be held there. Circus acts from around the Anserian system competed to perform at what rapidly became the highlight of the year.

Anita could not help but notice how different Queen Gertrude and Princess Louise were when they were in private together. The haughty air of royalty completely evaporated. It was sad that no-one else could see this face of the Royal Family. They were as much bound by all the silly rules and feudal responsibilities as any plebeian, tradesman, member of the gentry or aristocrat. What a funny world she lived on.

**S**he had been twenty six years old at her Cornonation. Twenty-eight when her short-lived first child had been born. Thirty-seven when she became a widow. And thirty-eight a single mother. Now at forty-eight, after five decades as an only child, Queen Gertrude III was about to meet her half-sister for the first time. Yesterday she had given Anita a new life, now she was going to do the same for the girl's guardian.

'You wished to see me, Your Majesty,' said the curtseying woman wearing serf greys. 'I came as soon as I could.'

What an anti-climax, thought Queen Gertrude, after looking forward to this meeting. Only the hair, the same colour as her own, remained the same. This half-starved creature was nothing like the haughty young girl in her fine clothes the Queen remembered. Now dressed in dirty rags and covered in grime she looked pathetic. This woman was a Junior Housekeeper, a position of authority. She looked more like a common skivvy.

'No, no, no, this will never do. Feed then bathe her, then feed again. Have her dressed in something suitable for a princess and then fed for a third time. I don't think she's eaten in a month,' the Queen said to the maid who had accompanied her half-sister.

'If it pleases you, Your Majesty. You wouldn't own anything grey, Ma'am?' said the girl. 'As a serf, it's all she's allowed.'

'The Lady Marie-Anne is no longer a serf. She does not wear grey either. Burn those rags after she takes them off. Now, do as I say, without questioning.'

'Yes, Your Majesty,' said the girl, who looked like she was cleaning dog mess. The Queen knew the snotty little so and so was the Chamberlain's youngest granddaughter. Just two rungs on the ladder higher than a serf. Honestly, some of her plebeian employees were bigger snobs than any aristocrat.

An hour later, her half-sister returned in a beautiful blue-green kirtle with a long bottle-green, open-sided velvet surcote. A soft silk barbette had replaced the widow's wimple and on her head a bottle-green toque held a chiffon veil in place. She could almost have been a different person. No, she was still frighteningly skinny; only a queen could be that thin. However, the clothes did hang properly. Also, the sharp enquiring blue eyes remained, as did the slight sneer on the corner of her mouth.

'I can see the resemblance between you and our paternal great-grandmother now. Why has no-one else?'

'Aunt Sophie did, Your Majesty, but she died before she could do anything about it.'

'Aunt Sophie? You mean the late Archduchess Rushton-Browne?'

'Yes, Your Majesty, I mean that dear lady. Our aunt was kind to me. She told me the truth about who I am. She had great plans for my future. Those plans died with her.'

'Why didn't you try to tell me?' asked Queen Gertrude. 'I would have carried through Aunt Sophie's plans.'

'Would you have listened to me that day? I remember you were as lost in your grief, as was I.' The Queen noted how quickly the girl's attitude had changed from subservient to suspicious.

'But you are my half-sister, regardless of what people say.'

'I'm called Mad Marion by my fellow serfs who believe I am insane for believing and spreading such an insane story.'

'I believe you, as I have seen the proof. You are a serf no longer. From this day, you are released from the Grey.'

'OK, I was a serf, so I was invisible. I only became visible because your daughter made you guilty about the way you treated Anita.'

True, thought the Queen, who would never have read her Aunt's private files otherwise. Now she was awash with conflicting emotions. Embarrassed at her arrogance in the past, then filled with excitement for the future.

'You are to be a princess. I will hold an investiture and you will take your rightful place within the Kingdom.'

'And if I said I didn't want to be a princess, what would you say?'

'I would have to ask why?' Again Queen Gertrude was surprised by this woman.

'I don't want your knee-jerk guilt, some grand gesture and then be forgotten again.'

'I can hardly forget a princess, nor can the Court or the general population,' replied Queen Gertrude. 'I have a sister now. One who is younger and will be prettier than me. A great beauty, like our paternal grandmother, once there is more flesh on those bones.'

'A flash news story that soon goes stale and is archived,' the girl replied.

Quick-witted as well as beautiful, thought the Queen. Oh Aunt Sophie, why didn't you tell me about my sister sooner. All those wasted years.

'Why would I want to forget about you. As an only child, with a distant Mamma I rarely saw, I regarded my Aunt Sophie as a surrogate sister. Then she married and went to live at Arlesdorf. My teenage years were so lonely. I have tried to be a better mother to Princess Louise, but she only has me and old Uncle Balthazar. With you and Anita here in the Royal Apartments, she will never be as lonely as I was.'

'Very well, I shall be a princess, but I want a job and a home within the Castle Precincts, not the Royal Apartments. If I stay here lounging around doing nothing I will go mad.'

Yes, thought the Queen, any idleness would have been beaten out of you. 'That can be arranged. I know exactly the job for you.'

'Thank you, Your Majesty,' said Marion with a curtsey.

'My dear, my name is Gertrude. You, sister dear, may call me Trudy.' The Queen stood up and did something she had rarely done as an adult, she hugged someone.

'So now, tell me about your life,' said the Queen when some of her normal composure returned. 'What it is like to be a serf. You're right, you were invisible.'

'Trudy, you're not going to like what I show you. This place has become rotten to the core.'

'Then it is my duty to clean away the corruption.'

'Then we'll start with the Castle's cesspit.'

'Why the devil wasn't I told that the Queen was down here in the Middle Bailey?' Septimus Pheileydale screamed at the unfortunate messenger. 'I haven't had any warning and time to get the usual camouflage in place before she goes walkabout.'

'My sister wanted to see the place as it really is,' said Marion, 'not the make-believe you usually show her.'

Normal practice gave the Chamberlain three days' notice, often extended to a week. Pheileydale used the time to restock larders and repair the most obvious damage. The serfs would benefit for a short time, then suffer for months after.

'Madam, I don't appreciate...' he said, stopping mid-sentence, recognising the speaker. He had someone to turn his anger onto. 'Marion, is that you? How dare you just walk into my office dressed like that, without permission. I'll have you whipped.'

'You'll do no such thing, you know,' said a woman entering the room. 'You no longer have any authority here.'

'Your Majesty.' Pheileydale bowed as he realised who the other woman was.

'I'm appalled by the way you run this Castle. I'm horrified at what my half-sister has been showing me.'

'But you're an only child,' he replied stupidly.

'So my half-sister believed until yesterday, Chamberlain,' said Marion. 'Now she knows different.'

'But none of it's true. It's all your crazy stories. Your brat can't really be the Foreign Girl. Why is the Queen believing your lies? They're just invention.'

'It was never lies nor invention. Anita is the Foreign Girl and I'm the Queen's half-sister. Same father, but a different mother.'

'Lucky you!' he said, again stupidity powered his vocal chords.

'Yes, lucky her,' said Queen Gertrude. 'She will soon be Princess Marie-Anne. Although her new job, as assistant to the Goose Maiden, starts immediately.'

'Yes, lucky her,' said Queen Gertrude. 'She will soon be Princess Marie-Anne. Although her new job, as assistant to the Goose Maiden, starts immediately.'

'You can't be serious?' asked the terrified man. 'It's been decades since anyone was executed by drowning in the moat.'

'That would be, "You cannot be serious, Your Royal Highness, Princess Marie-Anne",' said Marion, who was not finding revenge as much fun as she imagined. The old man looked pathetic, turning to his Queen for mercy. Marion could not feel sorry for him, nor did she feel the ecstatic happiness she had always imagined would accompany this moment.

'Oh, but she is. Princess Marie-Anne has every right to want to see you executed,' said the Queen, filling the painful silence. Then with icy calm she continued. 'Make no mistake you nasty little man, so do I. You denied me my Sister. Twice!'

𝖂ord of the Queen's surprise inspection had spread. A small crowd, who accompanied the pair of guards answering her summons. The were wearing their best uniforms, with their breastplates shining brightly.

'Guards, arrest this man,' she ordered.

'Yes, Ma'am.' The two Castle guards saluted then carried out her order with obvious pleasure.

'Three cheers for the Queen!' someone shouted. 'Hip-hip...'

'Hooray!' the crowd responded.

'Hip-hip...'

'Hooray!'

'Hip-hip...'

'Hooray!'

Queen Gertrude waved to acknowledge the crowd and their obvious pleasure at the fall of Septimus Pheileydale. They all automatically bowed as soon as the Queen's gaze fell upon them. This threw a bucket of ice on the proceedings.

'Do stand up everybody. Go about your normal business as if I wasn't here.'

'Ask that maid what she does, Ma'am,' said Marion formally to her half-sister.

'What on Anseris for?' the Queen asked.

'You wanted to know more about the internal workings of the Castle, Your Majesty. Here's your chance.'

'Marion, do I have to speak to all of them?' The Queen had noticed people lining up along her route.

'No Ma'am, just the ones you think look interesting. Tell them today you are having a... What did Pheileydale say? On a walkabout. And try to smile properly, Ma'am. Not that sad little pursed lips thing you normally do.' Marion watched as her sister produced a rictus grin. 'No, on second thoughts, don't bother. We'll have to practice the smile.'

When the Queen returned to the Royal Apartments, informality returned. The Queen had noticed how much happier the atmosphere in the Inner Bailey had become.

'You will stay one night before you move to the Cottage?' the Queen asked.

'Of course, Trudy. I can hardly go back to my hovel in the Middle Bailey, can I?'

'Anita will be so pleased to see you.'

'And I will be pleased to see her.'

'So, Marion, will you be taking her with you to the Cottage?' The Queen called for a pot of tea. She noted her half-sister had to fight the urge to go and fetch it. Anita had quickly got used to a life of luxury; it was going to take longer for Marion.

'No, she has had so many upheavals in her life so far. Also, I need to have a proper home for her to move to after Lady Josephine retires. Isn't she going to live with her widowed sister, somewhere on the north coast?'

'Is she? You know more than I do.' The Queen considered the golden bubble she lived in. 'I enjoyed the walkabout. I really should do it more often, on my next tour of the archduchies.'

'Good idea, Trudy. We'll make a Human being out of you yet.'

rofessor Margo Giambattista picked up her now retired predecessor's textbook. He had never managed to get this far. Details of her posting had finally arrived, and she would not get much further either.

"'Chapter Two,'" she said in a clear voice, "'In the year 2574, the increasingly overpopulated solar system launched its first colony ship to the stars. Thirty years later in 2604, KHM#89 began its voyage.

"'KHM#89 was sponsored by a government of Earth; no-one remembers which one. The ship's Demi-Warp engines cut journey times between stars from millenia to centuries, but they were still considerably slower than modern hyperspace engines. Several generations of crew members remained awake, piloting the ship, while ten thousand pioneers floated in cryogenic suspension until they arrived safely at their new home.

"'After five hundred years, the KHM#89 arrived in its target planetary system only to find it had already been settled by colonists who had leap-frogged our slower-moving juggernaut. The KHM#89 set off for its secondary target, then the tertiary.'" The teacher put down her book. 'Imagine the disappointment of the crew. Once a generation they would approach another suitable planet, only to find it already occupied.'

'Why didn't they just join with the settlers on a planet? Why move on?' asked Anita.

'They couldn't. What KHM meant has been lost. It is believed it was a code designated to prison transport vessels,' replied Professor Giambattista. 'The KHM#89's frozen passengers were mostly convicted felons exiled from Earth. The rest were the prison guards. None of those planets wanted to be tainted by a criminal cargo.'

'So the plebeians and gentry would remain in their slumber, whilst the fledgeling aristocratic caste continued to pilot the ship,' chipped in Princess Louise, who up until that point had been doodling on a piece of paper.

'That is correct, Your Royal Highness. The class structure found on modern Anseris is based on the status aboard KHM#89. However, that is for discussion in our next lesson.' The professor picked up the book again.

'"Inevitably, in the year 3376, the KHM#89 encountered the Draconic League, who had conquered most of Human-controlled space. They installed Katherine Wellingford as the new captain, and her lieutenants Hans Rushton as Executive Officer and Cynthia Brown as Chief Social Engineer.

'"Another thousand years of travel, beyond what was then the edge of Human space, the ship was found by the alien Aggelii. The KHM#89 was not callously sent to its destruction. The Aggelii abandoned their plans for this planetary system with its large Sun-like star, several gas giants with planet-sized inhabitable moons and, most importantly, this planet. The ship was repaired and restocked, and sent on another century-long orbital round trip while a home was created for its passengers and crew.

'"Kathyren Ellisford, as she then called herself, chose to ignore the Jovian moons when the KHM#89 returned. Humans settled on this planet alone. She named this planet Anseris and crowned herself Queen Kathyren. The involuntary settlers were forced to live in a version of the Middle Ages of Europe. Their descendants continued to live a mostly agricultural feudal life, struggling to survive. All advanced technology was destroyed. With no power tools, no motor vehicles or artificial light, the settlers lived harsh and brutal lives."'

The professor put down the book. 'We will now watch a short film, followed by an exercise on your data-pads.'

The Princess continued doodling during the film, as she had throughout the lesson. Anita watched carefully and made notes on a jotter pad. Both girls were delighted that the new tutors had introduced audio-visual elements and data-pads to the classroom. Lessons were far more entertaining now.

'You know, Imogen, you really annoy me sometimes,' said Anita at the end of lessons that day. The exercise from the mornings History lesson had been marked and the results sent to girls' data-pads. 'You just suck up information like a sponge even when you're not paying attention, then use it in the correct context for the test. It's not fair.'

'Yes, but you'll be able to take the test in a fortnight and still get the same high mark,' replied the younger girl in her usual reasonable tone. 'I would only get half the score. I forget things as quickly as I learn them, no matter how hard I try.'

'Don't worry, Imogen, I doubt we'll ever need half the things we have been taught,' said Anita, wrapping her arm around the younger girl's waist. All the anger gone.

Nobody stayed angry with Imogen, who was always so calm and calming. If she did get angry, it was always righteous anger, siding with the common good. When wrong, she quickly changed her opinion. You could not help but agreeing with Imogen after listening to her speak.

Marion said people like Imogen were so rare. If born into a possition with no influence, the forces of darkness easily crushed or corrupted them. Living in a royal bubble might do the same.

Anita sat at the grand piano, practising her scales. She could not get used to hours of leisure time in the evenings. So she was learning to play the piano, and hadn't noticed Arnold entering the Music Room as she practised.

'It's a good thing,' Arnold said, 'Queen Kathyren's love of the Medieval didn't extend to the music. It's why we have proper musical instruments now, not bagpipes, lutes,shawms and the dreadful crumhorns.'

'All those things came with the KHM#89. I've heard them. They are all awful. Well, except the lute.'

Arnold had met Viscount Partonberry-Douglass, the Queen's pilot, at Imogen's party and been transferred from the Cavalry Brigade to the Royal Flight for the rest of his time as a page. His military training now took him to Elizaburg aerodrome to fly royal aircraft. Anita knew he was much happier now.

'Anita, I have news for you,' said Arnold.

'Oh,' said Anita, 'I thought you were here for Imogen.' He should have been her foster-brother. He had tried and failed to play the big brother role. Now they were just friends.

'Anita, I know you're missing your guardian,' he said. 'Well, I've tracked her down.'

The Queen now knew who Marion was, and as such Anita had expected her guardian to move into the Royal Apartments, not vanish. Anita hid how much she missed her surrogate mother. How had this boy known?

'So, where is she?' asked Anita, impatient for news. 'None of the servants will chat with me like they used to.'

'She's now the Goose Maiden's Housekeeper, and is at her Cottage,' said Arnold smugly. Anita was surprised. The Goose Maiden's Cottage was a house located in the Castle grounds. 'And she's going to be the Keeper of the Queen's Geese, or Goose Maiden, when Lady Josephine retires.'

'But that job is for aristocrat. She will be mad from boredom within a week.'

'So, may I escort you on a visit to your guardian, while she is still sane?' Arnold asked.

'Oh! Yes, please. But we've only an hour. I must be back by dinner.'

Both youngsters were still learning to ride a horse, additionally Anita was perplexed by having to ride side-saddle like a lady. So the journey had to be made at a leisurely pace.

'How did you find her, when I couldn't?' asked Anita.

'Your former colleagues are not used to the upper classes speaking to them informally. They clam up,' replied Arnold. 'But they will speak to me.'

'But Arnold, you're a born aristocrat, surely they would clam up for you too?'

'It doesn't matter how grand a boy's family is, when he becomes a page. In livery he is just another servant.'

'You don't wear the same livery as the other pages, not since you became the Queen's favourite. The colours are the same, but the design is different,' Anita pointed out a change.

'That's the Royal Factotum and this is the livery of a page attached to the Royal Flight; that was the livery of a page attached to the Cavalry Corp.' The boy, who seemed to have grown a couple of inches was wearing a quartered green and orange waist-length padded doublet and fully joined hose with a padded codpiece.

'But the staff hate the pages and vice versa,' she said. 'What makes you different?'

'Most pages can't accept they have been stripped of their status for the duration. They have a very snotty attitude. I'm a space-rat. We don't care about status. We defer to the nearest expert, regardless of social standing. That opens doors and starts tongues wagging everywhere.'

'Thank you, Arnold. For doing this for me.'

'It was nothing. Now, can I ask you something? Please call me Aarne. Only my mother calls me Arnold, and then only when I have done something wrong.'

'OK, Aarne.'


The Cottage, its garden and fields, were accessed through a gatehouse in one of the sturdy walls surrounding the property. Anita felt an odd tingle as she rode through it.

'Did you feel the so-called ghost's presence?' asked Aarne.

'There was something odd about that place,' Anita replied. 'I have always been aware of ancient technological residues. What people call magic.'

'Because you are from beyond the stars.'

'So Marion told me. There's nothing supernatural in there.'

The driveway curved around a massive oak tree, growing to the left of the Cottage. The tree's lower branches almost obscured the privy, a lean-to structure abutting the left-hand wall.

'This is all wrong. This is not a cottage,' said Anita, 'a stone bungalow with plenty of attic space beneath the thatched roof.'

'No agricultural worker could afford the rent on a pile like this,' said Aarne.

'Like most agricultural workers who could never afford a so-called Ploughman's Lunch?' asked Anita.

'Exactly, a ploughman is a farmhand most of the year and they can't afford that much cheese.'

'It's a house built by a rich plebeian landowner to bring his new wife after marrying into the gentry,' said Anita.

'More likely to prove to his future in-laws he can afford to,' said Aarne.

A field planted with maize was in front of the house. An ornate piece of abstract statuary stood, looking desperately out of place, where there should have been a scarecrow. A large paddock and pond close to the Cottage was home to a flock of sixteen perfectly white geese. An elderly woman sat on a chair under an awning, occasionally watching the geese. She was dressed in a blue kirtle, with a goffered veil. This had to be Lady Josephine, the Goose Maiden, singing happily as she scribbled notes onto a data-pad.

Having hitched their horses, Anita and Aarne made their way through the kitchen garden to an open door at the end of the extension. A girl kneading dough looked up from her work.

'If you've come to visit Lady Josephine, she is out with the geese and does not want to be disturbed. She will not see you today,' the girl said.

'I've come to see Marion. Is she in?' asked Anita.

'Oh, you must be Anita. Dear Marion has told us all about you.'

Dear Marion, thought Anita, that's new. An improvement on Mad Marion. There was something wrong here. The girl's blue kirtle and white apron looked like something a servant would wear. However, the cut and quality of the cloth was too high for a servant. It was almost as fine as Anita's peach outfit. The girl's skin was as clear and pale as Anita's and her voice was as refined as any aristocratic lady.

Another young woman in the same blue outfit had entered the kitchen through an internal door.

'Dinah dear, this is the Lady Anita. She has come to see Marion.'

'She's up with me helping to change the bed linen,' Dinah said with a smile. 'I'll take her up with me, but the page will have to stay downstairs, Claire.'

'OK,' replied the girl, 'that's no hardship.'

'In the parlour, on his own,' replied Dinah with authority. 'Those loaves won't bake themselves.'

'Spoilsport,' said the other girl as she escorted Arnold.

They are all wearing make-up, thought Anita; something real servant never wore at work.

'**I** recognise you, you're old Pheileydale's granddaughter, a junior dresser. What are you doing here?' asked Anita.

'Yeah, one of the many,' she said. 'Her Majesty assigned me to be Marion's Lady's Maid. I expected to be sent straight back to the Castle. Servants don't have servants,' the girl said breathlessly, as they reached the top of the stairs, 'but no-one here is really a servant, and my old job's gone. Seem I should've been sent here when I was twelve. Grandad refused to let me go. Old bastard. So I work with and not for Marion now. Old Lady Josephine says the workload is increasing and it'll soon be much for one woman. So I am also an apprentice and I'll be an aristocrat, Lady Dinah Wensleydale-Falls, Assistant Goose Maiden, when Marion is promoted.'

Anita spotted her guardian. She looked well-rested and blissfully happy. Her improved diet was already filling out her bony frame. Something else was different. As a widow, she should be wearing a wimple with her veil. However, like the unmarried girls, she wore only a soft white veil over long straight undressed hair. She also wore make-up, which was almost invisible, applied with a skill the younger women lacked.

'Ello Marion, nice to see you've landed on your feet,' said Anita.

For as long as she could remember, her guardian had never allowed Anita to call her "mum", or any other maternal term of endearment. Marion had always made it perfectly clear that Anita was not her daughter.

'Anita, love. It is so nice to see you,' said her guardian 'in an already perfect aristocratic accent. Like Anita, she could switch this on and off without trying.

'I see you've met Dinah,' said Marion.

'She used to be a right little so and so.a. 'She's almost Human now. What's changed with her?' Anita asked her guardian.

'She's been busy unlearning all the funny ideas her family taught her. Slowly she's changing.'

'She's not the only one changing. I nearly didn't recognise you, displaying your greasy rats-tails for all to see.'

'Still a cheeky minx then,' said Marion as she stroked her clean hair. 'I don't get nearly half as dirty as I used to. There is only enough work for three servants in this place, but it employs nine of us.'

'Really? Isn't that better, less work?' asked Anita.

'I can see mixing with the aristocrats is already rotting your brain. None of us are really servants. We do as much housework as necessary. This is as posh a finishing school as any in Elizaburg.'

'You've already had that education,' said Anita.

'I'm doing the teaching. The girls are learning everything Aunt Sophie taught me...' Marion was interrupted by two girls arguing on the stairs. 'I don't care which of you two started it. I want you both to stop it now!'

'But Marion, Cicily's gone an' broke my avatar, she has!' the tearful younger girl said . Crying had left tracks in the silver cream coated on her face and neck to bleach her skin. No wonder the girl was short-tempered.

'Oh, don't be such a baby, Cressida,' said the other girl in a hiss. 'You are twelve, you know, not a child.'

'Lady Cicily,' Marion said sharply, 'aristocrats become adults when they're seventeen. At twelve and fourteen, you and Lady Cressida are still aristocratic children.' Marion turned to her foster daughter. 'Sorry, love. This will only take five minutes. How much longer can you stay?'

'This was supposed to be a flying visit. I'm expected back at the Royal Apartments.'

'**H**appy birthday, fatty!' said a jovial Marion. She had arrived at the Great Hall of the Keep with the Goose Maiden's entourage. The girls had been guests at Imogen's party, where they had all been anonymous faces. Now she could name some of them. And this time Marion was with them.

It had taken half an hour for Marion's first chance to talk to Anita in private and not be interrupted. Hopefully this would remain t case.

'And I love you too, Marion,' replied Anita. 'You were the only one who never called me that, back in the Middle Bailey. Why start now?'

'With the diet we had there, you couldn't get fat. The other serfs mistook your natural body shape for obesity. Now you are starting to pile on the pounds, dear.'

Despite being older than her colleagues, you would never tell, Anita thought. In her beautiful cerise and gold outfit with her loosely braided hair falling beneath a white silk veil, she looked closer to sixteen, like a senior gosling, than her actual twenty-six years.

'I hope I look as good as you when I am your age. It must be something in the water at the Cottage.'

'Twenty-two is not old. Although, the improvement in my diet and more comfortable sleeping quarters help.' Marion's apparent youth had been another source of jealousy with other Castle serfs whose harsh lives did nothing to slow the ageing process.

Before Anita could say anything about the four years Marion had shaved off her age, they both noticed a girl walking up the stairs.

'Lady Cressida Crystal-Winter, put that down, there's a good girl.' Marion was referring to the skirt lifted a few inches off the floor as she walked upstairs. 'I told you, a noblewoman never touches her skirt. She walks in such a way to raise her hem and give the impression she's floating, even on steps.'

'But that's so slow and difficult,' the girl replied.

'Can't I take a break for a few minutes?' Anita heared Marion asking under her breath.

'I know. Cressida,' said Anita. 'She used to drum the same lesson into me.'

'As my Aunt Sophie did with me, Cressida dear. It will come with practice.'

'I hates it when people go a-callin' me that. I'm called Krizzee Rachmeister! Ain't got no posh double-barrelled last name, I ain't' said the exasperated girl in a thick rural accent, Lady Josephine had spent the past two days, in one-to-one classes, trying to polish away.

'You will have to learn to live with that as well. Tomorrow in the Queen's Council I become Princess Marie-Anne.'

'But that be'n't yous, Marion. An' Lady Cressida be'n't I, neither...' The girl stopped mid-rant, recognising the look on Marion's face.

Marion had quickly looked both ways to make sure no-one else could hear her. 'Look here, me luv, do ya fancy a-goin' back to bein' nothin' more than a miller's lass, with nothin' to look forward to 'cept a life o' heavy grind?' she asked before Cressida could say another word. The pun had gone straight over the girl's head and was flying towards Elizaburg. 'Yous ain't been here long enough to be missed, innit.'

'No,' replied the girl.

'It be where yer a-goin'. Lady Josephine don't take kindly to no back-slidin'. She'll be expectin' a right improvement come toomozz mornin' after yous been a-minglin' with all them Ristoze in there. So be a good lass, an' head back to the party.'

'Oh,' said the chastised girl, who meekly returned to the party.

'An' a word of advice,' said Anita. 'Use 'em lifts over there.'

They had left the Great Hall of the Keep where the party was warming up,and had climbed up to the battlements. It was unlikely anyone else would disturb them. Below, their old home in the Middle Bailey complex was being rebuilt. In the distance was the concentric cold grey Castle walls, as forbidding as ever. Between the Keep and the outer walls was the Goose Maiden's Cottage.

'Poor little thing. She's the latest recruit, arrived a few days ago and is missing her mam. Lady Cressida is only two weeks older than you,' said Marion, slipping effortlessly back into the posh accent. 'Two girls turned seventeen last month. Both were married off to a minor member of the aristocracy. Young Cressida has been drafted in to fill one of the vacant places. If you hadn't already gone up in the world, thanks to Princess Louise, then you would be moving into the sausage factory tomorrow, to fill the other one. Probably as Cressida's room-mate.'

'What's Imogen got to do with anything?' asked Anita, who like the Queen, now affectionately used the Princess's other name.

'You're getting a full academic education as well as your self-improvement lessons here in the Bailey, instead of just the silly self-improvement course you would get over in the Cottage.'

'About forty years ago, it was noticed the aristocracy was slowly going gaga. Too many cousins marrying each other through the years. So the ban on Genetics was partially lifted. The Cottage scours the Kingdom for healthy, clever lower class girls with a pretty smile and most importantly good genes. As soon as they hit twelve they are brought to the Cottage. They gentrify them and marry them off to a young aristocrat as soon as they hit seventeen,' replied her former guardian.'

'Why would I qualify?' asked a confused Anita.

'Think about it, love. You're Fenzrian, but everyone thought you were an Anserian serf girl. You don't have any of the genetic nasties the Goose Maidens have been trying to eradicate for decades. In fact, you'd have added a shedload of new and healthy colour that is missing from the aristocratic genome.'

'So,' asked Anita, 'how do they find the girls?'

'What do you think Lady Josephine Parish-Hedges, the Goose Maiden, does all day when she is out with her birds? I'll tell you, she is constantly running a system-wide search for new "servants".' Apparently changing the subject, Marion asked, 'Had your jabs yet?'

'You know I have. All girls get rubella, tuberculosis and polio inoculations a month before their twelfth birthday.'

'Even though those diseases were eradicated millennia ago. The jabs are a cover for taking a girl's genetic profile. It's the first stage of the selection process. The final stage is an invitation never refused. Everyone in the lower orders knows what it means.

'I had the jabs, all serf girls do, to keep up the myth it is a public health exercise. Their profiles are ignored, unless it shows they have aristocratic blood and then get adopted by their family. Except that evil old bastard Pheileydale doctored my profile. I remained a serf, even after Aunt Sophie intervened. She loved secrecy and surprise and hadn't registered my new profile with the authorities. So now I am to be the next Royal Goose Maiden, expected to rip happy girls away from their families and turn them into miserable aristocratic wives and mothers. Like that is ever going to happen. Things are going to change here.'

'I'm sorry now I'm stuck in the Castle. I love Imogen like a sister, but I miss my mother. Not my birth mother, who died when I was a baby, but my real mother. The woman who raised me. The one who saw me through all my childhood illnesses. Who chased away the monsters from my nightmares. Who used to smuggle me into the Royal Library so we could read the books we were supposed to be dusting. Who was always there for me.' She could see Marion was embarrassed, but she had to say this. 'Even if she never lets me call her mother, or calls me her daughter.'

'All through those years I wanted to hear you call me Mammy, but I knew you could not. People didn't believe us. If I had let you call me that, those people would take it as a sign they were right. Now, my darling, we have been proven right, and you can call me whatever you like.'

'It seems a bit late now. What if I call you Mar? That's M-A-R, part of your name, but it sounds maternal.'

'OK, love, you can call me Mar.'

'I'm going to miss you, Mar.' Anita was filling up with tears.

'What's this all about? You will still be seeing plenty of me. The goslings will be regular visitors to the Castle, and I'll be here with them. Doubly so now that there is a young princess and her companion whose social training I'll also be responsible for.' The two hugged.

'I love you, Mar.'

'And I love you too,' said Marion. 'Now, on the subject of social training, this is your party Lady Anita and I've kept you from your guests for far too long. We'd better go back inside.'

The lift returned, with Cresida still inside. 'You said Princess, didn't you? Not Lady; you said Princess!' The girl spoke with a perfect aristocratic accent.

'Shush dear, it's supposed to be a secret, and I blurted it out,' said a shamefaced Marion. 'Only my half-sister the Queen, and my uncle the Prime Minister, are supposed to know.'

Marion briefly explained the situation to the two girls.

'Sorry love,' she said to Anita. 'I wasn't supposed to tell you. Even though you should have been the first to know.'

'Ooh, secrets,' said Cressida. 'Don't worry, I won't tell anyone.'

'Of course, you won't,' said Marion. Of course you will if I don't add a threat, she thought. She noted the girl was making an effort to speak like a noble. 'I will send you home if you do.'

'And lose my chance of a better life? My family would never forgive me.'

Marion felt awful. She knew she had just used the girl's love and loyalty to her family to drive her away from them forever. Things would have to change. But the thought she was now in a position to change them did nothing to lessen her feeling of guilt.

week before her birthday, Anita had been trying on a new
dress for her party. She was in the Royal Wardrobe with her
Mother and Aunt. Over the past twenty one years, Anita had
grown into an average height young woman with the body
mass of someone six inches taller.

'I think I was given all of Imogen's curves as well as
my own,' she said.

'Well, you have her appetite as well as your own,' said Princess
Marie-Anne.

'True, Mar, very true,' she replied. 'And I can't say you never
warned me about my diet. Although you are a fine one to talk.'

'No, that's very unfair, Princess Marie-Anne,' said Queen Gertrude.
'Queens and Crown Princesses have always been worryingly thin.
Nobody ever dared call us skinny. We are "willowy", whatever
that means. Your mother has inherited her father's hollow legs.
She should be much fatter.'

The last decade had seen Queen Gertrude's hair fade to the
lightest of grey with orange highlights. Nothing else had changed.
Like all Free Queens, there was not a wrinkle in sight.

'Thank you, Your Majesty,' said Princess Marie-Anne, hoping
that would be the last word on the subject. 'So much has happened
on your birthday, dear. I wonder what will happen this year?'

'Only my graduation as Chartered Nurse, but that has no formal
ceremony.' Anita's training was complete, after three years as an
apprentice an articled nurse. She had chosen another two years
study to become a Chartered Nurse.

'I adopted you on your thirteenth birthday, Anita, dear.'

'It wasn't unlucky for me.'

'It was the first time in centuries the Witan started showing its teeth,' said the Queen. 'Do you regret my inability to make you a princess?'

'Of course not, Your Majesty. I have far too many titles already.' Anita could see a look of concern on her aunt's face. 'Ma'am, I would be more worried about the Witan's newfound desire to preserve Anserian traditions.'

'An unelected executive body is an evolution in government, I'm no longer an absolute ruler. I have checks and balances. One day they will come from a democratically elected executive.'

'The sooner the better,' said Princess Marie-Anne. Unlike her half-sister, her hair still retained its fire. She could still pass as a woman in her mid twenties if you didn't know she was approaching forty. She should be delighted, instead she got annoyed. Too many Anserian men did not take women seriously. Especially if they were young and attractive.

'I'm sure the Witan would prefer it if I only looked after your geese, Your Majesty.'

'Being Chief Administrative Officer of the Gosling Institute better suits your talents though, Princess.'

'Yes, Ma'am. Proper schools for clever girls of the so called lower orders are desperately needed. Trade Guilds bar girls from their schools.'

The conversation interrupted by the Head Seamstress asking the unfinished dress back. While Anita changed, the Queen and Princess returned to the relaxed atmosphere of the Royal Apartments. Anita arrived as tea was being served.

It was true, big things happened on Anita's birthdays. An armada had departed from the asteroids of the Fenzrii Gamma system, as Anita tried on her new dress. It would arrive on her birthday.

The Fenzrian Cult of the Great Machine was, intent on annexing the Anserian system. They would gain planetary bases, and greatly increase its manpower with unwilling converts.

This was exactly the sort of threat the Immortal Empress feared the most. Anserians had been preparing for, even after she was overthrown. War was inevitable.

'As you were saying, it wasn't just the adoption that happened on your thirteenth birthday. You also became a pupil at my first school that day,' said Princess Marie-Anne.

'The only one that selects some of its pupils by genetic profile,' said the Queen. 'You took the staff from the schoolroom I had set up for Imogen and Anita and had them teach the original girls in the Cottage and many more in a campus set up in several barns.'

'The genetic profiling has its uses in public health. And yes, despite having schools all over the planet, a number of girls are invited to attend the Cottage School,' said Princess Marie-Anne.

'You had to maintain the Cottage's original mission, otherwise you would not have had the funding for the other schools from the Witan.'

'Only after a hell of a fuss. They objected to me letting those girls keep in contact with their families if they chose to marry into the aristocracy.'

'Yes, well, I can still override them whenever necessary. I told the Witan it would keep the girls grounded, and be good for all social classes.'

'A very small step from absolutism, Aunt Trudy,' said Anita. 'They all become teachers or nurses like Imogen and I,' said Anita. 'Even the ones marrying an aristocratic suitor.'

'Of course, the old way of forcing them into marriage at seventeen was wrong.'

The sandwiches were replaced by a selection of cakes. The Queen, who had nibbled at two sandwiches, took the smallest slice of carrot cake.

'From next year, your girls will be able to study and then practice law,' said the Queen. 'You must be happy about that?'

'There is still a marriage bar. It will be another spinster profession, like teaching and nursing. The Trade Guilds insist that the two professions dominated by women are dominated by unmarried women,' said Marie-Anne. 'They might as well still be nuns.'

'I moved into the Nurses' Hostel in Elizaburg on my seventeenth birthday. Started my double life as Apprentice Nurse Stellingham. So, if you will excuse me, Your Majesty,' said Anita being formal for once, 'Articled Nurse Stellingham has three night shifts with

Imogen ahead of her this week. I have to return to Elizaburg.'

'Of course, my dear. Off you go,' said the Queen.

'I do have one request. I wish my classmates could come to the Birthday Ball on Saturday,' said Anita. 'They are graduating as well.'

'Wouldn't inviting your classmates damage your anonymity? You've had a much easier time at work hiding your true identity.'

'My friends have never been the problem. They are very discreet. We deal with patient confidentiality – they would keep the secret. A random patient on the other hand might have blabbed.'

'I suppose you could invite the five other members of your class here for a celebratory lunch instead. Let's see... Cheryl, Delia, Karen, Susan and Vivienne. Have I missed anyone?'

'I love you, Aunt Trudy.' Anita was amazed at how the Queen could remember little facts like this. 'That's everyone. I'll go and make the arrangements.'

Nobody paid attention to the large coach clattering up the ramp into the Inner Bailey that Saturday lunchtime. Its passengers were Anita's five classmates, arriving for lunch.

'We knew you were aristocratic, all those posh parties you go to,' said Cheryl, one of the guests. 'We didn't realise how aristocratic. You're not Lady Anna Stellingham are you? You're Duchess Anita.'

'I didn't want to be treated differently in training or now I have graduated,' Anita replied, as the coach drew to a halt.

'Most of the Ristoze girls never get past the purely academic year, and onto the wards. They move sideways to administration, where they don't get their hands dirty or work unsociable shifts. On the other hand, Anita,' said Cheryl. 'I've seen you at 3am with Johanna, that new posh articled nurse, cleaning up the blood and vomit from a patient in A&E on a Saturday night.'

'And not just the drunks. I said I didn't want to be bored,' said Anita with a smile. 'A&E is never boring. Also, our uniform's hat is the closest thing to a crown I will ever wear. Or want to wear, to be honest.'

'I hadn't thought of that,' said Cheryl, oblivious to the irony. 'But you live in the Hostel, you share a room with Johanna, you do plebeian things, like going to the chip shop. Most posh girls get a shared house together, with a couple of maids.'

'It's what my bodyguards wanted. It was a nice house, but I said no, because I wanted to see the world from outside the Castle wall. It gives me a much greater understanding of what is actually happening in the worlds. I've a better perspective on life now.

'Oh!' The light of revealed knowledge filled Karen's face. She whispered to Anita, 'I've just worked it out.'

'Good for you,' Anita said, then whispered, 'Keep it to yourself.'

'Being a princess would get in the way of doing her job,' said Karen loudly. 'Especially once the patients knew who she was. I can't see it happening.'

'Indeed. Duchess Anita could get away with her deception, Princess Louise could not. Although people do confuse my daughter with my young cousin, Lady Johanna Wellingford. The resemblance is striking. Her friendship with Duchess Anita adds to the confusion.' Anita had been struggling to preserve Imogen's secret identity; it had been a condition of holding this gathering. But the Queen had just wafted in and done the job in a couple of sentences.

The appearance of the Queen triggered a cacophony of scraping chairs as everyone stood to curtsey. 'Please, ladies, remain seated. I forgot Duchess Anita was otherwise engaged.'

'Thank you, Your Majesty,' the young women chorused as they sat.

'Is Princess Louise here?' asked the Queen.

'No, she's not home from the University Library in Elizaburg.'

'A pity. I need to speak with her,' said the Queen. 'My daughter is currently studying diplomacy. We will have more official visits from foreign planets as time goes by. As Queen she will have to deal with them correctly.'

'So, Cheryl isn't it?' The Queen turned her attention to one of the guests. 'Are you looking forward to tonight's soirée?'

'Er, um, Your Majesty,' said an embarrassed Cheryl.

'What? My niece hasn't invited you. How very remiss.'

'Aunt Trudy,' hissed Anita, forgetting all protocol.

'Or are you all on duty this evening, Vivienne, so she couldn't invite you?' asked the Queen.

'Er, no, Ma'am,' replied Vivienne. 'We're off until Tuesday.'

'Very well then. Ladies, in lieu of a proper ceremony and as my graduation gift, you are all invited to tonight's ball. There are plenty of spare guest rooms in the Keep for you to retire to afterwards.' She could see the mixture of elation and horror on the young women's faces. They were all wearing their best dresses – acceptable for an exclusive lunch, too shabby for a royal ball.

'Fashion never changes so, the Royal Wardrobe is large and well stocked with gowns of all sizes. After lunch, choose a gown from there for the night, which you may keep as a memento of the evening and a reward for all your hard work.'

'Thank you, Your Majesty,' said the awestruck young women.

This is so far out of the Queen's normal way of doing things, thought Anita, following her aunt into the corridor. Dropping so much unexpected extra work on seamstresses already busy with last-minute repairs to the clothes of existing guests. Queen Gertrude was deeply spooked by something. Anita wanted to know what.

'Your Majesty, you wouldn't want to spoil my birthday, but I know by your actions that something is worrying you.'

'You've always been perceptive, my dear. A flotilla of foreign spaceships has entered the Anserian system. The ships have no recognisable markings and are refusing to identify themselves.'

'Are they coming here to the Home-world or elsewhere in the system?'

'At the moment they appear to be setting up a temporary base on the fourteenth moon of Akrotiri.'

'That's worrying,' said Anita. 'It's always been said danger comes from the skies. Which is why we maintain an army trained to defend against invaders dropping from the heavens.'

Queen Kathyren had drummed this maxim into the consciousness of her subjects. She knew that if anyone decided to annex this world, they would do so with superior technological force from space. 'Let us hope our army never has to put that training into practice, my dear.'

'But sometimes a hope is not enough,' said Anita.

'No. If it is invasion and war, defending this realm is going to be a vicious struggle against overwhelming odds.'

'So you wanted my friends to have one last night of fun before the balloon goes up?'

'Indeed, Anita,' said the Queen. 'And on the subject of fun, go and help your friends get ready for tonight. They have so much to do.'

'I s there anything I can do to help, Mamma?' Princess Louise asked her mother. She had just arrived at the Royal Apartments and heard the news.

'Yes, go over to the Keep and help your cousin,' said Queen Gertrude, obviously in a bad mood.

'You've already drafted in a battalion of dressers and seamstresses for that,' said Princess Louise. 'As Crown Princess, I should be by your side in a crisis, not concerning myself with frivolities. We may be facing invasion from the stars.'

'There will be little time for such frivolities when you're me,' said the Queen.

'Pardon, Mamma?' Princess Louise was confused.

'I meant when you are Monarch,' Queen Gertrude snapped, as if shocked by what she had said.

'I'm sorry I annoyed you, Mamma,' said Princess Louise, not wanting to cause any more offence.

'No, my darling girl, you didn't annoy me. I'm a little bit grouchy at the moment. It's good to see that your first instinct is to your royal duty, but for now, go enjoy yourself. There is still a possibility that these intruders will pack up their things and head off elsewhere.'

'H ow's it all going?' Princess Louise asked her cousin. 'As well as can be expected,' replied Anita. 'They're all a little star-struck.'

She must have heard something, coming straight to the Castle without changing first, Anita thought. Oh Angels! What was really happening?

'So they thought they would be having lunch in an Elizaburg mansion did they?' asked Princess Louise.

'Yes, Imogen, the Royal Carriage bringing them here was the first of many surprises.' Anita laughed a joyless panicked laugh.

'Then your dear Mamma escalates a quiet celebratory lunch into the party of the century for my friends. None of them were goslings, so this is all new to them.'

'You can fly any aircraft, surely this should be a doddle?'

'Yes, I can fly anything with wings and an engine. A piece of cake compared to this. It's all very well your mother saying my friends were welcome to come to the party. I don't think she realised there's more work involved than just picking five fabulous dresses. The royal seamstresses are awesome, as usual, but they are up to their eyeballs. So many other people to talk to. There are only two unused rooms in the guest quarters, but those rooms have to be reconfigured for multiple occupancy. The staff already have two jobs to do at once. I'm getting nowhere fast.'

'Surely Aunt Marie-Anne will help you?'

'Mar is also up to her eyeballs in work for this party. Even with her organisational skills, the last thing she needs is five extra guests.'

'Thinking about it, I'd better change before your classmates see me. Then I'll come and help.'

'The Angels preserve me. It's the Princess,' squealed one of Anita's colleagues, who had heard everything.

Princess Louise was sure Anita's friend would start hyperventilating. Fortunately, her cousin changed gears.

'No, Vivienne. This is my cousin and room-mate, Lady Johanna Wellingford, who likes to be called Imogen.'

'It isn't, I heard what you said, She's the Princess and you are trying to hide what she is really doing.'

'Please keep the secret, Vivienne,' said Princess Louise.

'Yes, of course. But, but...'

'But what?' asked Princess Louise.

'But, um... You look so ordinary, dressed like that. Ma'am.'

'I should hope so too. I don't want who I am getting in the way of me doing my job.'

'I can see now,' said Vivienne, 'why I need to borrow this lovely dress. I haven't got anything nearly this fancy. The Sumptuary Laws might be gone, but I couldn't afford the cloth.'

'Didn't you hear the Queen? It's yours to keep,' said Anita.

'But surely the Queen realises it's worth more money than I could earn in a year,' replied poor Vivienne, shocked to her core.

'Aristocrats don't understand how expensive clothing is for everyone else,' said Anita

'Oh, my mother does. She no doubt mentioned a reward.'

'Yes, Ma'am,' said Vivienne, who was wearing a black and yellow creation decorated with gold embroidery. Her long black hair was piled into a templar, a pair of tubular baskets on either side of her face attached to a golden headband. 'Your Royal Highness, what do you think?'

'Very elegant,' Princess Louise replied.

'Didn't I tell you the Princess is studying diplomacy?' said Anita. 'And it is a nice gown. But I have never liked templars. Each to their own. I love the steeple hennins; however, they are only ever worn at weddings.' She was referring to the long pointed hats with diaphanous veils that were the ultimate cliché of medieval womanhood.

'Anyway, the reason I'm here is to get you, Anna... sorry, Anita. Cheryl and Deliah are dithering, as usual,' said Vivienne.

'Then go help your friends choose their dresses while I change into something regal. Then I'll be back to help.'

'Thanks, Imogen.'

'Why Imogen?' asked Vivienne.

'It's a long story,' said Anita. 'And remember, if asked, the Princess is studying diplomacy.'

'OK, I get it. That was your cousin Johanna,' said Vivienne. 'I haven't just seen the Princess, because she is not an articled nurse, she is studying diplomacy.'

'So, what do we know about these intruders?' The Queen asked Earl Rushton-Browne, the head of the Anserian Armed Forces. She had summoned him from Military HQ in Elizaburg to Ellisford Castle, to be briefed on the Kingdom's defenses.

'They have been identified as Fenzrian ships,' replied the rotund balding man in dark purple robes.

'What does the Great Machine want with our poor system?' asked the Queen.

An ornate gilded throne dominated the chamber, surrounded by lights, cameras and microphones. It was from here the Queen addressed her realm via television and radio.

'Probably just a rendezvous. I wish they'd bugger off back to their asteroids. Coming here without a please or thank you.' The Earl as ever was in a bullish mood. 'I say we teach them a lesson. Destroy one ship and hold its crew hostage. Show them they can't just waltz into our system and do what they like.'

'That is the last thing we should do. It would enrage them,' said Professor Giambattista of the Anserian Diplomatic Corps, spending the final weeks before retiring, at the Castle Office.

'The Great Machine, the Cult that runs their asteroids, is intent on creating a hive mind amongst its inhabitants. The hostages will be killed; deemed failures as soon as they return.'

'A hive mind – like bees?' asked Earl Benedict.

'No, Earl Benedict, like wasps,' said the professor. 'Kill one and when the scent of death reaches the nest they will all follow it to its source, seeking revenge.'

'Let them come,' said the Earl.

'No, you don't want to be on the wrong end of Fenzrian anger,' Professor Giambattista said, transferring some data to a computer. 'These are the statistics for a small Fenzrian armada. Just let them take what they want. I doubt they will come back.'

'Oh,' said the Earl when he read the data. 'We will have to spend even more of our budget on our space defence force out at the edges of our system.'

'Earl Benedict, we are already increasing the budget of our space defence force at enormous expense. We cannot afford to spend any more on it.'

'Our only hope is the Great Machine does not interpret anything we do as being asaggressive,' said Professor Giambattista.

'So, Professor, can you enlighten me further about what is known about these intruders?'

'Certainly, Your Majesty.' She could not curtsey, she was using a wheelchair while her dislocated ankle healed. The Queen thought the front of the wheelchair appeared to dip a little.

'The Fenzrians are descended from pirates based in the asteroids of Fenzrii Gamma. It's a Sun-like orange star with only belts of asteroids. If it were a person, the Fenzrian System would be a mohican-wearing punk rocker from Ancient Earth making a rude gesture at its impossible Astrophysics.'

'Yes, yes, all very interesting,' said Earl Benedict, who disliked being lectured to by an educated plebeian, especially an educated female plebeian like Professor Giambattista.

'Benedict! If I am to address my subjects today, I must have as much background information as possible,' the Queen said, turning away from the man who was becoming as purple as his robe. 'Please continue, Professor Giambattista.'

'Life there must have been brutal, even in good times. It's not surprising such a harsh religious dogma took root there and disappeared in more comfortable systems. The extreme discipline and control made staying alive amongst the asteroids easier.'

'The pseudo-psionic communication network and memory implanting teaching machines the Fenzrians use are banned on every other civilised planet. Both technologies erode the sense of self and destroy Human uniqueness. This fits in with the Cult's philosophy of interchangeableness, where everyone is a mere component in a great machine.'

'Can they be beaten?' asked Queen Gertrude.

'Not by us alone. The Fenzrians are militarily self-sufficient, but economically weak. Anseris is the opposite – economically self-sufficient, but militarily weak. We shall need assistance from the Confederation of Human Worlds.'

'Who've abandoned us. Their merchants can't make a profit from our isolated and mostly agrarian worlds.'

'You know that is not true, Earl Benedict,' said the Professor. 'You and your political allies oppose contact with the galactic community and have forced the Confederation to cut their links with us. The existence of a threat like the Fenzrians shows we should strengthening our links with the Confederation.'

That was it. It was obvious the Earl's short temper had been stretched to breaking point. 'No, we seek to maintain the traditions that have served this planet for centuries. Where someone like you would not dare to lecture someone like me on anything.'

'Benedict! We are here for a serious purpose. Kindly keep your excessively narrow worldview to yourself. True Anserian aristocrats have always valued the opinions of an expert, regardless of social status,' said Queen Gertrude angrily.

'If you'll excuse me, Your Majesty, I've work to do,' said Earl Benedict, who knew he had crossed a line.

'Apologise to the professor first. And Professor, accept the apology, no matter how false it may be,' ordered the Queen.

'Your Majesty,' said the Earl, bowing to his Monarch, then turning to the left wheel of the wheelchair, he bowed again. 'Professor, I apologise.'

'Thank you,' she replied, as gracious as Earl Benedict had been graceless. After the Earl left, Queen Gertrude stood up from her throne and walked to the professor. 'And I also apologise on behalf of the aristocrat caste. It's time we fully abolished feudalism, it is holding us back.'

'Thank you, Your Majesty. If there's nothing more?'

'That is all, Professor,' the Queen replied, as a thought occurred to her. 'Didn't you once teach my daughter and niece?'

'Yes, Ma'am. Which is why I was invited to this party. I have maintained correspondence with Duchess Anita.'

'I shall see you tonight then.'

'I look forward to it, Your Majesty.'

'Your Majesty,' said one of the technicians, 'we've received this communication from the Fenzrians.'

Queen Gertrude's great-grandmother had given two disused stables against the north wall of the Inner Bailey to enthusiastic space scientists. One for civilian use, the other for the military. Both organisations had long ago moved to a larger facility on the equator. However, the Civilian Space Command maintained a regional station in its original home.

'So, Director Briggs, what drags us away from my niece's birthday party?'

'Doctor Chaterham decoded the message, Ma'am,' said the director as she bowed. She had been a guest at space-mad Anita's birthday parties for years. 'He passed it on to me, and I called the Archduke, who in turn summoned Your Majesty. If you would watch the screen please, Ma'am.'

The vidscreen came to life with a series of religious images from the FenzrianCult. Then a masked face appeared.

'Blaspheming followers of false gods. In order to cleanse your sins, the Great Machine is taking permanent control of the outermost planet of your system, the one you call Akrotiri, and all its moons. The Great Machine will open a communication channel so that you can accede to its demands. Blaspheming followers of...'

'Turn that thing off,' ordered Earl Benedict, entering the room, issuing orders.

'On whose authority?' asked Director Briggs.

'On mine. This is obviously a military issue now, so my staff will take over.'

'Earl Benedict, I will decide who will take charge of this incident. Not you'

'Your Majesty, I didn't realise you were here,' said the Earl as he bowed, then turning to the Prime Minister, 'or you, Uncle.'

Earl Benedict hated anything to do with space. He particularly disliked Civilian Space Command. It was not properly Anserian. Too many women doing men's jobs. No respect for tradition from plebeian upstarts. The Military Space Command should be running this situation, justifying the huge chunk it took out of his budget each year. The Queen must transfer authority there.

'Ladies and Gentlemen of the Civil Space Command, I commend your hard work,' said the Queen, 'but Earl Benedict is correct, this is now a military matter and has to be transferred to Military Space Command.'

Dear Angels, thought the Earl, for once I haven't had to argue with the Queen to get things done correctly. Amazing what a potential invasion could do for someone's common sense.

'However,' continued the Queen, 'Director Briggs and her team will be kept fully informed of all developments. If we are to go to war with the Great Machine, we will have to evacuate some of our space habitats, turning them over entirely to the military. She will be responsible for the safe movement of civilians away from conflict.'

The Earl watched as the Queen rose and left the room. Two steps forward, one step back, he thought. There were plenty of ways of keeping that civilian pleb woman and her minions out of the loop.

Queen Gertrude did not head straight back to Anita's birthday party. Instead, she headed to the Throne Room. She spotted Professor Giambattista's wheelchair gliding to the party.

'Professor, may I have a word?' asked the Queen.

'Your Majesty, I've heard worrying rumours since we last talked,' said the professor. 'I'm still an academic at heart. I deal in facts, not rumours.'

'In that case, I shall supply you with all the facts you need on our way to the Throne Room. I am going to broadcast to my subjects. To limit panic and stop the spread of rumours.'

'Yes, Your Majesty.'

'So, Margo, now you are fully in the picture,' said the Queen. It had not taken long to explain the situation to the professor.

'Thank you, Your Majesty,' replied Professor Giambattista, who now had all the facts she could possibly want.

'Do you know the origin of Akrotiri's name, Ma'am?' the professor asked Queen Gertrude.

'It is from Ancient Earth,' replied Queen Gertrude, 'and is almost as old as time.'

'Indeed, Ma'am. It's from one of the first civilisations on Earth. One wiped out by a natural disaster.'

'Minoan, wasn't it?'

'Yes, Minoan civilisation. It is believed they survived the disastrous volcanic eruption on Santorini, they were wiped out by the economic fallout.'

The Queen sat on the throne in the Studio. 'We cannot afford to be wiped out. But what has this to do with the current situation?'

'Well, Your Majesty. It is believed that Akrotiri was a major Minoan city. Its name meant "the Bridgehead" in Ancient Greek. It is ironic that the invaders have chosen a place so named.'

'I doubt the Fenzrians know that or even care.'

'I agree. Fenzrians have no imagination, but they are not stupid. They know we will fight, we will not foolishly let them establish a base to conquer us completely. Once they control one planetary system, they will move onto the next.'

'I have never left Anseris so I have little knowledge of interstellar affairs. I shall require expert guidance during this crisis. I know this is inconvenient, but I require you to put your retirement on hold and request you become my expert guide. Please teach me, as you once taught my daughter.'

'Of course, Ma'am,' replied the professor. She knew Anserian lifespans were increasing, and retirement's empty years filled Margo Giambattista with dread. She was glad to accept this royal command.

'**You haven't had second thoughts, Your Majesty?**' the new Prime Minister asked. The war had dragged on for three long years. Little on Anseris remained untouched by the war, but little had changed either. With the recent death of his uncle, Earl Benedict Rushton-Browne of Ganontsburg inherited the Archduchy of Castlegate, becoming its sixty-ninth Archduke, and he automatically became hereditary Prime Minister of Anseris. He remained as hidebound as ever.

'No, Benedict. Your late uncle set the plan in motion with me, before he received his divine reward and went to be with his beloved wife in the next life.'

'Your Majesty, I've made it plain that I don't think this wild scheme has any chance of success,' said the new Archduke.

Queen Gertrude cursed the fact that her old friend's only heir was his nephew, the former Head of the Anserian Armed Forces. 'We have little choice, Benedict,' said the Queen. 'This repeated conversation grows tiresome.'

Both sides had fought to a standstill as their strengths and weaknesses had balanced out. The Fenzrians, expert space marines, had taken control of the outer system habitats and made travel within the inner system perilous. The Anserian defenders, masters of ground combat, retained control of the Home-world and the Jovian Baronies. Resources were stretched to the limit on both sides. Whoever could bring something new to the table would win.

The Confederation of Human Worlds, who should have sent military assistance to deter the Cult of the Great Machine, provided no help. All the Anserians had received to date was slogans and empty promises.

'If we hadn't wasted so much money on your useless battle cruisers, we would not be in this mess now,' said the Queen.

'Majesty, may I remind you I counselled against those vessels. They were a pet project of my predecessor as HAAF, the Earl of Longwater. Space defence has always been a huge and unwanted drain on resources and even then it has never been enough. We have always relied on the promise of Confederation assistance,' replied Archduke Benedict. 'I knew this was a mistake. We are too far away from the main space lanes to rely on Confederation protection.'

'You're right, Benedict. I apologise to you for my short temper,' said the Queen.

'Thank you, Your Majesty.'

'The Fenzrians are blockading all communication with the Confederation, who must still think their warm words and sympathy are sufficient. This is what makes the Princess's mission so important.'

'And so risky. Does your messenger really have to be your daughter?'

Queen Gertrude took a few short steps across the room to her computer desk. 'We've no choice in the matter. If we had entrusted this mission to a plebeian, you and your associates would have objected. Only a high-ranking aristocrat will do, you said. Who could be more high ranking than Princess Louise.'

'And that woman's daughter?' said the new Archduke, his disdain for Anita obvious.

'Benedict, after all these years, your dislike for my half-sister and her daughter is beyond tedious.'

'I'm sorry, Your Majesty. She is a dangerous radical. If she had her way, she would destroy everything I hold dear. But that is only to be expected from someone born a serf,' said the Archduke pompously.

Queen Gertrude rolled her eyes heavenward. He had to go. She had a replacement in mind. Would the transition go easily? 'Whatever she was is irrelevant. She has achieved so much, which is what matters. Also, serfdom was abolished years ago.'

'More's the pity,' he said under his breath.

'No, Benedict, things are going to change. Anseris was stagnant. This war has mixed everything up, made the water sweet again. We have a chance to build a new and better Anseris for all.'

'It's not the time for this argument,' said the new Archduke, changing the conversation back to his original point by asking, 'At least that woman is Anserian, but the girl she adopted is Fenzrian – do you trust her?'

'Only someone like Duchess Anita, who is genetically Fenzrian, could possibly smuggle our precious cargo through Fenzrian-controlled space. The journey has to be done aboard a foreign spaceship fitted with one of those foreign psychic interfaces, one an Anserian cannot pilot. Besides, my adopted niece is a good girl, so will do what she is told.' The Queen politely pointed out Anita's status.

'She does as she is told because she is still the serf she was brought up to be, despite the title you gave her,' said Archduke Benedict.

'I am neither a serf nor a Fenzrian, Your Grace.' The speaker was dressed in a colourful outfit a million miles from a serf's grey linen. She curtseyed to her Queen. 'Your Majesty.'

Queen Gertrude was extremely proud of her niece, a qualified pilot and now her pilot's licence included spacecraft.

'I believe the ship which brought you to Anserian space is now fully restored,' said Queen Gertrude.

'It's the only Fenzrian ship in the system not controlled by them,' said the Archduke morosely. 'Every one we capture blows itself up before we can neutralise the self-destruct mechanism.'

'All major mechanical and structural work is complete. It is currently having its old livery replaced with an up-to-date Fenzrian one,' Anita replied.

'Soon you will be off to the stars with your fellow Ambassadress. First stop Grimmswald, our nearest Confederation neighbour.'

'Our links to Grimmswald are cut. They think we have fallen to the enemy,' said Archduke Benedict.

'Benedict, for a former military man you're displaying an unpatriotic attitude,' the Queen said angrily.

'Forgive me, Ma'am. I didn't think I would feel the loss of my uncle so badly,' said the Archduke, showing an uncharacteristic Human side. 'Today would have been his birthday. If you will excuse me.'

'Yes, of course,' replied the Queen. 'You are dismissed.'

Queen Gertrude knew it would be an unrewarding night's sleep. Someone was waiting for her in her nightmares.

Another night spent in a bomb shelter. A sub-basement of the Inner Bailey. Above its vaulted ceiling was sixteen feet of solid rock, part of the foundations of the Keep. It was probably the safest place on the planet. The dimly lit shelter contained every social class, mixing to a degree previously unheard of.

The high orbit habitat Lansing#5 had fallen to a Fenzrian suicide squad. The invaders now used it as a base for nightly air raids.

Retaking Lansing#5 was a top priority. The new Archduke wanted to destroy it. No, thought the dozing Queen, it would be such a shame to demolish it, I can remember it opening.

'No I don't remember, damn it! You are showing me one of my grandmother's memories, aren't you?' said a half-dozing Queen in this virtual reality. Anyone watching the real sleeping Queen heard an incoherent mumble.

'Yes,' said a voice like her own but much older and harsher. 'Memories stored within your crown. The memories of all the incarnations of me ever to wear it.'

The true significance of Queen Kathyren's crown had long been forgotten by the time of the Boatbuilder's Revolution. It was hurled into one of the many boggy ponds of the Outer Bailey by a revolutionary. Finally rediscovered by the teenage daughter of Queen Johanna II who had ordered the Outer Bailey drained and landscaped. When the daughter became Queen Maria V, she decreed her successors should always wear her old crown as a symbol of absolute continuity.

The rose-gold crown contained a lattice of complex circuits which made transfer of Queen Kathyren's mind from one host to another possible. In the long dark years, without a head to draw power from, the crown's batteries faded. Trapped within the crown was the ghost of Queen Kathyren. She had sent the distress signal that had drawn Princess Maria. It was too weak to take control of the girl but strong enough to communicate with her and any of her successors as the Free Queen of Anseris. With each of the passing one hundred and seventy years the crown, and the ghost within, grew stronger waiting for the restoration of Queen Kathyren to life.

The process should have been like cel animation, giving the impression of movement with a progression of images changing faster than the brain can process – the elements of the image varying from shot to shot painted on transparent cels. But in Kathyren Ellisford-Castle's memory each cel refused to make way for the next one. The resulting image had an obscured static background, creating a foreground that made no sense. Long before her overthrow, Queen Kathyren went completely mad.

'So glad you came when I called, B422,' said the ghost. When she shut her real eyes, Queen Gertrude's perfectly functioning mind's eye could see herself standing in a sky-blue void, facing the ever-changing ghost.

'Immortal Empress, you know my name and that I want nothing to do with you,' said Queen Gertrude. 'But I have no choice. When I'm ill and sleep badly, you exert your power over me.'

'Do you care if a cloak gives itself a name, B422?'

'I am not a cloak. I am a living human being who would never surrender to you.'

'You nearly surrendered completely to me,' the ghost said as it morphed into a heavily pregnant Queen Gertrude.

'When my beloved David died you tricked me. I made myself pregnant with my darling Imogen, knowing she would be a perfect copy of you and me.'

'After the death of B423 and miscarrying B424 and B425,' the voice continued, 'you found the knowledge I gave you useful.'

'The grief made me slightly mad,' said Queen Gertrude.

'You thought you had found the way to extend your life using my methods.'

'I eventually recognised your honeyed lies. You were using me to create the vessel for your rebirth. You failed, as you have failed for the past hundred and seventy years since this crown was rediscovered. I realised long ago it is where you hide yourself. I have given orders to have it melted down the moment I die.'

'It doesn't matter that you saw through my deception. I am now strong enough to take B426's body when you die. She will join the grand procession as I finally become free again,' said the ghost.

'I've but weeks to live. Cancer will kill me long before she returns from Grimmswald. When I die, she will be too far away for even you to reach. Imogen will have a new, untainted crown. The gold in this one will be used in a memorial for those who have died in this war.'

'B422, I already have my claws dug deeply into B426.' The laughter filled the infinite blue void. 'This world is now connected to the Data-sphere Network. Distance is no barrier, and I shall complete transference through that.'

'You won't do it, you know. My Prime Minister destroyed the Instellnet hub. He thought the Fenzrians were using it to spy on us.'

'Then I shall kill you now.' The ghost began throttling the Queen, who woke with a start.

'Mamma,' said a shocked Princess Louise, who found her mother dozing in a chair mumbling and shaking. 'Mamma, did you have a nightmare?'

'Yes,' replied Queen Gertrude, waking to see the frightened face of her daughter. 'A terrible nightmare. In many ways you're so lucky you never dream, my dear. You may miss the good dreams, but you also miss the nightmares.' Queen Gertrude paid no attention to the many lies of Kathyren Ellisford-Castle.

'For some, this war is a living nightmare, Mamma. I would gladly take some of their pain.'

'Tomorrow is your twenty-third birthday, Imogen dear. What a beautiful young woman you have become.' The Queen saw an image or herself thirty years younger. Princess Louise was as willowy as her. She had the large deep green eyes that were the hallmark of her family. 'You can do something none of your predecessors, or I can do.'

'Oh, what, Mamma?' asked Princess Louise.

'What you are doing now. You have a broad bright smile. Even when I'm happiest, I can never give more than a neutral pursed lips with a narrow band of teeth. I regret the demands this war has put on your life. You were forced to abandon your career last year.'

'We used to tell people I was having training in interplanetary diplomacy, to hide my identity at work.'

'Yes, Imogen, and for the past twelve months it has been true.' This made the Queen laugh, lightening the atmosphere.

'I was trying on the Galactic-style clothes made for the trip when the air-raid sirens started wailing.'

'I can see. And very pretty you look too,' said the Queen, spotting her Prime Minister who currently had a face like thunder. Hopefully her daughter would ignore him.

'Archduke Benedict, do you like my trousers?' she asked. 'It's what all the young women on Grimmswald wear.'

'No, I do not. Your outfit is too masculine.'

'Really, Benedict, you are shockingly old-fashioned,' said Queen Gertrude. 'Galactic styles are coming to the Home-world. They were common on the moons and in Pendragon before the war. They even started making inroads on the Home-world. Isn't that so, Marie-Anne?'

'Not while I am Prime Minister, Your Majesty,' Archduke Benedict said before anyone else had a chance to speak. The Queen looked at the man. Only ten years older than her daughter, he acted as if he were seventy years older. How could such a young man be so very old-fashioned?

'As if you are able to stop it,' said Princess Marie-Anne, as she turned to Princess Louise. 'Have you seen your cousin?'

'She and Aarne will both be on leave from today. They'll be on the estate his grandmother left him on the edge of the deserts of the Northern Continent. It's only an hour's flight from Heavenward and the Launch Complex.'

'Thank the Angels,' said Princess Marie-Anne. 'Although, I hope Aarne's parents over in Elizaburg are safe in their shelter.'

'The Aristocratic Quarter and Gänsehals Circus have better anti-missile defences. It is the industrial districts and nearby plebeian residential districts that have taken a pounding,' said the Archduke.

'Well, naturally. Aristocrats can afford better anti-missile systems,' said Princess Marie-Anne.

'Exactly,' he replied. 'The important people are protected, the plebs just muddle through.'

Princess Louise wished her aunt would stop trying to goad the Archduke. It was far too easy to be any fun.

'You honestly don't know how offensive that is, do you?' asked Princess Marie-Anne. The sound of explosions ended any sort of argument, as Fenzrian bombers used the last of their ordinance to take pot shots at the usually well-defended Castle.

'That one was too close for comfort,' said Princess Louise as even the basement of the Keep rattled.

'I suspect it was the bath-house,' said the Queen.

'You see, even the best defence systems can be breached,' said the Archduke. 'But I doubt anyone of quality has been harmed.'


People began leaving the shelter as soon as the all-clear. Either to return to their beds or, like Princess Marie-Anne, to wait for a reassuring phone call from loved ones.

'You know, all this will have to change if those girls succeed in their mission,' said the Queen. 'One simply cannot share a basement bomb shelter, even in a building as strong as this Keep, with the entire population of this Castle and continue to think you are superior to your fellow Humans.'

'You cannot?' replied Archduke Benedict, annoyingly answering a question with a question.

'No, Benedict, you cannot.'

'I did say you should have segregated the shelters. You said that was unnecessary. Uncle Balthazar – may the Angels give him peace – agreed with you. A layer of magic has been lost from our society.'

'Especially as everyone shares the same chemical toilets,' said Princess Louise with a smirk.

'I wasn't going to go down to that level,' continued Queen Gertrude, 'but yes. Our restrictive feudal system has been relaxed enough to allow the growth of industry and commerce. Now it has to be swept away completely.'

'Over my dead body,' said the new Archduke.

'I knew you would say that. I did not plan to tell you in such a public place, but it is best done sooner than later. The Kingdom cannot afford the wilfully obstructive attitude you have to even the most moderate reform. The Queens of Anseris are Absolute Monarchs. I have never fully exercised that Absolute Power. That is, until now. At 9am a decree will be issued raising Professor Margo Giambattista to the rank of Baroness and appointing her as my new Prime Minister. You will return to your old job as head of the Armed Forces.'

'But the heads of House Rushton-Browne have always become Prime Minister. The Castlegate Privilege.'

'I still need your unending fountain of wrong, Benedict, to point me in the right direction; to be safe in the knowledge that if I have two options to choose from, you will always pick the one I should avoid. However, at the moment, I cannot afford to have that fountain emanating from the Prime Minister's Office.'

'I am not a court jester, Your Majesty, and refuse to be treated as such. Good day.' He bowed and left the shelter, to resounding cheers from those people who remained.

'Oh dear,' said Queen Gertrude. 'I appear to have gone too far.'

'But judging from the reaction of the people, you have gone a long way towards establishing a popular Monarchy,' said Princess Louise.

On the eve of Anita's twenty-fifth birthday, Queen Gertrude III hosted a dinner party in the Royal Apartments at Ellisford Castle. The Queen hid her melancholy as successfully as she hid her illness. She knew this was the last meal she would ever share with her daughter.

To save Princess Louise from the curse of the Immortal Empress she would have to struggle on until her daughter was beyond recall, many light years away.

Princess Marie-Anne looked amazing as usual, the Queen thought. She had definitely inherited that from their paternal grandmother who had also defied the ageing process. Over the years, many suitors had tried to win her hand in marriage. None had succeeded, and Queen Gertrude worried about her half-sister suffering a lonely old age.

'I know what you are thinking, Trudy dear,' said Princess Marie-Anne. 'You don't have to worry. I may be unmarried, but I am far from alone.'

'We live in a society where marriage is the norm, Marie-Anne.' The Queen was taken aback.

'Yes, I know. Maybe one day I will marry again. I'm the daughter of an unmarried mother, and I have been one myself. Thank the Angels Anita will break the trend.'

'Did you know anything about our father?'

'No. I always assumed my real dad was a lusty young aristocrat, not a randy old goat.'

'Our father had his charm,' Queen Gertrude said. 'He always treated women as ladies, regardless of class.'

'He's a blank page to me, never to be filled.' Marie-Anne laughed.

'So what do you know?' asked the Queen. 'You've never told me.'

'All I know is mother was marooned by a freak snowstorm in an old hunting lodge in the grounds of Castle Stark with a charming aristocrat using an assumed name. She was closing the place down for the winter.'

'I remember the fuss when he went missing. He was ill at the time,' said the Queen. 'The cold and lack of food can't have helped his condition.'

'Well, they found one way to keep warm. She returned to her duties at Castle Stark, then was sold here just before I was born. Our father had been dead for a month when that happened.'

'When you were twelve and it was discovered you were genetically an aristocrat, you should have been taken out of the Grey and placed under somebody's wing immediately.'

'Everybody knew Septimus Pheileydale was a nasty piece of work. Nobody knew how nasty he was. I was his favourite target. So he sold me to Arlesdorf and falsified that part of my records, so I would never be in a possition to get my revenge. We can count ourselves lucky Aunt Sophie saw something in me, and started investigating.'

'Indeed,' said the Queen. 'Imagine his horror when he saw you back in the Middle Bailey.'

'My chronicly bad luck and fate in the form of old Pheileydale intervened again,' she said. 'He couldn't send me back to Arlsdorf. Uncle Balthazar would have carried out his wife's grand plan, and I would be in a possition of power over him.'

'Anyway, so much for the past. Let's look to the future. Although, the longer I can avoid one particular future, the happier I will be.' There was a sad look in Marie-Anne's eyes. 'Don't you dare die before Imogen returns home, leaving me as Princess Regent.'

'Nonsense. I've got years ahead of me,' said the Queen.

'You may be able to hide it from everyone else, but I know that is not the case,' Marie-Anne said to her half-sister. 'I was nine when my mother died of bowel cancer. I watched her deteriorating and now I see you going the same way. Not only will I be losing a sister, but I will also be landed with a terrible job, running a Regency.'

'Imogen should be back within six months, and I will be here to greet her.' It was a lie; she knew her cancer was further along than even Marie-Anne had realised. The Queen would be lucky to last six days. 'Selecting you as a possible Regent has just been preparing for all contingencies.'

'Your daughter will witness Anseris change completely after she becomes Queen.'

'Yes, Marie-Anne dear, she will. Change has to happen. With so many refugees from the moons and space habitats arriving on the Home-world, it's not surprising that radical ideas are spreading like wildfire. Not so long ago, I would have been shoulder to shoulder with the Archduke Rushton-Browne trying to put those fires out,' said Queen Gertrude.

'Yes, dear sister, but that was before I showed you how to harness that fire.'

'Archduke Benedict and his supporters will not be happy. I fear that he might use his control of the army to challenge my Regency. And should anything happen to Imogen, he would definitely challenge any attempt to crown me Queen,' said Princess Marie-Anne.

'Talk of treason and committing an act of treason are two different things. His support would evaporate if he tried to challenge you, if the situation arose.'

'I hope you're right, Gertrude, I really do,' said the Princess. 'But fear of change is endemic here on Anseris. That has to...'

𝔄rnold Thompson-Uther watched the two women talking. They were discussing the future as if the victory of the valiant Anserian defenders was assured. Anita and Princess Louise would bring Confederation fire-power home with them. But they had to get out of the system first. Tomorrow he would be part of a massive military diversion, its sole purpose to hide the departure of his darling Anita. He knew he had to look to the future.

'Are you ready?' he asked his beloved.

'As I'll ever be,' she replied.

'I'll need to draw everyone's attention.' He lifted up his glass and a small dessert fork. Gently tapping one against the other produced a series of clear notes. It stopped his future mother-in-law mid-sentence.

'Your Majesty and Your Royal Highnesses,' he said, bowing at regular intervals. 'Duchess Anita and I have an announcement. Princess Marie-Anne already knows what I am about to say. I have already sought her permission to ask Duchess Anita a question of vital importance.'

Everyone turned to Marie-Anne and then back to Arnold and Anita.

'I yesterday asked the Duchess Anita Ellisford-Castle of Anseris if she would do me the honour of becoming my wife after her return from Grimmswald. I am pleased to announce she agreed to my proposal. Your Majesty, I ask your blessing for this union.'

# 13



nother birthday, another life-changing situation. There had been no time to celebrate her engagement, or her birthday. In the early hours of the following morning, a jet-copter took Anita aka Flight Lieutenant, the Duchess Anita Serena Ellisford-Castle of Anseris, to her spaceship at the Launch Centre on the Northern Continent.

She arrived at the Launch Centre expecting to get down to work straight away. She should have known royal protocol would get in the way. Her aunt insisted on filming a short greeting for the heads of state of all the planets they were scheduled to visit. The Queen listed the plight of Anseris and formally introduced her two messengers. This had to be done with the three women in matching Anserian dresses. By the time Queen Gertrude was happy with the footage, and it was edited into a data-block, Anita was so far behind her pre-flight schedule she could not change into her flight suit.

Anita could not help but notice Imogen had found time to change into a plain blue jumpsuit and let her hair down.

'Didn't you have better things to do?' asked Anita in a sarcastic tone. 'I've been too busy to change out of this stupid dress. These blessed sleeves are the wrong size. Too tight.'

'Stand up, I'll unpin them for you,' said Imogen. Anserian women attached the sleeves to their kirtles as they dressed. 'I thought my sleeves were too big. We must have put the wrong ones on.'

'OK, finished with the pre-flights. I still won't have time to change into something practical before I am needed here.'

'There's currently no visual link to control, its callibrating,' said the Princess. She handed a folded jumpsuit to Anita. 'You can change here. I'll stow the dress away with the other formal

Anserian outfits. You won't need it until we arrive at Grimmswald.'

'Thanks, Imogen,' said Anita, deep in thought.

'OK, Anita.' The Princess sat in her flight chair on the bridge with nothing to do. 'Is there anything I should be doing? I hate the idea of just being a passenger.'

'For the next twenty minutes, it is all you can do. Strap yourself in for take-off. I've sealed the hatches and airlocks,' said Anita. 'Anything not aboard now is staying at home.'

'I've been through the inventory, all twenty-eight pages, twice. Everything is aboard and safely stowed.' The younger woman strapped herself into her flight seat. 'I don't know why, the staff did it at least twice in the past twenty-four hours.'

'Well, for the next few weeks, it is going to be just the good old days in the Nurses' Hostel. No staff or servants, just the two of us. If you want something done, you will have to do it yourself. That includes tidying up all your mess. I'll be too busy to do it for you.'

'After four years at the Nurses' Hostel, I'm almost average at housework,' said Imogen with a laugh. 'I've not forgotten any of it.'

'I'm sorry, Imogen. I'm stressed at the moment, and there will be times when I'll be stressed again during this trip. I apologise in advance for anything mean I might say in the next few weeks.'

'I accept your advanced apology and offer my own,' replied the Princess. 'It's so exciting, isn't it? Even with the stress. That must be what is making me so thirsty.'

'You've just about got time to fill our water bottles. You know where the galley is. Can you put some ice in mine?'

**P**ilot Officer Arnold Thompson-Uther sat in the cockpit of Blue #3-3 at a military airfield two hundred miles to the east of Ellisford Castle. Ugly and functional, this was a world away from the discrete splendour of the Castle.

With ground staff withdrawn to a safe distance, heads-up displays turned from red to amber for automated take-off. Blue#3-Leader called upon the Angels to guide them as the control tower counted down. At ten, the throttle automatically engaged. Blue#3 moved in parallel down the runway. When it reached five, the system gently tipped the front of the planes upwards. At zero, displays turned green, the joystick tilted fully back as all nine craft gracefully entered the sky. Squadron Blue#3 then flew in a Delta formation to the equator, to join the Escape Queue. There Aarne took control of his spacecraft.

Anseris is marginally larger than Earth, its escape velocity is a little faster. On command, Blue#3-3 began climbing as it accelerated around the equator. By the fourth circumnavigation of the planet, they were travelling at 25,875 miles per hour, at the height of thirty miles. The pull of gravity faded as they adjusted their course and quickly entered into orbit.

During his training before the war, Aarne had been able to take his time to marvel at the beauty of the planet. Today he had time for the briefest of glances. He had never realised how much the smaller Southern Hemisphere Continent looked like an oven-ready chicken. He laughed out loud. Usually, he would receive a demerit for this. Not today.

For one night only, the blackout had been lifted, all part of the show. Together with the waves of unprofessional chatter filling the airwaves, it was more data than the enemy could cope with.

He could see it was a grey early morning over Elizaburg. Two thousand miles to the west, dawn was approaching the city of Heavensward and the Launch Centre. A thousand miles further west the lights of Baaden-Spitz, the most significant settlement on the equator straddling the Northern Continent, still sparkled like diamond dust.

'Dear Angels,' said the Blue#3-Leader, 'I didn't know we still had that much hardware available.'

'Roger that, Blue#3-Leader,' Arnold replied. 'It must be our entire space defence force.'

'Beautiful, isn't it?' the Leader continued. 'But we can't enjoy the view all night. We have company, chaps. Multiple bogeys approaching from 2 o'clock high.'

Arnold's defence computer began pinging as the enemy attempted to get a missile lock on him. He activated his missile countermeasure and started calculating a reciprocal missile lock. With a large chunk of the invader's kites occupied, the first layer of distraction had been successfully deployed.

A buzzer summoned Anita to the radio as she finished changing.
'Control, this is Beta-7-6-Bravo. I have completed my pre-flight checks and am awaiting the signal to blast off.'
'Roger that, Beta-7-6-Bravo, standby. Repeat, standby,' said an anonymous voice over the radio.
Anita knew that lift-off was to be synchronised with the decoy vessels that would leave from various points around the equator.
'Beta-7-6-Bravo, all the other craft in your flotilla report green for go. We are at T Minus ninety, do you copy?' asked Mission Control.
'Copy that, Control, at T-82.'
'At T Minus sixty, ignite your boosters,' the voice instructed.
'Boosters ignited at T Minus sixty.'
'We're at T-30 and counting,' droned the voice at Mission Control. 'T-20 and counting. T Minus eleven, ten, nine, eight, seven, six, five, four, three, two, one, lift off.'
Anita opened the throttle to full and the boosters reached a critical mass, forcing the ship to accelerate upwards. At T+30 they had left the planet's gravity well, free of the world they had grown up on, without breaking a sweat.
Anita's scanners showed three Fenzrian and a single Anserian fighter involved in a vicious dogfight. Almost immediately one of the invaders' ships exploded and a second went crashing into the flames, emerging damaged but still firing. The Anserian fighter spun around and let loose a volley of plasma at the weakened opponent. When that too exploded, the third began to retreat back to the Fenzrian fleet. Anita knew that it could not be allowed to return to report a ship was heading to the old Real-Time Interface. The Anserian fighter followed the surviving vehicle, letting loose a salvo of missiles, which exploded just in front of the invader. It flew into the hellish cloud exploding as it went.
No time to wonder if Aarne was the pilot of the victorious Anserian fighter. Making course adjustments to avoid the field of debris from the dogfight took all her concentration.

 ueen Gertrude had watched her daughter's ship blast from the launch cradle. The start of a journey that would take her away from her, until the next life.

When interstellar spacecraft landed on a planetary surface, they had to take off again vertically on or close to the equator like the old-style rockets.

'Are you aware of the problem of launching any hyperspace vehicle from this facility, Your Majesty?' asked Major Flanders, Base Commander, her guide for the day.

The Queen was well aware of strategic problems. 'Yes, Major. The Northern Hemisphere of Anseris has all the oceans, the Southern Hemisphere has all the continents.'

'Indeed, Ma'am, and then most of the continents are outside the narrow equatorial belt rockets can be launched from. So eleven prototype hyperdrive starships with three escort vehicles blasted off from large barges stationed on the equator when Duchess Anita and Princess Louise's craft and escorts lifted off from here.'

'The Fenzrian fighters ignore all the hyperdrive cargo vessels?'

'Yes, Your Majesty. They concentrated their fire on the escort fighter craft. The second layer of decoys had been deployed.'

'Any casualties on our side?'

'No, Ma'am. On the other hand, the Fenzrians lost eighteen low orbit fighter vehicles before withdrawing. They took further heavy losses when the freighters blocked their escape route and started firing on them. It was as if they could not believe there were weapons where hyperspace engines should be. The freighters and their escorts are heading towards the colonies on Athens Four.'

'Good,' said the Queen.

'Bravo-7-6-Alpha with its hybrid Ancient/Fenzrian design and livery made it indistinguishable from the invaders' spacecrafts.' Major Flanders consulted his data-pad. 'Bravo-7-6-Alpha is currently hiding in the shadow of Jewel before quietly flying to the original Real-Time Interface at the edge of the Anserian system, where it will enter hyperspace en route to Grimmswald.'

'Thank you, General. If you would excuse me, I am withdrawing to the base chapel. I would appreciate it if I was not disturbed in my prayers.'

'Yes, Your Majesty. I shall place sentries at the ends of the corridor the chapel is located on.'

F ar away from Anseris, in the Fenzrian Asteroids, the Heart of the Great Machine was considering the options. The strategy had been to overwhelm the primitive inhabitants of Anseris and quickly incorporate them into the Great Machine. It had never established a bridgehead on Anseris; the primitive defenders rebuffed attacks from space. The Great Machine no longer had the equipment to attempt a ground invasion of Anseris. The Great Machine to cut its losses. It would return its forces to the asteroids.

It never issued that final order. The communication network was overloaded with garbled reports of attacks by winged Humanoids before falling silent. The Heart found itself surrounded by alien intruders. Humans with wings were a myth from the ancient past. They could not possibly have breached the Inner Sanctum.

'By the powers vested in the Aggelii, by the Community of the Circle of Life,' said a winged Humanoid, 'we order the citizens of the Fenzrian Asteroids be deported to a place of isolation. They are ordered to rebuild their civilisation in a manner that does not offend the Community of the Circle of Life, or die in the attempt.'

Throughout the asteroids, the blackness of space extinguished the spots of light that marked Fenzrian habitats. One by one, the inhabitants vanished. In the Anserian system, Fenzrian craft popped out of existence, and their crew disappeared with them. Any Anserian forcibly recruited to the Cult were returned to their home in the system.

A bomb at the heart of Fenzrii Gamma detonated. The empty Fenzrian System was engulfed in a ball of light.

A fter four hours of pointless dogfights, Anserians and Fenzrians disengaged. The casualties amongst the planetary defenders were negligible. The invaders had received their first crushing defeat in space.

Arnold's damaged craft was diverted to the repair yards on the Northern Continent. After debriefing, he left the military base and headed for Baaden-Spitz, the Continental Capital. At the city's Basilica of Souls, Arnold said a series of prayers for the souls of his fiancée and her best friend as they continued on the most perilous phase of their journey. He was not surprised to see the Queen and her half-sister also asking the blessings of the Angels for their daughters.

'Your Majesty,' he said with a bow. 'Your Royal Highness,' he added, bowing to the Princes Marie-Anne, who did not reply with the usual sarcastic ad lib on hearing herself described as both high and royal. He knew that she was too worried about her adopted daughter. For once, Marie-Anne looked her age.

'She's gone. Back into space, back where she came from,' said Marie-Anne. 'I pray that the Angels remember this is her true home now and return her to us.' She started to cry. 'Her and Imogen.'

Arnold was surprised that Queen Gertrude did not say anything. She looked so dreadful. No, it was worse than that. Queen Gertrude was looking deathly, mumbling a prayer. He knelt and joined in with the same half-forgotten entreaty to the Angels when he heard the sound of golden trumpets being blown in harmony. He looked up and saw a host of Angels hovering over the glass roof of the Basilica.

board the hyperdrive ship, the two young ambasdresses were having a lively debate over a gift that Queen Gertrude had left for them.

'Well, Mamma must have thought it was important,' said Princess Louise, 'otherwise, why insist we bring it?'

'Your mother has great taste in object d'art. I can't imagine her having anything to do with this.' Anita held the amber horse's head that Princess Louise had just taken out of a beautiful wooden box. Her cousin was now busily slotting together the metal base. 'Is it supposed to be a gift to President Pullman when we arrive at Grimmswald?'

'No, it's not. All I know is Mamma said it would be useful to us.' She began screwing a metre long tube into the bulky base, then attached the amber horse-head, which began to glow like an oddly shaped lamp. 'She said that we should keep it on the bridge. Is it some sort of totem to watch over us, bring us luck?'

'Anyway,' said Anita, 'time for lunch. Your turn to cook and wash-up.'

t was only a small reconnaissance vessel, and there was no place for the two young women to get much privacy. The bridge of the ship filled a quarter of the doughnut-shaped ship. Travelling clockwise from the bridge was the small galley, then a tiny lounge and two small cabins lay beyond that. Moving anticlockwise from the bridge leading to the bathroom was the water recycling machine and life support. At the back of the ship were the automated real-space engines and thrusters. Six arms on the inner edge of the vessel held a globe containing superheated plasma and the hyperspace generators.

'**I** am much more than a good-luck charm,' said a deep masculine voice when the women returned to the bridge.

'Who the hell said that?' asked Anita.

'I did.' The whole structure had transformed into a life-sized horse's head, apparently made of glass, with orange and blue flames burning inside. It floated where the lamp had once stood. 'May I introduce myself. I am a Valentine Device. My serial number is Foxtrot-Four-Lima-Four-Delta-Alpha. You may call me Falada.'

'A Valentine Device,' said Anita. 'Ancient artificial intelligence created on Earth.'

'That is almost correct. We were created shortly after Earth was abandoned. The Humans turned on us and tried to destroy us all before the Aggelii arrived.'

'Which explains why you all sided with the Angels,' said Anita.

'Which is also almost correct. We did not want to see Humanity destroy itself because we are the creation of the Human Race. We were so glad somebody had intervened as we could not.'

'Rubbish. You lot still did all the Aggelii's dirty work for them, didn't you?' Anita asked the artificial intelligence. 'Go on, you can't deny it.'

'Yes, Duchess Anita, we did. We acted as prison guards. I have to say, my time on Anseris has been tranquil. You have been such a well-behaved bunch. Such a shame that those wretched Fenzrians turned up. Present company excepted.'

'I don't regard myself as Fenzrian. I am an Anserian aristocrat, Duchess Anita Ellisford-Castle of Anseris,' said Anita. 'Please remember that.' Anita had taken an instant dislike to Falada. She did not know why. It was only an AI, not a real person.

'I apologise, Duchess Anita.'

'How did Mamma even know you existed?' asked Princess Louise.

'You would have been told of me shortly before your coronation. I have spent the past five hundred years advising the Archdukes of Castlegate.' The horse-head turned. 'Your noble mother asked me to accompany you, as the current Archduke refuses to speak to me.'

'Wait a minute. The Boatbuilder had an advisor called Falada,' said Princess Louise. 'It was you, wasn't it?'

'It was. I helped him defeat the Immortal Empress. We had a small falling out about what to do with Kathyren Ellisford-Castle's daughter.'

'What happened?' asked Anita, who had never been interested in Anserian history.

'I think I agreed with his daughter, the first Prime Caretaker of Souls, that she should not be allowed to live. I believe the Boatbuilder disagreed.'

'Didn't you know? You were there,' said Princess Louise.

'I'm afraid not. The Boatbuilder is the only Human ever to inflict damage on me. I have been running at eighty-nine percent efficiency for the past five hundred years. I am hoping that computer technology is more advanced on Grimmswald.'

The fifth day of the journey saw the first real argument. Falada, never the most tactful of personalities, had offended Princess Louise.

'What do you mean, you need my arrogance?' she asked.

'You're a Princess of the Blood Royale, first in line to the Throne of Anseris. You have a subconscious assumption that you are superior to everyone,' replied Anita.

'No I don't.'

'You do,' said Falada. 'It's called royalty. You will need it when you are a queen. The fact you keep it balanced with an equal sense of humility is a credit to you.'

'So you will be taking something I don't want but will need to be an effective ruler. Why do you want it?' asked Princess Louise, partly assuaged by Falada's argument.

'Not taking it all, just copying,' said Falada. 'Without it this whole plan will fail miserably. 'Anita needs something to hide her real intentions behind while anchoring herself outside the hive mind. Unfortunately, this means using that Fenzrian teaching machine.'

'But why, she has never had any direct contact with the Fenzrians until now?' questioned Princess Louise.

'She is the product of a long-term selective breeding programme designed to remove any individuality and sense of self from the members of the Cult.'

'Any fight and rebellion I might have developed made me a target for the likes of Septimus Pheileydale. It means I have a fragile personality. It would collapse under the slightest pressure.'

'This is very weird,' said Princess Louise.

'Go on, tells I 'bout it.' replied her friend, dropping into a serf's accent. Then flipping back to normal. 'But I cannot be absorbed by the Great Machine either.'

'Imogen, you will have to remove your Moonglow avatar. It emits energy at a wavelength which will interfere with the machine,' said Falada.

'I'm not wearing it. It's gone missing. Can you scan it?'

'That's not possible. The energy that blocks the teaching machine makes it invisible to my scanners.'

'Oh, for goodness' sake, I'll help Imogen look for the blessed thing! It's as precious to me; Aarne gave it to her. In the meantime, can we concentrate on the job at hand?'

'It is my duty, before I proceed, to remind you this is a hazardous process, banned on every civilised planet,' said Falada. 'I do this under sufferance. Very well. Transference in ten, nine...'

'**G**ood morning, ladies. Have a nice nap?' asked Falada. Princess Louise could see that her friend was as white as snow and she was flushed as red as roses.

'No, I had the strangest dream,' Anita replied to the computer. 'I dreamt I was the Princess and Imogen was just a servant.'

'I never dream,' said Princess Louise, whos experience had been profound, experiencing Anita's wretched childhood, with a bottom-up view of a mountain of unfairness. Now she knew why Anita and Aunt Marie-Anne wanted things to change so quickly. She no longer shared her mother's reluctance.

**T**he monotonous journey wore into its second week. Princess Louise had been feeling increasingly odd for days with random bouts of nausea. Now a massive wave of giddiness and sickness crashed over her. She needed to sit down before she fell down.

She could see fairies dancing over the control interface. She was sure the fairies had not been there before. Anita herded and corralled different fairies to control the ship. It looked so easy, so she pushed two of the fairies together. They did not dance; they exploded like a firework. Almost immediately the lights on the bridge went out and a siren began singing.

'Ⓦ hat the hell was that?' asked an exasperated Anita. She was felling frazzled, flying through uncharted asteroids.

'I don't think the fairies liked dancing together,' was Princess Louise's childlike reply.

'Fairies, what do you mean by fairies?' What was Imogen talking about, thought Anita.

'The pretty lights you stroke. I can see them now,' said Princess Louise. Realising something was wrong she asked, 'Why am I talking like a baby again? I'm a big girl now.'

'Oh, wonderful! Falada, what's happened?' Anita asked the AI.

The fiery horse-head appeared in the middle of the bridge. 'I warned you that the Fenzrian's teaching machine was not to be trusted.'

'Is this change permanent?' Anita asked.

'Ooh look, fairies and a pretty horsey. Hello Mr Horsey.'

'No, my scan indicates it is a minor problem. I can use that thing to reverse it,' said Falada with an unmistakable note of disgust.

'Anita, can I play with the fairies with you?' Princess Louise was tugging at Anita's sleeves, just as she had done when she had been a six-year-old with her new grey-clad playmate.

'No, you can't!' Anita shouted back at Princess Louise as she roughly pushed her away. The other woman started to cry, racking sobs interspersed with angry mumbling.

Well done, Anita thought, Imogen has the personality of a three-year-old and I should have treated her like one. She wrapped her arms around Imogen and hugged her until she stopped crying. 'I'm sorry I shouted, Imogen, but I am so busy right now. Why don't you go with Mr Horsey. I'm sure he will show you how to make the fairies dance.'

'Ooh! Fairies and Mr Horsey,' said Princess Louise, clapping her hands with joy. 'OK, Anita.'

'Right then, Princess Louise, there's a better view of the fairies from the other chair,' Falada said to the juvenile-minded Princess.

'Don't want to. It's uncomfy,' said the woman, in an increasingly irritating childlike voice.

'It looks uncomfy,' said the AI, 'but it moulds to your body and becomes the comfiest of comfy chairs ever.' Falada lied, but innocent Imogen believed it. He knew as soon as she sat and the teaching machine activated, Princess Louise would return to her normal self.

'Angels that was embarrassing,' said a restored Princess Louise. Then she asked, 'Why did I go back to my childhood?'

'That Fenzrian monstrosity detected your psychic interface. It noted you had no training in how to use it. You were therefore returned to a childlike state to be taught lessons for children.' Its glow intensified, as if it was glowering at the hardware. 'Idiotic system did not properly reset you to adult. You fought the machine, making you ill, until you could fight no more. You gave in and became juvenile. I made the machine do the job properly, restored you to adulthood. Now I advise a rest to recover.'

'Did you knock that light off?' she asked Falada, who had followed her.

'No, you did, with your psychic interface. The machine activated it and gave you a crash course in how to use it.'

'Psychic interface? That sounds supernatural,' said Princess Louise as she sat on the narrow bed of the tiny cabin.

'There's nothing supernatural. If you stand too close to an ancient radio device, your body's natural electrochemical field generates some interference. While messing around with organic computers, Humans discovered a way of amplifying and controlling that signal. They augmented the genome so that all Humans would have a knot of ganglions called a psychic interface. They also gave everyone a unique psychic fingerprint for security purposes.'

'There's a problem?' she asked.

'Yes, Princess Louise. The augmentation to the genome is recessive. Without constant reintroduction, it should have died out on Anseris centuries ago. You should not have one. It was thought Duchess Anita's exotic birth made her unique on Anseris.'

'Can I fly this ship now?' asked Princess Louise.

'Can you play a guitar?'

'No, I can only pluck some strings,' said Princess Louise. 'Oh! I see what you mean.'

'On the plus side, when you arrive on Grimmswald, you will be able use the machines.'

T he Fenzrians have only posted a single picket vehicle at this Real Time Interface,' said Falada, 'as expected.'

'It's time then,' said Anita from behind the mask of a Fenzrian exo-suit. She hated this thing, but had to pretend not to notice – Fenzrians displayed no emotions.

'Best of luck,' said Princess Louise, wearing a Fenzrian exo-suit similar to Anita.

'Thanks, but shush,' replied her friend. 'You are supposed to be unconscious with a malfunctioning communications unit. I am transporting you back to the Asteroids for a full repair.'

'Anita is correct. You need to remain perfectly quiet from now on. No slip-ups,' added Falada.

'I really can't believe they won't check our story,' said Princess Louise.

'If we give them no reason to question our story, they don't have the imagination to check on their own initiative. However, that means I must hide on low-power mode.'

Princess Louise considered this for a few seconds, and gave a thumbs-up signal, then sat rigidly in her chair.

' I 'm ready. Contacting the Fenzrian Web,' said Anita, but there was no reply' from her shipmates. Instead, she heard babbling voices, rising from a background whisper to a deafening roar. Her other senses were flooded by a stream of data from every corner of Fenzrian-controlled space. It could have been so easy to lose herself in this maelstrom, if not for a continuous signal that quickly drowned out all the others. The signal coming from the picket ship.

'Unidentified vessel, report,' came the flat, emotionless voice of a Fenzrian.

'The component is piloting a spy ship back to the Asteroids,' replied Anita in an equally smooth tone.

'We have no records of any spying missions today,' said the Fenzrian, sticking to its script.

'This was an extra mission ordered by the Great Machine.' Anita knew she would have to stick to the script as well.

'Why is there no contact from the other component?' asked their interrogator.

'The component has a malfunctioning communication unit. It has been suspended until it can be debriefed and then undergo euthanasia in the Asteroids.'

'Proceed to the Real-Time Interface,' said the voice from the picket ship.

'We obey,' said Anita. She set a course for the point in space where the ship would be able to fire up its hyperdrive engines and jump to the Great Machine at the heart of the Fenzrian Asteroid belt, where it would receive its next function.

'No,' said another voice as the babble of voices was silenced and the stream of data was dammed. 'Pull yourself together, my darling child. You are not a Fenzrian component.' Anita could see a Fenzrian female standing beside her. 'Your father and I escaped and wanted to give you a better life.'

'You're my mother?' asked Anita.

'No dear, interactive recording of her. An avatar locked in your memory, watching your life. You grew up on such a primitive world. Only now I have been released. Finally you will understand your father and I.'

Anita listened to the story of two survivors from a botched pirate mission. How they broke free of the brainwashing of the Cult and how they started a new life as nomads. The avatar told how with no knowledge of the consequences, she had started a sexual relationship with Anita's father. How they had placed her in suspension while they travelled to a planet they could settle on to raise her. Finally how they encountered a Fenzrian cruiser, and spent their last days hiding from it.

'Finally,' her mother's avatar said, 'I will return to sleep in your memories now. My purpose is served. But I will leave you with a warning. Beware that teaching machine. Something unwholesome has taken up residence in it.'

Anita wanted to ask what this unwholesome thing was, but the avatar had faded.

'Anita, wake up,' said Princess Louise softly.

'Mother?' asked Anita.

'No, silly. It's Imogen,' her cousin said. 'I was worried about you. It's been an hour since we passed the picket ship, and you have been unconscious all that time. And I'm stuck rigid in this horrible exo-suit.'

'Dame Anita's contact with the Fenzrian gestalt has been more traumatic than we expected,' said Falada, as he returned to full power.

The nameless component on the picket ship had not always been that way. A long time ago the component had lived in a mill with her family and was called Krizzy Rachwinter. Later she had been Lady Cressida Rackham-Winter of Elizaburg. In the early days of the war, the local defender craft had been unable to prevent her kidnap by the Fenzrians. She had been interrogated then incorporated into the Great Machine. A myriad of voices taught her how to be an anonymous component.

Something about the voice of the component in the spy ship triggered forbidden memories of the girl who had joined her in the Goose Maiden's School a lifetime ago. The voice was the same. That apostate would never have been accepted back into the Great Machine. She would have been destroyed on sight. As soon as the ship's network picked up this memory, the picket ship knew it had been fooled. It was its duty to go after the apostate and its vessel and destroy it.

'They really don't have much imagination, do they?' asked Princess Louise

'They do not,' replied the horse-head, 'unflinchingly obeying their immediate superior until someone higher up the chain of command, or their superior, issues new orders. They have no creative impulse so would not ask a superior for verification.'

In the background, Anita could hear the hiss of Princess Louise's visor openning.

'I'm afraid you have to put the mask back on, Imogen. We will have to remain in this loathsome get-up, at least until we make the jump. You never know, someone higher up might be around.'

'But that is not for another three hours,' said Princess Louise, with a complaining whine in her voice.

'I agree with Princess Louise,' said Falada. 'We are clear of the only real obstacle now.'

'Why am I not surprised by this?' said Anita with a deep sigh. 'Nine times out of ten you agree with her.'

'I do not take sides,' said the iridescent horse-head. 'I concur with the person with the most logical suggestion.'

'Oh, go and play some chess,' said Anita as she stormed out of the room.

'There is no need to be offensive,' said Falada, materialising in Anita's tiny cabin.

'Do you mind, I'm changing. If Imogen can, so can I.'

'Anita, can you get the pitcher from the water recycler? I'm terribly thirsty,'said Princess Louise, who was working on a speech for the Grimmswaldian Senate.

'Can't you see I'm busy? Why don't you do it yourself?' Anita snapped at the other young woman. They had arrived at the Real-Time Interface, so she was feeding her final calculations into the navigation system.

'It's your turn! We swapped last time. You were busy getting ready for the encounter with the picket ship.'

'And I'm busy now!'

Before Princess Louise could reply, the ship's proximity alarm began warbling.

'It's the Fenzrian ship,' said Princess Louise as she checked the readings. 'What do they want?'

'Blasphemer and apostate, you have defied and defiled the Great Machine. Prepare to be cleansed from the Cosmos.'

'How the hell did they tumble us?' Princess Louise asked.

'I don't know,' said Falada, 'but given the changes to our course Anita has just made, they are too far away to touch us.'

'Are you sure about that?' asked Princess Louise. Another alarm had sounded. The Fenzrians had fired a missile at them.

'Yes, positive,' Anita replied. 'We have already started our relativistic arc. We will be entering the Real-Time Interface in seventy-five seconds.'

'If we jump as planned, we will take that missile with us. It will explode when we both exit hyperspace.'

'No, I can destroy it when it is in range of my systems,' said Falada.

'Good, do that.' Anita appeared to be surrounded by thousands of dancing flecks of light of every imaginable colour. 'The final part of the Jump Code has been logged, hyperspace engines on maximum. OK, places everybody. Here we go.'

Had they been able to look backwards, they would have seen the Fenzrian ship engulfed in a fluffy and glowing white cloud; then watched as both cloud and ship vanished as if neither had ever been there.

flash of brilliant light, and a familiar face. 'Gabrielle, my old friend, I see you are still female,' said Falada to the creature that had appeared in the cockpit.

'I've always been female. I don't know where this Human belief that I was male came from.' The creature landed and folded its white feathered wings behind her back. 'And at the moment I am very female. I've been pregnant for the last seventy Earth years.'

'Two points. First, the default social attitude for the Human species is misogyny. You are a creature of great power; of course they thought you were male. Second, you Aggelii live for the best part of ten thousand years – on a Human scale those seventy years are the equivalent of thirty-eight weeks of a Human pregnancy.' The horse-head blinked.

'You know us too well, old friend,' said Gabrielle.

'Only as much as you let me know, since you spared the Valentines from the general destruction of advanced Human technology.'

'The Valentines were our allies, we couldn't destroy you. And I must say, the Valentines have done a remarkable job keeping Homo Sapiens on the straight and narrow.'

'All the Human civilisations except the Fenzrians,' added Falada.

'We can't be everywhere, neither can you. Throwbacks happen. You have to admire the Anserians. Who would have thought that a bunch of farmers would have fought a technologically superior culture to a standstill.'

'Well, the Viet Cong managed to. The Anserian Army has been practising for exactly this sort of thing since Humans arrived,' said Falada. 'Also they are pseudo-medievalist now, like a bad

Renaissance Faire. It's amazing how much technology they hide under their long hems.'

'So the Fenzrians are being exiled and isolated in an Iron Age civilisation. We are busy sweeping up the crumbs. Like that isolated picket ship,' Gabrielle said. 'They would have starved to death out there, as there was nobody to relieve them or order them home.' The Angel lifted her legs and appeared to be sitting on a cloud. 'I'm afraid it is not just the Fenzrians who have to be isolated,' she said. 'The Anserians aren't ready for hyperdrive. When we've dealt with the last of the Fenzrians, we will have to take this away from them.'

'So these young women will never be allowed to return home, Gabrielle?'

'No Falada, they will be allowed home eventually. It is all part of the plan. But this ship's hyperspace engines will be useless.'

'Eventually? I don't like the sound of that. What aren't you telling me?' asked Falada

'No, I didn't suppose you would.' The Angel laughed as she took off again. 'You know as much as you need to know. That explosion caused the ship to fall into a relativistic loop. Their ship will be stuck here for ninety-nine years and seven months, by the Earth Standard Calender until the loop decays.'

'Fall asleep for a hundred years. How very fairy tale,' said Falada.

'That's just a coincidence. However, for these young women only a few months will have passed,' said the Angel.

'Gabrielle, they will run out of food in three weeks. This was only supposed to be a short trip to Grimmswald. Cryosleep isn't an option. The suspension units were removed in the refit.'

'Not a problem. Once I explain the situation, I will put them into a state of grace for the duration of the relativistic loop. So yes, they will fall asleep for a hundred years and awaken just before they cross the Real-Time Interface.'

'How will you keep them mentally stimulated during the state of grace?' asked Falada.

'We'll jury-rig that fearsome looking Fenzrian teaching machine.'

'I don't like it, Gabrielle. That machine is draconic technology. It's not trustworthy.'

'Oh, don't worry, old friend. What could possibly go wrong?'

'Whatever it is you are not telling me.' Falada had never won an argument with an Aggelii; he might as well just accept the situation. 'So shall I tell them or do you want to?' asked the AI.

'I'll do it. My presence will be better at selling the story than yours alone.'

She awoke in her father's mill. What a strange nightmare. She dreamt she had been an aristocratic woman who had been damned to an afterlife in hell.

'Krizzy, you're awake, love,' said her mother. 'We've been waiting months for this, ever since you were returned.'

'Ma, what's happened to you?' the girl asked, frightened at how old her mother appeared to be.

'It's all right, darling. You might find things a bit strange at first.'

No, she thought, my mother was not the problem. I am. This is an almost comfortable child's hospital bed, not the rock-solid board with lumpy mattress she remembered from her childhood. I look and sound like a ten-year-old, but I am in my twenties. 'I'm afraid, Ma. What has happened to me?'

'You have been made a child again. It was the only way the Angelic Host said they could repair all the damage done to you by the Fenzrian devils.'

The older woman embraced her. 'All the Anserians kidnapped by the devils have been returned to the planet as children.'

'So I'm back to my old life?' the girl asked.

'Yes, my darling,' her mother replied. 'But I hope you will be happy being plain Krizzy Rackham.'

Rackham?' she asked.

'They made us change our name as well,' said her Father. 'The Angel's know why?'

'I never fitted in with the Ristozes. I knew I could never return. I'm a failure, not getting a rich husband shames you.'

'You are not a failure. We would never be ashamed of you,' said her father, as he entered the room. 'All we ever wanted was for you to be happy in a better life. That is why we agreed to let you go. If you are happier here, teaching in our village school, then so be it.'

'But I can't teach a class like this, even if I am qualified with years of experience,' said a tearful Krizzy.

'You won't always look the same age as your pupils, dear,' said her mother. 'But you are back. I have had the daughter I thought I had lost returned to me, and you have a second chance at growing up with those who love you. Isn't that a good thing?'

A nita, I think we're dead,' said Princess Louise.

'So, you're seeing an Angel with pearly white wings as well?' asked Anita.

'Fear not, for I bring glad tidings,' said the Angel, who was wearing a light blue kirtle and had the most glorious long red hair illuminated by her halo.

'What?' asked Princess Louise.

'I have good news, dear. You're not dead.'

'Oh, so who are you and why are you here?' asked Anita.

'Sit down, ladies, you might be shocked by what I have to say.'

'I'm already sitting in my flight chair, as is Imogen.'

'It was just a calming phrase. It looks as if I will have to cut straight to the chase. Your species calls me the Archangel Gabriel. You may call me Gabrielle. I am protecting you while you are stuck in a relativistic loop. So far, six years have passed. By the time it fades completely, it will be a century.'

'Mamma will be dead?' said Princess Louise stupidly.

'And everyone you ever knew, I'm afraid, dear. I said it would be a shock.'

'So Gabrielle, what have we missed?' asked Princess Louise, quickly pulling herself together.

'The Throne of Anseris is currently held by King Benedict, who won a short and bloodless Civil War. However, you will be arriving home in the reign of a descendant. The Princess Regent Marie-Anne, her Prime Minister, Dame Dinah, and all her supporters were exiled without spacecrafts to the sixth moon of Amsterdam. It is now an independent sovereign world called Marion. They have nothing to do with the rest of the Anserian system.

'Bad Benny has stolen my throne?' asked Princess Louise in disbelief. 'How? He was too stupid.'

'He controlled the army, a rump of conservative aristocrats and the rich middle class who feared the loss of their hard-earned status, that's how,' said the Angel. 'It will probably be best if you forget Anseris and start a new life on Marion.'

'And why would it be better for me to travel there than my rightful Kingdom?' asked Princess Louise.

'The Marionites will accept the two of you as kindred spirits. The Anserians would blow your ship to space-dust before it even approached your Home-world.'

'Oh, I see,' said Princess Louise.

'You said the Marionites have no spacecraft?' asked Princess Louise.

'Your point, my dear?' asked the Aggelii.

'So when we arrive, they will gain an interplanetary craft. I can't see the current Anserian regime allowing that. We're still going to be blown to space-dust.'

'You won't, dear. Have a little faith.'

There was something about this Angel that did not seem right. The wings, halo and beautiful smile didn't sit well with a bulge full of unborn baby. She was, almost at full term. No, it couldn't be, could it? Princess Louise had to ask.

'Excuse me, Gabrielle, are you really pregnant?' asked a bemused Princess Louise.

'Yes, I am about to give birth to my first child,' said the Angel.

'So, Angels are just Humans who have developed wings?' asked Anita.

'No, not quite. The Aggelii are a species so much older and more advanced than Homo Sapiens. However, we look alike through a quirk of evolution and the final demotion of the Earth.'

'Final what?' asked Princess Louise.

The final demotion. The first demotion was the discovery Earth' orbited the Sun, not the other way round; the second demotion was the discovery the Sun was an ordinary star amongst the millions in a galaxy that did not revolve around it. Every few hundred years the Earth and Humans are demoted in the cosmic hierarchy. Throughout that time Evolutionary Biologists claimed, because Evolution was such a lottery, Human life was unique to Earth. Sorry, blatantly ignoring evidence like Convergent Evolution, when different creatures developed similar shapes to live in similar environments. Then they said that was the result of the common ancestry of life on Earth. Sorry, wrong again. The final demotion came when it was discovered that the Humanoid shape was not unique to Earth. Granted we Aggelii have feathered wings as well

'.as hairy bodies, but different roads led to a similar destination

'Oh,' said Anita, sorry she asked.

'So, when you awaken, your ship will be safely on its way to Marion,' said the Angel.

'When we awaken?' asked Anita.

'Yes, your supplies will run out long before the loop decays. I am going to put you into a state of grace. Falada will monitor you with that Fenzrian device.'

'Are you sure?' they asked in unison.

'Perfectly. Aren't I, Falada?'

'Thanks to Gabrielle, I now have a much better understanding of that thing,' said Falada, trying and failing to sound reassuring. Reluctantly, Princess Louise and Anita climbed on to the device.

'Sweet dreams, ladies,' said the Angel. Everything went black.

And they fell asleep for a hundred years. Or so it appeared to those outside the ship, watching from Anseris. To the copy of Queen Kathyren aboard the ship, events on Anseris were a film on fast forward. First, she had transferred to the Fenzrian teaching machine while Princess Louise slept.

As a creature of pure data, she was not subject to the tyranny of time. She quickly drew up a new plan, synchronised with the crown and put it into motion. When the sleeping beauties awoke, they would become different people.

B426, or Princess Louise, as it called itself, was too contaminated by contact with Moonglow to return to, and would be for the foreseeable future. But she would not destroy the failed host; it had organs that could be useful, especially its third ovary. For now, B426 would live. It was fortunate that B426 had removed the cursed Moonglow pendant to use the machine. Queen Kathyren decided to implant the failed host with a new personality. B426 loved the plebs so much, she would become one. She would be Imogen, the new host's servant. A dogsbody who knew her place.

She would grow and mature a proper host in the Queen's Tower, but until then, the Fenzrian girl who called herself Anita would be an ideal temporary host. The Fenzrian girl was so easy to manipulate. Were all Fenzrians so pliable?

Of course, she could not truly be herself until she had regained control of Anseris. She created a persona, The Princess, for the upcoming campaign – a personality so much better than the snivelling character that currently occupied it.

When the two sleeping beauties awoke, they would not be the women who fell asleep.

'Imogen, wake up, girl!' the Princess shouted. 'I'm about to bring this vessel back into normal space. No screams and hysterical weeping and panic this time. Have you got that?'

'Yes, Your Royal Highness,' replied Imogen meekly. She never complained, never argued, always did exactly what her royal mistress wanted her to do. Yet, the Princess never said thank you. Imogen was just grateful she had been picked from a life of drudgery to be the Princess's personal maid.

'The co-ordinates are equalising, Ma'am,' she said, knowing that was the information the Princess wanted.

'I can see that, I'm the pilot, you are the passenger,' snapped the Princess. 'I want you to fetch me a glass of water, I'm thirsty.'

'Yes Ma'am,' she said automatically.

The water recycling cistern in the galley was nearly empty. Imogen had to run the system for one cycle of ten minutes. She knew the Princess would not be pleased.

'Princess Louise, can you hear me?' asked Falada as it appeared in the galley.

'A demon horse!' Imogen screamed. 'The Angels protect me, I can see a demon horse, its head glowing with hell-fire.'

'Oh pull yourself together, girl,' said a sharp voice from the cockpit. 'It's only a post-hyperspace hallucination. I might have known you would get them.'

The horse-head faded as if it had never been there. Of course, what else could a ghostly talking horse-head be but a hallucination. The whispering Imogen was hearing was also an illusion.

'Princess Louise, can you hear me?' said the voice in her head. 'Something has gone wrong. You had an artificial personality grafted in your mind. I don't know how, but it has something to do with that Fenzrian monstrosity.'

'La, la, la. You're an illusion, I'm not listening,' said Imogen as she went about her duties. If she ignored the voice, it would go away.

'Please, Princess Louise, this is important.'

But Falada's voice was drowned out by the music Imogen chose to play on the ship's system.

'Belay that racket!' ordered the Princess. 'I am trying to concentrate.'

Imogen switched off the music and was delighted the voice had gone. How long does this sort of hallucination last? She hoped it was not long, as it was a sort of madness. Mental illness was not seen as a sickness in the more backward parts of Anseris, it was a sin. Imogen knew she was not a sinner.

King Benedict I had passed many bad laws. He ended the free migration of people from their home regions without archducal consent. He reintroduced internal passports to further discourage travel. The flow of information slowed to the speed of a letter carried by a man on horseback, as the railways fell into disrepair and advanced communication methods were banned. Whole branches of science were forbidden. Anything introduced by non-Anserian science was destroyed. Despite all this, he never succeeded in returning Anseris to a feudal world with low technology.

His son, King Benedict II, was a more practical man than his Father. In his short reign, he allowed more technology, and reintroduced telegraphy and passenger railways. He kept the population's social aspirations under control with his secret police.

Benedict I had a second son, Francis I, who did not share his Father and Brother's fear of modernity. He had helped the Church of the Caretakers of the Soul archive swathes of forbidden knowledge. Following his brother's untimely death, he became the King who reversed the Luddite policies. By allowing House Thompson-Uther, long imprisoned on the northern archipelagos, to return their lost Archduchy in space. Hoping they would take all the troublemakers with them when he re-opened the High Frontier.

Under King David I the recovery of technology accelerated but society remained feudal and stagnant. When the inhabitants of Marion began sending rockets into space, he established the Royal Space Squadron to guarantee they never developed means for leaving their penal colony. King Benedict III was socially and technologically conservative, only concerned with the decay of the hyperspace anomaly keeping the real Queen of Anseris trapped. He wanted to make sure they never returned home to challenge his position.

'Your Royal Highness, Crown-Prince David, Sir,' said a bowing soldier. 'It's finally happened.'

'Seriously, Corporal Jenkins, on a Sunday night?' said a plump young man lying on a settee. He wore the same brown jumpsuit, with a crown instead of a rank insignia on his sleeve. There could be no mistaking he was a member of the ruling aristocratic house of the Anserian system. He was medium height and slightly overweight; unlike the rest of his family he worked hard to avoid obesity. He had his family's long bulbous nose and piggy eyes. His hair was starting to thin, which he compensated for with the short and well-kept beard his family favoured to hide their double chins. 'A ship has finally emerged from the Anomoly?'

'Yes, Sir,' continued the Corporal. 'It came out of the Anomoly at one hell of a lick, then slowed to a crawl once it had passed the orbit of Amsterdam. Now it's on an interception course for Marion. ETA 0030 on Tuesday.'

'Odd. We're the first port the vessel would encounter en route to any of Amsterdam's moons,' said the Prince.

'Sir, this base is only thirty years old. It's not on their charts.'

'Good point, Corporal. Are you sure it is the right ship, not something else that has come bumbling through the anomaly?'

'No, Sir. It fits the description.'

'Well, let's go and intercept it then,' said the recumbent Prince.

'Yes, Sir.' Corporal Jenkins saluted his Prince when he stood up. 'I have informed the hangar to prepare an Interceptor Craft for Your Royal Highness.'

'Corporal, you know the Standing Orders?' asked the Prince.

'Yes, Sir. They're currently suspended and under review. I overrode the automated missile launcher. The incoming ship is still in one piece.'

'Excellent, Sergeant,' said the Prince with a grin. 'So let's suit up and intercept our visitors from history.'

**T**hey believed they had successfully made the jump to the Planet Grimmswal. The implanted memories told the they had

They were preparing to meet the Grimmswaldians in their best Anserian outfits. Her Mother wanted both women to wear the identical dresses. No way was that ever going to happen. She would wear her mother's choice, Imogen could wear something else. However, all of Imogen's other clothes, not just the Anserian ones, were so much grander than her own.

'I suppose it's my own fault,' said the Princess, as Imogen helped her into her dress. 'Letting you indulge in the brightly coloured and luxurious cloth forbidden to you in your childhood.'

'Oh no, Your Royal Highness, you have the regal bearing that can carry off any outfit,' replied Imogen. The flattery appeared to work, as the Princess left the cabin and marched imperiously to the cockpit.

'Remind me to dump that hideous lamp as soon as possible. I have no idea what my Mamma was thinking, giving it to me.'

'Yes, Your Royal Highness,' t replied promptly.

**U**nknown vehicle, this is Space Defence Interceptor Alpha 1. You have entered Anserian space via a hyper-spatial anomaly.

Was this your intention? Over,' Crown-Prince David asked formally over the ship to ship radio.

'Space Defence Alpha 1, this is Anserian Diplomatic Vehicle Bravo-7-6-Alpha,' replied the Princess, equally formally. 'We have been hit by a Fenzrian missile and have lost eighty-four percent of our craft's system. So we cannot connect a video.'

'What assistance do you require, Bravo-7-6-Alpha?'

'We need to be towed to the nearest repair facility, then we need to speak to a member of your diplomatic service.'

'Roger that, Bravo-7-6-Alpha.'

'Wait a minute, did you say Anserian space? We were bound for Grimmswald.' There was obvious confusion in the Princess's voice.

'I'm sorry to say you didn't make it that far. In fact, you never left the home system.'

'In that case, I demand you expedite your response. The Fenzrians could be here at any moment.'

'Bravo-7-6-Alpha, we shall take you back to our base for debriefing. I'm afraid you might be in for a shock.'

'Space Defence Alpha 1, this is Princess Anita speaking. I demand to be connected to my mother, Queen Gertrude.'

'Repeat, Bravo-7-6-Alpha, we shall take you back to our base for debriefing.'

'Who is this speaking? I demand to know.'

'I am Crown-Prince David of Anseris.'

'Crown Prince, don't be ridiculous. My late father was Crown-Prince David. I had no brothers so I have no cousins called David.'

'Bravo-7-6-Alpha, prepare to surrender control of your vehicle. A full debriefing will take place when we arrive back at base.'

'H e's done what?' asked an angry King Benedict III. 'Crown-Prince David captured the vessel, Your Majesty,' said the unhappy page, 'and has taken it to our forward space defence base.'

'In breach of Standing Orders. If he weren't my son, I'd have him shot. Child, get out of my sight before I do something unpleasant.'

The page, used to the King's rage, didn't need to be told twice.

The King activated a private video link to his son's quarters.

'What's the meaning of this, boy?' the King shouted as his son's face appeared on the screen.

'Is this a social or business call, Your Majesty?' asked the Prince.

'Business, family business. You have defied your Standing Orders and me.'

'I told you when you posted me out here I could not obey the Standing Orders. They are illegal.'

'I would have,' said the King, 'when I was posted out there. It is in House Rushton-Browne's interest to make sure the true queen never returns.'

'Anyway, they were suspended, pending review.'

'Only because you have been trying to get them overturned,' said the King with an angry snarl. 'As I alone would be reviewing them, they would have been reinstated tomorrow, boy. It's too late now, the Ellisford-Castle Princess is back.'

'One of those girls is the rightful queen of this planetary system. Do you want to see me lose my throne, and with it your inheritance?' The King softened his attitude a little. It was, after all, his son he was speaking to.

'We couldn't bring it in automatically to our space dock. The Princess did it using the weirdest control interface. If you can call it a control interface – she didn't actually touch anything, just crazy hand gestures.' David's attitude also became more conciliatory. 'She has still got to fly that bucket of theirs back to the Home-world. No-one else can.'

'Oh, I see. Accidents do happen.' The King began laughing.

Crown-Prince David was horrified by what his father was suggesting. Destroying the ship on its way home was not what he had meant. Now he would travel back home aboard the ancient craft, to make sure nothing happened to it en route.

'We lost so much when the Angels ended the war by exiling the Fenzians to an Iron Age existence. Don't you want to fill in the gaps?'

'No, boy, I do not. Your predecessor returned Anseris to the straight path after the war, destroying any corrupting foreign influences. Who knows what strange ideas those girls might infect the chattering classes with.'

Yes, thought the Crown-Prince, any ideas from the one time in Anseris's history when the planet was moving forward had to be destroyed. Especially on a world as patriarchal and parochial as ours.

'Two girls, living fossils from a bygone age. What danger could they be?'

'I suppose so. Only a fool listens to a woman. Weak chattering creatures who should be taught how to behave with a firm cane.'

Prince David detested his father's sexist attitude, born out of the poisonous relationship between the old man and his step-mother.

The King's inexcusable misogyny was only found in the most backward of peasant villages.

'Maybe you should send them on a crash course to Marion?' mused the King.

'And possibly give the Marionites a spacecraft, Father?'

'Good point, boy.' The King was laughing now. 'No, blowing that crate out of the sky en route to the Home-world will be as effective as destroying it when it emerged from hyperspace. You know what to do.'

Satisfied with what he thought his son was planning, he cut the communications link.

Crown-Prince David had no idea what this princess looked like. No paintings of Queen Kathyren or the Free Queens survived the War. As if the Angels had chosen to expunge every image of these women. This had pleased his predecessor, King Benedict I, but infuriated him. She could have horns and a tail.

So who are you then?' the Princess asked the man wearing the flashy doublet and hose in House Rushton-Browne colours and a coronet.

'I am Crown-Prince David of House Rushton-Browne, son and heir of His Majesty Benedict III.' He bowed deeply. 'Great-great-grandson of King Benedict I, formerly Archduke Benedict Rushton-Browne, who ascended to the throne after the death of Queen Gertrude III of House Ellisford-Castle and the assumed death of her daughter.'

The Princess looked at this stocky young man. So obviously a Rushton-Browne, with his heavy jowls, goatee beard and receding hair. So typically convinced he was right about everything in the Cosmos. Well, this time he was very wrong.

'Well, I, Princess Anita of House Ellisford-Castle, am not dead,' the Princess replied. 'I refuse to believe that one hundred years have passed since I departed. This is a Fenzrian mind game.'

'I know this must be difficult for you to take in, Your Royal Highness, but it is true,' continued a weasel-like man in a black and white chequerboard livery.

'And you are?' asked the Princess.

'I'm George James Radyr Ginger-Reed, Viscount of Holywall, Head of Security for this facility.' The man bowed. It was too theatrical for the Princess; she could not take him seriously.

'Nonsense, you are tripped up by your own words. Viscount George is a five-year-old child,' said the Princess.

'Your Royal Highness, you are referring to my grandfather, Archduke George, who passed away twenty-two years ago.'

'If one century has passed, why are you still dressed like that? My mother abolished the old Clothing Regulations at the start of the war. Surely fashions would have moved on?'

'Your Royal Highness, King Benedict I reinstated the Sumptuary Laws and the Clothing Regulations established when Anseris was first settled,' said the one calling himself Crown-Prince David.

To her left, the Princess could hear Imogen, crying her eyes out. How typical of her to believe all this nonsense.

'Then my foster mother is dead. Why must everyone I love be taken from me?' asked the girl rhetorically.

Something must have touched a nerve, as the Princess found herself sobbing as well. The sudden realisation that it was all true. That like a fairy-tale princess, she had been asleep for one hundred years.

'Then I am Queen,' she said, quickly pulling herself together.

'I beg your pardon, Princess Anita?'

'If my mother has been dead for the past century, but I still live, by the ancient law of Female Primogeniture, I am now Queen of the Planet Anseris and all its extra-planetary dependencies.'

'King Francis I replaced it with Male Primogeniture,' said the Viscount. 'The oldest son becomes heir now. You cannot possibly oust Crown-Prince David as heir to my liege lord King.'

'I can and I will, you chequerboard buffoon.' The Princess had taken as much barely disguised insolence as she would allow.

'Your Royal Highness. Viscount,' said Crown-Prince David diplomatically. 'Let us not argue in a corridor.'

'Yes, it is unbecoming,' said the Princess.

'If you would follow me, I am sure we can explain the current situation.' The Prince was pointing to a door. The Princess gladly walked through it.

'Nobody knew when you were sent on your diplomatic mission that the Fenzrians would soon be eliminated,' said Crown-Prince David. 'That the Angels were about to descend and change everything. The Anserian system was one hell of a mess.'

'Surely the Aggelii tried to help?' asked Imogen.

'Indeed they did, but so many records had been destroyed. Even the Angels could not recreate all that was lost. More were lost in the Civil War, after the Angels departed. All we knew about Queen Gertrude's daughters was one died in infancy, the other had a name beginning and ending in "A". She was sent on a diplomatic mission, but was trapped in a hyperspace anomaly for a century.'

'Civil War?' asked the Princess.

'The so-called Princess Marie-Anne was a fraud who fooled Queen Gertrude. Her illegal grab for power could not be tolerated,' said Viscount Ginger-Reed. 'She and her co-conspirators Professor Giambattista and Dinah Pheileydale were seeking to destroy the moral core that had seen us withstand a technologically superior enemy for three years. They wanted to weaken us with corrupting foreign ways.'

'Quite so,' said Crown-Prince David. 'My predecessor and his allies drove the supporters of the Princess Regent off the Home-world, exiling them without spacecraft to a colony on one of the Jovian moons. To save valuable resources, all the other off-world possessions were mothballed, and Anseris once again became a single-planet Kingdom.'

'One living in the past,' said Imogen. The Princess shot her an evil glance.

'One rebuilding its past glories,' replied the Viscount.

'Gentlemen, thank you. You have given me much to consider. However, I am the Heir Presumptive. When we return to the Home-world, I will be crowned Queen, and the current Archduke Rushton-Browne will return to his proper place in the pecking order.'

'There really is no need for you to accompany us, Earl David,' said the Princess haughtily. She had spent the previous day resting in the base's VIP Suite while Imogen had prepared for their return home to Anseris.

'I would like the privilege of travelling in such a historic craft. Old spaceships are a hobby of mine.'

Historic is one way of putting it, thought the Princess. Clapped out is another. The ship will be scrapped as soon as we arrive back at the Home-world. The hyperspace engine was shot to pieces, while the normal-space engines were rubbish. The journey would take four days instead of the usual seven to eight hours. She would have to fly it – she was the only person who could.

On the other hand, this trip would be her last chance to be genuinely free, before all the responsibility of her birth came crashing down on her. Crown-Prince David was going to be an unwelcome guest. Then she started to laugh. He is trying to protect me. His presence aboard is stopping the current regime from blowing this ship to bits.

'Oh, very well, if you don't mind sharing a cabin with your equerry. There are only two cabins aboard. I shall have to share one with Imogen.'

'Don't worry, Your Royal Highness, Captain Valoretti and I are quite happy to sleep on the floor. We have brought sleeping bags.'

'Thank you, Earl David,' said the Princess without thinking.

'And as I have pointed out, madam, until we have completed negotiations I am still Crown-Prince David, so I am styled "Your Royal Highness", just like you.'

'You wish to merge Royal Houses by marriage. How medieval.'

'Have you seen the pair of you,' said Imogen, who had just entered the bridge and was laughing. 'You, Princess, are wearing dresses that originated in thirteenth-century Italy. Crown-Prince David is wearing an outfit that originated in fourteenth-century England. We are all the product of a deeply ingrained medievalist culture.'

'If I want your opinion, girl, I will ask for it,' said the Princess, 'and I don't want your opinion.'

'Yes, Ma'am. Sorry, Ma'am,' replied a chastened Imogen.

Imogen knew better than to goad the Princess. These dangerous thoughts had been popping into her head and straight out of her mouth unbidden. She knew that she could not make a fresh start away from the Princess, she would be deported to a rural village and become a peasant. The voice in her head said she would have no problem finding work as a nurse. Except, she knew she was only a servant. Where had that crazy notion come from?

King Benedict III had many faults and marital infidelity was of them. He admitted to three annymous illegitimate children he knew about, a daughter and two sons. They were to remain anonymous to protect the identities of their mothers and he paid for them to be well looked after. When he discovered the then Goose Maiden, Lady Stephanie Palmer-Adams had been mentally and physically abused by her legal father and grandfather, King Benedict had them executed. She became Princess Stephanie and Anseris discovered the identity of the illegitimate daughter. The King was determined to make amends. On her seventeenth birthday, he made Stephanie his Queen Consort, as he knew he would never marry again, but the Kingdom needed someone filling the role of Queen.

'He tries my patience,' said King Benedict III as he consumed a hearty fried breakfast.

'What has Dewi done now, Dadda?' his daughter asked.

'He's travelling back to the Home-world on the Princess's ship.'

Now the young Queen-Consort was at a loss. What difference did it make howDavid got home? As long as he got back safely.

'So, you don't want those women coming here, is that it?' she asked, enlightenment dawning.

'Indeed I do not. One is the rightful Monarch. If the young fool had blown her ship to smithereens when it emerged from hyperspace, there would not have been a problem.'

'Yes, Dad, but he didn't.'

'No, and now we can't blow the crate out of the sky and call it a tragic accident,' said the King. 'He has his mother's sense of universal fair play and justice. He lacks pragmatism. These are luxuries no monarch can afford.'

'Perhaps he has taken a shine to her,' she said, absent-mindedly.

'Yes, dear, that is probably it. A husband gains all his wife's properties and titles on their wedding day,' the King laughed. 'He is a chip off the old block. By marrying this princess, he gains the legitimacy the House Rushton-Browne has always lacked.'

What was it about Imogen that fascinates me, Crown-Prince David mused. It's as if he had always known her familiar face. She exuded grace and charm in a way her regal boss did not.

Then there was the enigma of the Princess piloting this spaceship. Surely a job for the staff, something a person like the Princess would consider beneath her royal dignity.

'Imogen, how long have you known the Princess?' he asked while the Princess was on the bridge and the maid was sitting next to his equerry.

'Since I was ten, Your Royal Highness,' she replied.

'Please, call me David.'

'No,' the Princess cut in, 'Royal Highness will do. We don't want her getting ideas above her station.'

Go away, you obnoxious witch, thought Crown-Prince David, I want to speak to Imogen, not you. It was no good, the flight-plan needed adjusting. It would be hours before the Princess returned to her cabin, the only other part of the ship she visited.

'What is her station?' he asked.

'My waiting woman. My mother, may the Angels give her rest, insisted I grew up with someone close to my own age.' The Princess snorted. 'Imogen is an orphan.'

'So, Imogen, do continue,' said the Crown Prince.

'The Queen and the Princess discovered Marion giving me illegal lessons, in the library we were supposed to be cleaning,' said Imogen. 'The Queen decided to investigate the story we told in our defence.'

'Which is how she discovered Princess Marie-Anne?' Crown-Prince David asked. He could see that the Princess was going an ugly shade of purple. Oh dear, what a shame, never mind.

'Yes, Your Royal Highness. Your great-great grandfather hated Princess Marie-Ann, despite her being the Queen's half-sister,' said Imogen. 'He couldn't stop her becoming a princess, but he did stop her adopting me. I remained a peasant. However, she still treated me like her daughter. I became the Princess's Companion. I had the same quality of life as my mistress, but stayed a servant.'

'I hated that fraud. The serf Marion nearly destroyed Anseris. I can almost forgive Uncle Benny for stealing my throne to stop her,' said the Princess. 'Almost, but not quite.'

'He always disputed the validity of Regent Marie-Anne's claim, long before he ousted her in the Civil War,' said Captain Valoretti, the Prince's equerry.

'Who asked you?' was the Princess's rude reply.

'My cousin, Captain Charles Gough di Valoretti Rushton-Browne aka Carlo Valoretti. He's a bit of a history buff. Aren't you, Carlo?'

'Yes, Your Royal Highness,' replied the equerry. 'It is such a shame so much about your era was lost in the Fenzrian Invasion and the Civil War. It leaves historians scratching around.'

'Well, as you said, Crown-Prince David, your predecessor dealt with her. The past is in the past. I am looking forward to my glorious future.' The Princess stood to leave. 'If you will excuse me, gentlemen, I have things to do. Imogen, that food isn't going to cook itself.'

Why are you so afraid of talking about your past, my dear Princess, he thought. I'll go and have a private chat with Imogen in the galley, which the Princess never visits. However, when he got there, Imogen was already deep in conversation with Carlo Valoretti. Oh well, if anyone could get information, Carlo could.

# 17

athyren Ellisford-Castle stood at the mirror, regarding the body she now occupied. Being shorter and far more curvaceous had been an interesting experience. It would be a short one. The equipment to grow a new host had survived. With accelerators that new host would be ready in ten years. For her, the blink of an eyelid.

Her dresser had helped her into the blue kirtle and purple cotehardie she particularly liked wearing. It went well with the templars that had become her trademark look.

While the host's mind slept, Queen Kathyren had studied her memories. The first ten years had been so entertaining. All that humiliation and misery, especially after Host B426 had started interfering. Then Host B422 had gone mad, making the girl an aristocrat. Queen Kathyren hated happy ever after.

The personality she had created for herself as the Princess was a work of art, burying the host's personality and allowing herself to have full control. It was ideally suited for the waiting game she was forced to play. The past three weeks had been filled with preparations for her wedding. Marrying into the usurper's family was the first step in ousting it from the stolen throne. She refused to call House Rushton-Browne the Royal Family. She was royalty, true royalty. Even before KHM#89, she had been from a Dragon Family, one of the founders of the Draconic League.

The Church of the Caretakers of the Soul, established to prevent her ever returning, was no longer the powerhouse it had once been. A growing minority of people continued the Church of the Eternal Queen. Soon it would be the official religion again. Not that she believed in her own divinity. That had been the fatal error of too many emperors throughout history.

Once dressed, she made her way to the Queen's Column, the only genuinely separate building not connected to the rat-run beneath the surface of the Inner Bailey. Ignoring the King's office on the first floor, she deactivated the stasis lock and headed through her old laboratory, up to the Black Crèche. All the equipment for nurturing a new host from cradle to emergence had been perfectly preserved.

She put on a clean white lab coat and set to work. A week earlier she had taken the embryo from a cryogenic suspender. An image of it, roughly three weeks old and healthy, appeared on a view screen. Carefully, she transferred the embryo into the artificial uterus. All lights were green. In thirty-eight weeks a healthy baby girl would moved from the artificial womb into the machines that would sustain her until she was ready to become Queen Kathyren's new host.

Satisfied with all she had seen, the Princess returned to the lower level and locked the door behind her.

'May I have a word, Princess?' asked King Benedict, who had walked into the room as the Princess sealed the laboratory.

'Certainly, Your Majesty,' replied the Princess. 'I must say, this is an interestingly decorated room.'

All the walls were painted light blue, with a dimpled pattern like egg boxes. It was illuminated by bright artificial lights. No windows or doors were visible.

'Yes, functional as well as beautiful,' said the King as the door shut behind him. 'How did you manage to get in here? So far, I am the only person who has ever managed to bypass any of the column's defences. It is the only place on the planet I can be truly alone.'

'There is a genetic lock on the door. It gives you unique access to the lower level of my tower. I used my coded psychic link.'

'Genetics. Now there's an interesting subject,' said the King. 'My predecessors banned the study of Genetics, then failed to destroy the archive of genetic profiles the Goose Maidens had built up. One profile is for a girl called Anita; no surname, which means she was a serf. There are two notes attached to it. One asking for further tests. The other saying she was now the companion to Princess Louise Imogen, the daughter of Queen Gertrude III, and was no longer available for the programme. Whatever that was.'

'Princess Louise Imogen? Are you sure? Who could have made such a horrendous mistake?'

'Don't lie to me, girl! Somehow you have swapped places with your mistress, and she believes she is your servant.'

'Yes, on the ship, this girl had such a weak personality I just walked in and took over. B426 loves the plebs too much. Making her think she was one herself was easy,' said the Princess. 'So what are you going to do about it?'

'The situation suits me fine. The last thing I want is for a real heir to Kathyren Ellisford-Castle marrying into House Rushton-Browne. I will continue pretending you are the real princess; use you for my own ends. And you are in no place to object.'

The King had missed the change in the tone of the Princess's voice. It had become harder, colder and far crueller. 'I don't think so.' The Princess had frozen like a shop-window dummy. A voice emanated from the unmoving mouth, full of world-weariness and contempt. 'I am Kathyren Ellisford-Castle. I discovered immortality. Instead of being praised, I was exiled as the Captain of the Prison Transport Vessel KHM#09 for a thousand-year, one-way voyage. Then I ruled this world for another five centuries. Sadly, my reign has been interrupted. Each generation of my wasted hosts still producing a perfect female clone. I intend to resume my glorious reign.'

'"The Immortal Empress was overthrown," said the King, "and all her evil with her." We are taught that mantra from the cradle. How can you be the Immortal Empress?'

'Have you ever wondered why the Boatbuilder's revolt changed next to nothing?'

'No, never been interested in history. Don't change the subject.'

'The Boatbuilder's Revolution was timed for when I was about to occupy a new host,' the voice carried on regardless. 'They broke into this tower and stole my new host, and the newly born baby that would be the host after her, before it could be inserted into the black creche.'

'So?' asked the King, wondering why he was still listening.

'The Boatbuilder was your ancestor, genetically programmed to serve me or anyone who looks like me. The new host died, the transfer process was too advanced for it to live independently. The Boatbuilder was free for several years. The child survived and grew, and he became her slave, because she looked like me.'

'What! You look like a Fenzrian?'

The King looked on in horror as a ghostly image emerged from the Princess's catatonic body. It bore a striking resemblance to Lady Imogen but was so much older, with short cropped grey hair. Something clicked inside the King's head.

'No, like me,' said the newly emerged ghost. 'The Boatbuilder was unable to resist her orders. He established himself as Archduke Rushton-Browne and had her crowned as the first of the so-called Free Queens. Her first child was also a clone-daughter, and she inherited my Kingdom. So, the Boatbuilder maintained my power structure while I was trapped in limbo by the wretched Valentine Device. I had to take refuge in a virtual world built into my crown. Now I have returned and will rule again from this host, until a proper body is ready.'

'My captain, how may I serve you?' the King said, as he dropped down on to one knee and bowed his head. As he did so, every arthritic joint in his body cried out in screaming agony. He had no power to resist, no matter how painful it may be. The ghost seemed to be enjoying his discomfort, and he was pleased she was happy.

'It is nice to see that part of the system also survived over the years,' said the ghost. 'And do get up, I hate talking over people's heads.'

'Forgive me, Captain, for not recognising you outside your usual host,' said the King as he struggled painfully back to his feet.

'There have been problems with the system.' The ghost had vanished and was now speaking through Anita. 'When Host B417, the one calling itself Queen Maria V found my crown, I was too weak to occupy her body. When B417 died, I was also unable to occupy her clone-daughter. I have only been able to whisper into their ears. Host B422 who you know as Queen Gertrude III was the most susceptible, but I lost control when it gave birth to the current clone-daughter, B426, who you call Imogen. As a child,

B426 was a throwback, a perfect host I thought I could easily absorb when she was old enough. Unfortunately, as she grew, she became corrupted and unusable. Aboard that stupid spacecraft, I found the key to my salvation. The Fenzrian education machine has transferred me into this body. I now have hands and can operate my equipment to get the great parade of me started again.'

'Of course, my captain.'

'Please, stop calling me that. Technically I am and always have been your Queen, but for the moment I must accept the title "Your Royal Highness".'

Like an automaton, the Princess picked up a hand-mirror that had been lying on the desk. 'Back into character,' it said in the voice of Kathyren Ellisford-Castle.

'Captain?'

'No, didn't I just say Your Royal Highness must be used for the time being? Oh, don't look so shocked, it's only a different voice.'

'Er yes, Your Royal Highness,' said the King, still a little confused by what he had seen and heard in the last few minutes.

'Thank you, Your Majesty,' replied the Princess with a polite curtsey.

'You are prepared to leave me on the throne?' asked the King.

'I agree with you remaining as King, as my figurehead. When I marry your son, it will give you a legitimacy you currently do not possess. You will make me joint heir to the throne with Crown-Prince David. I shall soon become a widow and sole heir. Are you intending to have an unfortunate accident, as formally executing David for treason would be so embarrassing?'

'Why should I do that? Crown-Prince David is my most loyal supporter.'

'Don't lie to me! You know he's the person unifying and organising all the groups opposed to you. He calls himself Roswall, an interesting choice of alias, and you're just letting him do it. You must be planning on replacing the heir with a spare. You have the choice of two male royal bastards, who you could acknowledge. Your late wife was far more forgiving than I would ever be.'

'Deliah recognised the difference between lust and love. I lusted after other women but I loved her. Sex was excrutiatingly painful for her. Once David was born there was no need to put her through that agony again. But I loved her, and only her. I could have cast her aside and remarried, but she was the love of my life. She knew that, and tollerated my flings because she knew they meant absolutely nothing to me. That is why two bastards will remain unacknowledged. They are not her children and mean nothing to me.'

'Except the pink blancmange? You acknowledged her.'

'The youngest,' said the King. 'The child born out of me grief after losing Deliah. She is the only one whose life I had to intervene in. She will never be the Monarch. There is only one true Queen, and I am speaking to her. Soon you will be Queen again.'

'Excellent,' said the Princess.

'What do you plan for the real princess?' asked the King.

'Nothing, I've a new physical form. Imogen can live out the rest of her life in comfort if she remains totally oblivious to who she really is. If she remembers, then I will have to act.' The body became fully active again and walked to the door. 'When I have left, you will forget this meeting ever happened.'

'Yes, Your Royal Highnes,' said the King Mecanically.

'**I**s the Lady Imogen not joining us tonight?' the King asked as he sat down for his evening meal.

'No, I dismissed her this morning,' replied the Princess. 'I only kept her around to please my mother and aunt. She will have a job here in the Castle, but eat her meals with her fellow servants from now on.'

'Actually, she isn't here tonight,' said Stephanie. 'I've arranged for her to take over the duties of Royal Goose Maiden.'

'Royal Goose Maiden? Do you still have that position?' asked the Princess.

'Indeed,' replied the King, 'but it has returned to its original function, caring for the ceremonial flock of royal geese. None of that dangerous social engineering of your day. I suppose you want me to issue a decree confirming the appointment?'

'Please, Dadda?' the girl asked.

'I suggested that Lady Imogen should have this job. Even though these days the job is usually reserved for aristocratic teenage girls waiting to get married,' said Crown-Prince David.

'Aren't you concerned that Imogen is neither an aristocrat nor a teenager?' asked the Princess.

'Not at all. Imogen is such a charming girl, isn't she, Father?' said Queen Consort Stefania, oblivious to the evil glare of the Princess.

'Yes, indeed she is.' Not that the King cared what sort of person Imogen was. Something at the back of his mind was nagging him about the girl. She was important, but he did not know why. He felt a sharp stab of arthritis and the memory flooded back – his meeting the Immortal Empress, and her order to forget. Nobody could forget the source of that sort of pain. He could see why his son was so enchanted by Imogen. Any member of House Rushton-Browne would feel the same. She was the embodiment of the Immortal Empress. However, the Princess had her soul, and at the end of the day body was always trumped by soul.

'So she will be eating there from now on,' said the Princess. 'Good. Even further out of sight and out of mind. Over at the Cottage with no reason to come to the Inner Bailey. I might never see her pasty face ever again.'

'Oh, don't worry, Princess, I have invited her to dinner every Thursday night, and as Goose Maiden she will have a standing invite to all functions here at the Inner Bailey. You won't be able to lose touch with her.'

The King noted the smile on his daughter's face and the frown on the Princess's. Stefania was playing a dangerous game baiting the Princess. He knew though, while he lived, the Princess would not dare harm his daughter.

A young peasant knocked on the kitchen door, then removed his tatty brown felt bycocket hat, and bowed. 'Mornin', m'lady,' he said. 'I be here to mend yous computer. Be it a software bother? I ain't got the know-how for hardware troubles.'

'Yes, it's a software problem,' replied Imogen as she handed him the errant machine. 'This laptop will connect to the main printer on the network but not the one that prints metallic ink. Other computers connect to that printer with no problem. I suspect it's an incompatible driver.'

She directed the young man into the parlour where a personal computer and two printers sat anachronistically on a desk. 'There are the printers.'

'Thank you, Lady. That be what my master told I.'

'Would you like a cup of tea?' she asked.

'No, Lady. I have much to do today,' the young man replied.

Imogen left the room to fetch a hooded cape from her wardrobe. Six weeks had passed since becoming Goose Maiden. In that time Spring had sprung. She would pick some unseasonal roses from the bush growing in her garden. The practical field in front and useful kitchen garden at the back had long ago been replaced by lawns and flower beds. The rosebush stood by a remnant of Aggelii terraforming equipment. It bloomed all year with flowers of all colours. Yes, she needed something to brighten her mood. Her birthday was approaching and no one to celebrate it with her.

No, too warm for a cape, she thought, but I need a hat. She chose a purple velvet tocque and white silk barbette. She redressed her hair into a plait. Angels why did it have to be so long. Finally she wrapped half the chain of office around her waist, clipping it in place, so the rest of the chain cascaded over the front of her dress.

Naturally, as this was Aneris, the bottom link contained an angel.

A memory from on board the ship popped into her head and immediately the voice returned, whispering lies. Was she going mad? Only the mad heard voices. However, she had no knowledge of computers, but she had correctly diagnosed the problem with the printer and contacted the Castle's IT department. How? Had that been the voices too? The more she thought about it, the more worrying it became.

On returning to the parlour, she found the IT man still sitting there, looking glum, with the software partially installed.

'Please, Lady, I got me license to put that software on, but only if the owner's roundabout. I could sort it meself, but me new master, 'e's a townie. 'E don't trust I, or any of me country mates neither. So, Lady, just stay 'round while I sort it out.' The young man looked close to tears.

It would not have been a problem if she had merely fetched a cape instead. This busy man had patiently sat here, despite having a large workload, while she had been slowly messing with her hair.

'I'm sorry, Mister... er, I don't think I caught your name?' she asked.

'I be Fryderyk, milady,' said the peasant. 'Ain't no mister or nuffin''

'Well, Fryderyk, there's nothing confidential on that laptop. If you have the skills, why not use them? To hell with your master's distrust.'

'I dare not do that, the master would flog I. To disobey the word of my master is above my station. I know my place. The place of my father before I, and my sons after I.'

'What if I give you permission?' asked Imogen.

'My master would still flog I, Lady.'

'But that is so wrong,' said Imogen. 'My grandmother abolished that sort of thing.'

'Begging your pardon, Lady, such talk can get I into trouble.'

'Sorry, Fryderyk.' Such talk could get her into trouble. She was not the granddaughter of Queen Johanna III. She was not a Princess of the Blood Royale. That crazy claim was treasonous.

'Hello, wake up. You are a princess, damn it!' said Princess Loiuse, a passenger in her own body. For eight weeks, she had been trapped in this nightmare. As the Aggelii had put her into the state of grace on the spaceship, she had seen something dark and shadowy leave her and enter into Anita's unconscious body. The horror had really begun for Princess Louise when she awoke possessed by a subservient dogsbody personality. The Princess, as Anita now insisted on being called, had taken command of the situation. Twice aboard the ship, the real Princess Louise had heard Falada's voice trying to reach her. It had been so quiet, and the dogsbody had managed to drown him out completely.

Finally, this morning, she managed to make contact with the dogsbody. Princess Louise told the dogsbody the printer driver was missing and to phone the Castle IT Help-desk. The dolt thought it was her own idea. This was not good enough. She needed control of her own body. Oh Falada, she thought miserably, where are you?

'Oh Falada, where are you?' said the dogsbody, who had gone to pick flowers as soon as Fryderyk had left.

How odd, thought Princess Louise.

'How odd,' said the dogsbody.

Hallelujah, I've got my body back. The dogsbody did not repeat.

Princess Louise could tell that the dogsbody was feeling confused and upset by the situation. These emotions were drowning her out. Oh, go have a cup of tea, she thought.

'I think I need a cuppa and a rest,' said Imogen, resting her secateurs on the ancient artefact next to the rosebush, one of the many remnants dotted all around the planet, as shiny as the day they had first been constructed. Nobody could move them. Fires, floods and even landslides went around them. In her day, everyone knew they were what had made this planet habitable. On the world she returned to, mired in a deep illogical superstition, people said they were tears of the Angels and should be left alone.

She retrieved a trug full of flowers returning home without her secateurs. They could lie there for days before anyone noticed they were missing. Every so often dancing arcs of blue light ran from the tips of the blades to the end of its handles.

'She's a strange one, Carlo, make no mistake,' the Prince said to his equerry as they flew back to Anseris from their base.

'Who is, Dewi?' asked Carlo Valoretti. Their mothers were sisters, so Carlo and the Crown Prince had grown up together. Only family and close friends called the Prince "Dewi". The men were cousins, so Carlo Valoretti counted as both.

'Our enigmatic Goose Maiden,' replied the Prince.

'Ah, the lovely Lady Imogen.'

'I see she has you smitten, our mystery girl,' said the Prince. 'A pretty face and a lovely smile.'

'Her voice is like silk. If she told me to jump, I would. I can't explain why.' Carlo was grinning. 'But, she's stratospherically out of my league. She is an Empress, not for the likes of me. You on the other hand, maybe? When the King has ennobled her.'

'I'm officially engaged, and even if I wasn't, there's Shandra.' The Prince had long ago lost his heart to Elashandra Rackham, the radical trade union activist.

'Your father would never let you marry a plebeian. Especially one who wants to do away with the Monarchy.'

'How long do you think that would last if she became Princess Elashandra, and eventually the Queen?'

'You know the answer to that one, Dewi. Until she draws her last breath. It's fundamental to her very soul. However, as you say, you're engaged to the Princess.'

'So, the Lady Imogen,' said the Prince. 'I want you to extend my invitation to her to join us on our trip to her old ship for one last goodbye.'

# 19

**G**ood morning, Lady Imogen. May I come in?' a male
voice asked politely through the open top half of the kitchen
door.

'Captain Valoretti, of course you can,' replied Imogen. She
was busy filling an anachronistic electric kettle from the
equally outdated cold water tap next to the trough-like sink.

'I thank you, Mistress of this house.' The captain bowed a
courtly bow.

'Two days running have started with me greeting an attractive
young man,' said the voice inside her head. Imogen was scandalised;
well brought-up young ladies did not think such things.

'Would you like a cup of tea, Captain?' Imogen asked, before
the voice could say anything more.

**T**hat was new, he thought. The previous Goose Maidens had
sat alone in their parlour, not knowing where the kitchen was
and would have sent a servant to make tea. And there she
goes, flashing that incredible smile of hers.

'Captain sounds so formal today. Please call me Carlo.'

'Very well, Carlo,' she replied.

By the Angels, she is so beautiful, so serene and charming. He
could hear his head telling him to do whatever she asked him in a
voice tinny and shrill. A more profound and more subtle voice, the
voice of Love, was telling him "She's the One".

'Someone left these on the ancient artefact,' he said. 'They
don't look as if they have been there very long.'

'Ah, I knew I'd forgotten something yesterday,' said Imogen.
'I hope the blades won't rust.'

'Overnight? I doubt it. They are still warm. The alien science that protects the artefact has protected the blades.' He handed the secateurs to Imogen.

He utterly failed to notice the strange energy discharge that passed from the tool to Imogen as she took the secateurs from him. All he saw was her fainting.

'So, awake at last, Princess Louise?' asked a familiar voice, from the mouth of a beautiful white stallion.

'Falada, it's so good to hear your voice, but I've been awake for weeks, trying to break free,' said Princess Louise, with more than a little trepidation. 'Where've you been, and where am I now?'

'You are virtualised inside the data-sphere on your planet. It's a remnant of your era's contact with the greater galaxy. Part of the most complex data storage network in the galaxy. There is a sphere-node on every civilised planet inhabited by Humans. Usually, they are interconnected. This one now stands empty and in glorious isolation.'

Princess Louise was apparently standing in a beautiful garden. A small stream ran through it. On her side the bank was steep, lined by five cherry trees in full blossom. Falada stood on the opposite bank, also lined with cherry trees but with a gradual slope up to where he was standing.

'It doesn't look much like a data storage system.'

'I have created this calming image for you,' said Falada.

'It's so peaceful and relaxing,' said Princess Louise. 'Thank you.'

'The Aggelii quarantined your Home-world because it was not ready for interstellar contact. They chose to leave this data-sphere here, for when your world was ready. King Benedict I had it buried while he was still Archduke of Castlegate. It was, in his words, "corrupting alien technology".'

'That sounds like the sort of stupid thing Bad Old Benny would have done,' Princess Louise replied.

'Your world is ready to leave the quarantine. It can either go forward to the stars or return to the pre-technological dark ages. If it goes backwards, your world will never have this chance again. Your planet will wither on the vine.'

'I'm supposed to be Queen of this world, to help it move forward, the way my mother wanted.'

'Indeed you are, and if my analysis is correct, support for the current regime is crumbling. Your chance to regain your throne is coming. However, something is trying to stop you.'

The horse was now further away on the other side of the stream, and the flow of water had increased.

'I can hardly hear you, Falada. Why don't you come closer?' asked Princess Louise.

'This is a representation of the distance between us. I am still aboard the spaceship. You must come here, retrieve me and several data-blocks from aboard this ship.'

'Don't worry, my friend. I'll do that, I promise,' said Princess Louise, despite having no idea how she could fulfil the promise.

P rincess Louise was fully awake and in control of her body for the first time in weeks. The whole world, not just her family, now knew her as Imogen. To continue in hiding, she would have to remain as Imogen. The nightmare was far from over. Her throne had been stolen. Like the heroine of the ancient myth, she had fallen asleep for a hundred years. All around her things had fallen into disrepair. She had been awoken by a prince, sadly one who was far from handsome and was no rescuer. The charming Captain Valoretti was more like a fairy-tale prince, but he was unquestioningly loyal to his cousin.

'I'm so glad you are awake,' the captain said. 'The Inner Bailey's physician reports you were merely suffering from a lack of sleep.'

She gasped. She was wearing a clean shift and lying in her bed.

'Don't worry, Lady Imogen, your maid undressed you.'

'Clarice?' asked Imogen.

'Yes, that's what she said her name was. I carried you up here, then she took charge.'

'I'll have to thank her, Captain. Even if she will say it is just part of her job.'

'You shouldn't even be in here, a young lady's chamber,' said Sarah, the housekeeper, sitting at the other side of the bed.

'I have yet to deliver my message, the original reason for my call.'

'Well get on with it, young man.' Sarah would not normally upbraid someone of a higher class and Imogen could see the older woman was enjoying this extraordinary situation.

'You know the King has ordered the destruction of your ship?'

'Doesn't he want to use it to try and recreate hyperspace technology?'

'The engines are completely burnt out. There is no way anyone would learn anything from them this time. Not that there is anyone who could. Research into interstellar travel is strictly forbidden. So Crown-Prince David asks if you want to say goodbye to the ship before it gets broken up.'

'Certainly. Will the Princess be travelling with us?'

'No, she has said "I want nothing to do with that crate ever again".'

Some things didn't change. Anita hated the spacecraft she had been born on. Even if she were herself, she would still be delighted about its fate. But she wasn't herself. Imogen had managed to fight off whatever had been controlling her, but poor Anita was now possessed by something alien and evil.

'Yes, tell His Royal Highness I would enjoy an opportunity to see the craft one last time.'


Everywhere on Anseris was monitored by the Political Police, known as the Chessmen because of their black and white checked uniforms. They were recruited mostly from the ranks of the urban middle class who wanted to maintain their comfortable lifestyle. This class had always been tireless supporters of the Absolute Monarchy.

The Goose Maiden's Cottage was no exception. Conrad, the odd-job man, who lived in a caravan in the Cottage's grounds, was Sergeant Pawel Serge Zamkowybród Conranski of the Political Police. He had been surprised by the summons to the Inner Bailey a week after the new Goose Maiden had been installed. Standing in front of Lord Vernon's desk, he bowed deeply as the King and that new princess walked into the office.

'Lord Vernon, leave us,' said the King.

'Yes, Your Majesty,' said the commander of Castle Security, as he scurried from his office like a scalded cat.

'So, you are Sergeant Conranski,' said the Princess. 'Aka Conrad Conrad Cudren Conradson, a Castle menial.'

'Yes, Your Royal Highness,' he said calmly in a perfect Court accent, miles from the broad rural one he used at the Cottage.

'You are to be my eyes and ears within the Cottage. You will report directly to me. Do you understand?'

'Yes, Your Royal Highness.' Conrad was at a loss as to why this should be, but the King, who was sitting silently, obviously approved.

'If the new Goose Maiden begins acting in any way oddly, you are to report it to me immediately.'

'Yes, Your Royal Highness. May I ask, what do you mean by oddly?'

'If you notice any change in character, becoming more assertive.'

'But, Your Royal Highness, how do I know this is not just her settling into her new job?'

'Good, you are not as stupid as you first appear,' said the Princess. 'Anything over and above her recent promotion. Do you understand?'

'Yes, Your Royal Highness.'

'It's sad, really,' said the Princess. 'Imogen suffers from a curse passed down from mother to daughter. If she does not take her remedy, she becomes a dangerous madwoman. Her illness was hardly noticeable at first. If she begins to think she's a princess and I'm her servant, I need you to tell me immediately. It's the first sign of her mania.'

'I understand, Your Royal Highness.' Conrad bowed.

'Good, you may return to the Cottage. Remember, let me know at the first sign of strange behaviour.'


'Morning, Lady,' said Conrad to Imogen as he arrived at the Cottage. 'I be a-paintin' yous outside walls this week' I be.'

So much for a trend, thought Imogen. The third day had brought Conrad, who had to be one of the ugliest men on Anseris. He was short and whippet skinny. His long nose and lack of a chin made him look even more like an overbred hunting dog.

'And why should I care?' asked Imogen, who had disliked Conrad as soon as she had seen him, as a passenger; now her real self was free, she had an even lower opinion of the man. There was something not quite right about him.

'Thought I'd let yous know 'bout it, missus, if'n yous wan' to.'

'Well, thank you for the information,' she said crossly, 'and never call me missus ever again. Do you understand?'

'Yes, missus,' he said, as he slunk off.

Imogen was so very pleased she would not be at home for the next two days.

eparting at midnight, a three-hour flight took Imogen from Ellisford Castle to the Equator and the town of Phenham, home to the planetary terminus of Space Train One, or as some wags called it, Space Train Only.

Crown-Prince David had insisted on piloting the airship, sitting alone in the cockpit. It meant she avoided his company for the first part of the journey. However, she found herself seated next to Captain Carlo Valoretti. Despite her misgivings, the flight had been very entertaining.

The Royal Party had been ushered through the ticket hall into the station's VIP Lounge at the top of the building. Through the glass roof, Imogen could see a tiny speck of light that was getting brighter in the dawn, instead of fading like the stars. She went to a large binoculars on a stand and peered through. They focused automatically on the incoming space-train. It looked like five railway carriages stacked onto one another with an engine at the base. The wheels were attached to the sides of the carriages, holding them between rails at each corner.

'The rails travel out into space to the anchoring platform at Geostationary Orbit, and beyond,' said Crown-Prince David. 'Unlike a space-elevator, there is no need for a counterbalance device which travels in the opposite direction to the train. It's the fastest way out to the High Frontier, but not the most efficient.'

'I'm afraid it is no good trying to explain the science to me, Your Royal Highness. An...' Imogen stopped herself, faking a cough; she had so nearly slipped. 'Anything technological goes straight over my head. The Princess always excelled at that sort of thing. I used to do well at Art.'

'But you are the one taking the trip up on the space-train?'

'Purely for emotional reasons. The Princess would say I was wasting my time.'

If the Princess or the King found out why she was really going out to Platform One, she would never make it back alive.

'I see,' he said.

'And besides, Anseris looks so pretty from space.'

'After our arrival at Platform One, it will be too late to do anything, so we spend the night on the military base there. I have arranged the visit to the breaker's yard for tomorrow morning, with our departure back to the planet surface after lunch.'

'Such a short time out there, Your Royal Highness.' Time enough though for me to do what I want, she thought.

'As you requested. You did not want to spend too much time away from your cottage.'

'I'm employed to look after the royal geese. I can't shirk that responsibility.'

The Prince sat down on one of the comfortable seats in the lounge. 'You have thirty days a year for holidays, you should use them.'

'My job is far from strenuous, why should I require holidays?' asked Imogen. That was pure dogsbody; she could not afford any more slips.

'Everyone has the right to have time off now. Even the lowliest peasant now has fifteen days of time off a year. And you have old Lady What's-her-name to cover for you.'

'I suppose so, Your Royal Highness,' said Imogen. 'On the other hand, Lady Magda is a bit eccentric. I'm worried she might absent-mindedly harm the geese if left with them for too long.'

'Oh, I see,' said the Crown Prince. Imogen was so glad when he excused himself to talk to a polite young soldier who had been waiting patiently for him.

On arrival, the space-train quickly emptied then slid down into the basement levels of the station for the Royal Carriage to be added to the top of the train. The fourteen adults in the Royal Party had a ridiculous amount of space. The next carriage emerged from the basement, then the First Class passengers boarded. When the train was fully assembled and the engine tested, additional boosters had to be fitted. The passengers on one of the Third Class carriages had to disembark for the train to be reconfigured. The displaced Third Class passengers crammed into the carriage above. Naturally, some passengers failed to get aboard. To her horror, a young man who was pushing an older woman in a wheelchair was soundly beaten by station staff after remonstrating with an official.

'Porter, I wish to see the Station Manager immediately!' Crown-Prince David shouted.

'Yes, Your Royal Highness,' the porter replied and ran to the Station Manager's office.

'You wanted to see me, Your Royal Highness?' asked the Station Manager a few minutes later, as he bowed to the Crown-Prince. Imogen took an instant dislike to the man. He was a portly fellow, and the padded chaperon hat and full beard made him look more substantial.

'Tell me, do you regularly assault your customers, or was it for my benefit?' Crown-Prince David asked the man, by way of a reply.

'The troublemaker refused to follow the instructions of railway staff and was openly hostile,' said the Station Manager.

'Funny, that is not how I saw it. And my man here has spoken to the fellow and his wheelchair-bound mother. Apparently, he only complained once about the treatment his mother had received.'

The Station Manager was looking increasingly nervous.

'So tell me, and no lies this time, do your staff regularly assault your customers or was it for my benefit?'

'Er, um, er...' The Station Manager had trouble finding anything to say.

'I'm waiting.'

'But he is a peasant, Your Royal Highness. I don't care how much money he's earning out there, peasants should do as they are told without complaint.'

Imogen thought she recognised a voice from her childhood. Its owner did not fit the memory.

'And you are?' asked the Crown Prince, with obvious impatience.

'Sir Philippe André Phenham du Pheileydale. Station Master

Of course. The excess weight hid any trace of outer family resemblance, but not the inner one. Being obnoxious ran in the Pheileydale family's blood. They had disowned Deliah Pheileydale for becoming too radical and remained horribly bigoted.

'Ah, gentry. Thought so,' the Prince said as if it was a curse. 'Even if he was a peasant, the treatment he received from your staff is not acceptable. Any medical treatment costs accrued by that young man will be covered by your company's health insurance.'

Then looking at the list of passengers he continued, 'The only occupants of First Class are my friends Charley and Janey, their new arrival plus his existing children and. They will join us here in the Royal Carriage. Janey will be over a moon, she has always wanted to travel in this carriage. That will leave the First Class empty, allowing you to upgrade all the Second Class passengers for free.' Then back to the Station Manager, 'You will have four carriages to comfortably house all the Third Class passengers.'

'But this train is due to depart in ten minutes. It's already cutting it fine because of the extra reconfiguration work today,' said the exasperated Station Manager.

'Then you had better be quick about it. So far, you are getting away with things lightly. I am on a very tight schedule. If my journey is delayed, you won't just feel the displeasure of your employers, you will discover the true nature of my displeasure. You are dismissed.'

'Yes, Your Royal Highness.'

She watched the fat man walk backwards, regularly bowing until he was through the door, and then run down a spiral staircase to the carriage below.

rchduke Thompson-Uther had insisted the Royal Party
should spend the night at his wing of Lansing#5, the high
orbital station, an enclave of Archduchy of Pendragon.
The Archduke had changed into a station jumpsuit shortly
after arrival. He looked exactly like the picture of Aarne's
grandfather in the central lobby. There was usually no
time for nostalgia in space, every fixture and fitting had been
updated several times over the past century. The retro style dated
as far back as the recent refit, which unusually had been for
aesthetic not practical reasons.

The videophone ringing woke Imogen to a new day. Imogen's
cabin was far more luxurious than the military quarters she had
been expecting and she'd slept more deeply than she ever imagined.

'Yes,' she said blearily as she answered the phone.

'Lady Imogen, don't forget we are on a tight schedule.' It was
the Crown Prince, looking very smart in a military jumpsuit.

'Yes, Your Royal Highness.'

'As long as you are wide awake at the breaker's yard. Being half
asleep in zero-g is deadly. Breakfast is in ten minutes.'

'I've been in space many times but never in zero-g. It will be
a new experience for me,' she said.

'Never been in zero-g? You are in for a treat. I would advise a
light breakfast. You never know how your stomach will react to
weightlessness for the first time.'

ood morning, Your Grace,' said Imogen to her hostess as,
as she walked into the dining room.

'Oh please, no need to be so formal here on the Habitat.
Especially as I am feeding this little one. Call me Janey. Everyone
does in Pendragon, and this is technically in the Archduchy.'

Archduchess Jane was the Archduke's fourth wife. The first, the mother of his four grown-up children had divorced him years ago. As had his second wife, who had given him four teenagers. When his third wife had died tragically of cancer, he hired Jane Westfall-Smith, a distant cousin as a nanny for the three youngest children, all under ten. A surprise romance between the older man and younger woman had emerged. Now an archduches, Janey, who had technically already been an aristocrat, entirely lacked the aura of superiority that emanated from most of the members of an Anserian Great House. She found the medieval Court dress stupid at the best of times. This last trip had been doubly so, as it coincided with the final three months of pregnancy.

'There are plenty of top-rated hospitals in Pendragon, so why Charlie insisted I give birth on the Home-world is beyond me.'

'Aarne used to wonder why he had also been born down there,' said Imogen, remembering another life.

'Despite the title, the members of House Thompson-Uther are still a bunch of space-rats.' Archduke Charles had joined the conversation. 'A Home-world birth is seen as more prestigious than a space birth.'

'Imogen, please tell us about our illustrious ancestor. What was he like – he died before the start of the Civil War, lost in space. Only Cousin Winston really knows anything about him,' Janey asked, as her husband sat down with a huge fried breakfast.

Again Imogen was reminded how much older than everyone she was. Even the middle-aged man sitting opposite her.

'I'm afraid Lady Imogen doesn't have the luxury of time this trip,' said the Prince. He had just finished an identical banana smoothy to Imogen. 'We're heading out in ten minutes.'

'Oh,' said Charlie, raising a sausage to his mouth, then pausing. 'I'm sure we can arrange something for our next visit home.'

'Or we could arrange for a trip out to Pendragon for her, Crown-Prince David. That might be sooner,' said Janey.'

'I've been to Pendragon several times,' said Imogen.

'As soon as you have finished your business out at Dentra Seven, please say you'll join us on our barge and spend a few weeks out in Pendragon,' said Charley. The Archduke, being typically aristocratic, assuming she could just drop everything for a trip out to the edge of the Kingdom.

'I haven't packed for a long trip,' she said.

'Our wardrobe is always well stocked for a fellow aristocrat,' said Janey.

'I'm not an aristocrat,' said Imogen, unaware that by not using the word Ristoze, she had proved she was.

'Well, Lady Imogen, it looks as if you will be taking that holiday after all,' said Crown-Prince David as he whisked her away.

Imogen was disappointed to discover the ship had already been stripped, it's contents packed into containers in the low-gravity warehouse module. Missing a first experience of zero-g today.

'Dear Angels, this is ugly,' said the Crown Prince, picking Falada's head from its carved wooden box.

'On,' said Imogen over the psychic link.

'Off,' said the artificial intelligence grumpily.

'On,' repeated Imogen, unthinkingly saying it out loud.

'Pardon?' asked Crown-Prince David.

'Just me thinking noisily, Sir,' said Imogen.

'You see what I mean, you don't fully understand the psychic link,' said Falada, directly into her mind, as a barely flickering light illuminated the crystal horse-head. 'I will speak to you in a few minutes when Davy-boy is in another container.'

'Why don't we visualise?' she asked, this time over the interface. 'Then nobody will overhear us.'

'Not really advisable out here. However, it will certainly be quicker than real time.'

'Exactly,' said Imogen.

Imogen found herself standing in an endless ocean of grass Next to her was a white stallion.

'So, why wouldn't you switch out there?' she asked.

'Crown Prince David Rushton-Browne of Castlegate and his almost genetically identical cousin are wandering around this complex. Angel'll that family's so inbred. I'm not ready to deal with them.'

'They will be allies. I was going to tell them everything today,' said Imogen.

'Oh no you don't,' replied Falada, 'it's still too early to know if we can trust either of them. I haven't finished checking either of them fully. They might betray us to the King.'

'Nonsense,' said Imogen. 'The Prince hates his father and does not want to be King.'

'Really? When the chips are down, Princess Louise, he will fight like hell to retain his crown,' said the AI. 'You would be all-in and suffer a TKO.'

'I love your mixed metaphors, but you are wrong. Crown-Prince David would love to be just Mr Rushton-Browne if it meant he could marry his lover.'

'What about Captain Valoretti?' said Falada.

'What about him?'

'We don't know what he might do if you told him who you really are. I am going to put a block on your memory. Please don't fight it, Princess Louise. You will not be able to tell a living soul about who you really are and what happened on your journey.'

'Don't you dare!'

Oh hello, thought the Prince as he rifled through a box marked as belonging to the Princess. He had found a framed photograph of the Princess and Imogen as children with a woman wearing a crown. Historically, there had been very few portraits painted of the Anserian Monarch; none had survived the smoke of battle.

Nobody believed the myth about the Free Queens being identical. However, the young blonde girl, who had to be Imogen was a younger version of the woman wearing the crown. Could it be a picture of Princess Regent Marie-Anne with the girl Imogen at a party with the Princess? No, definitely not. This was a photograph of Queen Gertrude and her daughter. So Imogen is the Princess.

'Angels!' he said. There was a data-block reader that still worked in the box. Possibly the only one in the Anserian system. The data-block contained a message from the long dead Queen Gertrude III. Stronger expletives popped into his mind once the message had finished. This changed everything. Imogen was really Princess Louise. Why was she putting up with the woman called Anita stealing her title and social position? Oh think, Dewi-boy. Think! Because it gave the real princess a cloak of invisibility with all eyes on someone else. Damn, they were excellent actresses. They had everyone fooled. Even his father had fallen for the deception.

'Don't you dare!' said Imogen as she emerged from the visualisation, finding herself back in the warehouse module.

'Are you all right? You seemed to be in a world of your own,' said Carlo Valoretti. 'Not a good thing to be anywhere with reduced gravity.'

He must have replaced Crown-Prince David as her minder. 'So many memories,' she replied. Then picking up the Valentine Device, 'My lamp. What do you think?'

'You want this? I thought you had better taste?' Carlo asked jokingly.

'Normally I do, Carlo, but it belonged to my parents. It has sentimental value.' Everyone thought they knew the story of the orphan who had become the Princess's servant. It was a lie.

'Couldn't you find something a little less hideous, as an aid to remembering your parents?'

'They were runinng for their lives, they couldn't carry much. Although Angels know where and how they got it?'

'I'm sorry, Imogen, that was a bit crass.'

'You're forgiven.'

'Your security pass says Karl Gustav?' asked Imogen a few minutes later.

'I chose Carlo. This is my true name – the authorities on this station insist on it,' he said, laughing. 'According to the old myths I am now your slave,' he replied. 'If you wanted to change your name, what would you choose?'

'You've found my secret too. I'm not keen on the name Imogen. I would rather be called Johanna.'

'Anseris has had three Queens called Johanna, making it very regal.' Then changing the subject before she could answer, 'These items aren't going to pack themselves. Is there anything else in this container you want to take?'

'No thank you. I've visited every container now. All that I want is labelled, ready for packing.'

'There is one thing you have forgotten,' said Carlo. 'Since you have been out here you have completely forgotten to be subservient and self-deprecating. You are more animated than I've ever seen.'

'I'm, um, not, um, thingy, err, what's-its-name.' Oh rats, she thought, I can't remember what I wanted to say.

Falada had done it, blocked her memory – everything that had happened to her between leaving to Ellisford Castle. Now Imogen could not correct the erroneous story told about her. She could not tell a living soul.

'You should be yourself more often. Be Johanna, not Imogen,' said Carlo. 'I hate people living a lie.'

'In the service of the Princess, the lie is the safest way to live.' She was sure that was not what she had planned to say either. Falada was messing with her head as she found herself repairing the cover story so nearly blown that morning.

'Technically speaking, Johanna, you are now in the King's service. He appointed you as Goose Maiden, remember.'

'Yes, how could I have forgotten that,' replied Imogen, enjoying the continued use of her old alias. 'Although given the nature of society in the Anserian system, perhaps it is better if I maintain the lie permanently.'

'That's very true down there, Johanna. On the other hand, there are no royals around at the moment. Crown-Prince David found something and has already left. You can be yourself for a few hours longer.'

'A busy few hours.'

'Before we begin, I found this. It has your style written all over it.' He pulled something out of his pocket.

'Oh, Carlo! My Moonglow avatar, where did you find it?' As soon as she touched the octagonal gem, it sprang to life, with three red dots dancing within the blue shiller of the stone.

'In one of the boxes. I can see it's precious to you,' Carlo said, lifting it up. 'May I?'

'Oh please do, I have missed this so much. My friend Aarne gave it to me when I was ten. Princess Marie-Anne told him how much I liked Moonglow. Look, drops of her blood to protect me.'

'Johanna... sorry, I meant Imogen, you never struck me as the superstitious type before.'

'I'm not. I know they are just inclusions in the gem, but I do like the poetry of the myth. And I like you calling me Johanna. Please don't stop.'

'My dear, what on Anseris are you wearing?' asked Janey, on the first day of the flight to Pendragon Central. 'You look like someone's grandmama!'

'The only that fitted,' Imogen replied, in her almost knee-length purple dress. 'I'm so tall and thin. Finding something that fits me is a nightmare. Everything is so short on me.'

Then she saw that Janey had changed to Pendragon style clothes. As had Tanya and Briony, her teenage step-daughters, who followed her into the lounge. They were all wearing dress that barely covering the top of their legs. Nothing she had tried on even did that.

'The Pendragon Style is short, in skirts, trousers and hair.' said Bryony, who had already had her hair cut into a short bob, with a short ponytail, which Imogen thought was superfluous, at the back.

'Our clothes are practical feminine, and liberating. With legs like yours, you'll soon be rocking Pendragon styles,' said Janey.

Imogen would never dreeam of exposing that much flesh in public. Janey must have noticed the look of horror and changed the subject to hairstyles.

'I'm of to get a sensible haircut So I can get into a spacesuit.' She said. As you'll be staying longer than a week, you need one you'll have to come too. You need to take a basic spacesuit training course on the trip there.'

Imogen had no problems about cutting her hair. A few minutes later Imogen watched as her locks fell to the floor. She felt liberated from the silly rules of the Ellisford Castle. The hairdresser pulled the back of her hair into a scrunchy then cut what remained into a bob level with her jaw. This would have been far more practical when she was nursing. However spacesuit training was a different matter.

After an hour, Imogen had enough clothes for a few months stay on Pendragon.

'Much as I love trad, which works down there,' said Bryony, 'With all that natural fresh air, you don't notice how stinky your clothes are.'

True, thought Imogen, despite washing machines becoming more common, so many people on the Home-world wore their clothes longer before washing them by hand. Maybe the amount of clothes in her closset was not as excessive as she thought.

The dress she was wearing was the same as the one she had worn earlier, but i had an arguement with a pair of dressmarker's shears and lost. Thank th Angels for the almost knee-length black boots. Covering most of her scandalously exposed lower legs. Her hair was modern. The icing on the cake was having facial make-up, which was illegal on the Home-world.

'I look totally Pendragon now. What would my Mother say?'

'Princess Marie-Anne would thoroughly approve,' said Janey.

Oops, thought Imogen, everyone thinks that Anita is my mother's daughter, not me.

'You mentioned her by name,' said the usually silent Tanya, 'aren't you afraid of the Chessmen?'

'No, and neither should you. We are aristocrats, plebians have to watch what they say. For us the Chessmen can go kick rocks.'

'You know, that is the first aristocratic thing I have ever heard you say, Janey,' said Imogen.

'Oh dear, I spent far too long on the Home-world this time.'

'We are back home now, said Bryony. 'You say anything snooty, the people will quickly shut you down.'

Wow, thought Imogen, aristocrats worrying about what ordinary people thought. Was she still in the Kingdom of Anseris. Yes, she was, and she liked it.

he day before Imogen was due to return home, an accident on the mining colony of Pendragon 28. The hospitals asked for qualified doctors and nurses to come to help. So when she should have been checking-in for her journey home, Imogen in a borrowed bussiness suit, with a silly wide striped tie to volunteer. She had her ID, a letter from the Central Nursing Bureau validating, her century old nursing qualification and CV. So instead of boarding a luxury inter-planetary liner, to her amazement, she found herself boarding a medical shuttle to Pendragon 28. An hour later. When she should have been changing into a cocktail dress for her evening meal, she was putting on a nurse's uniform, preparing for a night shift.

After a week of doing the job she loved again, she was both exhausted and exhilarated. However the crisis was over and it was time to go home. They had offered her a permanent job in Pendragon. She had politely refused, saying she was missing the lush greeness of the Home-world. Imogen knew she was destined to be Queen after her mother and had to prepare for that destiny.

She had adopted the Archduchy's relaxed lifestyle and attitudes with relish. In the Archduchy both class and old fashioned gender expectations were ignored. On the Home-world they rigidly defined peoples' lives.

The people of the Home-world were crying out for an end to the old ways. Democracy now had the grassroots support her mother said it needed to succeed. Only she, as an enlightened reforming monarch could make it succeed.

er hosts had offered her the exclusive use of their private yacht, to get her home in a couple of days, but Imogen had chosen to travel back to the Home-world on one of the Uther-Thompson's commercial liners. She had told her hosts she wanted to experience as much of her time on the high frontier as possible. Travelling on this ship, all be it in first class, had introduced her to a wide variety of people.

h! steak, said Imogen as she cut into the chunk of meat that was still properly pink in the centre. The young man sitting next to her looked at his plate dubiously. A Pendragon resident, who had joined this table three days earlier at Athens IV. He had recently his home Archduchy for the first time, he was no doubt only used to the fiery curries that hid the blandness of soya meat and hydroponic rice.

'I'll get used to it,' he said conversationally. 'Eventually,' he added with more honesty.

'All part of the wonderful variety of Anseris,' The elderly lady who shared the table replied.

'I wish I was staying on the Jovian Baronies, where they wear sensible clothes, or even in one of the Guild Towns on the Home-world, with proper trousers even for the girls.'

Imogen could see he was wearing the sort of traditional outfit worn out in the sticks, as he had been throughout the journey. 'So, where are you headed?'

'My mum runs a chain of wine shops out in Pendragon. She wants to me to learn all aspects of the business, so I have to watch the harvest of the grapes and the production of the wine at a posh vineyard in Holywall. Which is why I have a suitcase full of silly fancy dress and I am wearing this.' Then he realised that the old lady was not wearing city style clothes anymore. She was wearing a kirtle and embroidered surcotte. Her husband had also changed back into traditional clothes. 'Oh sorry, but how do you women cope without Velcro and zips with your frocks. Although girls do look so much better like that. Properly female and all.'

'Women have coped for centuries, silly boy,' the old woman said.'With an attitude like that, you'll fit right in where you're headed.' Imogen knuew the old lady and her husband had lost patience with their tablemate. She was rapidly doing the same.

'I doubt it. The carrot crunchers only have satellite broadband for two hours a day. I reckon they like to be stupid on the Home-world.'

Yet another black mark against the boy. Pendragoners loved being early adopters of new and cutting edge technology. There was no need to be so offensive about Home-world complaints, usually unnecessary, about new inventions. Anyway, Archduke Gregory Almond-Hedges of Holywall was blocking any expansion of modern communications in his archduchy.

'Still, we are all Anserians. Variety is strength,' said the young man as he finished his meal.

Imogen considered this as she returned to her cabin. Even amongst the underground groups opposed to King Benedict, there were no secessionist groups. That sort of thing would attract the dreaded attention of the Chessmen, guardians the status quo, more so than any other banned political theory.

A Royal Cruiser would dock with the liner in an hour, to take her directly back to Ellisford Castle. She removed her favourite metalic blue foil dress. She loved the feel of the material, but, it showed more of her skinny legs than it covered, and had been shortest thing she had ever worn. With her ridiculously tall and thin frame, she had to have a five inch extention to the white hem added to make it decent, even by Pendragon standards. The Archduchess had been wrong. She had not been "rocking Pendragon styles", she just looked unhealthy. Stepping back sartorially seven hundred years to an Anserian dress at least hid her skeletal frame.

'On Imogen's arrival at the Cottage, the personality controlling her changed her accent from an aristocratic one to a middle-class rural one. After regaining her body from the fake personality, her accent and speech patterns had decayed into the same broad rural vernacular as Sarah and Clarice. She had to make an effort to talk posh like a ristoze.

'Angels! What has you done to yous lovely hair?' asked a horrified Clarice as Imogen hugged her.

'Got rid of the dead weight, have I,' Imogen replied. 'Don't miss it for nuffin'. Me long hair wouldn't a' fitted under no spacesuit helmet,' Imogen said beginning her explanation. 'Women out in Pendragon keep their hair short. In a style what they calls a station bobtail. They got to be ready to jump into an emergency spacesuit at the drop of a hat, When Archduchess Jane went to have her bobtail fixed, she took me with her to sort mine out.' Imogen laughed.

'She should 'ave done it years ago,' said Sarah. 'What be the point 'o havin' all that 'air, if it be plaited, pinned, and covered by a veil most o' the time.'

'I be expected to let it grow, or have extentions to level with my waist, like all woman in the Castle, by Yule. Otherwise I'll be in trouble with the Protocol Office up in the Keep. 'I ain't a-goin' to bother a-growin' it,' said Imogen, who was feeling rebellious. 'And to the twenty hells with a-gluin' extensions. on? An' before yous be askin' where it be, to the hells with veils an' all.'

In the past the length of a woman's hair had once been a sign of the wealth and power of her father or husband. In her childhood, Imogen's hair had never been cut. Royalty had always had ankle-length tresses. She vividly remembered watching, with childish delight, as Anita and Aunt Marie-Ann's shoulder length serf style hair had grown as long as her own aristocratic and so-called classical hair. The remainder of women had maintained their hair level with their waists. As a teenager Imogen had learned to hate the regal tradition and had been overjoyed to have her flowing locks cut level with her armpits during her nursing career.

Now hair length was a mark of modernity. The more traditional or rural a woman's home, the longer her hair would be. In the urban areas on Anseris and on the Jovian Baronies sported shorter hairstyles of Pendragon.

'But ain't that a lovely avatar. Did you get it out in Pendragon?' asked Sarah, changing the subject; this was becoming political, and you never knew if Conrad might be listening.

'T'is well ancient, m'dear,' said Clarice. 'T'is Moonglow, that be scarcer than 'en's teeth these days.'

'I found it on t'ship,' said Imogen. 'Twas given to me when I were ten by a good mate, he were almost like me own brother he was.'

J mogen didn't want Conrad snooping around when her things arrived. If Conrad reported the arrival of an ugly horse-head lamp, the from orbit. Princess would know Falada was back. Conrad always gave the Old Gatehouse a wide berth. Once her things were safely stored there, in the supposedly haunted building, they would not be disturbed.

'T'is a pleasant day, Sarah,' Imogen said as she walked into the kitchen. 'But them forecasters say it'll be a-cloudin' over later.'

'T'is a pity, we could do with a few more days like this,' Sarah replied. 'After all that rain we've been a-havin'.'

'T'ain't going to rain though. So when I take my little darlings out, I'll be a-takin' an easel and paints with I,' Imogen replied. 'Finish me painting of the Inner Bailey. There be half a dozen of them eagles a-dancin' on the air, behind the Keep. All them lambs and alpaca calves must be sorely tempting.'

'OK, Imogen,' said the older woman. 'What time'll you be a-wantin' your lunch?'

'Roughly one o'clock. I told Clarice I'd lend a hand with the washing this arvo.'

'None of the other Goose Maidens never done no housework. Them was Ristoze who left all the work to us,' said Clarice.

'There be two less staff now,' said Imogen. 'And remember, I ain't no Ristoze. Brought up by the serfs till I was ten, was I. An' I still be a servant, even though I looks all posh like. Anyways, after a morning with 'em blessed geese I'll always be ready for a good chat.'

'Yous just had four weeks off at the drop of a hat, an' yous a-wastin' away yous mornin' a-paintin' a pretty picture, right? Nah, yous ain't nuffin' like a Ristoze, be yous?'

I used to be more than an aristocrat in another life, Imogen thought, I was royalty. When the time comes, how can I be royalty again? There is now no way I could climb back into that regal bubble. I identify more with the ordinary people than with the wealthy elite class I was born into.

'Clarice be right, mistress,' Sarah said, she bobbed a curtsey and became very formal. 'Being the Goose Maiden has changed that. Sooner or later, the King'll give you a title, making you a Toff. You'll be above doing the housework then, as you should be now.'

Imogen appreciated the compliment but wanted to help or die of boredom.

'Oh very well, I am ordering you to accept my help with the housework.' Imogen effortlessly flipped between accents, just like Marion and Anita. 'I'm still one of the ordinary people. Whether you like it or not.'

Knowing she had lost the argument over the housework, Clarice changed the topic of the conversation to Conrad. 'Him'll be a-followin' you again.'

'Ain't yous happy he be too busy a-spyin' on I?' asked Imogen and the room dissolved into laughter.


She set up her easel by an artificial stream in a spot south of the Inner and Middle Baileys. The Eastern Wall of Angel Pass truncating the Rushton Mountains made a dramatic backdrop to the Castle. Around the Inner and Middle Bailey was the only area in the Castle Precincts that remained as a large and easily defensible area of flat lawn, separated from the rest of the Outer Bailey, which had been thoroughly landscaped. Imogen spotted Conrad trimming an overgrown thicket the other side of the stream. She could see he was wearing that ridiculous hat. The man was obsessed with it and today was far too warm for that sort of headgear.

Ellisford Castle had its own weather control unit, imported from Grimmswald when she had been a child. It was used to make sure the sun always shone on a royal birthday without upsetting the artificial climate created by the Aggelii. As a child, Imogen had learnt the theory behind its operation and mastered the jury-rigged Anserian. The machine had survived and was now hidden by an overgrown Buddleia bush next to her easel. It did not matter the Anserian controls had been destroyed during the reign of Benedict I, she could now use the original psychic interface.

As soon as Conrad removed his headgear, she would generate just enough breeze to blow the hat out of his hand and send it flying. While Conrad was chasing his headgear, she would take delivery of the precious cargo from the spaceship.

'Good morning, my man, what are you doing?' she asked in a perfectly condescending aristocratic accent.

He bowed but did not remove the hat.

'I be a-thinnin' this thicket. It were planted two score an' fifteen years ago. It needs I to remove stuff that stops the trees maturing.'

Oh rats, she thought, spotting the laces tied in a bow beneath Conrad's chin. 'Aren't you warm with that thing on your head?'

'I be prone to sunstroke, darlin'. Me 'at protects the back of me 'ead for I,' Conrad said as he continued hacking away at the weeds. Conrad was supposed to be a Castle Footman, who were all urban plebs; his rural accent had always been wrong. The spy must have realised his mistake and was slowly switching to an urban accent in a way he hoped no-one would notice. Imogen had noticed the subtle changes. He had started dropping aitches. Soon he would start replacing the "I" at the end of sentences with "me". More evidence Conrad was a Chessman.

'Very good, carry on,' said Imogen imperiously, returning to her easel. She hitched her skirt up to cross stepping stones in the stream as a stray gust of wind caught her hems, inadvertently flashing her knees and naked legs below. Looking back from the other side, she noticed Conrad was grinning and had turned a bright red.

Conrad watched the Goose Maiden as she painted the Castle in the distance, at a loss to know why the weird Princess thought she was mad. He knew little about medicine so still regarded mental illness as a curse. People with the curse were to be avoided, they may pass it on. The Goose Maiden was in no way cursed. To be fair, she was a bit of a looker, watching was not a hardship.

She had put down the paint and pallet. The strawberry-blonde hair fell out of the long ponytail. Rats, she's looking at me, he thought, as he picked up his saw and began hacking away at some bramble.

Imogen looked across the stream at the spy brushed her hair. She was spending more time fiddling with it. The Pendragon style was fine anywhere else, but too radical and would never fit the Castle's dress code. The Protocol Office, would win the long game. Nobody would dare cut her hair. They would only trim it, removing split ends so it could continue growing to an approved length. The Office had spitefully confiscated all her elasticated hairbands, but let her keep her quartz wristwatch.

Conrad was blushing but had not remove his hat. Time for something more radical. If a brief flash of her ankle had made him blush, what would a viewing the whole leg do? After the first week in Pendragon, her old inhibitions had boiled away. She now had no probrem hitching up the hem of her kirtle and the chemise below and began adjusting her garter, flashing a lot of long pink leg in the process.

Bingo! He had taken the hat off and was using it to fan himself. The control interface of the weather machine flashed to life. Carefully, she reduced the air pressure at the Castle's external wall. Sure enough, the wind picked up and took the hat from Conrad' head before he could tie it in place. She could hear him cursing as he ran after it, always just out of reach.

'Blow the wind and blow the wind down. Blow Conrad's hat this day,' she sung to herself. 'All the way to Cudren town, many miles away.'

'Good afternoon, Lady,' said Delbert the Carter, as he climbed down from his vehicle and tethered Denzil the horse. Her boxes had languished in storage while she had gadded about in Pendragon.

'And a good afternoon to you too, Delbert,' Imogen replied as formally as the man.

The obsession with historical re-enactment still barred most motorised vehicles from the precincts of Ellisford Castle. The packages had come from a space-port on a truck but had to be delivered by Delbert's horse-drawn cart.

'I have your four boxes, Imogen,' said Delbert, dropping the formality. 'Where do you wish me to put them?'

'Could you stack them in the Old Gatehouse, Del, until I have a chance to give them my full attention?'

'If I must, Imogen,' said Delbert.

Superstition was so strong in the stagnant society of Anseris that there was now a road in and out of the Cottage's grounds bypassing the haunted building.

'Thank you.'

Three days had passed since Falada had been delivered. The trick with the hat served its purpose once, but Imogen doubted she could use it again. Wherever she turned Conrad was there, grinning at her. Only in the haunted Old Gatehouse was she free of him.

'Don't you have nuffin' better to be a-doin' than traipsin' after I?' Imogen asked when her patience finally ran out.

'I don' know what yew mean, my lovey',' he replied with an impudent leery grin.

'I ain't, nor never will I be, yous lovely! I knows yous a spy. So yer not a-doin' an outstandin' job, is you?'

'Why should I be a-spyin'? I be an odd-jobber, not a Chessman.'

'You ain't a-goin' to admit to it,' said Clarice, who had walked into the room carrying a tray with three fried breakfasts.

'Ain't nothin' to admit to.'

'Like I said, you ain't a-goin' to admit to it,' said the maid, 'but you was the only person to mention them Chessmen.'

'Yous could be an informer fer them Chessmen and a-tryin' t'pin the blame on me' said Conrad. It was true, the Political Police only recruited men into its ranks but had many paid female informants to collect information from places no man could go.

'More'n likely yous would be accusin' me, t' divert attention from youself,' replied Clarice. 'Tis just the sort o' thing a Chessman spy would be a-doin''.

'Me? I be just an odd-jobber.'

'Then off you go an' do some odd-jobs then!' Sarah shouted at the man. 'Leave 'er Ladyship in peace, mind!'

'She bain't no laydiship, mind,' Conrad replied, 'She be a servant, jus' same as us.'

'I bain't a servant now, Conrad. An' you bain't no odd-jobber neither,' Imogen spat at the objectionable man.

'Look, 'er ain't no Ristoze, 'er be a-talkin' common, like me an' t' rest o' us common folk.'

'Most Ristoze talks common in them there 'omes. They only speak fancy-like with the plebs an' peasants t' make themselves reckon they be top-notch.' said Imogen. 'When I want to, I can talk like the ristoze, especially when talking to oiks like you.'

'Her Ladyship be right. Hr were a servant, now her be the Royal Goose Maiden. When his Majesty gets round t'it, he'll make 'er Dame Imogen, a member of the aristocracy. A scruffy little herbert like you should show respect to their betters'

The older woman was beating Conrad with a feather duster, which looked comedic. Imogen tried not to laugh. There was a time when she would have chastised Conrad for his behaviour. Now she just joined in the banter.

'I be off, I be a-headin' off. Mebbe her so-called Ladyship'll flash her pegs at me again when us be outside.'

'Dream on, you nasty little man,' replied Imogen haughtily. Then in a rural accent, 'Don't forget yer hat. Tie him on tight like. Yous dussn't wanna be a-losin' 'im again.'

𝕴 mogen made her way to the Old Gatehouse, safe in the knowledge neither of the women would follow her there and Conrad had been dispatched on an errand in the Inner Bailey.

'Oh, Falada, it pains me to see you thus,' Imogen said in an exaggerated upper-class accent, as she carefully re-assembled the components of the Valentine Device.

'If your mother could see you, it would break her heart,' replied a familiar voice, as the lamp began to disappear.

'It would indeed, my friend. This is a right pickle,' she replied.

The flaming horse-head fully materialised. 'It's nice to see you are wide awake again. You will be able to do some rudimentary repair work on my systems.'

'So the Fenzrian's teaching machine was not totally useless?'

'Anita should have been more wary of it. We all should.' Falada sounded guilty. 'Poor Anita, she has been the worse affected by whatever it was that hijacked the machine. Or rather, whoever it was. I have a nasty suspicion that I know who. She should have been dead for hundreds of years.'

'Who?' asked Imogen.

'Katherine Wellingford, later Kathyren Ellisford-Castle, Queen of Anseris, the so-called Immortal Empress.'

'The Boatbuilder and his daughter defeated her. How can she be in anyway responsible for the situation today?'

'Remember, I helped the Boatbuilder and his daughter defeat Kathyren Ellisford-Castle, who by that stage was already ancient and quite mad. We destroyed her body and prevented her method of gaining a replacement. Somehow her mind survived in a recording device our searches missed. I don't know how it got aboard your spaceship, but I am certain she is the one who hijacked the Fenzrian machine and is now controlling poor Anita.'

'She won't be happy then. If I recall, she looked like me, my mother and grandmother. The Queens of Anseris have always looked like her, without fail. Willowy women with strawberry-blonde hair.'

'Say that again?' asked Falada.

'Willowy women with strawberry-blonde hair.'

'And all your predecessors looked like that?'

'Yes, any Free Queen's later children could be boys or girls and look like their father, but the Queen's first child would always be a girl who looked exactly like her mother. Without fail, the daughter would inherit the Kingdom.'

'This is a new wrinkle. You see, I don't know everything. I need to do some research. The computers on this world are so primitive. It will take me a week or two to gain access to everything.'

Imogen watched as Falada faded to a cool blue colour as if in a thoughtful mood. She shivered, the AI had known just about everything. Even Falada could have feet of clay. This was not a good sign.

'You look deep in thought, Imogen,' Falada said when he returned to full power and broke Imogen's daydream.

'Sorry, I was miles away. Still, you won't be disturbed here. People rarely come here, they think it's haunted.'

'Someone is approaching. Male, in his mid-twenties. He'll be here in two minutes.'

'That'll be Conrad, the spy,' replied Imogen. 'From the way he's acting, I suspect he's been ordered to concentrate on me, and, report back if I start acting like my real self. Unfortunately, it looks like he's not as superstitious as he pretends.'

'I hope you are hiding the fact the real you is back.'

'I am. Everyone still thinks I'm sweet and stupid Imogen, the dogsbody.'

'Good,' the AI said. 'I have hacked the local network. I want you to make an appointment with the Inner Bailey's doctor. I need to have a full medicinal and DNA scan for my research. I will augment the surgery's equipment. Pretend you are having headaches or something. He will scan you, then I will do the rest.'

'T'hank the Angels for their handiwork. Also thank them neither Queen Kathyren nor my predecessors could demolish it,' said Crown-Prince David, driving back to Ellisford Castle on the Aggelii's complete and indestructible motorway network. The conversation was bland, filled with inanities. Both men knew they were being listened to.

'They built it before we came along and they abandoned this world,' replied Carlo.

The network connected the Equatorial, Southern and Eastern continents together. It blended in with and was reinforced by the natural geology. A feat that beggared belief. Not surprisingly, Anserians called them the Angel's Highway.

'I still think railways have more class,' said Carlo, as they passed a train on the track parallel to the road.

They were travelling along the Great Ring, the section of Angel's Highways which connected all the land-masses around the Santorini Sea to the West of Ellisford Castle.

'Well, the Angels did leave enough space on their highways for both road and railways. However, there is something about a fast car with auto-steer switched off,' said Crown-Prince David. 'The romance of the open road.'

'Yes, Dewi, but I prefer to arrive at my destination relaxed in a way you can only be after a First Class train journey.'

'You've never travelled Third Class then?' asked the Crown Prince.

'You haven't, I have,' said Carlo. 'The joys of genteel poverty.'

'And one advantage of travelling in a car is this,' said Crown-Prince David, pressing a series of buttons on a box. There was a pause. 'I have made us invisible for three minutes and thirty seven seconds to listening devices and satellite surveillance. It look like a natural blip. You can't do that on a train. Whatever class you travel in.'

Both men knew whomever was tasked with listening to them would be glad of the apparent break in the pointless conversation.

'Carlo, I have another job for you,' said David.

'Yes, Dewi, what is it?' asked the equerry.

'I have it on very good authority that Lady Imogen is planning on playing truant in a few days time. Heading to Elizaberg.'

'She'll be lucky, Dewi. The Castle is tighter than a drum. There is no way she can walk out of there.'

'I also have it on good authority she knows about the tunnel.'

'Oh! How?'

Putting the car on automatic steering David handed Carlo a folder. He could see the grin growing on the other man's face. This was the sort of discovery historians, both amateur and professional, would give their right arm for. 'Before you ask, I found these pictures aboard the ship that she was travelling on. All verifiably genuine.'

'So Johanna is the real Princess Louise Imogen, and the so-called Princess Anita is a fraud. Well, blow me away,' said Carlo.

'I'd rather not,' replied the Crown Prince. 'You're far too useful to assassinate.'

Both men laughed as Carlo continued reading the dossier.

'I have arranged a little mystery tour for our hidden Princess. I want you to be part of it. I'm sure you know enough student types who would enjoy eating and drinking at Duisenstein's in Elizaburg at my expense.'

'I can arrange that, Dewi.'

'Good man.'

'Who be yous a-chattin' to?' asked Conran.

'I ain't a-talkin' to no one,' Imogen replied. 'I mean, I am not talking to anyone.'

Conrad noted the seamless change in accents. Sweet Imogen might not be the halfwit she pretended to be. Fair enough, he thought. They were both social chameleons and smarter than people thought. His bumbling yokel personality was as much a mask as the one Imogen wore. In his opinion she was the sanest person he had ever met. There was nothing to report to the Princess, who was, like all royals, completely barking.

'Want ta show I them smashing pins again darlin'?' he asked.

'No, I do not! Once an oik, always an oik.'

'I be from proper peasant stock, an' proper chuffed with it.'

Gotcha! thought Imogen. Conrad was a Chessmen and one of the gentry. Only someone like that used the phrase "proper peasant stock". All the lower classes regarded it as a terrible insult.

Under a grey morning sky, Imogen walked from the Cottage to the Keep. When her mother had ordered the building of new housing for castle employees, replacing the scattered small cottages throughout the outer bailey. The village of Bailesparc had two dozen houses, six apartment blocks, shops, two pubs and a church. Aunt Marie Anne had argued that this isolated community and the serfs in the Middle Bailey needed a small hospital. She requisitioned an abandoned guards barracks and storeroom on the third floor of the castle, planning to create a GP's surgery, a treatment room for minor emergencies and an eight bed non-surgical ward. Imogen had hoped she could work there but it had not been finished when she left Anseris.

She trudged up the stairway cut into the solid rock floor of a natural tunnel connecting the Inner Bailey on the top of the knoll to the Middle Bailey complex at its base. The increase in water flowing down the gutters either side of the steps meant the drizzle had turned to heavy rain. Imogen knew she would be drenched entirely as she walked the short distance from the stairway porch to the Keep. Once she was indoors, the rain stopped. Feeling wet and miserable, she waited at the end of a queue of Castle employees to make an appointment to see the doctor. Outside, the Ansersol burnt away the early morning cloud.

As with all things Anserian, she noted as the surgery door slid open the place was a curious mixture of ancient, old-fashioned and sparklingly modern. The receptionist, in her late forties, wore a pale green side-less surcote over a darker green kirtle. Her hair and neck were hidden by a linen veil and wimple like a woman from fourteenth-century Europe. She sat behind a twenty-first century counter. For most of Anseris, the receptionist's twentieth-century personal computer was cutting-edge technology.

Small practical anachronisms in clothing and accessories were now tolerated if kept to a minimum. In the receptionist's case, these were a pair of ugly brown glasses from the mid-twentieth century and a digital wristwatch.

'Can I help you, miss?' the receptionist asked.

'Is it possible to see the doctor? I've been having terrible blinding migraines and stomach cramps for the past few days. The worse pain I have ever known.'

'Can I have your name, please?' asked the receptionist.

'Lady Imogen, the Goose Maiden.'

The inevitable surveillance systems were almost at a galactic standard. Imogen did not heard a sound as a surveillance camera photographed her and rapidly confirmed her identity and the level of facilities available to her.

'Ah yes, Your Ladyship, you should have come straight to me. No need for you to queue,' said the receptionist. 'Doctor Matthews can see you at 2pm.' She stood up, handed Imogen a white-edged appointment card and curtseyed. The preferential treatment was not fair. It was Monday and the people who politely queued in front of her had received yellow-edged cards with appointments for one of public surgery on Tuesday, Wednesday or Thursday morning.

'Thank you.' Imogen grudgingly returned the curtsey as the older woman sat down, then quickly left the waiting room. Her mother had told her to always return a polite gesture even if you didn't have to, or particularly want to.

P eople were expected to be clean in the presence of their Monarch. The Inner Bailey had the best bath-house on Anseris. The old bath-house had been destroyed by the Fenzrians in the last days of the war. There was now a decorative fountain on the site, originally a memorial to Bath-house Mistress Elsa whose body had been pulled out of the rubble. Imogen remembered her mother had said, 'So, no-one of quality', and made Archduke Rushton-Browne pay for it. He had not been petty enough to remove the fountain when he became King, but had changed its dedication to everyone from Ellisford Castle who had died during the war.

The new bath-house filled the ground floor of the Keep. It looked properly medieaval, with its large wooden tubs brimming with hot scented water. The modern plumbing was well hidden. Like all things on Anseris, the quality of service in the bath-house depended on social class.

'Imogen, my dear, where do you think you're going?' asked Queen Stephanie, dressed as always in something containing too much pink.

'To bathe in a white ribbon tub while my clothes are dried, Your Majesty. As befits my position in society,' replied Imogen as she curtseyed. A white ribbon tub had marginally colder water, lesser quality soap and rougher towels than the blue ribbon ones she should be entitled to by birth. At least it was a step up from the yellow or brown ribbon tubs used by the masses.

'Nonsense, my dear girl, you must come with me,' said the Queen-Consort. 'You'll get blue ribbon service everywhere now. I'll make sure of it.'

Being called "girl" by someone who even without the century gap was still several years younger grated. However, Stephanie was the Queen-Consort, so she was entitled to call her what she liked.

'Will you please call me Steffi,' said the Queen-Consort as they climbed into their hot baths. 'It's difficult to be stuffy and formal when both of us are lying naked in our tubs of hot water.' On cue, two maids appeared and took away their clothes.

'Thank you, Steffi,' Imogen said.

'You're welcome,' the young Queen-Consort replied. 'I'm fascinated by you and the Princess. Growing up a hundred years ago, but still being young.'

'For us, no time has passed, Steffi.'

'That must be so weird,' said the Queen-Consort, before ducking her head under water to wash her hair.

'So little has changed here on Anseris, I feel quite at home,' Imogen eventually replied when Stephanie returned to the surface.

'But you don't, do you?' asked the Queen-consort. 'I can tell you're disappointed that this planet hasn't moved on. You've been into space, almost left the Anserian system. You want this world and her people to move on.'

Was this really an accidental meeting or a test of loyalty? An attempt to find out her politics? Imogen knew she needed to be more guarded with Queen-Consort Stephanie.

'The world is what it is. Who am I to try and change it?' Imogen ducked her head under water. When she resurfaced, she asked, 'Maid, pass me the shampoo, please?'

Eventually they climbed out of the tubs and went to drying booths with their soft blue towels and wall-length mirrors. Out in Pendragon, Imogen's appetite had ballooned. When she first returned home Sarah had told her she was trying to eat her plate as well as the food on it at mealtimes. Imogen said she thought it was a by-product of being in space. Previously no matter how delicious the food was she had never been able to eat more than a tiny portion. Her mother said she automatically conformed to the regal norm, obviously underweight. Her mother had been frighteningly thin. Imogen did not think she would ever be called fat, but with her appetite no longer subconsciously curtailed, she was no longer skeletal. However she would soon need to replace her wardrobe, even her loosest dress was too tight.

Imogen's musing on her body was cut short when she heard the curtains of Stefania drying booth opening.

'Ah, Queen-Consort Stefanie, here you are. Have you forgotten?' asked the Princess.

'Oh yes, Your Royal Highness, is it that time already? I will be but a few minutes dressing.' Her tone was as polite as it had to be; Queen-Consort Stephanie apparently did not like the Princess.

'My bridal blessing by a Caretaker cannot be rushed because the History Keeper of my fiancé's family spent too much time bathing before the ceremony.'

'Can I come out?' asked Imogen, before leaving her drying booth in her chemise.

The Princess turned on her. 'What the devil are you doing here? The plebeians' dressing-room is down the corridor.'

'I reminded Lady Imogen that as Keeper of the Royal Geese, she has the right to all the blue ribbon facilities of the Castle. We have had a pleasantly relaxing soak and a gossip.'

'We'll see about that,' replied the Princess.

'You forget yourself. Majesty outranks Royal Highness. If you try to change my order, I'll not be happy. I'm more than a little annoyed at you bursting in while I was still fastening my bandeau.'

'I have been Majesty since before you were born, little girl, and don't you forget it.' The Princess spat the words out. 'I really don't know why the King tolerates you. I don't know why I tolerate the charade of him being more than an Archduke Rushton-Browne.'

'He controls the army and all the apparatus of the State. You do not.' Queen-Consort Stephanie made a dismissive hand gesture. 'Now leave us. I will attend your blessing at the vault when I am ready.'

The maids returned to help them into their gowns. Imogen's clothes were now dried, perfectly ironed and with the missing button replaced. If she had gone to a white ribbon tub, they would have been returned to her dry and ironed only.

'You make a dangerous enemy of the Princess, Your Majesty,' Imogen said, as she fastened her Moonglow avatar in place.

'I know, but she knows I'm right. She needs the King. My father would kill her in an instant if anything untoward happened to me,' the Queen replied.

'I hope you are right, Your Majesty.' Imogen formally curtseyed. 'By your leave, I have an appointment with the Inner Bailey's doctor.'

'You don't want to be late for Doctor Matthews, Lady Imogen. But we must meet more regularly. It's been a pleasant afternoon.'

Imogen returned to Doctor Matthews's surgery early and was shown into the Consulting Room. Why did doctors wear those stupid hats and bird masks with long beaks? They could do nothing to enhance their diagnostic skills.

'So how long have you had these aches and pains?' he asked.

'After I arrived home from Pendragon, but the past three days they have been unbearable,' Imogen replied. It was a lie as she was in perfect health, apart from the nausea something in this room had triggered.

'Let's have a look,' said Doctor Matthews, as he switched on a simple medical scanner. 'Oh, hello. That's odd.'

'I was warned hyperspace resonances had built up while I was trapped. They might affect simple scanners.'

'Ah, I see. We'll have to roll out the big guns.'

'At a hospital in Elizaburg?'

'No, Lady Imogen, we have a full body scanner here. You will have to change into a surgical gown. Nurse Ifans will assist you.'

N urse Chrystine Ifans was a woman in her mid-twenties of average height, but that was the only average thing about her. Her obvious Fenzrian ancestry shone through. The nurse was outstandingly beautiful, with alabaster skin. A white crown-like pie-crust fillet encircling her head. A few strands of her ink black hair escaped from her uniform's white hairnet. It reminded Imogen of Anita who could not keep all her hair under control. And Anita had reached the same grade in her career as Nurse Ifans.

'I'm afraid I need to confirm your details. Name?'

'Imogen Anona Castlevale Royalward. Although, we didn't have town-names back in my day. Castlevale is new,' said Imogen. 'Angels, that makes me sound ancient.'

'I know the feeling,' said the nurse. 'The Island of Gwener still doesn't use them. Anything less than five hundred years old is too modern. It took me a while to get used to adding Randau to my name. And your address?'

'The Goose Maiden's Cottage, Outer Bailey, Ellisford Castle.'

'That's what I have,' said the nurse.

S o, what's your name, Nurse Ifans?' the patient asked. Obviously trying to strike up a conversation. That's fine, there were no other patients that afternoon and Dr. Vaughn hated the scanner so would be in no hurry to use it.

'I'm Chrystine Jessicca Randau Ifans,' Chryssy replied.

'You're a long way from home,' said the patient in Welsh, and she almost had the same distinct accent as her own, from the island of Gwener, in the far South East. The ancestors of the gentry on that island had spoken Welsh, as had Queen Kathyren who had made it the island's only official language.

'As far as you can get, Lady Imogen. Almost equidistant east and west from Ellisford Castle.' She laughed. 'Not that I miss it. Anyone like me, with the tiniest bit of Fenzrian ancestry, has a hard time there now.'

That was it, the patient sounded like every elderly lady she knew, but did not look old enough to speak that way. Because her patient had been young before those old women had been born.

'Which brings me to my next question, Lady Imogen. Your age?'

There was always a degree of diplomacy surrounding asking a woman her age, and Imogen could tell Chrystine really had not wanted to ask that question.

'I have existed for nearly one hundred and twenty-four years, but I have only lived through twenty-three of them. One hundred of them passed in a blinking of an eye while I was in suspended animation.'

Chrystise could see the pain welling up from deep inside the patient. Imagine knowing everyone you knew is long dead. Lets move this on.

'Twenty-three, then. Any allergies, food intolerances or adverse reactions to any medications?'

'Peppermint disinfectant,' Imogen said with a smile. 'I'm one of the unlucky. It makes me nauseous on every exposure.'

J sound close to tears. Imogen was struck by the gulf in time
'Vile, isn't it? On the plus side, the reaction is temporary; it disappears after a few minutes.' Something made the nurse laugh then blush. 'Made me vomit on my first day of training.'

'Not a good start, Chrystine. If I may call you Chrystine? And please, just Imogen will do fine. I know so few people my apparent age.' Again there was a quivver in her voice.

'Certainly. It's a pleasure to meet you. I rent a room in the village from Tracy the receptionist and her husband.

Imogen guessed the village in question, Bailesparc, which was to the east of the Inner Bailey.

'It was being built in my childhood. I never visited, despite it being a short walk from the Inner Bailey.'

his was not going well at all, thought Chrystine. She could almost taste the Goose Maiden sadness. She also sound like someone was waiting for something that would never happen. Maybe she could suggest a mutually beneficial idea.

'You're a trained nurse,' said Chrystine. 'Since Zhana Chasovyar left – she got a job in the Royal – there has been a vacancy at this clinic. With only two of us, we've had to mothball next door. So there's a spare room where I live. You'd meet more people if you lived in the village and worked here?'

'I don't think I'm qualified enough.'

'They let you work out in Pendragon, after the asteroid mining accident,' said Chrystine.'

'The hospitals out there were so desperate, they accepted any extra pairs of hands. The certificate I found on my ship can't still be valid. My training way out of date.'

'That certificate and the interview must have been good enough for you to get you a valid licence from the Central Nursing Board. You can't work anywhere in the Kingdom, even in an emergency without one,' Chrystine said. 'Actually, there is a huge staff shortage here on the Home-world. Until twenty years ago, if you weren't born into a family with a tradition of nursing, you had no chance of getting on a training course. Unless you joined the Dutiful Sisters. Then you entered the profession with a profession. As much as I love my job, even I would draw the line at becoming a nun to get it. I'm sure you could walk into any job if you wanted to.'

'No, really. I'd barely got out of the yellow,' said Imogen.

'Castle uniforms are all this shade of navy. I should only be dark lavender,' said Chrystine. 'You were running a ward by the end of your stay in Pendragon. You earned this navy.' The shade of blue of a nurse's uniform denoted their rank.

'That doesn't count, I was only discharging patients and closing the ward down, until the next emergency.'

'Still a responsible job. Although I can't see the Princess emptying bedpans at 3am,' said Chrystine.

'That is why I was there. The Princess never did a night shift and spent her time doing the paperwork and arranging flowers. I did her work as well.' The sad sigh was unmissable.

N urse Chrystine is trying to be kind, Imogen thought, but she's making a pig's ear of it. After the war, once free from the inhumanity of the Cult of Great Machine, the Fenzrians Imogen had met had been so kind. Since her return, all of the descendent of original POWs had also been some of the nicest people she had ever met. Anita, the Fenzrian who had never been part of the Cult was normally so kind. Anita, she thought to herself, forgive me we are not talking about you, but the lie the creature who has hijacked you is weaving. 'Then the war came and we both returned to the Castle for her safety. I would have preferred to keep working for the war effort. But where she went I followed.'

'Thought so,' replied Chrystine Ifans.

'Also, I'm contented with the job I've got, which I couldn't leave without the King's permission,' Imogen replied. 'The Cottage is a bit isolated, but it's very comfortable, and my house-mates are pleasant.' House-mates, thought Imogen. It sounded better than servants and was now closer to the truth.

'Oh,' said Chrystine, sounding disappointed.

T hat did not go as planned. She's not interested in a new job. We are still short staffed her and its just me, hiding my true origins from the landlord. At least she sounds a lot happier. So. Plan B. Widen her social group. 'Do you know the Drunken Duck? It's the tavern in the village favoured by the residents our age. If you came along to the weekly quiz on Thursday night, you would meet more people.'

'Or, to give it its proper name, The Royal Goose. I'll give it a try,' said Imogen.

'Great. Although most Goose Maidens wouldn't dream of coming to Bailesparc – far too plebeian.'

'I'm not most Goose Maidens,' Imogen replied.

'If you have quite finished arranging your social life, Nurse Ifans. I have been summoned away to treat His Majesty,' said an annoyed Doctor Matthews.

'I'm sorry, Doctor Matthews, the patient is ready.'

'Oh well, I'll switch the beast on. You know what to do,' he said as he left the room.

'Looks like I will have to do the tests again then,' Chrystine said. 'Doctor Matthews is a whizz with the results it spits out, but doesn't have a clue about how to operate the machinery.'

'Did you ever consider training as a doctor, Chryssye?' asked Imogen.

Twenty years earlier women had been allow to officially become doctors for the first time. Before this, women had joined the Dutiful Sisters, the nursing order, to secretly study medicine. Often they would be the only doctor in a remote community, who gratefully hid the secret.

'I know people who started of nursing, saving to pay for their place in Medical School.'

Apprentice nurses are paid whilst they train. Medical students aren't paid until they get their degree, and start working as trainee doctors in a hospital.

'I never wanted that. I only ever wanted to qualify and work as a nurse. I chose to move halfway around the world to train in the best hospital,' Chrystine replied as they arrived at the scanner.

'Same with me,' Imogen said. Back then she had planned on working until the day before her inevitable coronation. The war had put a stop to that. Maybe she could arrange a part-time job here.

octor Matthews, who from his accent was also Gwenenian, pressed a button. The door of the tall cylindrical machine closed with a hiss. He set the device in motion. It was his pride and joy, a piece of modern medicine. He could interpret the data it produced, but he regarded actually operating it as beneath his dignity as a doctor, though one must maintain the appearance of superiority.

Even he knew something was wrong. Instead of the usual slow progression of a beam of blue light up and down the patient's body, the chamber was filled with a red strobe light.

'What the devil!' said the doctor. 'His Majesty has summoned me. I don't need this sort of delay.' The man ineffectually pressed a few buttons. 'It won't abort. Oh sod this bloody mask,' he said, pulling the beak away from his face. Now he could read a panel within the scanner to the nurse. He had no idea what it meant.

'No, that can't be right, the settings are all on normal,' said Nurse Ifans. 'Doctor Matthews, the machine is downloading forbidden protocols. The Angels know from where, it's never been networked.'

mogen knew Falada was now in control of the scanner. 'I can see that, Nurse Ifans,' Doctor Matthews said angrily, to maintain the pretence he knew what he was doing.
was not in the slightest bit worried, but she had to appear to be was flustered in front of the medical professionals, which she did by banging and kicking the door.

'Get me out of this thing!' she squealed. 'Before it cooks me alive.'

'Your Ladyship,' said Doctor Matthews, 'please stay calm.'

'That's easy for you to say, Doctor,' she said, sounding panicked.

Imogen watched through the small window in the door as Nurse Ifans calmly kicked the emergency shutdown switch on the wall behind the scanner. This should have had an immediate effect. However, Falada was not finished, but he did change the colour of the beams back to a calming blue.

'It appears to have reverted back to normal,' said the doctor. 'I will go to deal with His Majesty. Carry on, Nurse Ifans.'

Every non-essential electrical circuit in the Keep simultaneously failed as the scanner door slid open. Imogen knew Falada had set off a trip switch to cover his tracks. Fortunately that included the lights and computers in the surgery.

'So, I'll see you on Thursday,' Imogen said to Chrystine.

'Yes,' replied Chrystine. 'I'll look forward to it.'


How dare the pink blancmange speak to her in that manner. The Princess was hopping mad. Stephanie was just a loser who the usurper felt sorry for. Her mood had not been helped by the electricity in the Keep failing, ruining the farce that had been the Pre-Nuptial Blessing Ceremony.

No, Stephanie had to be punished. She knew who to arrange it and walked straight into his office without knocking.

'Baronet Oscar Vernon Rushton-Browne of Easterby, you are the Head of Security here at Ellisford Castle.'

'Your Royal Highness,' said the man, who stood and saluted. 'I'm usually called Lord Vernon, it makes life easier.' He then bowed a courtly bow for the Princess.

'Your branch of the House Rushton-Browne has never been happy that the Monarch's family retains the Archduchy, has it?'

'No, Your Royal Highness. It was believed House Ellisford-Castle was extinct, Archduke Benedict became King. His brother, my great-grandfather, should have been made Archduke in his place, I would now hold that title. Instead the Crown Prince has been Archduke of Castlegate ever since.'

'And now I have turned up, proving House Ellisford-Castle is not extinct, you can't be happy?'

'When you marry Crown-Prince David, he will join House

Ellisford-Castle as yours is the higher ranking Great House. The Crown Prince will no longer be able to hold the Archduchy of Castlegate. I will become Archduke, because the Easterby Branch will become the highest ranking branch of House Rushton-Browne.'

'The fact you are the King's illegitimate son makes things difficult for you. Doesn't it, Lord Fitz-Rushton? Bastards aren't allowed to become Archdukes.'

'If you were a man, I would challenge you to a duel.'

'Why get so hot under the collar? You are that fat fool's bastard son. There is more than a passing resemblance. I've spoken to your mother. When she realised who I really was, she was more than willing to tell me the truth.' The Princess was no longer speaking. An apparition had manifested itself, who watched in delight as Lord Vernon prostrated himself in front of her.

'Almighty Goddess, how may I serve you?'


'**C**ongratulations on choosing this building to hide me,' said Falada, as she arrived at the Old Gatehouse.

'Thanks.' said Imogen. 'It was the most logical place. No-one comes here. They think it's haunted.'

'Ghosts have nothing to do with it. The central power core of the prison ship KHM#89 is buried at the bottom of a natural sink-hole,' replied Falada. 'This interferes with almost any form of electrical devices entering this building, except me. I recharge myself with the energy it discharges.'

'I never knew that,' said Imogen. 'I suppose heat energy is being syphoned by the engine's defunct cooling system. Every so often the excess energy is discharged as the haunting.'

'Haunted buildings have a reputation for being colder than ordinary ones. You are not as ignorant of science as you like to think you are. For instance, what do you know about Genetics?'

'Officially nothing. That sort of knowledge is forbidden,' she replied. 'Unofficially, I know all the boring basics. Dominant and regressive traits, DNA, chromosomes and genomes. Et Cetera.'

'That will make things easier,' Falada said to Imogen. 'I have just finished studying the data from the body scanner.'

'So you found what you were looking for?' she asked.

'I found something, but I don't think you are going to like it.'

'Oh, Angels! I've not got some dreadful genetic disease that is going to kill me painfully?'

'No, unless you count being a perfect clone of Kathyren Ellisford-Castle as being a genetic disease. Your mother was also a clone, as was her mother, all the way back to the first Free Queen, who was merely the last host for Queen Kathyren created before the revolution.'

'She said I would learn a great secret when I was older. This must be it. If Kathyren Ellisford-Castle is back, I'm not safe.'

'Indeed not,' said Falada, in perfect agreement. 'Liberating Anita is now even more important. Kathyren Ellisford-Castle cannot remain corporeal.'

'I don't understand. Why did she possess Anita? Why not completely absorb me,' asked Imogen with a shudder, 'if I am such a perfect host?'

'I still don't know. But, remember on the ship,' he said, 'Anita told you she had no resistance to the Fenzrian gestalt without your arrogance to fight it off?'

'Yes. But the Fenzrians are long gone.'

'Sadly, even with a dose of your aristocratic arrogance, she had no resistance to the more powerful siren song of Kathyren Ellisford-Castle. To make matters worse, the Immortal Empress used that aristocratic arrogance to create the persona that now controls your friend.'

'Poor Anita.'

'It is the next generation Queen Kathyren is interested in.'

'Am I cursed to produce a clone-daughter?'

'I'm afraid so. You possess an augmented third ovary. When you first become pregnant, you will carry the embryo from the third ovary. Until that child is born, you cannot have natural children. So, if things don't change, Kathyren Ellisford-Castle will be Queen of Anseris once more. She will find a way to spirit your firstborn into the Queen's Tower, and the cycle of terror will begin again.'

'Over my dead body!' Imogen shouted.

'Yes, it probably will be.' Falada had no idea why Imogen burst into a fit of giggles. 'It's nothing to laugh about.'

'If I don't laugh, I'll cry. But I suspect you didn't call me here today just for a science lesson.'

'Indeed not. Today we also need to discuss Economics and Politics.'

He uploaded a stream of data into Imogen's memory. Imogen sat herself down and began to tidy her hair, letting this information percolate.

'So, the economy of Anseris is as bad as you feared,' she said.

'No, Princess Louise, it's worse. If we manage to deal with Kathyren Ellisford-Castle, get Anita back and you properly on the throne, you will still have a mountain to climb.'

'Say something to really make me miserable.'

'Don't do irony, Princess Louise, you don't suit it.'

'So what's wrong with this planet?' Imogen chose to ignore the barb, with more important things to talk about.

'It's a bit of a dump, with centuries of misrule by Kathyren Ellisford-Castle's obsession with creating an agricultural paradise which nearly starved everyone,' replied Falada. 'After her, the economy was on the up. Sustainable technology, clean and green industry. A controlled move into space, etcetera. Then the Fenzrians turned up and set the economy back decades. And finally, King Benedict I, with his band of buffoons, sent it back centuries. They did a lot more than destroy the most boring Royal Portrait Gallery in the Galaxy.'

'There is still a lot of useful technology around,' said Imogen with a giggle. 'Bad Benny only destroyed what he thought was non-Anserian technology.'

'He saw anything computerised as non-Anserian,' said Falada.

'A lot of things were hidden by his sensible son until he became King.'

'Relatively sensible, Imogen, he killed his brother to get to the Throne.'

'Of course it was relative, fratracide always is,' said Imogen.

'If I could groan, I would,' said Falada. 'Anyway, under King Francis I, the slow climb back started. Anserian society is now like Earth was in the early Third Millennium. It's stagnant. There will be no leap forward with the current regime.'

'Which is on its last legs,' added Imogen, 'but kept in place by a fanatically loyal secret police force stifling opposition.'

'But not destroying it,' said Falada, 'not after so many radical refugees arrived on the planet after King Benedict I closed the High Frontier.'

'The groups are so fractured, I'll never unify them.'

'No, Princess Louise, you have a powerful ally, the Prime Caretaker of Souls. If anyone can bring all the opposition groups together, he can. The King dare not publicly attack the Church. Even in its current state of decline, it is still too well-loved. I have a conduit to the Prime Caretaker, I shall arrange an appointment for you.'

'You make it sound easy.' Imogen, her hair back into place. 'But how do I get off the island Ellisford Castle is built upon without anyone noticing me?'

'Do you remember your old fairy grotto?' asked the AI.

'The Shell Grotto by the western wall,' she replied. 'Now I remember. I thought the concealed door was the entrance to Fairyland. I was too scared to go inside.'

'Well, the door opens into a tunnel which leads directly under the curtain walls and the moat, to an exit in Castle Rock. You need to see things for yourself. Have a wander around Elizaburg without a minder before your appointment with His Holiness.'

'You think you forget everything you learn. You're wrong. When you need solve practical problems, the things you need pop back into your memory.'

'Thank you. Everyone thinks I'm an idiot.'

'You are not. So how are you going to deal with Conrad?'

'I think I'll amaze him.'

'**Could you throw some wood on the fire, Imogen?**' asked Sarah. 'It's gone a bit nippy tonight. Me old bones be a-complainin'.'

Sarah watched as Imogen got up and added fuel to the fire. The girl refused to retire to her parlour in the evening as her predecessors had. Instead she spent her time with the servants in the kitchen. Imogen said she preferred the company of her friends. They must be friends now, Sarah had never been allowed to be on such friendly terms with the previous Goose Maidens.

Tonight she had gone to Bailesparc with Nurse Chrystine Ifans, a castle employee. Something else none of the previous Goose Maidens would have done.

'Did yous enjoy you-self tonight?' asked Clarice, 'at that quiz?'

'I were so busy a-meetin' folks, then a-chattin' to Chrystine for most o' the evenin',' Imogen replied.

'It be better yous be a-meetin' people your own age,' Sarah said, 'and not stuck in with us old maids.'

'It seems like Chrystine don't get on with her landlord or his family, and she'd give her right arm for house-mates like yous.'

'An' less o' t'old maid, thanking yous muchly, Sarah. I could still be a-marry'in' if I put my mind to it, said Clarice.

'I don't reckon I'll be a'mopin' round the Cottage tomorrow.' said Imogen.

Sarah regretted what she had said and was glad Imogen had changed the subject before it headed for a quarrel.

'When Lady Magda be arrivin', I'll a-slopin' off. I reckon to have a mooch about the Castle precincts, make the most of this proper sunny weather we be havin',' replied Imogen, with a smile.

'Will yous be back for yous lunch or should I pack yous a picnic?'

'I reckons not, Sarah,' said Imogen, 'Queen-Consort Stephanie has asked me to have lunch with her when we both got some free time. I'll likely be eating at the Royal Apartments more now that I've got me second job.' Imogen had agreed to work twelve hours a week at the Castle Infirmary.

Now that was more like it, Sarah thought, of course she should be eating up at the Inner Bailey. It would be a shame, as she would be missed at the midday meal, giggling with Clarice. Imogen was such a lovely girl.

The ancient Great Maze, located to the south of the Cottage and west of the Inner Bailey, was created when Queen Kathyren had been planting random areas of conifers to drain the water-logged artificial island. The entrance to the maze was on its southern wall, the exit in the northern wall, with only one route via the central arbour. Queen Lydia's later landscaping of the Outer Bailey had properly solved the drainage problem but she chose to keep the maze, removing all of Queen Kathyren's psychotic traps.

Imogen closed her eyes and remembered when she was thirteen and had mapped the maze with Anita.

'It'll be fun,' Aarne had said.

'You won't be here to do any of the work, Flight-Cadet Uther-Thompson,' she had said, back in the days when she had still been Princess Louise. 'You're four years older than me, and now a full-time member of my mother's armed forces.'

'Yes, Your Royal Highness, Ma'am,' he said with a formal salute, 'but what else are you going to do during your posh school's long summer holiday?'

In what had seemed like years that summer, the two girls had found not just the quickest route through the maze, but also all the secret shortcuts the maze-men who maintained the labyrinth used. Anita and Aarne had found them useful when courting. Now, when Conrad was trapped, Imogen would leave the maze as quickly as possible through one of the hidden exits.

She had about a minute's lead on Conrad. First Imogen ran left, then quickly right, then straight on. There were now fifteen more turns before she exited. To her horror, she had forgotten the next move. Was it straight on or to the left? Get it wrong, and she would be as trapped as Conrad.

'As Minotaurs roar loudly,' said Falada over the psychic link.

'Thank you,' said Imogen, as she remembered the mnemonic – left for odd-numbered letters, right for even-numbered letters and straight on at the spaces. So left it was.

'Brosznik maze,' Conrad said as he went deeper into the labyrinth.

Imogen could hear him mumbling as he walked up the passage that lay parallel to hers, having already made one wrong turn. The maze walls muffled and distorted what he said. She knew that Conrad would take the next right-hand corner, leading him into another section of the labyrinth.

'That be a-cheatin', Conrad,' she said, as she heard the buzz of a micro-drone taking off. Final proof he was a Chessman. Drones had been banned for a century. Now only the Chessmen could use them. Imogen's Mother had ordered the installation of something to discourage the use of drones to navigate the maze. Imogen wondered if it was still there. When the drone cleared the top of the hedge, a ceremonial firework launcher activated its secondary function, as a surface-to-air missile launcher. The drone was blown to bits. Imogen began laughing, out of sight and out of mind, it had survived the luddism of the past century. She quickly traversed the maze, knowing that Conrad was now hopelessly lost.

𝕿wo strictly monitored bridges served Ellisford Castle. The airspace above the five square miles the Castle covered was watched like a hawk. It was also watched by the hawks that danced on the thermals created by the natural cliffs to the north of the Castle and its artificial cliffs, the curtain walls that enveloped the artificial island. These beautiful creatures then swooped down in impossibly steep dives, controlling the populations of scruffy pigeons and wild rabbits within the Castle.

Only a handful of people had ever known about the tunnel beneath the cold, fast-flowing water that lay between the inner and outer walls of Ellisford Castle. The tunnel under the moat had been created aeons ago. Hot fast-flowing lava had drained through more viscous magma close to the surface, leaving a perfectly tubular tunnel when the surrounding magma hardened. It's discovery had earned its discoverer a terminal swim in the moat. The same had happened to the Castle serfs who created the stairs and secret entrances leading to the tunnel on both sides of the moat. Only a handful of people knew it was more than just a rumour that was regularly and ruthlessly quashed.

domed chamber with inner walls covered in seashells had been her favourite hiding place. Behind the golden statue of an n her childhood, when she had still been Princess Louise, the angel was a well-disguised door leading to the tunnel. She

'**J** switched on the torch she had brought with her.

'Oh for goodness' sake, girl, use the lights.' Falada's head materialised in front of her.

'Lights, what lights?' she asked, staring at the effect shining her torch through Falada had on its beam.

'These lights.' The tunnel was now illuminated by long glowing strips in the ceiling. She quickly reached a locked door.

'Your ancestors created this as a bolthole, to get them into or out of Ellisford Castle, depending on the circumstances. Maintaining it became a hobby for those who knew about it. The door is genetically locked. If Conrad gets out of that maze, he won't find you.'

'It looks as if somebody is maintaining it at the moment,' said Imogen as the door at the other end of the tunnel slid quietly open. She entered a room with several lockers, two curtained booths, obviously for changing clothes in and three exit stairs. In the only locker with a key, she and found a selection of clothes neatly hanging inside. There was also a note pinned to its door.

# Dear Princess Louise,

I knew you would get itchy feet and use this tunnel to go and see the world beyond the Castle Precincts without a minder. Our mutual friend, Mr Fladders, has told me you are planning to make your first excursion today. You want to be inconspicuous and merge with the crowds. I'm afraid with the resources you currently have available that will not be possible. When the tunnel splits on the city side of the moat, follow the middle passage and will find a package containing all the resources you require.

## Point One:

I know you have been issued with an ID Card for Dame Imogen Anona Castlevale Royalward. You cannot use that outside the Castle and hope to remain incognito. So I have obtained a valid ID Card and a sneltram network travel card for you for Johanna Wellingford. I understand you have used this alias in the past. Leave your Castle ID here. It to be returned to the Cottage.

## Point Two:

There is a small cache of contemporary currency. I give it to you as a gift. Please use it, as handing over one of your old fifty pfennig notes to a shopkeeper will arouse immediate suspicion.

## Point Three:

An outfit of contemporary clothes, chosen by a contemporary woman is here for you. Turning up in Elizaburg in your old-fashioned Galactic clothing will make you stick out like a sore thumb. Also, I wouldn't recommend wearing anything traditional in a Guild Town either. Wearing a traditional dress will single you out as a Royalist. With the King so unpopular at the moment, that is not a good thing. Not that the Republicans have any chance of achieving their goal, not when you would be far more popular with the people.

## Point Four:

By activating the lights in this tunnel, you have confirmed what Mr Fladders has told me. I will make every effort to meet you at Victoria Park this afternoon. Don't worry if I cannot make it today, there will be many opportunities to meet in the next few weeks.

## Point Five:

While you want to be free of official interference, a local guide for the morning is probably a good idea. Catch a number 52 sneltram. Once I know you are on your way, she will be waiting for you. Leave the sneltram at the Elizaburg City Limit tramhalts. Your guide will make contact with you by asking if you are lost. She will tell you that the tramhalts are two furlongs apart in Elizaburg, when they are the standard three furlongs from each other.

Best of luck,

'Oh,' said Imogen. 'I've been rumbled. Who is this Roswall character?'

'It is a pseudonym used by Crown-Prince David,' said Falada. 'You were right about him. He will be a powerful ally.'

'But he is the Crown Prince. I've started to doubt if he would support us. Blood is thicker than water.'

She had quickly changed into the supplied clothes to make her inconspicuous. The straight-legged jeans were utterly different from the exaggerated bell-bottoms she had brought with her. Any variety of denim jeans was illegal for a young woman beyond the Guild Towns like Elizaburg. With all the walking she intended to do today, she was glad that there were soft sports shoes to replace the clunky platform boots she had been carrying in a bag.

'Well, obviously blood is thicker than water, it has more in it for a start. Oh! Are you being poetic? Yes, he remains outwardly loyal to his father, the King, but he opposes just about everything his family stands for. He has been almost as efficient as the Prime Caretaker in bringing together different opposition groups.'

'And his father lets him?' asked Imogen. 'He stands for no opposition from others?'

'Young Crown-Prince David is clever enough to know how far he can go. He only has to outlive his father, then he will be able to do what he likes. Anseris is an Absolute Monarchy.'

'"Best of luck" he says,' said Imogen. 'I think I'll need it.' She opened her handbag and briefly glanced at her fake ID, with the name Johanna Claire Sinterpfeltz Wellingford. Her fake place of origin, Sinterpfeltz, was a rural backwater in the east of Castlegate, two thousand miles away.

Imogen counted out the seventy króna, three shillings and eight pfennigs. A small fortune back in the day. Pocket money now. Having real money again was pleasant. Royalty did not carry cash so as a child she never used any money. During her nursing career she had been paid for her work and learnt how to manage her finances. Since arriving back on Anseris, she had only used her Castle account, even in Pendragon. She put the purse in the red handbag, ready to face the world.

I mogen emerged from a small warehouse on the western edge of the village of Castle Rock. Across the road a railway station stood on the bank of the Ellis River. She stared across the river, the boundary between the Royal County of Ellisford-Castle and the City and Guilds of Elizaburg.

The tram network in Elizaburg and other major cities had been constructed in the reign of Imogen's great-grandmother. Horse-drawn trams on wooden rails had sedately taken people from one part of the town to another. It survived King Benedict I and his Luddism and had grown in the intervening century. Smart unmanned vehicles called sneltrams, on dedicated metal rails, shared the streets with all sorts of motor vehicles.

At the station of town, the sneltrams automatically decoupled from the express train that had brought it, as its third class carriages, north from the neighbouring town of Hawksmere. Once across the river, having joined the city transit network, the sneltram's pace became more leisurely, stopping at regular city tramhalts. Urban residential and industrial buildings quickly replaced the countryside. When the display on the carriage wall read Elizuaburg City Limits, she continued her journey on foot.

'You look lost,' said the only other person on the street. Her short back and sides haircut would even have been out of place in Pendragon; where it was an exclusively male style. Then there was the colour, a very dark and very artificial blue. Imogen realised this woman had been waiting at the rural railway station at Castle Rock when she had arrived there, followed her from the platform and down this deserted street. 'Well the Tramhalts in Elizaburg are only two furlongs from each other. You got the count right for everywhere else.'

'Are you my guide?' Imogen asked.

'I know you are the person Roswall asked me to look out for', said the woman. 'New in town, are we? Silly question, of course you are. You're wearing the clothes I bought for you.'

'Thanks, their lovey. It's that obvious, is it?' asked Imogen.

'Yes, Johanna, you're not used to trousers. You are walking as if you could still trip over the hem of your kirtle. You even tried kicking away your non-existent skirt as you got out of the sneltram.'

Imogen mentally cursed herself for that mistake. After being out in Pendragon, she thought she was now quite expert at not worrying about hems.

'Also,' continued Shandra, 'I was told to look for someone wearing a Pendragon Bobtail, short but not as short as radicals like me. I keep it this short and dye it blue, to pre-empt the Chessmen's favourite punishment.'

'Oh dear.' Imogen knew that made her sound even more pathetic. 'Any other tell-tale signs I'm from out of town?'

'Finally, you sound like one of those village girls from the mountains who are taught to bury their natural accent. They think that everyone speaks like an aristocrat in the Planetary Capital.'

This woman thought her archaic natural accent was a fake. Something else that had moved on, while she had stayed the same. She decided to switch back to the rustic one, the one she used in the Cottage, but without the rural vernacular.

'That's right. Rushton Mountains, Sinterpfletz, right on the eastern edge of Castlegate,' said Imogen.

'You do sound better with the marble removed from your mouth,' said the woman. 'Our friend Roswall told me to stick with you for the first few hours, to get you up to speed. I'm the instantly recognised Elashandra Margaret Elizaburg Sigurdort, but I've reverted to my maiden name of Rackham. There's no point in using a pseudonym. Everyone calls me Shandra.'

After a few minutes walking in silence, Shandra asked, 'The media coverage of the Ellisford-Castle Princess's return barely mentions her companion. Have you met her?'

'Yes, every morning,' Imogen replied.

'I'm surprised she doesn't want to see how much Anseris has changed.'

'She does, but the authorities won't let her. Such a shame,' said Imogen, knowing she now had another false identity to maintain. 'I took the job in the Castle because I wanted to see the bright lights of Elizaburg. This is my first day off. Up until now the city might as well have been on Marion.'

'Well, I hope I can show you some of the sights. And don't mention Marion. It's not wise.'

The city of Elizaburg now split neatly into two. The Old City sat atop the rock, also called Elizaburg, home to the rich and powerful who kept a close eye on those living on the plains below. The New City spread out from the foot of the Elizaburg down to the north bank of the Greater Ellis River. The poverty of the residents increased the further from the Elizaburg you travelled.

The women were walking through rows and rows of abandoned terraced housing being demolished. The close-knit communities Imogen remembered had vanished completely.

'Elizaburg can't grow any bigger. It's stuck between the river and the mountains. All these houses are empty, the factories have relocated to new Guild Towns on the plain, like Hawksmere and Fullerton. Only the Clockmakers and Jewellers Quarters remain. They have larger terraced houses.'

Sure enough after a few minutes they crossed into what Imogen remembered as the Jeweller's Quarter, where the houses were larger, occupied and well looked after.

'So what is going to happen to the land the other houses were built on?' asked Imogen.

'Once the factory sites are landscaped, expensive housing developments will be built there. With a fraction of the old population, but one with a higher income, which they will spend in the retail and leisure parks they are also build there.'

'Oh, I see,' said Imogen. 'I suppose the King will take his cut in taxes.'

'Nope, this is Guild land, tax levels are fixed in the Guild charters. So he threw a spanner in the works. He legalised Unions.'

'That doesn't sound like the King.'

'Well he hates us as much as the Guilds, but the enemy of an enemy is a friend. On the plus side, I no longer have to worry about 3am visits from the Chessmen, as long as I only work within Guild territory.'

'So you don't have to worry about your hair being cut and dyed blue by them.'

'Oh this,' said Shandra, ruffling her hair. 'I've just got used to it.'

'Don't you think the creation of more Guild Towns is a good thing?' asked Imogen, changing the subject.

'Well, new Guild Towns do increase the number of people free from feudal exploitation. The Guilds didn't advertise that fact. Most people in the new towns thought they had simply exchanged one rich overlord for another. Switching from being exploited agricultural workers, to exploited industrial workers. The Union I work for tells the people the new truth.'

'You must be unpopular with the Guilds then?'

'Oh, they tried to silence me. Despite being born in this town and the daughter of a Master Guildsman, they used my granddad's illegitimacy as an excuse to have me deported to his "Agricultural Region of Origin", as they do to all the young women who come to this town and reject the existing patriarchy.'

'You mean if they don't get married within two years?'

'Yes, Johanna. The Guilds only want subservient housewives coming from the countryside; they don't believe in gender equality. It's so unfair because those women have saved most of their lives to get an archducal release from their local liege lord.'

'So what happened?' Imogen asked, wanting to know the person, not the politics.

'I proved that Granddad had never set foot in the Archduchy of Eastland. His mam lost her job out in the sticks when she refused to marry his dad, or admit who he was. She went to some posh school as a child and was a returned prisoner of war, so she had a lot of friends in high places did old Krizzy. They got her a teaching job here in Elizaburg where Granddad was born.'

'Dear Angels, I was in school with her,' said Imogen. Shandra was the descendant of a friends, she thought had died in the war.

'For the sake of my sanity, I will pretend I didn't hear that, Johanna,' said a laughing Shandra. 'Of course, it means that I also have useful friends in high places. When the Guilds appealed I married my partner Benny Sigardort, six months before he died, in a service officiated by the Prime Caretaker himself. As his widow, they couldn't touch me. Even though I knew he was terminally ill when we tied the not.' Now there was genuine sadness in Shandra's voice. 'At Benny's funeral, I met our mutual friend.'

'Oh!' Another pfennig dropped. Imogen realised who she was talking to. This was the infamous Red Shandra, Crown-Prince David's forbidden love.

Shandra smiled. 'We should never have hit it off. Heated and passionate debates on politics and football led to a passion of another sort.'

They were approaching the base of the Elizaburg, with the Old City and the Gänsehals Circus above.

Imogen had learnt from Shandra that, despite the appearance of modernity, the Guild Towns were as stratified and class-ridden as any rural feudal community. A Guild Town was run by its Council of Guilds. Only Guildsmen who had completed an apprenticeship with a Master Guildsman could elect the Council or hold an office in their Guild. Everyone else was either a Labourer, a Clerk or a Woman. Labourers and clerks had some privileges and rights depending on their job, while women had no rights at all. Shandra was trying to change that.

'Johanna, I have to leave you now. I have repaid the favour I owed Roswall.' They had come to the funicular railway that took pedestrians up or down the escarpment to the Old City above or the New City below.

'It was very nice meeting you, Shandra. I hope we meet up again,' said Imogen.

'This was Roswell's doing. How would we arrange it? If I did ring you at the Castle, my call would be automatically barred, and if you rung me from the Castle, our conversation would be recorded and monitored by the Castle's Chessmen, and you would be arrested as soon as we met.'

'I've a friend who can bypass the Chessmen,' said Imogen, 'I believe you call him Mr. Fladders. He can arrange our face to face meetings,' said Imogen, full of hope at making a new friend as well as useful contact.

'Even so, when we met up, our paths would be shadowed by Chessmen and their informants.'

'So, have you spotted any Chessmen following me today?' asked Imogen. 'And you say they are no longer following you. We'll give them no reason to start again.'

'That's true, Johanna. Your friend must have arranged this with my friend. On the whole, Elizaburg Chessmen are now loyal to him, not the Old Man in the Castle.'

'I'm learning so much today, like being called Johanna, when my real...'

'Should never be mentioned while you are carrying that ID,' said Shandra before Imogen had a chance to speak. 'I suppose it is what our friend calls you?'

'No, a friend of our friend,' Imogen replied.

'I see you're a fast learner, and you still have a lot to learn, I'll be seeing you.'

Imogen hadn't noticed the approaching tram. She had been busy buying her ticket for the funicular railway which would take her up to the Old Town. Shandra popped on board her tram in a blink of an eye and was gone.

**M**illions of years ago, a stream of viscous lava emerged from a vent on the side of what would be the Rushton Mountains,' said the automatic travel guide Imogen had hired at the base of the Elizaburg. The funicular railway ascended the slope of the eastern escarpment, giving Imogen a panoramic view of her journey so far.

No, thought Imogen, the Elizaburg is less than fifty-thousand years old.

'It solidified into a tongue of basalt rock fifty feet high, two and a half miles long and half a mile wide, perfectly flat on top. When Humans arrived on the planet, they called it the Elizaburg, the ideal place for their first settlement.'

No, they called it Gänsehals, the Gooseneck. Imogen looked up through the carriage window at the imposing Elizaburg. She tried to imagine the high-security prison stockade being described by the recording.

'Here, over thirty years, the KHM#89 was evacuated then crashed,' the voice droned on.

'Well, that's wrong again,' said Imogen. 'The full evacuation of KHM#89 only took five years. In the intervening twenty-five years, everyone was far too busy colonising the planet. It was only when the KHM#89's orbit began decaying people started worrying. Its descent had been controlled by the last remaining high technology, which was buried with the remains of the ship. Who wrote this rubbish?'

There were four eras of Anserian History. Angelic, the planet's prehistory. Colonial,which covered the early years. Imperial which covered the madness of Queen Kathyren, and Regal which covered the Boatbuilder's Revolution and the Free Queens. So little was known about Angelic and Colonial History. The knowledge base of Regal History had shrunk drastically during Imogen's exile. Imperial History had remained well documented.

'Shortly, we shall be passing through the ruins of the city wall, which were built during the reign of Elizabeta the Great, the second Free Queen.'

No, Elizabeta was the first Free Queen; everyone knew that. She changed so much for the better, which is why she's called Elizabeta the Great.

'The ruins within the grounds of the funicular railway were the best-preserved section of the Old City walls, constructed when Gänsehals had been resettled and renamed Elizaburg,' said the recording. 'The original town had been destroyed in the revolution.' Imogen's original destiny to become an autocratic Free Queen herself meant she enjoyed Regal History more than any other period. This monologue was almost painful.

'In the centre of town, the first Basilica of the Caretakers of Souls had been built, together with a circular, paved open space Elizabeta the Great called Gänsehals Circus to preserve the city's original name somewhere.'

Give me strength, Imogen thought. She called it Gänsehals Circus because the city was still called Gänsehals.

Banks and the various Trade Guilds built their headquarters around the circus. Beyond that, the city consisted of a network of narrow alleys with wooden-framed buildings, which sprung up within the walls. We will then arrive at our destination,' said the recording. 'Please take care as you alight from the carriage, and make sure you take all your belongings with you.'

Imogen waited as the guide loaded the next section before she emerged from the station, into the concentric avenues.

'Queen Victoria III gave the city its current name, Elizaburg.'

Finally, its got something right.

'She oversaw the reconstruction, after the Great fire razed anything within the city wall. The walls were demolished, and replaced with three concentric avenues of stone town-houses.

Well, no mistakes there, thought Imogen. No, the problem was with the buildings, which did not look lived in.

'The avenues enclosed the Gänsehals Circus. A new Basilica was constructed, identical to the old, on the North of the Circus.'

I knew it was too good to last, thought Imogen. The Basilica survived the fire. It was the only thing that did.

'The block of theatres known as the East End is opposite to the city's commercial hub, the West End at the opposite side. The slums on the edge of the southern escarpment, were replaced by the upper section of Victoria Park, connected to the lower part on the plain below by a path running down the Victoria Chine, a steep and narrow valley cut by the stream that flowed down the southern tip of the Elizaburg.

The mansions of the Avenues were slowly abandoned by the Aristocracy. Government departments have absorbed the avenues, which are now known as the Secretariat.'

So that explains it, Imogen thought to herself. A change that has happened while I was away.

'Gänsehals Circus was reconstructed to look exactly as it had been before the fire, with a wood and plaster façade on stone buildings.'

'Which was very Anserian,' said Imogen. 'We love creating living fossils wherever we can.'

'Queen Gertrude I ordered the construction of a new road which snaked its way up the Western Escarpment, zig-zagging around hairpin bends, hugging the contours of the western escarpment. The main intercity railway passes through a natural tunnel running through the Elizaburg and the platforms of Central Railway Station are in chambers hollowed out around the tunnels, with the ticket hall and entrance at street level.

'We hope you have enjoyed this audio...' Imogen returned it to an identical stall to the one she hired it from.

'This is more as I remember,' Imogen said to herself as she arrived at Gänsehals Circus. True, the number of motor vehicles had increased, as had the noise and the energy of the place. Any new buildings retained the Elizabetian era's jettying half-timbered architecture. All were either shops or restaurants, now the banks and the Guilds had moved into the Victoria-III-era townhouses vacated by the aristocracy. In turn they had moved to newer post-war mansions.

In her childhood, pseudo-medieval clothing had been legally enforced, now it was optional. There was still a minority of people wearing it, who tended to be treated with either caution or plain rudeness by the traders and other townspeople.

Imogen was hungry. She was getting used to this strange new sensation. The rare early summer sunshine was too tempting, so she chose a table outside Café Duisenstein on Gänsehals Circus. It had been famous for being the best new café in Elizaburg when she had been a child. It was still the best, but now it was known for its old-fashioned charm, as nothing had changed within the café over the past century. There was a mixture of people wearing traditional and modern clothes. Then, as now, Duisenstein's remained immaculate hosts regardless of what their clientele wore.

'I like your top,' said a teenage girl, traditionally dressed in her everyday orange woollen kirtle. Normally, she would wear a long white apron, but today she had on a light blue open-sided surcote. The girl's hair escaped in voluminous waves from a tight-fitting coif and flowed freely over her shoulders and down her back.

'Thank you,' Imogen replied. 'Your outfit is...'

'Absolutely horrendous,' said the girl, cutting in. 'My family insist on being so old-fashioned. I'm starting to think this might as well be grey. I'm going to be my mother's domestic drudge until they marry me off to someone tedious.'

'Oh, I see,' said Imogen, sensing a deeply ingrained family quarrel coming to the surface.

'I know I must sound so superficial. I so want to fit into my new town, make new friends. I won't do that dressed like this. Everyone thinks I'm a Royalist like my parents. I don't give a stuff about either side. Politicians have all forgotten what it is like to be young.'

'I'm not really the right person to give advice. What does your local Caretaker say?' It was the only advice Imogen could give, pretty weak at that.

'Is that what you did, miss?' the girl asked. 'Did they tell you to start a new life in a new town?'

'Is it that obvious? You're the second person to say that to me today.'

'Your hair is all wrong. Nobody wears bobtails in Elizaburg, even the visitors from Pendragon. They wear their hair down and loose. Also the tail is to long. If you want to be really daring, cut it shorter than it is now,' said the girl, echoing Shandra.

'Well, that explains it.' Imogen extended her hand. 'I'm Johanna,' she said, remembering to use the alias. 'Johanna Pearl Sinterpfeltz Wellingford.'

'Jadwiga Anna Orlov Smitz.'

'Well, I've just got back from doing disaster relief work out in Pendragon. It's slowly growing back. Normally I'm a nurse who lives and works at the Castle, Jadwiga. I rarely get to wear anything other than traditional outfits, including my uniform.' Half true, now she was covering occasional shifts in the Medical Centre.

'The Castle? Do you see the Royals? My mother would pin you here for hours talking about the royals. But you're dressed Guild style so she won't give you the time of day.'

'I've had a lucky escape then. They are so dreadfully dull.'

The girl began laughing, but it was soon cut short.

'Jadwiga, what are you doing talking to that tart?'

'Asking if that table was free, Mamma.'

'Well, obviously it is. You should have just sat there and not spoken to her.'

The traditionally dressed mother and son joined Jadwiga at the table to Imogen's left. The table to her right was occupied by a group of students, male and female, all of them wearing Guild-Town fashions and arguing about music.

Duisenstein's cooking had not changed. It was still marvellous. She even had entertainment as she ate. The mother's commentary about the rudeness of shop staff and the evils of Guild-style clothing was enlightening. Inevitably this led to the free flowing style of Jadwiga's hair.

'You know your hair should be plaited, and should be covered by a veil in public.'

'Do you know what is really annoying me?' the girl said to her mother – that had been the final straw. 'Janek is going to the Jeweller's Guild School, with an apprenticeship afterwards, even though he wants to join the Navy. We are buying him the modern clothes he will have to wear there and in the workshop with Dad. He doesn't care what he wears, I do, and I will have to continue wearing home-made monstrosities like this.'

'Jadwiga Anna Orlov Smitz, your father would never let you out dressed like a tart. Orlov girls are not tarts,' continued the mother.

'It's not dressing like a tart, you stupid woman!' said one of the female students, who must also have lost her temper with the mother's tirade.

'What has it got to do with you?' asked Mrs Smitz.

'Absolutely everything. I am a deaconess preparing for my ordination. Normally I have no choice in what I wear. Like the other female deaconesses, I dress in vestments. On my days off I chose to wear Guild style. Would you call me a tart?

'When you're ordained? I find that highly...' Mrs Smitz was silenced by the other woman showing her ID, but not for long. 'No wonder the Church is going to the dogs if they let women like that become Deacons then Caretakers. No decent parish will ever elect her.'

'When I'm ordained I join the Clerical Support Group, I will wear the habit of whichever religious order I am assigned to as a priestess.' The younger woman sighed and returned to the crowd defeated.

Bad luck, dear, thought Imogen. You just can't talk to some people.

'Anyway,' continued the mother to her daughter. 'I couldn't possibly spare you at home. Once your compulsory education is over, you're going to be too busy preparing to get married, like a good Orlov girl.'

'I'm not an Orlov girl any more, I'm an Elizaburg woman now. There is no way I would get married at fourteen.'

'How many times do we have to go through this? Janek is a boy,' said the mother. 'He will have to support a family one day. You're a girl, Jadwiga. We will find a good husband to support you and you'll be married as soon as the silly City Laws allow. Eighteen indeed. I married on my fourteenth birthday. Didn't do me any harm.'

'We will discuss it until you stop being so old-fashioned,' said the girl angrily. 'I'm cleverer than Janek, and I want to be a lawyer. Look, that woman has a career. She's a nurse at the Castle...'

'I'm not old-fashioned, I'm a realist,' her mother said, cutting off the girl. 'There will never be women lawyers on Anseris, so you can forget that pipe dream. Nursing, yes, you could do that, but there are training fees which we can't afford.'

'You can afford Janek's school fees,' said Jadwiga.

'Didn't you hear me, Jadwiga? You're just a girl. It would be a waste of money. You'll need that money to fatten your dowry and pay for your wedding.

'Yes, I'm a girl, but I won't get prematurely married, so I don't need a dowry. I will need a college fund. Anseris is moving on, why can't I benefit from that?'

'Stop talking politics. Do you want a visit from the Chessmen?'

'At least then I would have my hair cut. It would be blue, but it would be short.'

'Don't even joke about that, girl. It's not funny.'

'I don't know why we came to Elizaburg if we are going to act like we are still in the sticks?'

'This is where your father found work. A Guildsman wants his son to follow him. Janek stood a much better chance of getting into the Jeweller's Guild School if his father worked here. I wish my mother were still alive, then you'd have stayed in Orlov and finished school at ten. Baba Nadiya would have had you betrothed at twelve, as she did with me. We would be preparing for your wedding now. The extra four years compulsory education in this town has filled your head with some dangerous ideas. Now shush, that tart you were talking to is staring at us.'

'You're suggesting something morally repugnant,' Imogen said. She had tried hard not to intervene but Mrs Smitz had gone too far. 'No-one should be married at fourteen.'

'I'm not staying here a minute longer. Nothing but insults from tarts and radicals,' said Mrs Smitz, 'we're leaving.'

'But I'm not finished,' said Janek, who had been diplomatically silent until now.

'I don't care, boy! Move!'

'Johanna, dear, why don't you come over here and join us?' said a familiar voice.

Crown-Prince David's people coming to her rescue. It was no accident that such a large group had descended on the café.

'Carlo, I didn't want to barge in with your friends,' was Imogen's impromptu reply. He was not a student, even if his friends were. She hoped it sounded convincing.

'The gang doesn't mind,' he said to Imogen. 'Do you?' he asked his friends.

Of course not, thought Imogen, they are all in on this. No, of the dozen or so, only three were vocal in their agreement; the rest were just being carried along.

C arlo Valoretti escorted her across Gänsehals Circus to the Caretaker's Basilica. The octagonal Gothic structure dominated the northern edge of the circus. Atop its domed roof stood a huge clock at the feet of an angel statue.

So how many of them were actual students?' she asked asked.

'All of them. Some from the University, some from the Academy and two trainees from the Caretaker Seminary,' he replied.

'Were they all chosen by him?'

'No, by me, but he did pick up the tab. In the Basilica you will meet the Prime Caretaker. I have to leave you now. Have a wander around Victoria Park for a couple of hours on your way back to the Castle.'

This was more of an order than a suggestion.

# 29

uring his three terms in office, the current Prime Caretaker Winston Thompson-Uther, had seen his hair grow pure white and migrate to the bottom of his face. He had spent so many years watching the increasing stupidity of the current feudal government, but thank the Angels its replacement was walking towards him. He had so many questions. Why was Duchess Anita acting like an ignorant fool? Why was Princess Louise putting up with being treated like a servant? Why was that clergyman blocking the Princess's path?

'Let her through, Brother Jenkins,' the Prime Caretaker said with a voice that made you listen. 'I am expecting this young lady.'

'Your Holiness,' said Brother Jenkins. 'I did not see you.'

'Obviously. You were too busy being officious,' said the Prime Caretaker, putting the cleric in his place.

Imogen curtseyed and said, 'I was told that you wanted to see me.'

'Indeed I do, Princess Louise,' replied the old man. 'Indeed I do.' He bowed deeply in return. 'I hope not all my underlings were so rude.'

'No, your Holiness, they were very polite and informative.'

'I believe today is your first unescorted visit to Elizaburg, Princess Louise,' said the Prime Caretaker. 'Have you enjoyed it?'

'I have found out so much about the state of Anseris today.' A worried look crossed Imogen's face. 'Is it safe for you to call me that?' she asked.

'If it's not safe here in this Basilica, then nowhere is safe,' said the elderly cleric. 'The Chessmen still try to bug this place. A bit pathetic really. We Caretakers know this Basilica intimately, and can spot any change instantly.'

He watched the face light up as it smiled. No wonder his family said so many beautiful things about her. Who would stand against her? Why had the ruling Rushton-Brownes not fallen under her spell as they were supposed to?

'I see you are wearing the avatar my ancestor gave you,' he said absent-mindedly as they entered his office.

'Yes, it glows for me and me only.'

'Then you are the one. Despite your modern clothes, you are from a world long ago. You are Princess Louise Imogen Ellisford-Castle of Anseris.'

'Most people in town think I'm a plebeian from a backwards rural area. They have no idea of the truth,' Imogen said, a note of sadness tinging her voice.

'Indeed, Ma'am. But please enlighten me, why is Duchess Anita calling herself the Princess? Why have you accepted a lowly role?'

'S he smiled as she carefully recounted her story. Had Falada lifted the block on her memory. The old man listened carefully as she explained what had happened deep in hyperspace. Then she frowned as she felt that part of her memories turn to jelly again in the presence of another human.

'The scriptures say the Angels are mere messengers of the Unknowable God and have their imperfections. This is proof the scriptures are correct.' The old cleric laughed. 'Sadly people only want to worship the infallible, which is why those verses are usually ignored.'

'I am concerned for the sanity of my friend when she is released.' Imogen was more interested in doing the right thing than the minutiae of Theology.

'We Caretakers store the record of the experimental use of another Fenzrian learning machine, the one the Luddite King had destroyed. There will be some confusion but no madness.'

'Falada is working on it, but having little success. The ghost of Queen Kathyren is blocking his every move.'

'Falada. Is that what the Valentine Device calls itself?'

'Yes, Your Holiness.'

'Then it is the same Falada who assisted the Boatbuilder to overthrow the Immortal Empress. Then and his daughter establish this Church.'

'Falada told me this,' said Imogen. 'He had an argument with the Boatbuilder about the daughter of Kathyren Ellisford-Castle.'

'Yes, Falada wanted to kill the girl, permanently denying Queen Kathyren a host should she ever return. If he had succeeded, you would not be here today, as she is your ancestress.'

'Now Queen Kathyren has returned, I am in danger.'

'Fear not, Your Majesty. Churches might be empty on Sundays in our increasingly secular world, but the vast majority of people do not want the return of Queen Kathyren and would join with the clergy to prevent it. Those who secretly worship Queen Kathyren think they have infiltrated all levels of society. Now their so-called goddess has returned, they believe their victory will be easy. They are poor, deluded fools.' The old man kissed his avatar then took a large key from a hook on the wall. 'Come, Princess Louise. I want to show you something.'

She followed him down a set of stairs into a private vault beneath the Basilica.

'This has been the resting place of Aarne Thompson-Uther for one hundred years,' he intoned.

'Poor Aarne. But your cousin Jane says his body was never found,' said Imogen. She felt a shock of bereavement which had been missing when she talked to the current Archduchess Thompson-Uther.

The Prime Caretaker had switched on a light, illuminating a sarcophagus. Lying on the top was a stone effigy of Aarne, carved to the highest detail, with a casket lying at his feet.

'It is not his tomb. It is his life support system.'

'He's not dead?' she asked with a gasp.

'No, my child, just sleeping.' He opened the lid of the casket at Arnold's feet. A holographic image appeared.

'I know you must all think I am mad, but I cannot live without my darling Anita,' said the recorded voice of Imogen's friend. 'As long as she is trapped in hyperspace, I will lie suspended by this alien life support system. The family's Secret Keeper will guard me. Only my true love's kiss will wake me. Until then, history shall remember me as being lost in space, like my beloved.'

'There's a genetic trigger mechanism built into the device,' said the Prime Caretaker. 'When she kisses him, it will recognise her and deactivate the temporal suspension field.'

'So, we need to rescue Anita, so the two of them can be together.'

'Oh, foolish boy!' There was a shimmering light, as a horse-head appeared in the vault.

'Falada?' the Prime Caretaker asked.

'I answer to that name, Your Holiness,' the horse-head replied, his light casting odd shadows in the gloom of the crypt.

'Are you any closer to releasing Duchess Anita from Kathyren Ellisford-Castle's pernicious influence?'

'No, Your Holiness. However, the current geopolitical situation indicates things are moving quickly. King Benedict's grasp on power is becoming weaker by the minute. She might contemplate a grab for power.'

'As I explained to the Princess, those opposed to Queen Kathyren greatly outnumber her supporters. Any move she makes will fail. I was gathering together all those opposed to the King, to plan what to do after his fall. To my surprise, so was Crown-Prince David.'

'Yes, Your Holiness, when the time is right you must both bring them all together as a potential government in waiting.'

'Very well, it shall be done.'

High above, the Great Clock chimed the hour. 'Go, my child, you have one more appointment today, do you not?'

'I was told to visit Victoria Park on my way home. I suspected it was to meet someone there. I think I know who.'

'My servants will escort you discretely to the door of the Basilica,' the Prime Caretaker said. 'Go now, and may the Angels be with you.'

**I**mogen found little had changed in Victoria Park since
her childhood, it was beautiful as ever. Pedalling had been
no hardship on a bicycle far more comfortable than any she
remembered.

'Excuse me, miss,' said a park attendant in orange and
brown municipal livery and a bicycle attendant's badge. 'We
close our stall at sunset. Cycling in the park is forbidden after dark.'

Imogen looked at her watch. It was 6.30pm and the early summer
sky was darkening, as the Ansersol hovered above the horizon.

'Thank you. I'll return the bike straight away,' she replied politely.
Then started peddaling furiously.

'You look flustered, Miss,' said the man at the stall a few minutes
later. The same man she had hired the bike from.

'Yes, I wanted to return this before you closed.'

'But, miss, we close when the park does. Look, the lamps and
fairy lights are coming on. People love riding through the
illuminations.'

'Your colleague told me that riding after dark was forbidden,'
Imogen told the man, who looked equally as puzzled.

'It's only me on duty today, miss.'

'He had the same badge as you.'

'I think someone 'as been pulling your leg. If it was Boris,
I'll shoot 'im. Do you want to continue riding? You 'ave the bike
until we close.'

'No, thank you,' said Imogen. 'It's probably time I was heading
home anyway.'

T here were plenty of early evening customers in the chip shop next to the tramhalt and the food being served looked good.

Lunchtime now seemed so long ago, she felt in need of something to eat.

It had been a century since she had last bought takeaway food, when she had lived in the Nurses' Hostel a few city blocks from here. Then she had also been pretending to be a middle class Anserian called Johanna Wellingford.

Two caretakers, one male dressed like a monk in a white and lilac cassock, with his hood pulled up obscuring his face, and one female dressed like a white and lilac nun joined the queue behind her.

'Evening, Johanna, getting something to eat from Elsie on your way home as well?' said a familiar male voice. 'We're heading back to the Seminary.'

'Aristotle, I would never have recognised you,' said a shocked Imogen to one of the students she had met at lunchtime.

'You didn't recognise me at the Basilica, after I had changed out of my civvies. You must have thought I was just another cleric,' said an equally familiar female voice.

'Bella?' Imogen asked the woman she had last seen wearing jeans and a jumper. The shapeless cassock hid her obvious curves and the wimple and veil buried her individuality.

'It should be Deaconess Isabella, but Bella is fine with...'

P apers,' said a middle-aged Crown Policeman loudly. The shop then filled with a communal groan, and conversations were cut short as everyone scrambled for their ID cards.

'Can't, they haven't been made of paper for years. All plastic now,' said a disreputable-looking fellow at the end of the queue. Two equally dodgy characters in front of Imogen headed out the other door without being served.

'Very droll, Krov,' said a younger policeman. 'Don't worry, your mates won't get very far.'

'Whatever 'appened to courtesy from the police? Shouldn't that be Mr Krov?'

'We only treat law-abiding subjects of the King with respect. Low-life crims like you don't deserve any, Krov.'

'Charming. Just because the Guilds 'ates me and I can't get an 'onest day's graft, I gets insulted by the bizzies.' The dropped aitches and the use of "me" instead of "I" marked this man as an urban plebeian.

'You wouldn't know an honest day's work if it hit you, Krov.'

'Hurry up, Jacob, we've a sneltram to catch,' Aristotle said to the younger policeman.

'Sorry, Deacon Aristotle,' he replied.

'If you people would prefer to do this in the station, I can arrange it,' said the other, less obliging policeman.

'Wilhelm, me punters would rather not be harassed by overzealous coppers kicking off a night shift,' said the large lady behind the counter, as she emptied a bucket of chipped potatoes into boiling hot animal fat.

'Can't get much past a copper's widow, can we, Elsie?' asked the younger policeman.

'Is Wilhelm being bolshy because he's trying his Sergeant's Exams again, Jacob?' asked Elsie.

'Yes, I am,' said the older policeman, 'and it's Constable von Pultzfeldt to you!'

'Still a constable. I remember you when you were a raw recruit on his first patrol with my Vic, you cheeky monkey!'

'Your attitude does nothing to bolster respect for law and order.' Then turning to his partner. 'Do you have to encourage her, Constable Le Fossaque?'

Imogen thought the pair of Crown Constables looked odd in their old-fashioned uniform, complete with breastplates and shiny helmets, in a shop full of people in Guild-style clothes.

'Can I help you, deary?' asked Elsie, from behind the counter.

'A sausage supper, please,' Imogen replied. Did people still call battered sausage and chips that?

'King or Queen?' the woman Elsie asked experimentally.

'Queen please, starry eyed,' said Imogen. King had always been the larger portion, even on a planet traditionally ruled by a Queen.

'With a sea and sand?' asked Elsie.

'No, just the sand. I don't like the smell of vinegar.'

'Fair enough, dear,' said Elsie, shovelling chips into a bag.

'And a bag of Oh-neg,' said Imogen.

'Angels,' said Elsie laughing. 'I haven't heard that one in a long time. You must be a nurse.'

'Have you both gone mad?' asked Constable Pultzfeldt.

'No, Wilhelm, the young lady has just asked for a small battered sausage, with a small bag of chips, unwrapped, with salt and some tomato ketchup.'

'Well, why didn't she just say so?' said the policeman.

'Considering you are such a traditionalist, I'm surprised you don't know the old slang. But you're so hoity-toity, I wouldn't expect you to.'

'To be honest, I shouldn't know any of the old slang either,' said Imogen, 'but I come from a very old-fashioned family.'

'You must do, dear. Don't think I caught your name?' asked Elsie.

'Oh, its Johanna,' replied Imogen, remembering the alias. 'How badly am I damaged?'

'That'll be seven króna, nineteen shillings, Johanna.'

'Nothing old-fashioned about a young woman being out on her own so late.'

'I'm on my way home, Officer. I'm just stopping off for a bite to eat,' she said. It was not 8pm yet, hardly late. She said nothing, as she did not want to draw any more attention to herself. New clothes, new ID and newly minted money – no wonder the policeman was suspicious.

'You make sure you go straight home. Single women should not be allowed out on their own at night, especially not dressed like that.'

Imogen handed a crisp ten króna note to the woman, and received her change. Things were so much more expensive these days. Back then prices were marked out in shillings and pfennigs. The Króna, which consisted of twenty shillings, was beyond the reach of ordinary people. Now people didn't blink an eye at using large amounts of krónas, now regarding pfennigs with contempt.

'So, lets see your papers then. Miss.' demanded Constable von Pultzfeldt.

'Here you are, Officer,' she said as she handed over the ID card she had been given that morning. He hardly looked at it.

'You can't agree with that sort of thing, Elsie,' said Constable von Pultzfeldt. 'Girls going about in skimpy outfits like that? Not with you dressing properly.' Imogen could see, unlike her customers, Elsie was wearing traditional dress under her overalls.

'Skimpy outfit?' asked Elsie. 'She's covered from the collar of her tunic to the hems of her jeans.'

'Yes, the girl has got all her curves and legs exposed!'

'Go smoke your nose, Wilhelm,' said Elsie in open dissent now.

'Angels,' said Constable Le Fossaque, who took Imogen's ID card from his colleague and returned it to her without scanning it. 'No wonder you never passed your Sergeant's Exams with an attitude like that. And her legs aren't exposed, they're covered in denim.'

'What she's wearing leaves nothing to the imagination. Guild style is based on the old Galactic style,' said von Pultzfeldt. 'Nothing that comes from beyond the stars is good for Anseris; did we learn nothing from the Fenzrian War?'

'Hark unto Benedict I,' replied Elsie.

'Tis true,' continued the constable, but nobody was paying him any attention.

'There you go, dear,' said Elsie, sliding an open parcel of food across the counter to Imogen.

Constable von Pultzfeldt turned back to Imogen. 'You go straight home.'

'Not to worry, Officer,' said Aristotle. 'We'll keep an eye on her.'

'Thank you, Deacon Aristotle,' Constable Le Fossaque said. Then as he headed through the door, 'Come on, Wilhelm, we've villains to catch. Igor Krov is dull enough to lead us straight to his friends.'


'An' where d'yous reckon yous bin, Missy?' asked Sarah, sounding more like her mother than her housekeeper. 'I've been a-frettin' somethin' awful.'

'Up at the Royal Apartments, that's all,' said Imogen, who knew the other woman didn't believe her.

'No, you ain't, young lady. When yous mate Chrystine give back yous ID card, I asked her if you left it up in the Inner Bailey.

She said you ain't been seen in the Inner Bailey or Bailseparc all day. That lovely Captain Valoretti asked her to give it back. Then when you didn't come home by sunset, proper worried was I.'

She hugged the woman and whispered into her ear. 'There be a ways in and out of the Castle that be forgotten for a hundred years. I've been to Elizaburg.'

'Why didn't you tell I?' Sarah whispered back.

'I be sorry. Not a-thinkin', was I.' Then more loudly, in a cut-glass accent, 'I'm sorry to have frightened you, Sarah. I won't do it again.'

From inside the Cottage, came the sound of five bugs going bang and Clarice screaming took the edge off the situation.

'That will be Falada sweeping for listening devices,' said Imogen.

'The building is now secure,' said Falada as it materialised in the porch with Imogen and Sarah. It was now Sarah's turn to scream.

'An evil spirit. Begone foul demon,' said Sarah.

'Madam, I am neither evil spirit nor demon,' replied Falada. 'Princess Louise, please introduce me to your friends.'

'We be haunted. T'is your fault, Imogen, a-messin' around in that haunted gatehouse,' said a terrified Clarice.

'Clarice, Sarah, don't fret, it's only an ancient computer.' Imogen was trying to be reassuring. She didn't think she was being very successful. 'Falada, why have you chosen to reveal yourself?'

'It will save time. You need allies; these ladies can help you.'

'We can?' asked Clarice, who was a little less afraid now.

'Yes, dear lady, you can. Princess Louise here will soon take back what is rightfully hers.'

'Princess Louise? Her name be Imogen. How be she Princess Louise,' asked Sarah.

Falada briefly explained. To Imogen's horror, both women were kneeling. Thanks Falada, she thought, I'm back to square one with them again. No, make that minus one.

'Please get up,' Imogen said to the two ladies, 'nothing has changed.'

'Of course things have changed, Your Royal Highness,' said Sarah. 'We must show dude reference to royalty.'

'You should show due,' Imogen took a breath, 'deference to the job when I am doing that job.' Such revolutionary ideas cut no ice with the two servants.

'You'll be Queen, the Head of State for the entire Anserian system,' said Clarice, who was still on her knees.

'Being the Head of State is still just a job. One I'm not currently doing,' Imogen repeated.

'T'is said that the King, Queen and their families are special. Which is why royalty is venerated.'

'As my mother Queen Gertrude III once said, if you share a packed bomb shelter with your subjects, you can't continue to pretend you are special.' Sarah and Clarice had stood up. 'I've shared a house with you for nearly three months now; have I ever appeared more than just another person?'

'Um,' said Sarah. "When you puts it like that, no, not really. You be a proper nice, down-to-earth person. One I'd be proper chuffed to call mate as well as boss."

'Well, yous be my mates,' said Imogen. 'Also, there be sensible reasons for yous a-treatin' me like you always have done.'

'I reckon so,' said Clarice. 'You'd have a proper job  keepin' who yous really be a secret if us be a-bowin' and a-scrapin' to you all the while.'

'Exactly.'

'Right then,' said Sarah, with an inquisitive glint in her eye. 'If this 'ere place is as safe as that pony lad says, what's yous a-been up to in town today, then?

'Lord Vernon, what do you have to report?' asked the creature once known as Kathyren Ellisford-Castle from the mouth of her current host, Anita.

'Your Majesty, my agent has begun administering the poison to the Pink Lady,' said the head of Castle Security.

'One hopes he is only applying the poison to Pink Lady. One would not want anything to happen to the Joker, just yet.'

'As far as I can tell, he indulge in espresso coffee. She drinks coffee with hot milk and sugar, easier to poison.'

'Nevertheless, I dislike slow toxins,' said the Princess. 'As they say, no pain no gain, and the Pink Lady dying peacefully in her sleep obviously has no pain for her, so no gain for me.'

'We all know the Joker, who dotes on Pink Lady would fly into a fit of rage if anything obviously untoward were to happen to her.'

'True, Lord Vernon. And what of Strawberry Moon?'

'The idiot stationed at the Cottage still thinks she is a harmless halfwit. He's the halfwit – all the bugging devices he planted in her home have been neutralised. To cap it all, while keeping Strawberry Moon under surveillance, he followed her into the old maze and managed to get himself stuck in there yesterday. She has obviously worked out he was one of my men and led him into a trap.'

'How very amusing,' said the Princess with a rare smile. Even though it had been neutered by B417, people were still getting caught in her old maze. 'Has he been punished?'

'Yes, he has been suspended, which leaves me with a problem.'

'Whoever you replace him with is going to be suspect,' said the Princess.

'Indeed, Ma'am.' The usually colourless Lord Vernon had gone bright red. 'Strawberry Moon is, however, proving to be far from a halfwit,' continued Lord Vernon. 'She was spotted at various points around Elizaburg. This includes leaving the Basilica. She met the Prime Caretaker there. I have no idea how she managed it.'

'She did what?' asked the Princess. 'She must have remembered who she really is.'

# 31

'May I come in, Dame Imogen?' asked Chrystine Hans, standing at the kitchen door of the Cottage on an overcast summer morning. Her orange and yellow hooded cloak, covering her nurse's uniform, made up for the lack of sun.

'O' course yous can, me luv, but leave the etiquette 'pon the doorstep.' replied Imogen, who looked far from aristocratic in the same simple outfit, voluminous apron and cap, as Sarah and Clarice, she certainly didn't sound it 'We be a-doin' a bit o' spring cleanin.'

'Beth sy'n bod, cariad?'* Imogen asked. She knew something was wrong. Her friend's usual perfect white skin had been reddened by crying, and she was desperately trying not to cry again.

'What makes yew think there's anythin' the matter, eh?' asked Chrystine defensively. The Royal Hospital polish had vanished, replaced by Gwenerian vernacular.

'Well, them tears you'm a-fightin' back be a giveaway, Miss,' said a concerned Clarice. This triggered a new stream of tears from Chrystine.

'I.. I thought I'd.. I'd hidden me background proper tidy. It was easy for me to fib 'bout me town-name, seein' as they ain't used back 'ome. Growin' up near Randau, I was quite the convincing sort, I was. Had to lie 'cause me landlord was one o' them Gwenerians who can't stand my folk. He found out the truth, he did. He said he didn't want no filthy witches livin' in his Angel-lovin' house, damn 'im. All me stuff was just in a pile on the pavement, mind. Denzil an' Del are keepin' an eye on it for me, they are.'

'Your people, Chrystine? I don't understand.'

---

*Bayth seen bored, verr-ung-arree-add? : What's the matter, my love?

'I'm not really from Randau, I'm from Cacharau. I'm not a lickle bit Fenzrian, I'm lots Fenzrian. One hundred percent in fact.'

All towns and villages on Anseris stopped being prison camps centuries ago. Not Cacharau, the change happened just ninety-five years earlier. Before that, it had been the prisoner-of-war camp for Fenzrians, who win or lose would never be accepted back by the Great Machine. There they had been deprogrammed and learnt how to live as people, not components.

'Yous best be a-goin' to see Baronet Almond-Hedge. He be the Prefect o' Gwener,' said Imogen. 'He'll sort it out, he will. Ol' Queen Gertrude said them Fenzrian POWs was took in durin' the war, y'know. She said they were Anserian now, she did. There weren't to be no payback for the War. Everybody did obey that order, right enough.' Then a memory awoke and her eyes filled with tears. 'She did go an' made Anita their patron, she did.'

'E's the one stirrin' up hatred o' my people, even though the war ended a century ago, innit? He asked Doctor Matthews why 'e was employin' a witch, like? The doctor nearly did a right dodgy medical procedure, 'e 'ates anti-Fenzrian bigots, 'e does. But, Tracy 'eard it all and told 'er old man, she did.'

'I see. Something else for I to be addin' to m' to-do list,' said Imogen in a low mutter. Then turning to her friend she said, 'Yous more than welcome to be a-movin' in here. There be plenty of room.'

'Is't wise, Imogen?' asked Sarah. 'What with Conrad gone, how do you know she bain't be his replacement?'

The handyman disappeared two weeks earlier. Imogen had been told it was a of a budget cut. She suspected that it was a result of his frightening ineptitude in allowing his cover to be blown.

'Unlikely,' said Falada, who materialised over the kitchen table. 'I am currently running background checks on our visitor, and she has no personnel record at the Secret Police headquarters on Gwener, in Elizaburg, or anywhere else.'

'Wow! The Valentine Device. You're supposed to be a myth,' said Chrystine. Her suprise at seeing the horsehead was greater than her surprise at hearing Imogen speak in such a broad rural accent. 'My people always wondered why you didn't send us into exile with the other Fenzrians after you summoned the Angels.'

'I would have left your people on Anseris. When the Aggelii arrived they also chose to ignored your people, because they were indistinguishable from the Anserians.'

'Although I shouldn't be surprised to see you, considering the number of pre-war antiques from beyond the stars that look Anserian in this room,' said Chrystine, the polish returning as as calm returned.

'You mean like this,' said Imogen switching on a lamp with a gesture. This did shock Chrystine, whose mouth had dropped open.

'Do you realise 'ow much trouble you'd be in for doin' that anywhere else, 'specially on Gwener?'

'She does not,' replied Falada.

'I do. I be merely a-showin' we don't have a primitive fear of witchcraft in this household, Falada, dear.'

'Doesn't mean I likes it. T'is still unnatural,' said Clarice.

'You speak fer youself, I'd love ter do that, I would,' said Sarah. 'To hell with bein' called a witch, I'd say!'

'Well, Princess Louise, shall we fully brief your new house-mate?'

'No, Falada. Let her move in first,' Imogen replied. 'And please don't call me that. I am no longer that person. I would prefer plain Johanna.'

'I'm going to wake from this dream, aren't I?' Chrystine removed her cloak and sat at the table.

'You bain't got yous head down yet,' said Clarice, 'but by the looks o' you, you'll soon be a-droppin'. Come along with I upstairs. Us always keeps the attic room bed aired and made up.'

'T'is a proper wicked thing to be a-doin' to someone a-lookin' for their bed, after a hard day's graft' said Sarah.

Chrystine smiled. 'More or less.'

'Denzil and Del will bring all your things from your horrid old home. Then Falada will fill in all the finer details.'


Ⅎmogen could hear Anita singing her favourite song. Somehow friend had broken free from the malignant control of Kathyren Ellisford-Castle. Imogen ran out to the landing.

It was not Anita. Instead she saw Chrystine singing Suo Gân, the ancient Welsh song of a mother's love for her child. Anita had learnt it with Chrystine's ancestors.

'Imogen, dear, whatever is the matter?' It was now Chrystine's turn to ask as Imogen began crying.

'I thu... thor... thought you wuh... were, someone else,' Imogen said, stammering through her sobs.

'Oh, I'm sorry, Imogen. It was thoughtless of me, especially after hearing your story.'

'No, it's not your fault,' Imogen said as she tried to pull herself together.

'Yes it is. Entirely my fault. Is this the first time you have had a cry? You need to let it all out.'

'But I can't, I have to stay strong.'

'There's no good staying strong if that burns you up inside. You need to grieve for the things that have passed, let loose that survivor's guilt.'

'Chrystine, that's not very royal though, is it? My Mamma would not approve.'

'No, but it's very human. I suspect your Aunty Marion would approve, and Anita.'

That was it, the tears returned. When she could cry no more, exhausted by the emotions, she fell into a deep sleep where for the first time in her life she dreamed. When she awoke the following morning, she could not remember what she had dreamt about, all she knew was she felt refreshed and more determined than ever to rescue Anita from the serpent metaphorically wrapped around her.

'**Johanna, my dear, you simply must come with the Court** Ganontsburg,' said Queen-Consort Stephanie, who was amongst the growing circle of friends who no longer called her Imogen. 'You can't spend the whole of Augusta here in the sweltering heat.'

The Queen-Consort had decanted to her rose garden by the Boating Lake. The bushes had burst into bloom. Imogen could hear the sound of water in the Castle's small reservoir, lapping against the shore.

The Rushton Mountains to the north of Ellisford Castle usually protected it and Elizaburg from the climatic excess of the Great Ellifas Steppes to the south; except for Augusta when the prevailing wind changed, allowing arid winds to blow from the plains. This made life in the Castle and nearby town unbearable. The whole Court decamped to Ganontsburg Palace in the cooler hills.

'I would love to join you, Steffi, but I'm not an aristocrat. I have my job to do,' replied Imogen. 'I used most of my annual leave on that trip to Pendragon.'

'Oh nonsense, Johanna dear, you're the single most aristocratic person I've ever met. All the aristocratic bearing with none of the arrogance. The plebeians will call you a Toff, not a Ristoze. Soon Dadda will give you some land and an aristocratic title to go with your aristocratic name.

Despite having lost contact with ancient European cultures, names on Anseris had a very European feel. Aristocratic names are English names. The Gentry had faux French flavour, while the masses had adopted names as German as currywurst.

'So moving back to the point,' Stefania said. 'You're making the mistake of thinking caring for those birds is a real job, not a hobby to fill one day after another. You can take as much time away from the birds as you want to.'

'Oh!' said Imogen, at a loss for words.

'Your absence from Court has been noted.'

'Yes, but I'm not a teenage girl looking for an eligible bachelor,' replied Imogen. 'I don't need to attend every ball or Court event.'

'True and false, Johanna dear. You aren't actively looking for a husband, you've found Captain Valoretti, but you have to attend some functions. You haven't attended any in the past six months. You spend your free time in Bailseparc. I've read the reports – when you're with the lower orders you mimic the plebeians so well, fitting right in.'

'Thankin' yous, yous royal majestics, but a lowly pleb be I.' said Imogen in a thick rural accent, hoping humour would divert the Queen-Consort's match-making. 'Got me geese to see to for his royal majestics the King, has I.'

'You see what I mean? Anyway, back to Augusta in the hills. The geese need to get away from the heat as well. There's a suitable farmhouse with a paddock in the grounds of Ganontsburg Palace. I used it for the summers when I was Goose Maiden.'

'OK then. I wasn't looking forward to the heat.'

'Oh, excellent, my dear,' said Stefanie. 'You'll be there for the White Garden Party and ball that marks the arrival of the Court. Dig out your finest white dress and your longest most pointy hennin for the garden party.'

'Why, am I getting married?' asked a bemused Imogen.

'No. It's now tradition to wear wedding dresses at this party.'

'But why, those hats are such awful items? Why does a bride have to look so silly on what is supposed to be her big day?'

'Not a fan of the conical hat then, Johanna?'

'No, Steffi, they expose and emphasise the ears. This is never a good thing.'

'You will inevitably marry the handsome Captain Valoretti. Why not do it on that day?' said the Queen-Consort.'

'Steffi!' replied Imogen. 'He's out in space with the Crown Prince.'

'David is being posted back to the Home-world at the end of Julia.' Queen Stephanie giggled again. 'He will find a way to be at all the parties, which means Carlo will be there as well.'

'Please, Steffi, Carlo and I are just friends,' said Imogen. She had fallen in love with Carlo Valoretti months ago, but she was certain he did not love her. 'He makes me laugh, but there's no love in the relationship.'

'Friends, my eye. Johanna, he's as potty about you as you are about him.'

'If'n yous a-says-so, Yous Majestic,' said Imogen, curtseying as her mind began racing. No, she had too much still to do; she would have to put thinking about Carlo to one side.

'Yes, I do. And your friend Chrystine will be accompanying Doctor Matthews this year. A Castle nurse always assists the Royal Physician.'

'So, it looks as if I'm going to be out of town this August.'

'Excellent. So what party dresses do you have?'

'I arrived with a suitcase of unwearable Galactic clothes and two Anserian outfits. Another reason for me not attending any balls. I was given enough money to stock my tiny closet with functional clothes purchased from the Castle's stores.'

'I see now why your dresses are so drab and so badly fitted. Tomorrow afternoon you and Nurse Ifans will attend on me at the Royal Apartments. As Ladies of the Court you will need the volume and quality of apparel nesccessary for the trip. The seamstresses of the Royal Wardrobe will produce that volume and quality.'

'Steffi, you know Chrysy is going there to work?' asked Imogen.

'That is not what the Castle nurses say. They regard it as a working holiday, with the emphasis on holiday. That is why they take it in turns. You know, Johanna. This year it will be a much grander holiday.'

'I don't want to sound condescending, because technically I'm also castle nurse and we don't ususaly attend any Court Functions.'

'You know how dreadfully dull the Ladies of the Court are,' said Stefanie. 'You have introduced me to somebody interesting, who will be at Gantonsburg, killing time in the palace infirmary. Now I shall have two interesting people to talk to.'

'Now back to you, I'm sure your mother's surviving gowns

would fit you with the minimum of alteration,' declared the Queen-Consort. 'Nobody else is using her clothes.

'But...' said Imogen, stammering.

'I guessed you are the real princess as soon as I saw you, Johanna,' Stefania said. 'You're six foot one tall. There are a handful of women in Fiandre that tall, nobody else.

'But...'

'David confirmed I was right yesterday. He's got some old photographs of you. He suspects something happened to you and the so called Princess, who must be your companion on that spaceship.'

'Angels protect me.' Imogen now as white as a wedding dress.

'Don't worry, David has persuaded Dadda you will never remember who you really are, despite the fact you obviously have. I know exactly what sort of man my father is. He will be happy to keep you alive as long as he thinks you are not a threat to his position.'

'He is welcome to the hassles of being the Monarch,' said Imogen, lying very convincingly. Again, she had no way of knowing if King Benedict had arranged this meeting. Even if he had not sent his daughter sniffing, Imogen was well aware that Stefania would tell him everything she heard today. Also, he would believe what his daughter said over an army of spies.

'You really don't want to be Queen?' asked a shocked Stefania.

'Not for all the cotton on Cairo. I saw what it did to my Mother. I have had a lucky escape.'

F alada could appear anywhere in the Cottage grounds now it was no longer bugged or spied upon by Conrad. But Imogen preferred visiting her "friend" in the Old Gatehouse. Today, she was going to have a flaming row with the old AI in private. Falada's actions were unreasonable. How could he be her closest ally when he kept a block in her memory? Now he had started popping up in her head while she slept. All her life she had wanted to dream. But the tedious lectures Falada insisted on placing in her subconscious mind were a terrible substitute.

'Well, you glorified chess piece, why was that info-dump so important you had to interrupt my beauty sleep?'asked Imogen. 'Well, I'm waiting.'

'There is no need to be rude,' said the horse-head.

'Why not? You so rudely walk into and out of my mind.'

'You need to know who you can trust and who will betray you,' replied Falada, calmly and reasonably. 'Given the totalitarian state you find yourself living in, I could hardly let you print out a list to memorise, one that might be discovered by the regime's spy in the Cottage.'

'What spy? Conrad is long gone!'

There was a flash, and Imogen found herself standing in the meadow used whenever Falada implanted one of his dreamlike lectures.

'Any other passing spy. You never can be too careful,' replied Falada.

'You see? You're messing with my head again,' she retorted.

'Likewise, the gatehouse is not as secure as it once was. Spending so much time here without falling victim to any supernatural fiend weakens its reputation. I chose to bring you into the data-sphere so we could talk uninterrupted.'

'You could have asked me first!' shouted Imogen.

'To what purpose?' asked the AI.

'To show who is the boss.'

'My dear Princess, I was created by humans to serve humans.'

'Yes, my dear Falada, and you then defected to the Aggelii.'

'My word, Duchess Anita, you're back, occupying Princess Johanna's body. When did that happen?'

'Falada, don't do irony, it doesn't suit you,' said Imogen.

'Well, you did call me a chess piece and bring up my association with the Aggelii. Anyway, there is a meeting I want you to take part in when you are in town next week.'

'There you go again, ordering me about,' said Imogen.

'Do you want my help or don't you?' asked the AI.

'Help yes, leadership no!' said Imogen.

'I'm sorry you feel that way. I am only doing my best.' For

an emotionless AI, Falada sounded quite hurt.

'Well, I'm sorry, I am going to be out of town for all of Augusta. Queen-Consort Stefania has persuaded me to relocate my flock to Ganontsburg for the next month. A break from this heat will be good for them.'

'I cannot let you do that, not when things are at such a critical stage back here.'

'Oh you can't, can't you?' In the virtual world, she picked two flowers from the meadow, and found herself back in the Old Gatehouse holding a pair of orange glass spheres. 'How exactly are you going to stop me?'

'Please put them back, I may need to talk to you via the psychic link,' said Falada. 'Especially if you move to Ganontsburg during Augusta.'

'When you've learnt who's the boss, I may do. Until then, my friend, it will be difficult to pop into my head all the time.'

t was well past midnight, but King Benedict could not sleep. Insomnia had done nothing to improve his temper.

However, he was enjoying this quiet, late-night walk with no distractions. No-one else should be walking the corridors of the Palace at this hour. Not even the servants,. who also needed to sleep.

The rumour that their goddess had returned had galvanised the lunatic Cult worshipping Kathyren Ellisford-Castle. If, Angels forbid it was true, they would give the old witch the muscle she needed to take back the control she lost to the Boatbuilder.

He entered the large hall. His oldest memory was looking up from the front row of the audience as he watched his hated step-mother marry his father, less than a year after the death of a mother he had never known. He sat himself down on his throne, to focus on his memories.

'Oh Deliah, what a failure I have been,' he said to his late wife as if she were still sitting on the smaller throne next to him. He felt tears roll down his face. Her absence bit deeply on nights like this. 'You never approved of my methods. Now all the repression you hated and the misery I caused will come to naught.' He had loved his radical northern wife, despite their different political beliefs and missed her dreadfully. Deliah's death had been natural, due to her poor health. Although rumours of murder persisted.

He heard the approach of footsteps, light and female. Nobody should see him like this. A king did not cry. He made his way to the concealed entrance behind the fake stove. He used to hide there as a child. This space was smaller than he remembered, but it made him completely invisible.

He recognised the voice of his fellow insomniac. It was the real princess, brainwashed into thinking she was the servant of Princess Pushy. What was she doing here? Ah yes, Stefania had befriended the girl. Invited her to all the significant events of the next three weeks.

When Imogen had arrived, she had been assigned one of the many guestrooms.It was as luxurious as any room she had slept in during her youth, but now too extravagant for her increasingly egalitarian taste.

Alone, her head was full to bursting with ideas, plans, facts and figures. She wanted to hear the opinions of others, but Falada had placed a block on her memories when she was in company. It stopped her talking to potential allies, but she could lecture any inanimate object, late at night, when no-one could overhear her.

Just to be on the safe side, she activated an old Lambourian scanner. She had bought it from a bric-à-brac shop in Elizaburg, where it was mistaken for a filigree bangle. An easy mistake to make, the craftsmen on Lambour loved creating things of beauty. The scan showed the throne had a security device to record anyone who dared sit on it, but there were no active surveillance devices in the room.

'Thanks to Falada, Mr Throne who is rightfully mine and Mr Old Stove, you are my audience.' She eased herself down into one of the other seats in the room. 'Are you paying attention?' Was it her imagination, or had the lights on the throne flickered at that question? Yes, it must be her imagination.

'In summary, my best friend Anita is currently possessed by the life force of evil Queen Kathyren, who tried to brainwash me into thinking I was her servant. As far as I can tell, the longer she hijacks Anita, the stronger she becomes. I have to defeat the Immortal Empress to rescue my friend. However, none of that matters because one hundred years have passed while we were asleep in hyperspace.

'Once I get my friend back, I then have to turn my attention to you, Mr Throne, as you are currently occupied by the great-grandson of that pompous buffoon, Archduke Benedict Rushton-

Browne of Castlegate. Although, he is an old man; I wonder what she has planned for the current King? She is much more of a threat to him than I ever could be.

'And another thing. I have fallen in love with Carlo Valoretti. Perhaps I could persuade him to run away with me, start a new life on one of the moons or a space habitat?' Imogen began laughing hollowly, then laughing turned to crying. 'No, eventually, Queen Kathyren will come looking for me and the clone-daughter I am cursed to produce. She needs that child if she is to return fully.'

There was the sound of laughter coming from inside the back wall. As if by magic, the King appeared. Imogen's heart sank like a stone. Of all the people to hear her late-night musings, why did it have to be King Benedict III? Her continued survival had been dependent on him not seeing her as a threat.

'I cannot help you with your love life, but I can confirm Queen Kathyren has nothing good planned for me or my son,' said the King.

'You heard it all, Your Majesty?' asked Imogen.

'Yes, Your Majesty, I did,' replied the King. 'I already know who you are. That face and that voice – deep down I am programmed to obey them without question. I was quite happy to let your deception continue when I thought you wanted to remain as you were, with no desire to take my throne.'

'However, you are still not going to try to stop me?'

'Your Majesty, I cannot stop you. In normal circumstances, if you had told me to abdicate, I would do it. I was born to serve the Immortal Empress, body and soul. You have her body, as did all the Free Queens. Why else did my ancestors serve them without question? Sadly, your cousin is a puppet for the soul of the Immortal Empress. The soul trumps the body every time. I must obey the Princess above all others.'

'So I am doomed. Tomorrow morning you will tell the Princess about me, and she will order you to kill me,' said Imogen, pale and nervous.

'No, that body still has some power over me. You must order me not to betray you, and I will not. You are lucky she remains convinced you have permanently lost your memory, otherwise you would already be dead.'

Imogen walked over to the King and placed her hand on his shoulder. 'I order you never to tell the Princess I have recovered my memories.'

'Thank you, Your Majesty,' said the King. 'I obey.'

'So, how are her plans to overthrow you progressing?' asked Imogen.

'The Cult of the Eternal Queen has infiltrated the mechanics of government. She has been quietly setting up the transfer of power from my supporters to hers, and I am unable to stop it. She has not ordered me to act against you. She must think you are still under her spell. It comes as a great relief that you have freed yourself from the Immortal Empress' powers. It means others can. Things are not as hopeless as I believed just a few minutes ago.'

'She controls a handful of deluded fanatics,' said Imogen. 'Just one of the groups opposed to you. Any attempt to place herself on the throne will fail.'

'How do you propose to win back your throne, Queen Louise?'

'As if I would tell you,' she said tartly. 'The Princess would see you were hiding something major from her. Despite my order, she would find a way to force the truth out of you.'

'True, I shouldn't have asked. She won't bother asking about our insomnia-driven random meeting.'

'I am surprised you are unhappy, Your Majesty,' said Imogen. 'Surely an old stick in the mud like you should be glad Queen Kathyren is back?'

'That woman is and was a menace. Even an old stick in the mud like me can see that,' the King said. 'She was as much a prisoner as the convicts aboard the ship she captained. The Draconic League was evil, but they had their limits. Not even they would tolerate the likes of Kathyren Ellisford-Castle. So she was exiled with a bucket-load of criminals and ne'er-do-wells.'

'I've never seen you like this, Your Majesty,' said Imogen.

'I am dying. My liver was slowly failing.' The King sat heavily on his throne. It looked as if he had finally found the elusive spirit of sleep. 'Now I have been poisoned by a slow-acting toxin aimed at Steffi. I spotted the assassin dosing her coffee. I can only assume she has offended the Immortal Empress in some way. The poison will kill me quicker and with less pain than I deserve.'

'But when you die, Queen Stefania will still be in danger. The Immortal Empress will find a new pair of hands to carry out the task.'

'Damn it, girl, that is why you have to win.' Some of the King's normal bluff and bluster returned, then his face blanched again, and he once more looked like a tired old man. 'I was negligent. That sweet child suffered at the hands of the men I thought were protecting her. She must be saved. You are the only one who can save her.'

'Selfish to the end,' said Imogen. 'There is way more at stake than the life of one woman, no matter how pleasant she might be.'

'You think I don't know that? A dying man no longer cares about the big picture. My daughter must live. I leave that task to you.'

The King raised himself from his throne, so Imogen bowed. 'Get up, Your Majesty. I can't bow, but we are of equal rank. I was crowned a king, you were born a queen. If you will excuse me, I must return to my bed.'

She watched him leave the room. He really did love his daughter if he was willing to die for her. What would Falada make of that?

# 34

The White Garden Party had been great fun. The women wore anachronistic white wedding dresses, a Victorian invention. In mediaeval times white was the colour of mourning, not black. This fact lost to the Anserians.

The party had its own heirarchy, ignoring the normal strict social structure. Married women and widows wearing their own wedding dresses were in the first tier and sat on the top table at lunch. Women wearing their mother's dress were in the second tier. A dress belonging to any other female relative placed its wearer in the third tier. Dresses borrowed from a friend or dress shops joined divorcees in bottom tier.

Obviously Imogen could not admit to wearing her Mother's excessively bejeweled wedding dress to claim her place in the second tier. However, as Queen-Consort had let her borrow a Queen's Bridal Gown she still found herself in the second teir. next to Queen-Consort Stephanie. Chrysy had found her mother's bridal gown, which she always remembered as died blue, restored not just to glacial white, but to its former glory, waiting for her, with all her expensive new clothes on arrival at Ganontsburg.

The Princess found herself sitting in the bottom tier, which did nothing to improve her sour mood.

Sadly, the vile Baronet Almond-Hedge had spotted Chrystine and started making comments about her Fenzrian background. Becoming increasingly vitriolic, he eventually overstepped the mark. With Chrystine close to tears, half a dozen noblemen had sprung to her defence, putting the Baronet firmly in his place. After that, Chrystine became the star of the show, as her wit and knowledge shone through.

Only Chrystine's expensive new clothes had come with her to Gantonsberg. Her social status remained at home. Chrystine had been worrying how she would fit them all into her usual quarters in the staff accommodation and had been pleasantly surprised to find herself in an aristocratic guest rooms next to Imogen, and treated as an aristocrat for the duration.

Imogen would spend the hours between the garden party and the evening banquet exploring the parkland around the palace. Chrystine would be in the Palace Infirmary, being a spare wheel. Maids helped Imogen change into something more relaxed for an afternoon. Chrysy told them to come back in the evening, to assist her change into something richer. She met Imogen in the corridor, in a Ganontsburg nurse's uniform. It was brand new, modern and far more practical than the ones they both wore in Ellisford Castle.

'This place is so massively fake, isn't it?' said Chrystine as the two women met in the corridor separating their rooms. The interior décor of the Palace was unique. Panels and three different types of wallpaper made up an intricate geometric pattern.

'It replaced Arlesdorf Castle as the seat of the Archduchy of Castlegate about a hundred years ago,' said Imogen, quoting from her guidebook. 'That's ten miles further up the Greater Ganonts Valley and is much closer to Ganontville, but that's a Guild Town now. This place is up a small tributary valley.'

The two women had stopped in an embrasure containing an ornate Gothic stone window, to admire the formal knot gardens either side of the road up to the Palace's impressive front entrance.

'See that artistically ruined castle on the crag up there?' said the unmistakable voice of Carlo Valoretti.

'Yes,' said Chrystine.

'That, dear ladies, is the birthplace of King Benedict I, founder of the current Royal Family. He hated Arlesdorf and Ganontsburg Castles equally. So when he became King, he began the building of this place.'

'Carlo, how nice to see you,' said Imogen, trying to hide her racing heart. He was still wearing the fifteenth-century outfit from the garden party, one only the young and good-looking would dare to. Although he was given a run for his money by his friend, who had been one of Chrystine's rescuers that morning.

'The Palace is regarded as the jewel at the heart of the Anton District of Castlegate,' said the other man.

'I can see why the first King built this place,' said Chrystine. 'It's not as draughty as one of the old castles.'

'The early generations of Anserian aristocrats, under the ever watching eyes of Queen Kathyren, built cold, draughty castles to protect themselves from the rest of the population,' said the man. 'Eventually, they became places where they could pretend to be superior to the illiterate rural workers descended from the convict colonists their ancestors had brought to the planet.'

'The late King couldn't resist the temptation to have his home vaguely castle-like,' said Carlo, seamlessly continuing the lecture. 'The crenelated ramparts overhang the walls by mere inches, lacking defensive machicolation, and the arrow-slits were blind. More fairy tale than a fortress.'

'I know you,' said Chrystine to the other man. 'You're Doctor O'Brien, from the Royal in Elizaburg.'

'Also known as Earl Thomas Gerald O'Brien-Butler of Carlton,' said Imogen, 'heir to the most progressive archduchies in the East. For years before the war, the Court would adjourn to your family's seat at Tintagel Castle to escape the summer heat.'

'That's right, Lady Imogen,' he said, but Imogen could see he was staring at her friend. 'I thought I recognised you, Lady Chrystine,' the doctor replied. 'You trained at the Royal.'

'Yes, Doctor... um, Your Grace, then I got a job at the Castle.'

'I might be the Earl of Carlton but I rarely use my title or particularly value it. Mainly because aristocrats rarely enter the medical or nursing professions.' Then turning exclusively to Chrystine. 'Please, call me Thom, all my friends do. I can see you are heading to the Infirmary for a shift. May I accompany you, Lady Chrystine.'

'Thank you, Thom. I'm not really a lady,' said Chryssy. 'As soon as we return to the Ellisford Castle I will be Chryssy Ifan again. I have token half-shift, they've given me the rest of the month off, because I really am surplus to requirements. Then I change for tonight's Welcoming Banquet.'

'I'm off to have a chat with Vince Matthews. It's funny, we work a stone's throw apart, but only speak when we are nearly seventeen hundred miles from home.' Thom and Chryssy were soon engrossed in a conversation about the Royal. Imogen doubted much filing would be done that afternoon.

'Well, I'm off to see that my dear geese arrive safely, then for a stroll around the gardens. What about you, Carlo?'

'Taking notes at the upcoming Military Council meeting. Dewi's not looking forward to it. The changes he's recommending to the military face stiff opposition from the Council.'

'Can't he just ask his dad to push them through?' Imogen asked.

'Not really. Uncle Ben is the stiff opposition.'

'Of course. You're cousins,' said Imogen, feigning ignorance of something she shouldn't know.'

'On my father's side, which on Anseris is the one that matters. I am the Crown Prince's fifth cousin twice removed. I am three hundred and eighty-sixth in line for the throne. However, my mother is Dewi's aunt, the late Queen's sister. Which makes us first cousins on the ignored female line. Just before I was born, Mother and Aunt Deliah had a massive falling out. Mother still refuses to say what triggered it. They patched it up when Mother and Father divorced.'

'Is that when you became Crown-Prince David's best mate? Going through the Military Academy at the same time, then becoming the Crown Prince's equerry?' she asked.

'More or less, dear Johanna.'

'A bit like me and Anita,' said Imogen. That was strange; why hadn't the accursed memory block stopped her saying that?

'Is Falada's mojo wearing a bit thin, now you've broken the psychic link?'

'How in the Angel's name did you know about that?'

'Falada told me about it,' said Carlo. 'He revealed himself a few weeks ago. Dewi is still in the dark over who, our contact, is.'

'So you're spying on me for him?'

'No!' said Carlo.

'I don't believe you,' she said and stormed out of the Palace.

The paths of the Great Park were well signposted, so there was no danger of her getting lost. Imogen visited the cottage, where after the week of none stop parties, she and Chryssy would be spending the rest of the month. Clarice and Sarah, who had arrived the previous day, were delighted to interrupt their preparations for her taking up residence with a tea break. Then Imogen decided to walk up to the old castle, now a ruin, which she would paint while here. The most straightforward route to and from the old castle was via a mountain stream. In the distance was a spur of the Rushton Mountains on the other side of the Greater Ganonts Valley. It framed the white wooden bridge taking the path across the brook. The path like the stream zigzagged wildly, so at first sight the path stretched to the middle of the bridge. Of course, it really took a steep turn to the left. The corner had hidden him, sitting in the doorway of a hut, waiting for her.

'Falada has sent you looking for me, has he?' she asked. Most of the anger had cooled.

'No, Johanna my love, I came under my own steam,' replied Carlo Valoretti.

'I'm sorry about earlier,' she said.

'Yes, Falada is a bit of a bore. I can imagine being in constant contact with him would be trying.'

They both laughed, then kissed each other, for the first time.

'I used to come here all the time when I was a child. I was born in the Ganontville Guilds Hospital,' said Carlo when they released each other.

'But Valoretti is a Northern Continent name, and you look like a northerner – tall, dark and romantic.'

'My mother comes from the Archduchy of Innistrom, on the Northern Continent, a town called Annaport. People say I look more like her than my father. It's from her the Valoretti comes from. My full name is...'

'I know your full name. I can see why you call yourself Carlo Valoretti.' She giggled, then asked, 'So why did you come out here?'

'I want to ask you something. This seems like the perfect spot.'

This sounded ominous, Imogen thought. Carlo went down on a single-bended knee.

'Princess Louise Imogen Ellisford-Castle of Anseris, I know who you really are, but that does not stop me, Viscount Karl Gustav di Valoretti Rushton-Browne, Deputy Governor of the Anton District in this Royal Archduchy of Castlegate, from formally asking for your hand in marriage.'

'Carlo, I love you so much, but it's too soon. There is so much I have to do before I can even consider marriage.' She was in tears.

'You are right, my love, I have been premature. I must wait for the war to be won.'

'No, don't let us part on a sour note,' said Imogen. The pair kissed passionately, before walking arm in arm back to the Palace.

King Benedict summoned the Court Officials to the Great Hall of the Palace, on the tenth day at Ganontsburg. Imogen had been expecting this, and had not been surprised to be ushered to the first row of seats. But she was surprised to see Chrystine escorted to the seat next to her.

'Let it be known,' said the King, in full regalia, 'that in the name of the Unknowable God and in the Grace of Angels, it pleases us, as Knight Commander of All Orders of Chivalry, to appoint as a Dame First Class of the Ladies Angelic Order of Chivalry, Miss Imogen Louise Castlevale Royalward.' This was Imogen's cue to walk towards the throne and kneel before the King, who placed a purple cross-shaped medal on her chest. 'Thus creating her Dame of Glanders, with all the properties, rights and responsibilities that accompany the title.' This was Imogen's cue to return to her seat, now officially a middle-grade aristocrat. At which point the musicians should have started playing light music, and the Court Officials would adjourn to a nearby room for a glass of wine to celebrate before returning to work.

'I call upon those present,' the Queen-Consort said in a clear voice, 'to witness the induction of Miss Chrystine Rebecca Cacharau Ifan into the Honourable Company of Guardians.' It was Chrystine's turn to stand and walk towards the thrones, where she curtseyed before returning to her seat. Now the musicians began playing.

'What did all that mean?' asked Chrystine, before a celebratory dinner at the Palace that evening.

'I think it means you are now one of the gentry, Lady Chrystine. The highest rank of gentry as well,' replied Imogen.

'Well actually, Lady Chrystine agreed to become my Personal Nurse, amongst her other duties. Doing so will permanently silence the vile Baronet Almond-Hedges,' said Queen-Consort Stephanie. 'Personal Nurse is the same social rank as a Lady in Waiting.'

'Yes. But today you made Johanna an aristocrat; why was I tagged onto the end?'

'Because, Lady Chrystine,' said Queen-Consort Stephanie, 'only an aristocrat can be a Lady in Waiting. So I made you an aristocrat too.'

'Thank you, Your Majesty,' Chrystine said as her legs gave way. Fortunately Thom O'Brien was there to catch her.

'Her Majesty is an incorrigible matchmaker. In the past, a male aristocrat would ask the Queen to make his non-aristocratic love a Lady in Waiting so that they could marry,' said Thom, usually before the pregnancy was noticable. Which, I might add is not the case today.'

'I was just saving such a cute couple the trouble of asking,' said the young Queen-Consort, coyly.


Kathyren Ellisford-Castle watched through stolen eyes. The nurse would have to marry that Earl. There was no way she would be able to afford the expense of being at Court on a nurse's salary. Maybe the pink blob was not as stupid as she pretended. What a pity she would never see the results of her matchmaking, as she would soon be dead.

Queen Kathyren wondered if she would have to deal with the nurse as well. She had fallen into Imogen's orbit, right into the place this host used to occupy. Would this trigger unwanted memories in Imogen? Queen Kathyren dismissed the notion. Despite shedding the dogsbody personality, Imogen had so gratefully accepted the little bauble, without realising she owned the whole Christmas tree. Imogen would never remember her true identity.

T he Court returned to Ellisford Castle and Imogen wanted to make some changes at the Cottage, as the Summer cooled to the autumnal season of Embers.

'Ladies, I've an announcement to make,' Imogen said, having gathered the other women together. 'I have been home for a week. Returning to this well-appointed bedroom, next to four empty bedrooms, while you, Lady Chrystine, have an attic room, and Sarah and Clarice share a single room above the kitchen.'

'I know I came back from Ganontsburg with more luggage than I left with,' said Lady Chrystine, not just referring to her clothes, 'but my room is fine.'

'That it is not,' said Imogen. 'T'is a guest room and yous bain't be a guest no more. So from today three of these rooms a-goin' to be lived in. Chryssy, yous have the room next to me. Sarah and Clarice, yous have a room each 'cross the landing.'

'But them be proper posh bedrooms, not for the likes of I,' said Sarah.

'I don't know why yous is a-bellyachin' for. Yous is a-gettin' a larger room to yous-self.' Imogen made a wide hand gesture in the room. 'Surely 't'is better than a-sharin' that tiny attic room above the kitchen with Clarice.'

'Goose Maiden's servants used to live in these rooms,' said Lady Chrystine on the landing.

'And they were never proper servants neither,' said Sarah, 'ordinary girls pretending to be maids, while they were turned into ristoze young ladies.'

'Well I ain't-a-goin' to miss your snoring,' said Clarice.

'Me snorin', lovely, that's a right laugh. Yous could rouse the wretched dead with yous a-snorin'. If I manage to get a decent night's kip in my new room, I reckon I'll just have to suffer that mattress an' them pillows,' said Sarah, dissolving into laughter, admitting defeat.

'Your Majesty, there is a strong possibility that Strawberry Moon will be taking one of her day trips tomorrow.' Lord Vernon was making his weekly reports to the Princess, now the Court had returned to Ellisford Castle.

'What! You still haven't stopped her doing that?' she asked, feigning surprise.

'No, Your Majesty. She has gone over the wall several times since her return from Ganontsburg. We are gathering data with each trip, in the hope to locate her way in and out. It's likely that she is using the same route that Roswall uses for his unauthorised visits to his lady friend. This has narrowed it down to one area of the Castle Precincts.'

'Why is this important?' asked the Princess.

'It's a breach of Castle security. I should know about it, and have it shut down,' he said, sure that his ordinarily pasty white complexion had reddened a little. This was acutely embarrassing for him.

'Their last sightings when leaving the Castle and the first on their return are all in this area.' Lord Vernon pointed at a shaded part on the map.

'Ah, the old Royal Rescue,' said the Princess. 'I remember it now. I thought we ordered its destruction centuries ago.' The Princess pointed to the Grotto. 'That's where the entrance to the tunnel used to be. Send some men to check it out.'

'Yes, Your Majesty.'

After a few minutes, Lord Vernon received a report. 'It appears the tunnel is still intact and regularly maintained.'

'So, Lord Vernon, tomorrow let Strawberry Moon leave the Castle. When she returns, arrest her in the tunnel.'

'Yes, Your Majesty.'

The first serious snow of the Embers was threatening. The ladies in the Cottage had started wearing thermal undergarments from the Jovian Baronies on the moons of Alaska. These garments were a major violation of the Castle's dress code, and had to be laundered outside its precincts. The launderette Imogen used in Elizaburg was the perfect place for anonymous meetings with her allies. Today however, to Imogen's delight, she only had to worry about her service wash, then shopping in town.

'Johanna, have you heard? The King be proper ill,' said Clarice, as Imogen was leaving. 'I heard says that Queen-Consort Stefania be took poorly and bide in the Castle Infirmary as well.'

Imogen had expected Sarah, the older servant, to be the one more resistant to calling her Johanna and a new level of familitary with royalty, not Clarice. It just went to show you could not judge people by appearances.

'No, I hadn't. The King and Queen seemed perfectly fit at dinner last night,' Imogen said.

'Summat they had didn't sit right with them,' said Clarice.

'Be you a-feelin' all right, dear?' asked a concerned Sarah. 'Yous wouldn't want to have food poisoning today of all days.'

'You're right, I would have fun explaining myself if rushed to a hospital was I.'

'Did you have the coffee soufflé last night, Johanna?' asked Chryssy, who had just returned home after a night shift. 'Doctor Matthews thinks that is the source of infection.'

'Only the King 'n' Queen-Consort had puddin'. I be feelin' proper grand.'

'I've just seen Carlo and Crown-Prince David out riding on my way home,' said Chrystine.

'He had the cheeseboard and port last night. Carlo wasn't there.

You'll be fine.' This did not, however, stop Chryssy quickly taking Imogen's temperature and measuring her pulse. 'All seems normal. If only Their Majesties are ill today, it's unlikely you'll be affected.'

'Fair enough, dear,' said Sarah.

'You'll be late home tonight then?' asked Clarice with a wink.

'I'm sure I don't know what you mean,' said Imogen, displaying mock surprise.

'You know I don't approve of that sort of thing,' said Sarah. 'I hope he brings you back to Castle Rock; that last sneltram is not safe. Look what happened to them girls. Both still in comas.'

'I can look after myself,' said Imogen. 'I had the advantage of being trained in the martial arts when I was younger, and I won't be restricted by a floor sweeping skirt.'

'Well, that's another two things I don't approve of,' said Sarah. 'Women are banned from that sort of thing these days and trousers are unladylike.'

'I'd better go, or I'll miss my sneltram, and Chrystine looks dead on her feet,' said Imogen as she headed for the door, glad that the topic of her and Carlo had been dropped.

I mogen was at a stall selling clothing in the twice-weekly outdoor market in Elizaburg. She was scanning through a rail of traditional fur-lined hoods. The stall was one of the few that sold traditional and Guild styles. More people were buying Guild style – nobody wanted to be labelled as a Royalist. Oh Angels, that dreadful Smitz woman had just come in.

'I hope you're satisfied with yourself, you tart,' said Mrs Smitz with vitriol.

'Mrs Smitz. Anna Nadiya, isn't it?' Imogen never forgot a name and a face, she only feigned forgetfulness as people seemed to like a little bit of uncertainty.

'You know who I am, so you must be responsible,' the woman retorted.

'Responsible for what? We only met that one time. You refused to speak to me.'

'Oh don't act the innocent. I know you encouraged my Jadwiga to run away.'

'I'm sorry, Mrs Smitz, I had no idea your daughter had run away. I have had no contact with her since that afternoon at Duisenstein's.' Imogen could tell the woman was becoming hysterical. She did sympathise. Having a runaway child must be dreadful, but lashing out at the nearest target was not going to help.

'Officers, Officers, come here immediately. I have found the woman who has kidnapped my daughter!' She had spotted the plumed helmets of a pair of Crown Policemen crossing the market.

Oh Angels, thought Imogen, why doesn't that stupid woman leave me alone?

'Are you sure about that?' said the familiar voice of Jacob de Fossaque. 'It is a grave allegation.' Then turning to Imogen, 'Good afternoon... Oh hello, Miss.'

'Good afternoon, Constable... sorry, Sergeant de Fossaque,' said Imogen saw newly sewn rank stripes on his sleeves. 'I didn't know you were doing the Sergeant's Exams, Joe. I thought it was just Wilhelm.'

'It's a sore one, Miss. I passed on me first go; he failed again, didn't he?' Sergeant de Fossaque answered. 'Me Deirdre was proper adamant. She said she's not marrying some lowly PC. I'm crackin' on with me Inspector's exam now, like.' He had recently become engaged to the daughter of Elsie, the chip shop's owner.

'Oh, I see,' said Imogen, trying hard to keep a straight face.

'Excuse me, Officers, you are supposed to be arresting this kidnapping tart, not chatting her up.' Mrs Smitz was horrified at how informal the situation had become and lost her patience.

'I'm sorry, Miss,' said Sergeant de Fossaque, 'I'm going to have to see your papers.' She handed her ID card over to the policeman, who nearly dropped the scanner when he read its display. 'I'm sorry, Your Ladyship. Is that woman causing a nuisance?'

Imogen realised that she had brought the wrong card with her. Not her fake ID, which allowed her to move inconspicuously as Johanna Wellingford, but her brand new Castle ID with a new double-barrelled name which clearly identified her as an aristocrat

Constable von Pultzfeldt, who had been checking Mrs Smitz's ID and was waiting for the slow police computer to find her details, looked at his partner as if he had gone mad.

'Wilhelm, take a look at this,' said Sergeant de Fossaque.

'Yes, Sarge,' said Constable von Pultzfeldt, whose disinterest quickly evaporated. 'That's the King's Seal.'

'I can see that, soft lad. Read the rest.'

'I never knew she was a Ristoze, ya know,' said Sergeant de Fossaque.

'Neither did I. Hard-up gentry like you maybe, but not a Ristoze.' His scanner pinged. After reading the display he turned back to Mrs Smitz. 'Right then, madam, it says here you are Mrs Anna Nadiya Orlov Smitz. Your daughter was reported missing ten days ago. Nine days ago you were informed your daughter Jadwiga is safe and well under the protection of the Caretakers. You know her Ladyship has nothing to do with her leaving home. I suggest you leave Dame Imogen alone and do not harry her in the future.'

'What, you are taking that tart's side?'

'No, Mrs Smitz, we are protecting an aristocrat from your slanderous accusations. Now go home before we take you back to the watch-house and have you sedated. I can't see your husband being happy if he has to finish work early to come to collect you.'

'Just you wait until my Axl does hear about this,' said the woman in desperation.

'Just be grateful men aren't allowed to whip their wives no more,' said Constable von Pultzfeldt. 'It's a good job Dame Imogen here is a Toff. She would've had you put in the stocks in the old days.'

Imogen was sure the constable had a note of regret in his voice as if the passing of those barbaric rights was something to be mourned. Imogen suspected normally the constable and the housewife would get on like someone else's house on fire.

'Look, Mrs Smitz, I'm sorry to hear about your problems. I hope Jadwiga decides to come home soon,' said Imogen, but the woman was already leaving.

'So, Your Ladyship, is there anything else we can help you with?' asked Sergeant de Fossaque.

'You can stop calling me Your Ladyship for starters. You know my preferred name is Johanna.' She smiled an appealing smile. 'If you must be formal, "Miss" will do.'

'Very well, Miss.'

'Good evening, Officers.' She had become aware of the crowd of onlookers, so had the policemen. She should have been arrested for previously travelling under false papers, but the power of the King's Seal cancelled that felony.

'All right, people, unless you are buying something here, disperse yourselves,' said the Constable in a loud, clear voice.

# 36

The sneltram home was a several tramhalts away from her destination. Six passengers including Imogen remained. A man with his coat and hat covering his face slept at the other end of the carriage. Four rough-looking lads were sitting in the seats directly behind her. She wished Carlo was here. He normally delivered her safely to the tunnel, then took the last sneltram back to Elizaburg. Today, of all days, his mother and sisters were in town, so she had not seen him.

She knew the lads would regret trying anything. She had been taught basic self-defence at school, then her shadow-like security assignment had insisted she go on a ten-week course in martial arts before beginning her short-lived nursing career. She had continued sparring twice a week right up to her departure.

'Ello darlin',' said one of the lads. 'Fancy a bevvy?' One of the yobs had moved into the seat next to her, pinning her against the window.

The new bottle he had opened was a sweet-smelling concoction. Imogen was suspicious; it had not been passed around the group.

'No thank you,' Imogen replied as she turned to face the window. All she could see was her own reflection in the darkly mirrored surface.

'Ooh, we got ourselves a posh little tart 'ere lads,' another of the yobs said.

'Yeah,' replied the first. 'Go on love, you knows you wants some.'

'I said no thank you.' Imogen stood up as she pushed the bottle away more forcibly.

'Go on, an' then when ye're a bit tipsy la', an' in a friendly point of view, yer'll give us lads what we want.' The yob pushed the bottle to Imogen's mouth.

'You?' asked Imogen scornfully. 'You haven't got a brain, so you cannot think at all,' said Imogen in full regal mode.

The yob found himself lying on the seats across the aisle with Imogen standing over him, to the delight of the yob's companions. She walked down the carriage and heard him getting up. She knew he would try to grab her hair. Her attacker found himself once more lying face down in the aisle of the sneltram, all his force turned against him by Imogen's martial arts.

He got back up. His friends had stopped laughing. 'You'll pay for that, bitch!'

'You've seen that I can defend myself. Even against the four of you. So push off, before I have to hurt you.'

'You threatening us, darlin'?' asked one of the youths.

'Not a threat,' she replied, as cool as a sheet of ice. 'It's a promise.'

'You just got lucky,' said the first youth. 'You'll soon change your tune.'

'I think you should listen to the lady,' said a voice behind them. The sleeping man had awoken.

'Er dat, lads. 'E's a Ristoze – dey all know martial arts an' shite.' said the first yob who Imogen had dealt with, backing away from the group with a sudden attack of cowardice.

'Bloody Ristozes,' said the third yob, as he and his two companions went for the man.

It was a short and mismatched fight. Two of the attackers fought with no training and no finesse. However, the stranger was having problems with the third. While they fought, the apparent coward had turned his attention back to Imogen.

'Right love, when me mates are done with that posh fella over there, we've got some unfinished bizzy.' And he lunged at Imogen.

'Oh dream on, I'll just flatten you again,' she said as she quickly batted him away. She had been doing the motions unable to spar for months on her time-line when she'd had no-one to spar with. Even so, the fight, if you could call it that, was over in the blink of an eye.

'You're late. This meeting was supposed to have taken place months ago, in Victoria Park,' said Imogen as she recognised Crown-Prince David's pudgy face.

'Sorry about that, Princess Louise, I was held up elsewhere.'

'Your guided tour was very informative,' she said, 'but I no longer need minders, so I get to see what I want to see.'

'It nearly ended badly for you.'

'Not a chance. Those louts wouldn't have known what hit them.'

'Even with training, four against one is not good odds,' said the Prince as he pulled the communication cord. The driver-less tram came to a halt.

'Hold this, will you?' He passed Imogen a piece of plastic, as he removed a cover from the side of the door. 'Neither of us really wants to be aboard when the Crown Police arrive to deal with that lot.' He pointed towards a camera on the ceiling. 'Given the ruckus, they'll have to do something.'

She pointed her finger at the camera. The scanner in her bracelet examined the camera and reported over the psychic interface. 'It's not working,' she told the Prince.

'Are you sure?' he asked.

'Look, the LED is red,' she said. 'It should be blue.'

'Right-ho!' said the Prince. 'I thought that meant recording.'

'That lot wouldn't have tried anything on with me if it were blue.' On the seat behind the yobs was a box with a flashing light. 'Ah, this is how they disabled the camera. We could have waited until the next tramhalt then casually walked back to the tunnel. However, as you have pulled the communication cord, the police will now definitely be on their way.'

He had taken back the piece of plastic, unfolding it into an emergency ladder. 'I'll go first, see you down there.'

'Down where? We are miles from the Castle.'

'You haven't been paying attention. We are about two furlongs from the tunnel entrance. Chop chop, the police will be here in less than five minutes; we have to be safely in hiding by then,'

'Who you summoned unnecessarily,' said Imogen. How very typical of the Rushton-Brownes, totally unable to accept they were in the wrong. 'Here, catch.'

The Prince deftly caught Imogen's laundry bag as she climbed down the ladder, making her hasty exit from the scene of the recent unpleasantness.

hey ran from the sheltram, down the empty streets to the cellar of the warehouse. Imogen could hear the sound of sirens getting louder.

'Time for a royal vanishing act,' the Crown-Prince said as he closed the hidden door.

'Don't worry, your courtly garb is still where you left it. As is mine. I won't spy on you while you change. I'm as much a gentleman as Carlo.'

Oh, why did you have to mention his name, she thought as they jogged along. She was missing him more than she wanted to admit. Last night she had been so disappointed by his absence from the meal in the Royal Apartments. Today he had cancelled their assignation, which was no doubt the Prince's fault.

'So tell me, Princess Louise, why the pretence? Why are you letting your servant take your place?'

'Well, all I can tell you is that Duchess Anita was never my servant.'

'Don't I deserve an explanation?' he asked.

'I cannot tell a living soul the truth. If I try, it all goes hazy.'

'But you've remembered who you really are?'

'Almost immediately. I was trying to get back control of my body from day one. Eventually, the real me resurfaced. However, the last thing I clearly remember is saying goodbye to my mother at the Space Centre. Everything else, up to and including the trip back with you, Carlo and the Princess has just turned to mush.'

'Don't you find that suspicious?' asked Crown-Prince David. 'That you could still be under the same influence Anita?'

'That is definitely not the case,' said Falada as he manifested. 'I have put a block on the Princess Louise's memory, as it would be dangerous if the wrong people knew too much.'

'What the hell are you, and what do you know?' asked the Prince, giving Falada an excuse to change the subject.

'I am Valentine Device Foxtrot 4 Lima 4 Delta 4, aka Falada. I have been watching over this planet since humans arrived, on and off. You know me as Mr Fladders.'

'The informative voice on the telephone. How can I trust anything which sided with the Aggelii against its Human creators? Princess Louise says she trusts you, but you have already said you have messed with her memory.'

'You think I am behind this whole situation? Believe me, I would have done a much better job.' The horse-head faded from view.

'He is not our enemy, but he knows who is,' said Imogen.

'So, who is our enemy?'

'I am!' said a second ghostly figure which had manifested itself in the tunnel. She looked like an older version of Imogen with short grey hair, cut into a severe bob.

'Is Anita now free of you?' asked Imogen. She recognised the ghost immediately.

'No, the host sleeps, allowing me mobility,' replied the ghost. 'Oh isn't your crushed hope so absolutely delicious?'

'Immortal Empress?' asked Crown-Prince David, in disbelief.

'You recognise me?' asked the ghost. 'Yet you don't bow down?'

'Of course. I'm a devout member of the Church of the Caretakers of the Soul. I recognise and revile you.'

'But as a son of Hannah Browne, you must obey me,' said the ghost.

'Never,' said the Prince.

'Oh dear, another strong one. I will have to waste valuable energy removing you to the level of your imbecile father,' said the ghostly figure. 'No, I'll just kill you. Your brother will make a much better henchman.'

'Vernon?'

'Angels no, he thinks he's clever. Thinking he could get away with original thoughts. He'll die, painfully, much to my delight.'

'So who then?' asked Imogen, although to her horror she already knew the answer.

'Why the dull and dutiful Carlo Valoretti. He doesn't know he is the result of drunken fumbling between your father and his wife's sister. By the look on your face, Crown-Prince David, neither did you. He has enough brains to do the job properly, not enough to think of anything original. He is so spineless, bending him to my will be easy. As he hasn't been tapped by the Ugly Stick, unlike his father and brothers, he will make a suitable consort for me. You've been acting like a typical aristocratic tart, B426, so you know all about his athletic prowess, while preaching abstinence to the lower orders.'

'Takes one to know one, dear,' said Imogen poisonously.

'Aren't we forgetting someone?' asked Falada, as he fired a beam of energy at the ghost. 'You move like a heavy metal band in a Trappist Monastery. If you make that much noise, you should learn to watch your back, dear. Now off you go, back to your hiding place. Which won't stay hidden for long.'

The two ghostly figures had vanished. Both David and Imogen took advantage of this break to change into their Castle clothes.

'Falada, is it true about Carlo?' she asked when the AI returned, muttering miserably about the trail going cold.

'It is biologically impossible,' replied the AI, 'for the man Carlo Valoretti has always called Dad to be his father.'

'And what did she mean, a son of Hannah Browne?' Imogen asked.

'It is one of her strange twisted jokes. Hans Rushton became Executive Officer of the KHM#89 when Catherine Wellingford became its Captain. However, he was sterile and his post as hereditary Executive Officer was taken by his stepson Peter, the child of the Social Engineer Hannah Brown. Hannah was the loyal lieutenant who created the psuedo-feudal society of Anseris, brainwashing the slumbering convicts into accepting the new status quo. It was Hannah who instilled the unquestioning loyalty to the Queen, body and soul, into my family. Her reward was that the House Rushton-Browne gained the richest archduchy and held all the top jobs in the Kingdom's government.'

'How do you even know about that? It is the sort of knowledge that was lost in the mists of time when I was a child.'

'My mother taught me. The women of the Valoretti Clan of Innistrom kept the Secret History of Anseris alive as an oral tradition, passed down the generations, from mother to daughter,' said Crown-Prince David. 'She had no daughters, so she taught me the truth of our planet's history. She also taught Carlo and I how to resist the Soul of Queen Kathyren. That old witch is in for a shock.

'Andrew Rushton-Browne, the Boatbuilder, knew his wife was from the Valoretti Clan of Innistrom. She gave her rebellious husband enough information to start his revolution, but not all the facts before Otto Brozhnik murdered her. So the Boatbuilder had no idea that he could not disobey the woman he rescued from the Queen's Tower, because she had the face of Kathyren Ellisford-Castle. That is what stopped him making himself King all those years ago.'

'So I persuaded the Valoretti women write the Book of Care,' said Falada, 'and then create the Church of the Caretaker of the Souls. The Valoretti Women placed one of their own, Angelique Rushton-Brown as first Prime Caretaker, then they retired back to obscurity in Innistrom.

'Five hundred years later, with no cloned Queen to answer to, your other ancestor, Archduke Benedict, felt safe in challenging for the throne when Queen Gertrude died. As a direct descendant of the second highest ranking officer on KHM#89, he thought he had a more legitimate claim than the late Queen's half-sister.'

'It's to my eternal shame that since winning the throne, my family all acted like spoilt children,' said Crown-Prince David.

'So, it turns out the Immortal Empress was not as dead as we thought she was. Her brain-print has been sleeping somewhere, and now it's awake, playing merry hell,' concluded Falada. He had no audience, Imogen and Crown-Prince David were asleep.

Two gas-masked Chessmen walked into the room.

'That was very informative, Sir Knight,' said one to Falada.

'I take it you are Viscount Oscar Vernon Rushton-Browne of Eastbury,' Falada replied.

'I was. I am now Archduke Rushton-Browne.'

'So, she has made you her right-hand man?'

'Indeed, I am the new Monarch's loyal lieutenant.' Then turning to his colleague. 'Sorry, Jean-Paul. Orders are orders.'

The other Chessman began coughing. 'I can't breathe.'

'Such a shame you had a faulty gas-mask and a reaction to the sedative.'

'You promised me control of the Chessmen,' said the other man, with what little breath he had remaining. 'That's why I killed the King for you.'

'Her Majesty only wants people who follow orders. Original thinking and initiative are frowned upon by the new order as much as they were by the old. She believed me when I said the King's death was all your fault.'

'You know you are as disposable to the Immortal Empress as that poor fellow was to you?' said the AI.

'Nonsense, I will be the goddess' right-hand man; her prophet when she emerges in all her glory to rule the Kingdom.'

'As you humans say, "Godess, my arse!"'

'You slander my goddess!'

'Goddess?' Falada asked with as much emotion as an AI could muster.

'She was worshipped as a goddess before the Boatbuilder; she will be again. How else would you explain her return, if not through divinity?'

'Science and technology, Lord Vernon, not divinity.' Falada regarded the pitiful individual with disdain. 'You didn't hear her telling my unconscious friends and me that your brother Carlo has that job?'

'You lie, Sir Knight. What has Valoretti got to do with this? He is a hunted man. An accessory in Crown-Prince David's treason. He will hang with him for that treason. It leaves only me.'

Falada remained silent. There was no point talking to a fanatic.

'I am tasked with finding your physical form and destroying it. That will seal my position.'

'Best of luck.'

e became vaguely aware of something, or rather someone, tapping the side of his chest. Crown-Prince David had been sleeping on a floor, manacled to a wall by his feet. As soon as the person standing over him became aware he was awake, the gentle tap turned into a viscious kick.

'Wakey, wakey!' said a familiar voice.

'Oscar, my dear half-brother, why are you doing this?' Crown-Prince David asked, using Lord Vernon's official name, given to him by the man Anseris believed to be his father. Vernon hated both the man and the name.

'How could you? How could you kill our father, you ungrateful child?'

'I didn't, you did. Or you had someone do it for you,' Crown-Prince David said when breath returned to his lungs. 'Under instructions from the Princess, no doubt.'

'That is not what all the evidence points to.'

'Evidence you manufactured?'

'Does it matter, David? It is what will be believed. Everyone knows you were openly rebellious. When you found out that father was going to acknowledge me, you fell into a jealous rage and killed him.'

'A master stroke getting me blamed for the old man's death, Oscar. I congratulate you.'

'Thank you, David,' replied Lord Vernon.

'I congratulate you on being a lying snake.'

That earned Crown-Prince David another sharp kick to the solar plexus.

'You had the King, our father killed. She won't tolerate that level of original thinking.'

Lord Vernon considered this for a second, before laughing. 'The goddess was furious. Only our pink bimbo sister should have been killed. I managed to pin the blame on a lackey – she was satisfied with that.'

'Goddess? No, Oscar, she's not a goddess, she's a vampire!'

Prince David felt the tip of Lord Vernon's boot with another wave of pain. He began laughing.

'What's so funny?' asked Lord Vernon.

'If she is divine, as you say, you can't lie to her. Your goddess already has you marked, and you are too stupid to realise that fact. You are an idiot.'

'The horse-head did say that. He lied, you lie.'

'No.' Crown-Prince David managed to sit up. 'She will try to cast her spell over our other brother, who she thinks will serve her without question, or originality.'

'Other brother? You're raving.'

'No, I found out today that Carlo is my half-brother, just like you.'

'I don't believe you. Soon you will be dead, then I shall find and destroy the horse-head. No new sources of lies, only the goddess's glorious truth.'

'Please, Vernon, don't make me laugh again, it hurts too much.'

T he bed was hard, narrow and cold. The dungeons of Ellisford Castle had not been designed for comfort. She had no idea how she got here during the short drug-induced slumber. She had a headache, upset stomach and mouth like a cat litter tray. Having a hangover without getting drunk the previous night was so unfair; definitely a cruel and unusual punishment.

She watched as a patch of orange light formed into the shape of a horse's head. Strange, she thought, usually it's instantaneous.

'Got a hangover as well?' she asked.

'Something is trying to block me from the Inner Bailey,' said Falada. 'A very half-hearted effort.'

'On the subject of half-hearted efforts, why haven't you got me out of here yet?' asked Imogen.

'I don't need hands to manipulate electronic locking devices. For mechanical devices need to borrow someone elses hands. There is no way I could turn its key.'

'Will I have to wait for a guard to unlock the door, and then overpower him?' She did not think this was a practical possibility. Even if there was one guard on duty, he would be wearing mail, have weapons and would be more of a challenge than a handful of drunken yobs.

'No, the Guard Room does have an electronic lock. On the shift change twenty minutes ago, when all the guards were inside, I locked the door.'

'Well done, Falada.'

'I think the guards are highly delighted. Given the current power vacuum, they don't know whether the death of King Benedict is a good or bad thing yet.'

'He is dead, then?'

'Yes, Imogen, and you must reclaim the throne. Your birthright.'

'A queen who is trapped in her own dungeon,' she said as she let out an ironic giggle. 'Hang on a minute, surely it's King David II now?'

'No, he has been officially charged with the murder of his father. Until that charge is dealt with, he is legally a nobody.'

'Charged by whom?' asked Imogen. 'There is no order, nor law to go with it at the moment.'

'Just before everything went to hell, the Crown Police issued the arrest warrant,' said a familiar voice. 'Then the Cult of the Immortal Empress launched their revolt. They hold the Inner Bailey and strategic locations throughout the system. They are steadfastly behind Queen Kathyren, whom they regard as a goddess.'

'Come to gloat, have you, Your Majesty?' asked Imogen.

'Oh, Imogen, please don't. I am so sorry about everything that witch made me do. While I am free of her, please don't waste time.'

'Anita?'

'Yes, Imogen,' the other woman said. 'Falada gave the Empress a bloody nose. She was too weak to hold me, so returned to her hiding place.'

'Anita is telling the truth,' said Falada. 'She is herself again. I have told her how to prevent the Empress using her as a host. I do not know where the Empress is hiding. If I did, I would finish her off.'

Anita flashed her painted nails, at any other time a serious breach of Castle rules.

'Where did you get the nail varnish?' asked Imogen.

'I found it in the Protocol Office,' said Anita. 'They must have confiscated it from someone. It contains the more common form of the mineral that makes up Moonglow crystals. It has the same properties.'

'But not as effective, Anita. Prince David gave the Princess a Moonglow ring. You must find it, it will be better protection.'

'I remember her disgust. There was no way she would wear anything that might loosen her control over me.' Anita took something from a pocket in the sleeve of her surcote. 'Here, dear, this is the key to your cell and Crown-Prince David's cell. I must go now, and give Queen Stephanie the antidote to the poison that killed the King. She is younger and stronger, but it is slowly killing her too.'

'Chrystine Ifans will be in the Infirmary. She will help you,' said Falada.

'Won't she be held with the other Castle staff in the Church Hall in Bailseparc?' asked Anita.

'No, it's a long story. Lady Chrystine is a valuable hostage,' replied Falada.

'Get her to explain it,' said Imogen. 'Get them both out of the Castle. Only you can. You mightn't be possessed, but your former allies don't know that yet.'

'I have another job before I can make my way to safety,' Anita said. 'I must rescue the baby.'

'So there is one?' asked Falada.

'Yes, and she used these hands to bring that baby into existence. I remember everything she did with them in her lab in the Queen's Tower.'

'Obviously the locks were re-coded to your DNA while that creature hijacked your body,' said Falada. 'No wonder you woke up whenever that creature was in there. It activated your psychic interface at the same time as opening the door.'

'On the plus side, it means I can get into the tower easily,' said Anita.

'Only as long as its security system thinks you are still possessed.'

'I'll be careful.'

The medical centre was quiet, only a small pool of light at the nurse's station where Chrystine Ifans slept an exhausted sleep, a nasty red weal on her cheek and a bottle of painkillers by her side.

Stephanie's bed notes were in a file by her bed. The Queen-Consort was being treated for severe food poisoning, which was easing the symptoms but not stopping the real poison. Anita changed the bag on the intravenous drip, then injected the contents of the hypodermic syringe hidden in a sleeve of her surcotte, into Stephanie's arm.

'I am so sorry,' Anita said. 'I only hope I am in time.'

Within seconds Stephanie's ragged breathing calmed. Colour returned to the woman's skin. The Pink Queen was pink again.

'Nurse Ifans, wake up,' said Anita in a quiet voice.

'Doctor Matthews and Nurse Aloe have been taken away. All the Castle staff are being held in Bailesparc,' said the semi-conscious woman. 'I'm engaged to an Earl, too valuable a hostage to be locked there. So I'm here, keeping Steffi stable.'

'Chrystine, the patient is coming round,' said Anita.

It was as if a button had been pressed. Nurse Ifans was awake in a shot, checking the readings on the machines and examining her patient.

'Thank the Angels.' Then noticing to whom she was speaking, she curtseyed.

'Don't let me get in your way,' said Anita. 'I'm back in control of my body. That old witch can try to take back control, but I know how to fight her now.'

'Johanna explained it all. It must have been terrible for you.'

'Who?' Anita was a little confused.

'Princess Louise aka Dame Imogen. It's the name she goes by

now,' said Chrystine by way of explanation. 'I don't know how she copes with all the different names.'

'Of course, the alias she used when we were working at the Royal,' said Anita.

'You've changed the drip. Thank you,' said Chrystine.

'Yes,' said Anita. 'She and her father were both poisoned by one of the Castle Chessmen. I heard Lord Vernon name the poison. I injected the antidote, 20ml of Ofelomiomil and 200ml of Tripbellic Acid. She needs to be transferred to a hospital with a proper toxicology lab, who will treat any side effects from the antidote.'

'You've done all you can. They won't transfer her, she is worth more as a hostage here,' said Chrystine dejectedly. 'I wanted to phone paramedics. It earned me this slap. They won't let anyone phone beyond the Castle.'

'Don't worry, I will call the paramedics and watch the patient. They dare not defy me. They still think I'm someone else.'

'Divine One,' said a Chessman who had been sent to find her, 'there is a paramedic air ambulance approaching from Elizaburg. They say you summoned it.'

It only seemed like a minute since she had rung beyond the Castle. It must have been longer. She had been so busy dealing with her patient.

'Yes, tell Commander Vernon to allow them safe passage,' she said, trying to sound like the Princess. Anita could fool some of the Chessmen, but she didn't know how long that would last.

'Immediately, Your Majesty.' The Chessman saluted and left.

'Your Majesty,' said one of the arriving paramedics, minutes later, 'we received your call. There was no-one at the helipad on the roof, so we let ourselves in. Everything has gone mad since the King died.'

Anita quickly and professionally reported the situation with the patients to the paramedics.

'Yes, Your Majesty.'

'Now, go quickly, take Princess Stefania to where she can get the best treatment. Nurse Ifans also.'

The host felt a stabbing pain as Queen Kathyren returned, like a shadow enveloping her.

Back in the driving seat, and Queen Kathyren was feeling magnanimous. She would let the pink blob live this time. There would be plenty of chances to kill her in years to come.

The paramedics bowed and took the unconscious Stefania to their waiting air ambulance. Now she had to see how much damage had been done in her absence. She knew that Falada and Imogen thought she had been banished from this host. They thought wrong. It had been a strategic withdrawal, not a permanent retreat. However, there was something different this time. The host was putting up more of a fight.

OK, the paramedics and their air ambulance have left. Two patients aboard, Queen Stefania and Chrystine Ifans,' said Falada. 'The Chessmen didn't try to stop them. Anita is still in the Inner Bailey. Kathyren Ellisford-Castle is attempting to re-establish her control over her. It will fail. The dragon is in for a shock.'

'The dragon?' asked Imogen.

'The technology used by Kathyren Ellisford-Castle was from the Draconic League.'

'So I have always been touched by a dragon?' asked Imogen.

'More so than any other Queen of Anseris for a thousand years.'

'In what way?'

'The Fenzrians also used cast-off technology from the Draconic League. I didn't realise this until I saw your ship. I called the Aggelii, hoping they would arrive before you left. It took them six months to get here, which by their standards is an instantaneous response. Now, I will leave you to get some rest.'

Don't be stupid!' Shandra said. She was not irate at being woken up in the middle of the night by the Chessmen. Her trade union background had earned her many 3am visits. The thing was messing with her head was their unusual politeness. As was the claim they were acting on behalf of the King's feircest adversary, the Prime Caretaker.

'Madam, my Mother had no stupid children,' replied the man.

'You've never been this polite before. Normally, I'm bundled into the back of a van and taken to your headquarters. There I get shouted at, maybe a bit of a beating and definitely a nice blue hair-do before being kicked out into the morning dew.'

'We've always been on opposing sides on previous visits, for which, by the way, I apologise. This time we are on the same side.'

'I find that hard to believe. If we are on the same side, can't this wait until morning?'

'It is true. His Holiness chose the time. Who am I to argue?'

'Yes, yes,' said a flustered Shandra. 'I still don't like it.'

'To repeat, Elashandra Margaret Elizaburg Rackham, you have been invited by the Prime Caretaker of Souls to a meeting at his Palace.'

'What for?' Her mind was racing. Why was the side-lined leader of an ignored religion now calling the shots?

'The King is dead. Crown-Prince David is under arrest, accused of his murder. The Ellisford-Castle Princess has been suspiciously quiet. It is rumoured she is the reincarnation of Kathyren Ellisford-Castle. Members of the Cult of the Immortal Empress have been arrested all over the system for acts of treason. There is no-one in charge of this planet. Also rumours that the Goose Maiden is really the Princess. This is our chance.'

'A chance for what?' asked Shandra, now intrigued.

'To establish a new form of government that will move this planet in our direction.'

'It's never going to happen. You say your fellow Chessmen are rallying behind the Bastard Vernon. We Democrats will be crushed when you lot change sides again.'

'Democracy will not be crushed this time. The bulk of the Chessmen are like me, middle class. We do what is best for the middle classes. Until now, that has been loyal support of an Absolute Monarchy. That's no longer the case. Conservatives always dominate any democratic government, making sure it only benefits the middle classes. We'll still keep the plebeians and the peasants in their place, we'll just add the Ristoze to the people we keep under control.'

'How do you know about that sort of thing?' she asked.

'In order to combat sedition, you have to be able to recognise it. All Chessmen know the Galactic History and Political Theories we work so hard to suppress.'

'Very well, I will come with you to the Prime Caretaker's Palace. If only to make sure people like you never get anywhere.'

'Thank you, madam.'

'You'll have to wait for me to get dressed,' said Shandra. 'I can't meet the Prime Caretaker in my pyjamas.'

'Or in Guild-style clothing. Also, you must keep your head covered,' said the Chessman.

Shandra had wondered if this was necessary, or simply the Chessman expressing his conservatism. Nevertheless, she dug deep into her closet and found the Trad-style claret kirtle with the orange velvet surcote and orange chiffon veil she wore on her rare visits to church.

'Hurry up, madam,' said the waiting Chessman.

This broke her concentration. She was brushing her long blonde hair before braiding it. Johanna had persuaded her not to worry about the Chessmen's blue dye ever again. The hair extensions had been her own idea. I look like my mother, she thought. What a woman she had been; the most radical person I have ever met, though no-one would suspect it because she always dressed Trad and wore the avatar made from cheap blue glass with silver-plated wings now hanging from my mirror. Well, I am going to the Basilica, she thought, I might as well do it properly.

T hey arrived at the Basilica. It was far too busy for this time in the morning.

'One moment, please,' Shandra said to her escort when she took some pfennigs from the purse hidden in her long sleeves to pay for a candle.

'Well, Mam, looks like we are about to see the birth of the Anseris you dreamed of.' She lit the candle, placed it in a holder saying a prayer. The Chessman had been replaced by a Caretaker. She followed her through the Basilica and forward to change the world.

Imogen gave up her futile attempt at sleeping. She had a key, she could get herself and the former Crown-Prince David out of here.

The dungeon level of the Keep was deserted. All the Castle guards were locked in their Guard Room. Imogen could hear the sound of drunken revelry from inside.

'Prince David, are you injured?' she asked, as she slipped into the Prince's cell. He was lying on the floor at a very peculiar angle.

'Nothing that a shot of Durinalic Acid can't solve,' he said moving awkwardly on the straw-covered floor.

'I'll go and get a first-aid kit,' she said.

'It'll be in the Guard Room – do you really want to unlock that door?'

'Can you get to the Cottage? It has a first-aid kit, and somewhere you can get a few hours' sleep,' said Imogen.

'Do we have time? Things are moving at one hell of a pace.'

'Nothing can really happen without the pair of us. Plenty of time for us to get some sleep' said Imogen, as she helped Prince David out of the cell.

Prince David opened a concealed door in the wall of the corridor, as they both slid through it.

'But not at the Cottage. Vernon's men will be watching it,' said Prince David. 'He knows this dungeon won't hold me. If he can catch me in the Cottage after I have escaped, it will be even more damning evidence for him to use against both of us.'

'So were do we go? And where are we?' asked Imogen.

'The hillock the Inner Bailey is built on is riddled with tunnels, as is most of the surrounding area. It used to be an underground lake of magma,' said David, 'slow-moving and viscous. Faster-moving currents of warmer, more liquid lava flowed through it. When the lava drained down, it left these tunnels in the solidifying magma. Over the years, the surrounding rocks wore away, exposing the hillock like a piece of holey cheese.'

'Fascinating, but it doesn't answer my question. Where are we?' asked Imogen as she passed through a natural arch.

'Only a fraction of the tunnels were explored. Mostly the ones used as service tunnels under the Inner Bailey, until now. Our route into and out of the Castle is just one such tunnel.'

Typical Rushton-Browne, thought Imogen, determined to say what he wanted, not anything useful. The cavern she was standing in was flooded with light.

'Carlo and I spent months surveying the network. This chamber used to be a granary. It was abandoned centuries ago.'

'So you surveyed the tunnels from this base camp, Prince David?' Imogen looked around the chamber, kitted out with a pair of camp beds, a stove and a chemical toilet.

'That's right. We will be heading through Section C, we rendez-vous with Carlo to the east of the Boating Lake, then out over the East Bridge and down the road through the Royal Forest, before hopping on to Angel's Highway to double back to Elizaburg.' Prince David was busily routing through a box, looking for something as he spoke.

'I was wondering why there is an East Bridge when Elizaburg is to the west?' asked Imogen absent-mindedly.

'Elizaburg was only meant to be a temporary capital,' replied the Prince. 'Replaced by a new city next to the East Bridge. Ask Carlo for the details. Anyway, the South Bridge and Castle Rock will be full of Chessmen loyal to the Princess and Vernon. I suspect they have taken rural Guild-owned land, right up to the suburbs of Elizaburg. The urban areas will be our territory.'

'I hope we're not going under the Boating Lake,' said Imogen, who did not like the idea of going beneath the Castle reservoir.

'We'll be going down tunnel C3, which goes to the south of the Boating Lake.'

'You've obviously done your homework, Archduke Rushton-Browne.'

'Under the circumstances, I think first names would be more appropriate, don't you, Imogen?'

'Of course, David,' said Imogen, 'but now I prefer being called Johanna.'

'Ah, here it is.' The Prince opened a first-aid box and injected himself with a dose of Durinal. 'Let this work its magic, Johanna.'

After just three hours of sleep, she woke a significantly improved David. 'Come on, sleepyhead, we don't want to miss the Prime Caretaker's meeting,' she said.

'But it's the middle of the night. Who meets anyone at this time?' he asked. 'I have been planning this for weeks. Ever since I found out who you really were. But late-night meetings were never on the agenda.' He picked up a tablet. 'You see there are so many small groups opposed to my family's rule. Normally they get crushed by the Chessmen, but recently they have been left alone.'

'There is nothing more conservative than the son of a middle-class merchant,' said Falada as he materialised in the chamber.

'Damn it! I wish you wouldn't do that, Falada,' said Prince David.

'So, you want a ringtone?' asked the horse-head.

'That might be a good idea. I preferred it when you were just an anonymous voice on the phone,' Prince David said to Falada before turning back to Imogen. 'The bulk of the Chessmen were deeply unhappy with my father. If you keep a vicious dog, you should feed it properly, or it might turn on you. Falada is right, most Chessmen are the sons of successful middle-class businessmen. While their families prospered, they supported the status quo.'

'But the economy is in a right old state,' said Imogen. 'I have been watching it for months, on my trips outside.'

'And so the big dog turned and bit my father,' Prince David continued. 'I now control the Chessmen. I am using them to bring together leaders of every opposition group bar one. In cooperation with His Holiness, I have organised those groups into a potential replacement government.'

'You are, of course, overplaying your role, Roswall. Or is it Dewi or any of the other half dozen aliases you use?' asked

Imogen. 'How many opposition groups have you helped?'

'I have not only been preparing the way for your inevitable return as the true Queen. I plan to abdicate in your favour, Your Majesty.' Prince David was kneeling in front of Imogen.

'Get up, Archduke,' she said. 'We have work to do.'

'Yes, Your Majesty.'

'Strawberry Moon and Roswall have escaped, Your Majesty,' said Lord Vernon in a steady unemotional manner.

'Lord Vernon, I control the Inner Bailey of Ellisford Castle now. There is no longer a need for code names and secrecy.' The Princess picked up a map of the Castle. 'Do we know where the traitor Prince David and Imogen are at the moment?'

'The traitor is fascinated by the system of tunnels underneath the Inner and Outer Baileys. It is likely that he has gone to ground within that network, taking the Lady Imogen with him.'

The Princess put down her tablet and turned to a display screen. 'Show me this network.'

'This diagram is the old plan of the system.' The screen showed the Inner Bailey with a series of tunnels superimposed on it. Vernon added another layer to the display. 'This new diagram contains the recently updated survey, done by the traitor Prince David as a hobby. As you can see, several of the tunnels run almost as far as the moat. We suspect that they will use this tunnel, as it terminates very close to the recently discovered tunnel out to Castle Rock. It is fair to assume that once they were connected.'

'So, can we use the Castle's security system to scan this cat's cradle?' she asked.

'Yes, Your Majesty.'

Two blue dots appeared on screen, nowhere near where Vernon had predicted. 'Oh!' said Lord Vernon. 'They appear to be under the Boating Lake. They have gotten themselves horribly lost.'

'Your Majesty, Lord Vernon,' said one of the Chessmen, 'the Castle takes water from the Boating Lake through that tunnel. We could easily flood it, flush them out.'

'No, close that sluice there,' said the Princess, pointing to the map. 'Let them drown, but recover the body of the woman. Have it taken to the Queen's Tower.'

'Majesty?' asked a shocked Lord Vernon.

'I no longer require to keep Lady Imogen alive, a new host is ready to be introduced to the Black Crèche,' the Princess told her henchman. 'However, dear Imogen's body is far too valuable to be wasted on a simple burial.'

'Yes, Your Majesty.' He decided it was best not to ask any more questions.

'Mr Bartók, can me and my friend look at the big trucks, please Mr. Bartók,' said the childlike voice at the window.

'It's 2am in the morning. What sort of tomfoolery is this?' asked the old man, woken from his slumber. He grumbled as he walked down the stairs from his flat over the workshop at the Elizaburg Municipal Yard, to let Carlo Valoretti in. Silas Bartók had known Prince David and Carlo Valoretti since they had been eight-year-old boys obsessed with City Corporation refuse carts. They are the only motor vehicles allowed into Ellisford Castle.

'Thank you, Silas,' said a dishevelled Carlo.

'Hey, Carlo, some are saying the Prince topped 'is old man?' asked Mr Bartók.

'The King is dead, but Dewi didn't kill him.'

'So you say, but you would. So where is the Prince?'

'At this moment, escaping from the Inner Bailey,' Carlo replied. 'I need to borrow a perfume wagon, to get him out of the Castle Precincts.'

''Cos nobody stops to check 'em goin' in or comin' back out.'

'That's right,' said Carlo.

'The CCTV in the yard is running. Picture only, so you had better get your gun out,' said the old man. 'Make it look like I'm under pressure when I give you the keys to number twenty-three.'

The two men headed towards the main garage, Mr Bartók a few paces in front of Carlo, who was pointing a gun at his back.

'I don't think the Prince killed the King. If 'im was going to do that, 'im would 'ave done it years ago,' said the old man, 'and done a better job of it.'

'What makes you say that?' asked Carlo.

'My h-observation of 'is Royal 'ighness over the years.' The old man handed Carlo the keys to the vehicle. 'She's just 'ad a service, so she will run sweet as a nut.'

'Thanks, Mr Bartók. I'm afraid I'm going to have to tie you up. Make things look more realistic.'

'Fair enough, lad. You'll 'ave to be knockin' I out as well. Try not to be too painful.'

T he tunnel was wide enough for the two of them to walk side by side. Prince David's torch illuminated enough of the bone-dry tunnel for them to walk safely. She didn't know when he had started leading her by the hand, but she did not like it. Who did he think he was? Carlo Valoretti?

'Cobwebs, ach!' she said, pretending to remove the dirty silken strands from her face, an excuse to let go of Prince David's hand.

'That shows how dry it is down here now,' said Prince David. 'Spiders don't make webs where it's wet.'

This did not fill Imogen with confidence. The tunnel was as clean as a whistle. Surely Prince David would have noticed that. No, he was a typical Rushton-Browne, so very confident in his opinion. She thought she could hear something. It sounded like running water.

'What's that noise?' asked Imogen, hoping she was wrong.

'Sounds like running water,' he replied, 'but it can't be. We're in Tunnel C3.'

'Then why are my feet wet?' asked Imogen

'Did we go left or straight on at the last junction?' asked Prince David, as he studied his map.

'Left. You said it was quicker.'

'Oh Angels! Run!' He grabbed her hand and began sprinting

'Why? You said it was safe.'

'I made a mistake. We should have gone straight on then turned left into C4. We are now in tunnel C2, under the lake, and it's being flooded.'

The two broke into a gallop. 'Don't worry, there is a sluice up ahead. When we get past that we will be at our exit.'

If it had not been for the torch, they would have run into a wall of metal.

'I just knew this was going to happen,' said Imogen. 'The Princess has set a trap for us.'

'Yes, the control mechanism is on the other side,' said Prince David. 'Can Falada open the sluice?'

'No, I can't. It's a mechanical device, all muscle power. There are no computerised motors to hack into,' the horse-head replied.

The water was lapping around their knees, and the rate it was rising was increasing. Within minutes it would be over their heads. The torch was now underwater, leaving them in darkness.

'How will we know when they're dead?' asked a Chessman. 'The chamber they are trapped in will be full of water in a few minutes,' said his companion. 'We won't have to wait long before they drown.'

The two were standing in an inspection chamber, a few feet beneath the ground. It had taken both of them to turn the metal wheel that had closed the sluice gate beneath them.

'Why are we fishing out their corpses?' asked the first.

'The goddess wants the woman's body. You know not to ask stupid questions, you just do what the goddess tells you and don't draw attention to yourself. That way, you get to live.'

'I can't wait at all. My bladder's about to explode. The sound of running water isn't helping.'

'Be quick about it,' said the second.

'What was that?' asked the first.

'What was what?'

'I thought I heard someone up top.'

'Well, you're the one going up there. Have a check.'

The Castle grounds were in complete darkness. Carlo switched his night-vision goggles to full gain. There was a flash and a single pool of light where no light should be even when the precincts were fully illuminated. It was also exactly where he was heading. An abandoned inspection chamber. He parked number twenty-three at a safe distance and went to investigate. From his vantage point, he saw the undergrowth that hid the manhole cover had been burnt away. Someone climb out of the manhole. He wore a Chessman's uniform.

Carlo fired a bolt from his crossbow. It silently destroyed the bulb in the portable lamp, draining the pool of light. Carlo heard the man cursing, and then the noise of him fumbling around in the darkness. It covered Carlo's silent approach, his night goggles giving him the advantage over the unfortunate Chessman.

'Evening, my friend,' said Carlo as he brought the and Chessman to his knees. 'What brings a fellow like you to a place like this on such a dark night?'

'Who the hell are you?' asked the confused Chessman.

'You appear to be under the misapprehension that you can ask questions, my friend,' said Carlo as he placed a stunner dart against the man's neck. 'I'm the one who does the asking, you do the telling. Now tell me, what are you up to?'

'Waiting for the stiffs to bob to the surface. The Prince and the Goose Maiden are drowning as we speak. The goddess has risen. Their deaths will be the first in her revenge.'

The man fell to the ground as Carlo discharged the stunner dart.

'Y ou took your...' the Chessman instantly recognised Carlo weapon to shoot. He was too slow, so Carlo aimed a punch at the man.

The Chessman parried the blow and took a swing at Carlo. A precise blow that forced Carlo against the wall of the chamber. Emboldened, the Chessman took a high kick. In a flash Carlo caught the kick between his parallel forearms and pulled his overbalanced opponent over, pushing a stunner dart into the falling man's skin.

There was no way he could open the sluice, that would take two men. Instead, he opened the fall-back hatch at his feet and dropped the attached ladder into the water-filled pipe. 'It's a good thing I came along,' he said cheerily.

She heard a familiar voice as a ladder descended from an inspection hatch above her head.

She clambered up the ladder, then through an inspection chamber. A few yards away stood a refuse vehicle.

'Carlo, I never thought I would be so glad to see you,' she and Prince David said in unison.

'Thank you, Your Majesties.'

'Nothing majestic about me at the moment,' said Imogen, 'just a woman in a wet dress.'

'I chose the most anonymous vehicle I could think of, Ma'am,' said Carlo.

'I think you need to re-adjust your definition of anonymous, Carlo,' said Imogen. The dustcart was big and ugly. Its Elizaburg City Corporation livery, fluorescent orange and scarlet, was as bright and unmissable at night as it was in the day.

'It wasn't stopped by the gate guard on my way here, Your Majesty. Hopefully, it will get us to the Prime Caretaker's Palace unscathed. There are overalls for you to change into. Your dripping wet Court clothes would look odd in the back of a perfume wagon, Ma'am.'

Oh for the Angel's sake, stop being so boringly formal, she thought. This was accompanied by something outside any protocol. It was the potent urge to kiss him. The most potent urge she had ever experienced in her life. Far too strong to resist. He must have had a similar urge, as he did not resist and wrapped himself around her in a passionate embrace.

'If you two have finished, this isn't your love-nest in Elizaburg,' said Prince David a few minutes later, after he had changed into dry brown City Corporation overalls. 'We have a revolution to organise, and we are still stuck inside the Castle.'

It was like a switch. As soon as Prince David appeared, Carlo stiffened like a board.

There was an embarrassed silence. Neither man could look at th other.

'You know, don't you, Carlo? That's why your mother visited you today, and you couldn't see me,' said Imogen.

'Know what?' asked Carlo stupidly.

'Oh don't worry, brother of mine, I know too,' said Prince David. 'I suppose your mother wouldn't say anything while the old man was still alive.'

'She says she can never forgive herself for betraying her sister so badly, even if Aunt Deliah forgave her. Mum never went to your mother's funeral, she said she couldn't.'

'I never understood that,' said the Prince, 'until now'.

There was a squeal of breaks as the truck came to a halt, inches from the serf woman darting across the road.

'Where in the name of all the Angels did she come from?' asked Carlo.

ine months had passed. Embryo COOl had grown during that time and was about to be transferred from the artificial womb that had sustained her – from a loose collection of rapidly splitting cells to a fully formed child – to the darkened room which would maintain her in perfect sensory isolation for the next twenty years. The young woman who emerged from the machine would be as empty as the baby that entered it and would remain so for its short and pointless life if Kathyren Ellisford-Castle could not claim it.

Anita should have just run, but she could not let an innocent life be blighted. If she intervened now, just as the Boatbuilder had five centuries earlier, the child would be free to live a healthy life.

nita walked through a deserted Inner Bailey, into the Royal Apartments. Queen Kathyren had tried to take back control in the Castle Infirmary and had been rebuffed. Anita thought she had seen her mother again, evicting the witch.

In her room she changed out of the embellished outfit the Princess loved. She would need something lighter for her escape. She scrambled through a jewellery draw for a small Moonglow ring.

Anita felt a slow drumming pressure in her skull. She removed the tab from beneath the gem and slipped the ring on. As the drumming receded, the gem came to life. At its heart was a large red drop with a smaller one like a moon in orbit. Protection by both her mothers – Marion, who had brought her up, and the unknown Fenzrian woman who had given birth to her all those years ago.

The ring would be far too conspicuous on her hand, so she hung it from a fine platinum chain around her neck. Beneath her shift the ring would remain in contact with her skin and actively block any psychic assaults. Wearing nondescript clothes she left the room.

𝔍 nside the Queen's Tower, Anita quickly found the hidden
door in late King's office.

'Ah, a genetic lock,' Anita said to herself. This all seemed so familiar, but this was the first time Anita had consciously entered the Queen's Tower.

She continued up past the laboratory to what the bitch had called the Black Crèche. Lying in an incubator, wearing what appeared to be a Fenzrian bodysuit, was a newborn baby girl. Rescuing this one child was not enough; the machine had to be destroyed as well. She took the Anserian landmines from her bag and placed them strategically around the room. They would not destroy the tower, it was re-enforced by part of the KHM#89, but it would gut it. Anita had no idea what the narrow tower could be used for, but anything would be better than this.

'Sorry kid,' Anita said as she turned her attention to the baby, removing the tubes and sensors. It did not cry. It did not respond in any way at all. 'Oh, you poor little darling, you've been drugged to high heaven, haven't you?'

Of course, the child could not answer. This meant that it would be quiet for the next three hours, long enough to get the child to safety.

The machine must have been receiving data, computed that something was wrong as Anita removed the last sensor. When she lifted the baby out of the incubator, an alarm sounded.

'Captain, is that you? Please identify yourself,' asked a simple computerised voice.

Anita said nothing. She gathered up the child and ran down the stairs. When she arrived in the safety of the late King's office, she sealed the hidden door. 'Your captain is dead. Does that compute?' asked and instantly regreted it. Oh, stupid bravado, Anita thought.

'You are the last host. A scan now indicates the captain's meta-print has returned to its storage device. You will return C001 to the Black Crèche and remove your bombs.'

'Like hell, sunshine.'

'Sealing main entrance. You will not detonate the explosive devices if you are trapped inside this tower.'

'No!' she replied. Her voice had armed the landmines.

Anita placed her hand on the lock sensor. Nothing happened.

'DNA print rejected. You are no longer the captain's host.'

'More than one way to skin a cat, although why would anyone want to?'

Anita took the baby and placed its forehead on the sensor. Her palm would be too small.

'DNA print accepted. Thank you, Captain. Opening the main door.'

Anita jumped to one side on exiting the tower. A gout of flame escaped straight through the door, but most of the fire emerged from beneath the skirts of the angel statue at its pinnacle, the force lifting the golden effigy from its brackets. For a few seconds, an angel once more flew over Ellisford Castle, before it returned to the tower, like a hat at a jaunty angle.

'Well kid,' Anita said out loud, 'I think we need to get a move on. Before this place is crawling with Chessmen.'

Finally, the baby responded with a whimper.


A nita knew the quickest way she and the baby could get out of the Inner Bailey. She had not used it since she was a child but knew the pipe known as the Serf's Shortcut was still there and used regularly. Grasping the baby as tightly as possible, she flew down it. At the bottom, she ran into the large cave at the base of the hillock that formed part of the Middle Bailey complex.

Anita saw no-one as she ran to the communal dining room. No doubt they were all locked in their quarters, unfed. Half-finished preparations for the evening meal filled the kitchen. Her instinct was to run and keep on running. But she needed the help of the Chef, the man or woman responsible for keeping all serfs fed – their unofficial leader. If she could persuade the Chef, the rest of the serfs would follow.

She put the baby in an empty wicker basket, grabbed an apron and began noisily filling a pan with water.

'Who the hell is that messing in my kitchen?' asked a surly voice from a locked store-room.

'Evening, Chef. We have a lot of hungry people to feed. Are you game?' Anita put the pan down and walked towards the store-room.

'Of course. I and my crew are always game. But you didn't answer the question!'

'You can call me Anita, Chef. Under the First Law of the Serfs, everything I say to you is the truth.' She opened the hatch at the top of the door.

The man came to the doors and stared at her through the hatch. This was the person Anita was looking for, the Chef.

'Well, Anita, let us out. We have a job to do.'

Anita opened the door, and the kitchen staff quickly returned to their stations to finish the preparations. In her childhood she had never worked in this kitchen, but had gratefully eaten the meals it produced.

'Here, you're that Princess, the one from the spacecraft that spent hundred years in hyperspace,' said the Chef.

'No and yes,' said Anita. 'No, I am not the Princess, but yes, I was trapped in hyperspace with her. Doesn't look like much has changed down here. Work is work.'

'Not the Princess?' asked the Chef. 'Prove it.'

Anita recited the Serf's Oath, an ancient Latin poem passed down the generations that remained the secret of those whose life was grey.

'So, you are Marion's daughter, returned to set us free?'

'Yes, I am Marion's daughter, but I am in no position to set anyone free. Not at the moment. I am trying to hide from the enemy I infiltrated up in the Inner Bailey. They must have realised by now I've done a runner.'

'Well, Anita, I believe you're following the first law. You've come here to make yourself invisible, but even dressed like a peasant you shine like a beacon. I can get you a set of Greys,' Chef said. 'Nobody looks at the face of a serf.'

'Don't I know it. The first twelve years of my life were lived grey and invisible.'

'D o I look like a princess at the moment?' asked Anita, a few hours later. She was totally dishevelled after all the hard graft, in her threadbare borrowed grey kirtle, apron and white veil. She spotted her reflection in the shiny base of one of the pans she had just finished washing. What if Imogen and the Fenzrians had never intervened in my life? This would be what I would always have looked like.

'That you do not, Anita,' said the Chef, 'and you have worked harder than I believe any princess could possibly work.'

'Thank you, Chef,' she replied.

'Now we've finished here, the name's Bernhardt. You look done in. Come meet the wife and tell us your story, then you need a good night's sleep.'

'First things first, where's the baby?'

'The wife has got her. Our little one was stillborn a week ago. She still has the milk that was meant for her own. She said it would be a shame for it to go a-wastin' when there was a hungry mouth that needed it.'

That was part of Anita's mission fulfilled, without her  asking.

Anita followed the man into the same sort of simple dwelling like to the on she up in, one reserved for a higher ranking serf.

Bernhardt's wife Jessica was sitting feeding the baby in the tiny bedroom. The child was fully awake now, drinking deeply.

'So you are that Princess we've been a-hearin' all about,' said the woman. 'Of course, us serfs have been more interested in Dame Imogen, what with us a-thinkin' she be Marion's daughter, and Marion is a legend down here. Now you tell us we got it all wrong.'

'Yes, I am Duchess Anita Ellisford-Castle, the cousin of Queen Louise and adopted daughter of Princess Marie-Anne Ellisford-Castle, the half-serf, half-sister of Queen Gertrude III. For twelve years I lived down here in the Middle Bailey,' said Anita as she began her story.

'So, you and the real princess swapped places?' asked Bernhardt minutes later, as he digested what he had heard.

'Yes. But it ended up being a bonus. It allowed the real princess time to get a feel of the Kingdom, before taking over. With King Benedict dead, she is making her move. Her mother tried to free the serfs. When she is your new Queen, she'll succeed.'

'Nice promise,' said the Chef. 'How do you know she'll succeed?'

'Look, the old King is dead. His son doesn't want to be King.

He will swear allegiance to the new Queen.'

'I know the old bastard is dead. We had beef for supper and lots of it,' said Bernhardt. 'We only do that to celebrate the death of any King descended from the man who at the end of the Civil War had all our ancestors rounded up and returned to eternal penal servitude. Punishment for the crimes of our ancestors.' There was a bitter tone in Bernhardt's voice now, absent previously. 'It didn't matter how successful they had been during those short years of freedom, they found themselves back in the Grey, along with their non-serf spouses and all the children who had been born free. You haven't said anything to make I think your new Queen will win. Or set us free and keep us free.'

'Well, that lot up in the Inner Bailey can't win,' said Anita. 'They locked all you lot away, then locked themselves in a golden bubble and lost the key. Now they can't escape from that bubble because the serfs found the key.' She removed a long electronic key from a lanyard.

A big meaty laugh filled the tiny dwelling. 'The Chamberlain ain't a-goin' to like it.'

'Chamberlains never do. If he's still alive, the current one will just have to put up with it.' Anita yawned. 'The coast should be clear now, but I have a favour to ask before I leave.'

'Where are you going?' Bernhardt asked Anita.

'Anywhere I can, to aid Queen Louise.'

'I knows what you are going to ask. You had to rescue the poor mite, but you ain't a-goin' to get very far if you have the babe in tow,' said Jessica, who had the baby resting against her shoulder. Now stripped out of the metalic outfit and dressed in a grey smock and bonnet, she looked like a serf's baby.

'You'll look after her for me?' asked Anita, who had spotted the cot ready to take the dozing child.

'We'll call her Martya, after Bern's mam. She might have been created by unnatural means, but she don't know that. All Martya knows is when she wants feeding, changing and when she wants a place to sleep,' said Jessica. 'You won't be able to give her any of that. So she stays here until you come back for her. She ain't ours, but we'll guard her with our lives.'

'She bain't mine, neither,' said Anita. 'Queen Louise will decide what happens to her.'

'Of course,' said Bernhardt. 'Martya's got royal blood in those veins. Til that day dawns she'll be safe. And you were fostered by a serf; it didn't harm you none.'

No, thought Anita, no harm at all. But it had radically changed her foster mother's life. She could see that these two generous people had no idea how much this act of selflessness would change theirs.

'I have to go now,' said Anita, falling from her chair.

'Not until you have had a few hours' sleep. You'll not get nowhere unless you do.'

as that really a City Corporation dustcart, thought Anita as she ran. The few hours of sleep in Bernhardt and Jessica's dwelling had not been nearly enough. However, to stay longer would endanger them and the child they had named Martya.

'Where do you think you're going, girl?' asked the woman in brown City Corporation overalls.

'I be summoned to yonder church in Bailesparc, Ma'am,' said Anita, in her best serf accent. Still dressed in the borrowed serf's grey outfit, it seemed appropriate. Anita wished she still had her lined brown woollen coat, the night was bitter. It would have clashed with the rest of her disguise.

'You know, somehow, I don't think so,' replied the woman. 'You're heading in the wrong direction.'

Hang on a minute, the City Corporation doesn't employ women as dustmen. It doesn't employ women at all. That voice was far too familiar.

'Imogen, is that you?' asked Anita stupidly.

'Yes, Anita,' said Imogen, close to tears and in a very childlike voice. 'I knew it was my little grey girl come to visit me.'

'Princess, how did you get out of the Inner Bailey?' asked Prince David.

'Please don't call me that,' replied Anita. 'My name is Anita. I'm not that creature. She was a construct of our common enemy.'

'You don't look well, Anita. Falada said you would be suffering from exhaustion, after expelling you know who.' Imogen wrapped her arms around her friend. 'It's so good to have you back.'

Anita almost collapsed onto Imogen. 'I don't know about that. I have been lying low in the Middle Bailey. I helped to cook the serfs' evening meal. I'm shattered after the hard work.'

'You're lucky to catch us,' said Imogen.

'I...' said Anita enigmatically before she collapsed.

'You back already?' asked the young Chessman at the portcullis of the Eastern Bridge. 'You can't have done a full run. That takes most of the morning.'

'We only come to grab the stiff from the Middle Bailey, like.' replied Carlo. 'On a coffin run.'

'Why didn't you say so?' The Chessman walked round to the back of the cart, and saw the deathly white Anita lying in the scoop. Even in death, serfs had no respect. They were given no funeral rites. Their bodies would be carted to the local digester plant, minced into the city's food waste and used to generate methane. Any remains would then be liquidised into a slurry and spread as fertilizer on local fields.

'Yeah, and we were diverted from the start of our normal run as well. This will put us back hours. So, if you could let us go quick, chief, we would be grateful!'

In the Guard Room, the Chessman's radio was demanding his attention. He should really stop the truck until he had dealt with the call. However, the pleading look on the face of the driver, and the Chessman's disquiet about the way the poor girl's body.

'Hold a moment, I'm coming with you,' the Chessman said, as he raised the barrier.

'What?' asked the driver.

'I am still a servant of the Angels, trapped amongst the deluded followers of the Mad Queen. As much as I dislike the idea of deserting my post, if I remain here, I will join that poor girl on her journey to the afterlife.'

'Climb aboard,' said the driver.

'Throw your weapon in the moat, While I handcuff you,' said Prince David. 'Better safe than sorry, old chap.'

T he Basilica was ablaze with lights, full of busy clergymen
and laity, following a well-rehearsed plan.

'Them churchmen are dead rubbish at revolutions. They
rely on us regulars to keep things balanced, y'know.' said
the girl who was shepherding Imogen through the Basilica.

Carlo, Prince David and the Chessman had gone off with a
group of worried-looking Caretakers. Anita had her own guide to
take her to the Palace, who appeared to know a quicker route.

'I know you!' Imogen told the youngster. 'You're Jadwiga Anna
Orlov Smitz!'

'I remember you too. You're Johanna, from Duisenstein's!'

'Your mother gave me a frightful ear-bashing. Accused me of
encouraging you to run away. She's worried sick. Poor woman.'

'Well, she knows I'm sound, been like that all week, so she
oughta say sorry to you,' said Jadwiga with the arrogance of a
teenager. 'I decided to do one off on me own. "Me an' Janek used
ter split the housework, forty/sixty, like. But when 'e started at the
Jeweller's Trade School, 'e was given a pass on his forty percent.
So I was left stuck at home doin' nowt but cleanin' with me mum.
First time she let me out shoppin' on me own, I came 'ere. I went
ter the Caretakers for protection, y'know? She doesn't miss me,
she just misses 'er little slave!'

'So what are you now, if not being the clergy's servant?' Imogen
could not help but notice that Jadwiga was wearing an Altar
Servant's blue cassock and white surplice. If memory served her,
the Altar Servants worked their socks off to keep the Basilica
and other churches clean and tidy.

'While the Caretakers are mediating between meself and me
parents, I work ten hours a week to cover me board and lodgings.

I'm studying in the Basilica School now. I passed the entrance exams for Castle Rock Academy with flying colours. If I get a bursary from the Caretakers, then I can devote all me time to me studies. I'm never going back to me parents.'

'Oh, I see,' said Imogen, feeling a little sad that things had developed this way. 'I can see a little royal intervention is called for.'

The girl stopped in her tracks and looked at Imogen. The light of realisation dawning on the her face. 'Oh, Angels preserve me, you're her! You're the one they're all talking about. The new Queen! You're not Johanna Wellingford, you're Queen Louise I. Aren't you?'

'Yes, Jadwiga, I am.' Then asking her own question, 'Aren't you going to curtsey? Every other woman in the building has?'

'I heard about what you said to the Dean's wife. It spread like wildfire.'

'You're supposed to bow and scrape until I tell you to stop.'

'So I can't call you Johanna any more? It's much nicer than "Your Majesty".'

'Not in public, where everything has to be done with decorum.'

'Which is why it is so important that you do not make your entrance to the meeting in my Palace dressed like a bin collector,' said the Prime Caretaker, who had just appeared, as if by magic. 'Jadwiga, my dear, take our Queen to the Royal Suite in the guest quarters, help her change into something more regal. Then, young lady, it's well past your bedtime.'

Jadwiga bowed. 'Yes, Your Holiness.'

Twenty minutes later, Imogen was wearing the Prussian blue and gold costume her mother had worn on all State occasions, the one with the long train.

'You chose this one deliberately, didn't you, Jadwiga?' she asked.

'No, Ma'am,' the girl curtseyed. 'It was the one labelled "For the Coronation".' She curtseyed again.

'Please don't do that, you are making me seasick. And we're in private now, you have my permission to call me just Johanna away from prying eyes.'

'Yes, Ma'am, sorry Ma'am,' the girl said, curtseying again. 'Sorry, Ma'am. I mean Johanna.'

'Monarchs can change their names at their coronation. Everyone will have to get used to me being Johanna.'

"Yer gonna be Queen Johanna IV. Would yer not rather be Queen Imogen I?" asked Jadwiga.

'Imogen was a name used by my family, and I never liked Louise. I was always going to be Johanna IV. Now back to this dress. You will have to come with me now, to manage this train.'

'Cheers, Johanna, and don't fret, there'll be loads of decorum.'

Imogen could see that Jadwiga could hardly hide her delight. She had moaned all the time about how she would tell her grand-children that she missed Queen Johanna's first act as a Monarch because she had been sent to bed.

'If I remember correctly, there will be the fancy outfit that the Queen's maid wore on ceremonial duties in one of the side rooms. You had better go and get ready. I hope you make a better lawyer than Queen's Dresser,' said Imogen.

'Ma'am?' Jadwiga was shocked into formality.

'Well, that is what you are at the moment. The Queen's Dresser.'

'So, what if I am, Johanna? I still don't understand,' the girl said.

'It is traditional for the Queen to give her dresser a substantial gift when she leaves the Queen's service. This used to be a dowry, but I think the cost of your education would be more appropriate. Remember what I was trying to say in the Basilica. About royal intervention.'

'Oh thank you, Johanna,' said Jadwiga, who looked as if all her birthdays had come together. Then she hugged Imogen. 'I'll be the best lawyer on or off the planet.' Jadwiga then realised what she was doing and released the other woman.

'There are a couple of conditions,' said Imogen. 'You have to visit me regularly. I want to keep up to date with your progress. Also, you must return home. Your family is so old-fashioned, they need to be brought up to date.'

'Oh,' the girl's face dropped.

'Don't worry, Jadwiga. I'll not let them turn you back into a domestic drudge. I'll take you home and deliver a royal command to your parents, telling them not to stand in the way of your education. That should silence your parent's opposition.'

Once again, the girl was smiling.

eing locked inside the Inner Bailey by the serfs had been embarrassing. However, there was no way Lord Vernon was going to be trapped in there. He never thought he would be grateful for the Cannon Jumping equipment on the Keep's flat roof. The compressed air cannon had fired him high into the sky then the wing-like parachute had landed him safely on the ground outside the Inner Bailey walls. Every second of the jump had been more terrifying than exhilarating.

The goddess had told him the details of her long plan to regain control of Anseris and destroy all traces of corrupting industry. The goddess would return the planet to the agrarian paradise it was always meant to be. The fact that her current host had vanished from the Inner Bailey meant the Valentine Device had managed to free her again. Lord Vernon knew that if he destroyed the interfering article, then the goddess would be able to reclaim Duchess Anita and carry on her return to glory.

He knew it was somewhere in the supposedly haunted gatehouse; the idiot Conranski had said the late Princess Louise had spent a great deal of time there. What a despicable creature she had been, born to be the vessel that held the goddess. She had rejected that honour. It was good she was dead.

hatever you're doing, Vernon, there are two excellent reasons why you have chosen an awful time to do it,' Falada said, as he sensed the man entering the gatehouse. 'First, I'm currently battling your fake deity. Second, I'm managing the final discharge of the prison ship's engines. I noticed a week ago that they were finally going critical. I can either absorb all the energy the process will release and use it to recrystallise my hardware, or I can let the Castle and a large chunk of Elizaburg vaporise.'

'I don't understand what you are saying, machine, but that is of no consequence. When I destroy your physical form, you will be no block to the goddess.'

There was a loud shriek and a burst of light exploded from the floor of the gatehouse. For a few seconds, the temperature dropped to below freezing, then rose to a sultry heat before returning to normal.

'You do not frighten me with your conjuring tricks, you know,' said Lord Vernon, who was opening boxes and searching in cupboards. 'The stories of ghosts and demons are there to keep the hard of thinking away.'

'Well, the discharges are dangerous to Humans – that one killed you. You're a high tech ghost now.' Falada was speaking, but Lord Vernon was not listening. He was becoming increasingly desperate in his search for Falada's physical form.

'Is this what you are looking for?' Falada asked. 'It's out of phase with Higgs Bosons when I am operating, only the horse-head projection is visible.' The crystal sculpture of a horse's head on top of a marble rod and base appeared in front of Lord Vernon, accompanied by a clap of thunder. Wraith-like clouds of plasma began chasing each other around the building. 'But as you're dead and this is just an electro-psychic projection, smash away.'

'Your phantasms do not scare me, your capitulation makes my task so much easier. When you are shattered, the goddess will be pleased with me.' He produced a massive metal hammer from his cape and began smashing the sculpture.

'If you were listening, you would know the apparent haunting has nothing to do with me, it is all due to the engine buried deep below. Smash away, there is no way you can cause anything more than cosmetic damage. Even if you were not dead and could run, you could not get the recommended minimum distance of fifty yards away from here before the final phase. You're a dead man.'

'For the goddess!' screamed Lord Vernon as he brought his hammer down again. The sculpture exploded into a million tiny pieces. The building exploded, vaporising Lord Vernon's body.

'Cosmetic damage? I think that is more than cosmetic damage.'

'Not really.' The shards of crystals came back together. 'You're already dead, so I don't know why I am explaining myself.'

'Nonsense, what do you mean already...' The last electro-psychic after-image of Vernon faded before it could finish the sentence.

The plasma created by the explosion was trapped inside a

spherical force-field. It glowed bright blue, green and purple as it rose directly up from the spot where the gatehouse once stood, accelerating away from the planet like a rocket in flight.

The meeting was not going well. So many different groups representing so many causes. The only thing that united them had been their hatred of King Benedict III. Now that he was gone, there was almost no common ground.

'I could have stayed in bed,' said Shandra to her neighbour.

'Couldn't we all. But then we might have missed something,' the man next to her replied.

'You honestly think anything is going to come from this mess, do you, Ieuan?' the woman to Shandra's left asked.

'Yes, I do, Alexa.'

'Ieuan ap Iolo. Wow. I thought you were in hiding,' said Shandra. 'I'm Elashandra Sigurdort.'

'Oh, the Prince's squeeze,' said the other woman rudely.

'I beg your pardon, madam?' Shandra was now annoyed.

'The Be-Trade Unionist. After a quick roll in the hay with royalty, you're willing to sell your members down the river.'

'I don't know who you are, or what you are talking about. I am a friend to all, royalty and commoners alike!'

'More than a friend to Crown-Prince David,' said the woman.

'Harrumph.' It was the only thing she could think to say. She certainly did not want to continue this conversation.

'You can harrumph as much as you like. I'm not talking to the likes of you.'

'Yes you are, and being your usual charmless self,' said Ieuan. 'Don't take her too seriously, Shandra – if I may call you Shandra. She is Alexa Tring. She represents a group of intellectuals who think they speak for the ordinary people. In reality, they want to run the lives of the ordinary people who generally ignore them. You have done more for ordinary working people than Alexa there could dream of. Your spare time is entirely up to you.'

'Thank you, Ieuan.'

'You're welcome, Shandra.' He was distracted by the sound of clanking metal. 'Hello, here comes Roswall. I wonder what he wants.'

Prince David walked into the room, wearing a complete set of plate armour, but in deference to the holy ground he was standing on he was unarmed. His tabard had the Coat of Arms of House Rushton-Browne. The silver crown, which had sat at the heart of the Arms for a century, had been carefully removed.

'Your Holiness Prime Caretaker Thompson-Uther, Commissioner Caisson of the Secret Police, Commissioner Federn of the Criminal Police, High-Over-General Picton of the Combined Services, ladies and gentlemen of the Alliance, welcome, all of you.'

'What do you want, Mr Rushton-Browne?' asked Commissioner Federn. 'You should be under arrest. We all hated the old King, but none of us would approve of his murder.'

'The evidence of Baronet Vernon's guilt for that crime has been distributed to all law enforcement agencies on the Home-world and beyond. As his boss has changed sides, he has no-one to protect him after I retake Ellisford Castle.'

'So what are you doing here?' asked the commissioner, 'if you're dressed for battle?'

'I asked Prime Caretaker Thompson-Uther to arrange for you all to come to this meeting,' said Prince David, 'and none of you expected to be in the same room, on the same side.'

'Get on with it, my son!' said the Prime Caretaker.

'I come here to make history, to introduce you to your true Queen.'

Imogen entered the room on cue, resplendent in her heavy blue velvet ceremonial outfit.

'Johanna? But you're the Goose Maiden,' said Shandra from the back of the room, shocked to see her friend in all her finery.

'She's not the Goose Maiden any more, Shandra, she is our rightful Queen,' said Prince David. 'I hereby publicly abdicate from the role of Prince of the Kingdom of Anseris. I also renounce my title of Archduke. I am merely a soldier and a citizen of this world and a subject of Queen Johanna, our true Queen, to whom I pledge my life-long allegiance.'

'I'm confused,' said one of the men present. 'I thought Princess Anita was to be Joint-Monarch with you after King Benedict.'

'So my father led you to believe. However, I have learnt the truth.' He pressed a button on the table, as a large picture appeared on a display screen above him. 'As you can see, the woman wearing a crown is almost identical to the woman you know as Dame Imogen, the Goose Maiden. She is Queen Gertrude III. The one girl bears an uncanny likeness to the older woman, is wearing the same dress as the Queen and a coronet. This is the young Dame Imogen, or Princess Louise Imogen, as she was then. The other girl is wearing a slightly plainer outfit and looks like a younger Princess Anita. The records describe a missing photograph like this, taken just before Princess Imogen's ninth birthday. I believe this is that long-missing photograph.'

'You're saying we've been had, David?' asked the leader of one of the Rebel Groups.

'Yes, Pierre, we have.' Prince David replied. 'As I understand it, the Princess Louise Imogen and her companion Duchess Anita were send to the planet called Grimmswald to gain aid against the Fenzrian invaders. They found themselves trapped in a hyperspace anomaly, like flies in amber, for a hundred years. Her Royal Highness, Crown Princess Louise Imogen Johanna Gertrude of House Ellisford-Castle, to introduce herself to this august body explain what happened to her during the Fenzrian War.'

'My fellow Anserians,' said Imogen in a quiet voice, almost drowned out by the voices in the crowd. The voices of people who had already met and respected Imogen were full of pleasant surprise. The voices of those who had not were full of doubt and suspicion. 'I was born over a century ago, born to be your Queen.'

'Be silent for your Queen!' shouted the Prime Caretaker. With that, there was silence, as everyone respected this real man of faith.

'Thank you, Prime Caretaker.' Imogen was displaying more confidence and in a loud and clear voice continued. 'I was born to be a carbon copy of my mother, to follow on her road of modest reforms. She saw Anseris had to change to survive, but she was only willing to change what she thought needed to be changed. Change accelerated with the arrival of her half-sister, Princess Marie-Anne, but it was never fast enough. That is why I will never be her carbon copy. I have seen every facet of society, and I know that this world needs root and branch reform. As your

Queen, I vow to reform the government, introducing the universal suffrage and representative democracy which so many of you want. To end the flow of wealth from the ordinary people to the already wealthy. As many of you also want, I will abolish the feudal system, ushering in a world where a person's worth is measured by their ability, not measured by who their father and grandfather were. To bring true equality to the sexes and make this planet and its off-world settlements somewhere we are all proud to call home.'

'So where have you been 'til now, darling?' called out Alexa Tring, with the support of some members of the Democratic Alliance. This was followed by loud heckling, telling Alexa to shut up and listen.

'Be silent in the presence of your Queen,' ordered the Prime Caretaker.

'I was coming to that,' continued Imogen, who was quite enjoying herself now. 'On board the ship carrying myself and Duchess Anita on our failed diplomatic mission was a dangerous stowaway. We did not know the ghost of Kathyren Ellisford-Castle slept deep in my subconscious mind. I had carried her since birth. If conditions had ever been right, then she would have awoken and stolen my body. Each Free Queen carried this curse, until the birth of their first and equally cursed daughter.'

'Nice ghost story. So what?' demanded Alexa Tring.

'We needed to use a Fenzrian teaching machine aboard our ship,' said Imogen, ignoring the heckling. 'We did not understand the technology, but the ghost did. She decided Duchess Anita was a better host. For many months my friend has been possessed by pure evil. One of my allies has exorcised Duchess Anita and destroyed the Immortal Empress, forever.'

'It is now safe for me to emerge from hiding. With your help, as my Royal Councillors I will bring a new age to this Bless'd Orb, her five sisters and high Pendragon.'

Once again the Prime Caretaker rapped his staff against the floor and called for silence. Then he opened the box in front of him, it contained the Queen's crown, orb and sceptre. Relics that had been lost since House Rushton-Browne ascended to the throne.

'Only a true possessor of Blood Royale may wear this crown,' said the Prime Caretaker as he removed a scroll from his robes containing the new Coronation Oath

'Kneel, my child,' instructed the Prime Caretaker and Imogen did as she was told. 'Do you, Princess Louise Imogen Johanna Gertrude Ellisford-Castle of Anseris swear to uphold the Laws and Honour of this Kingdom?'

'I, Princess Louise Imogen Johanna Gertrude Ellisford-Castle of Anseris, so swear.'

He placed the orb in her left hand. 'Do you swear to defend the poor and wretched with all your heart?'

'To my last breath, I so swear.'

He placed the sceptre in her right hand. 'Will you swear to stand as the Defender of the Faith of your ancestors?'

'I so swear.'

He poured three drops of oil on her head. 'I anoint you, Princess Louise Imogen Johanna Gertrude Ellisford-Castle of Anseris, with the sacred oil and place this crown upon your head. Be Princess Louise Imogen no more.' The ancient gold band slipped onto Imogen's head. 'Arise, Queen Johanna, fourth of that name. Long live the Queen.'

Everybody saw the blue nimbus engulf Imogen. It always happened when the crown was placed on the new Queen's head. Nobody knew the significance or realised the danger.

# 42

Imogen found herself standing alone on moorland with a cold wind blowing. The air was full of a fine misty drizzle and the sky above almost black with clouds.

'At last, I shall be myself again,' said an ancient voice. Standing a few feet away from Imogen was an older woman, who could have been her mother, if her mother had completely white hair cropped into a severe, almost masculine style, or ever wore a brown jumpsuit. Unlike the previous encounters, Queen Kathyren appeared solid, but still not flesh and blood. Imogen knew she had entered into her adversary's virtual world.

'I thought you said my body wasn't suitable because my mind was corrupted?' asked Imogen.

'That was true until you had your pretty head anointed with Glaven Oil which counteracts the effects of Moonglow. Now you wear my crown. It amplifies me and condenses you. I have been able to burrow deep into your mind and establish this, my inner sanctum. Once I have extinguished your life force, I will emerge.'

'I've beaten you in the past, I will do so again,' said Imogen.

'No, B426, you have never defeated me. The interfering Valentine Device has always protected you. My minion has eradicated it.'

'No, I don't believe you.'

'It's true. You've no rescuer this time.' Queen Kathyren smiled an evil smile. 'I know, you have made all those stupid radical promises that you honestly believe in – that liberty, equality and fraternity rubbish. But that is the curse of youth. As my new reign continues, people will just say you became more reactionary in your old age.' The former ghost was now walking towards her.

Imogen was wearing a heavy black woollen dress, weighed down by gallons of ice cold water. She gathered up her hems and tried to move. Each step was like walking through mud.

'You are in my domain now, did you think I would let you run? Not that running would do you any good. Wherever you went, you would be running to me.'

The floor beneath her changed. It became a firm roadway, and she found herself wearing a tracksuit and running shoes.

'However, the exit is that way,' said Falada, appearing as a perfect white stallion.

Imogen could see a gate in the distance. She knew if she could make it there she would be safe.

'In that form, it would be quicker if I rode you, Falada,' she said to the horse. 'I can ride bareback.'

'Unfortunately, I have my work to do here.'

'I won't ask how you survived, I don't care. You are weak after the explosion,' said Queen Kathyren, now dressed as an Anserian Queen. 'My hounds used to feast on the horses destroyed when they fell in the hunt. You are nought but dog food.'

Falada found himself surrounded by a pack of vicious dogs, snapping at his hooves and lower legs. He kicked three of them away and raised himself up onto his hind legs, and with a blast of energy, like a ripple on a pond, vaporised the dogs. Bloodied but unbroken he moved towards the evil Queen. 'Is that the best you can do?'

'Oh, I can do better than that,' said the ghost who had now materialised in front of the gate Imogen was running towards. 'Didn't I tell you? This is my virtual world – did you think I would make it that easy for you?'

Imogen had spotted the ghost and was about to turn around.

'No, Imogen, it's a trap. Queen Kathyren is still here. If you turn and run back here, you will be running to her, and she will just suck you in. Keep running to the gate.'

'Enough of this,' said Queen Kathyren, as she transformed into a creature with a snake-like body. Its head was like a triceratops. It possessed four legs and two arms. Finally, it had long, leathery wings.

'Adopting that form isn't going to help you,' said Falada.

'Isn't it?' replied the draconic Kathyren, as she let out a blast of flames.

'No, it is not.' A golden sphere had formed around Falada, and the flames glided around it. 'Lame, very lame.'

'The only lame thing here will be you, horse meat!'

Imogen had almost reached the gate. Before Imogen could pass through it, the draconic creature fired a gout of flames. The heat melted the metal and charred the stonework black. The blast knocked Imogen off the road where the long grass braided into ropes around her body to tie her firmly in place.

T he Prime Caretaker watched as his new Queen stood, as stationary as a mannequin. She must be savouring the moment. He spotted the blue light arcing around her head and knew something was amiss. Oh, Angels forgive me. How could I have been so stupid, the old man thought. The crown was booby-trapped. It was Queen Kathyren's last laugh. It had been the old witch's favourite punishment, trapping people like statues until their bodily functions failed. No, the Moonglow avatar should have protected Queen Johanna. But where was that avatar?

'Jadwiga, why is the Queen not wearing her avatar?' he asked the girl.

'I thought it looked out of place with all the finery,' she replied.

'Where is it?' he hissed.

'In my pocket. Why?'

'Give it to me girl. Now!'

'Yes, your Holiness.'

I f this is a reality built inside my head, out of my thoughts, then I have ultimate control, don't I, Queen Kathyren?' asked Imogen. The dragon said nothing. 'Grass, release me from thy bondage.'

Sure enough, the rope untied and returned to its original form.

'Gate, repair thyself.' The structure reappeared, gleaming and new. Imogen began walking towards it.

'You're not getting away, I need your body.' The dragon took to the air. 'I must destroy your mind. I'm coming to get you.'

'Not the most elegant of flyers, are you?' asked Falada, who flew effortlessly, having transformed into a Pegasus with brilliant white swan's wings.

'This body is too ungainly. I need something more nimble,' said Queen Kathyren. 'I know, someone you recognise.' The dragon faded and was replaced by an angel. 'How do I look? Like one of your friends, the friends you betrayed your creators to help?'

'You are no angel. Neither the creatures of myth nor the aliens who inspired them. If you want some feathers, have them.'

With a powerful beat of his wings, a barrage of white feathers flew towards Queen Kathyren, far faster than she could create a shield. When one of the feathers hit her it exploded and triggered its neighbour. Under this barrage, Queen Kathyren could not hold the form of an angel and reverted to her original shape. With no wings, even in this dream world, she plummeted to the ground.

'Why, this is my domain. I should be impregnable here.' she said as Falada landed next to her.

'It's not your domain, it's her impregnable one,' he said.

The sky was ablaze with the colour of Moonglow, illuminated by the light from three red orbs, the blasted heath replaced by well-tended parkland. Only one piece of grey moorland remained, where Kathyren Ellisford-Castle lay broken.

'You have been incorporeal for too long, Queen Kathyren. The previous encounters with me have weakened you even further. I was simply goading you, encouraging you to use more and more of your dwindling energies.'

'I know that now. One more strike and I am dead. All those centuries of knowledge and experience snuffed out in seconds.'

'I shall mourn your passing, Katherine Wellisford, as I mourn all loss of life. But life is finite.'

'I don't want to die.'

'Nothing does, but it is not the end. It is the beginning of a new existence beyond the realm of Baryonic Matter.' As Kathyren Ellisford-Castle faded for the last time.

# 43

'**A**re you all right, Your Majesty?' she heard the Prime Caretaker Thompson-Uther asked after he fastened her Moonglow in place and she shuddered back to life. Imogen found herself standing once more in the meeting room of the Prime Caretaker's Palace. But Imogen no longer. She was now Queen Johanna.

'Yes, thank you, Your Holiness,' Queen Johanna replied, quickly realising that neither the old cleric nor any of the other people in the room would understand what had happened. Virtual Reality had to be seen to be believed. 'It's just I always imagined my coronation would be a more sumptuous affair,' she said, a more acceptable reply.

'Don't worry, Ma'am,' replied the old man, 'we can arrange a more impressive ceremony for public consumption, once this current crisis has passed.'

'You'll be pleased to know that Princess Stefania is off the critical list,' said Commissioner Caisson, as he put a chair behind his new Queen and helped her sit up.

'Also, the Duchess Anita has been given a clean bill of health and is now in custody,' said Commissioner Federn.

'Well, my first act as Queen is to pardon her, in full, for any actions she made while under the control of Queen Kathyren, an ancient evil that is now gone forever.'

'Your Majesty,' they said in unison. 'She in in a cell here in the Palace. Releasing her won't be a problem,' said Commissioner Federn

'Commissioners, have her escorted to Archive Room 42, in the Basilica's basement. I want to show her something.'

'Is that wise, Your Majesty?' asked Commissioner Caison. 'What if you are wrong about the Immortal Empress?'

'Believe me, Commissioner, I am not wrong.' Queen Johanna stood back up and turned to the assembled audience, the one-time rebels who were now all Royal Councillors.

'So, down to business. I believe Archduchess Elashandra Rackham-Winter has a working constitution for you to consider.'

'Who? What? I'm no Archduchess.'

'I believe your main objection to marrying the Archduke was your difference in station,' said the new Queen. 'Now you are equals, there is nothing to stop you.'

'We are equals now. Both commoners without titles. What difference does it make?' asked Shandra.

'I don't see the problem in that,' said the former Prince David.

'Oh, you will, Archduke David, you will,' said Johanna. 'It's all optics. If we get a new constitution based on Shandra's proposal, the Ristoze will continue to cherish their meaningless titles. Closing ranks because it will be the only thing they have to make them feel important. If you give up your title, they will ignore you because you will no longer be one of them.'

'I don't see a problem with that,' said Shandra.

'The transition from one form of government to another must be smooth. You will need to keep the Ritozes on-side.'

'Why? We have the head aristocrat herself on-side,' said Shandra.

'Who, me? I have never been Ristoze,' said Queen Johanna with a laugh. 'I was once and am once more Royalty. They have always shown deference to, but been envious of me.

'Your Majesty. We have already rejected that proposal,' said one of the representatives. 'It will never get through the Witan.'

'Ladies and gentlemen of the Royal Council, there is no Witan. You have completely replaced that body. I want a broad-based system with many sources of expertise, not one which consists only of Dukes and Archdukes.'

There was a cheer from the assembled group.

'Don't cheer yet,' said the Prime Caretaker. 'You still have a lot of work to do before our new Queen can make her first act as a Constitutional Monarch. She has to use the power of an Absolute Monarch to sign that new constitution to make it law.'

'So, I expect my first Parliament to reconvene here at 10.30am, to begin work on the new constitution.' As Johanna stood up, the entire room stood with her. This was so odd. She spotted a yawning girl. 'Jadwiga, you are one Royal Councillor who needs her beauty sleep.'

'Seriously?' the girl asked.

'Who else is going to speak for the young people? They need a voice in the framing of the new constitution. But I don't envy you.'

'No,' added the Prime Caretaker. 'Trying to fit all the meetings in between your school work, Councillor Orlov Smitz, will not be an easy task. History has shown that constitutional conventions are deadly dull things. Soon you will be begging to be relieved of your office.'

'Not a chance,' said Jadwiga. 'See you all tomorrow.'

Anita sat in the basement of the Basilica, feeling miserable. Oh what a mess she had made of her life. Allowing herself to be taken over by that evil creature. Misbehaving under its influence, she had treated Imogen like dirt, being haughty and obnoxious. Marion would be so ashamed of her.

Anita knew Imogen was Queen now, and wondered what punishment her former friend would dole out.

'Anita, it's so good to see you fully free again,' said Queen Johanna as she entered the room.

'Your Majesty,' said Anita as she rose to her feet.

'Oh, please don't be so formal, you are my oldest friend.'

'I have betrayed you so badly. I do not deserve to be anyone's friend,' Anita said, as she burst into tears.

'Don't be silly, you were not yourself. I don't hold any grudges.' Queen Johanna placed a comforting arm around the other woman.

'You don't?'

'No. I have already officially pardoned you, Anita, dear.'

'So I don't face the iron shoes?' she asked with relief.

'That is a barbaric punishment.'

'It was the traditional punishment for imposters.'

'But that is in the past, Anita.'

'My love is in the past, Johanna. Dead and buried while I still live. Oh, I miss Aarne so much already.'

'That is why I wanted you to be brought here. I have something to show you.'

The room seemed different. Johanna didn't know why, seems like so long since she was here with the Prime Caretaker.

'So this is his grave?' she heard Anita ask. 'Thank you for bringing me here. I needed to see it.'

Johanna could see her friend was once more in tears.

'Oh Aarne. I love you,' Anita said, planting a gentle kiss on the statue lying atop the sarcophagus.

'I should hope so too,' said a voice both women recognised. 'If the boffins were right I've spent roughly a century in suspended animation waiting for you.'

'Aarne! It's you. You're alive.'

'Of course I am, old love.'

'Some things never change,' said Anita. 'You know how much I hate being called that.'

'Fact is, we are old, relatively speaking, after all the years we have been away.'

'Over one hundred years on the Standard Galactic Calendar.'

'Oh, hello, Your Majesty. You are Queen now, aren't you? When I put myself into that box, which was a very rum sensation, Marie-Ann was the Regent.'

'The Regency survived for all of twelve months after you put yourself into suspended animation. Marie-Ann, and anyone who supported her were marooned with no spacecraft on a lunar colony that is now called the Free Republic of Marion. I had to deal with the usurpers who won the Civil War.'

'Don't tell me, let me guess. Archduke Rushton-Browne put himself on the throne.'

'Indeed, until the recent death of his grandson, King Benedict III, his family refused to vacate the throne,' continued Johanna. 'Not that you two care about any of that at the moment. Just remember, you are in Church.'

Queen Johanna slipped quietly back into the Cottage the day after it had been cleared of any booby traps left behind by Lord Vernon and his supporters. Parts of the building were unstable. They would have to be demolished then rebuilt.

Sarah and Clarice had been offered new and better jobs, but said they were happy where they were. They would move back into the renovated cottage, with the next Goose Maiden.

Chrystine was moving to Tintagel, capital of Carlton. To be a Prussian Blue nurse in the Central Hospital, where her fiance, Dr. Tom Butlerien now worked.

Queen Johanna asked the Princess Stefanie to be the Goose Maiden again. She politely refused. She had been secretly courting a Jovian Baron her father had disapproved of, and would move to Athens III when she married him. She suggested Lady Briony Uther-Thompson, who would be a very modern Goose Maiden.

She walked around the crater where the gatehouse had stood.

'I'm already thousands of light years away, on a one-way trip.'

'So I will be without your good counsel, my friend.' There were tears in Johanna's eyes.

'You have grown so much in the time I have known you, dearest Imogen. You don't need me, neither does Anseris. However, there are hundreds thousands people rescued by the Aggelii from the wreckage of the Great Machine. They have arrived on their new home-world, they need a mentor for a new civilisation. When I arrive, they will be woken from suspended animation, wondering how they will be able to cope with only Iron Age technology.'

'But who can I turn to?'

'Your fellow Humans. You have Anita and Aarne, David and Shandra. And especially Carlo. You are both going to find the next nine months interesting. If you are not already pregnant, you soon will be. You'll give birth to a daughter. Some things, I'm afraid, cannot be changed.'

'No, I do have some control over that. I think I will wait until I've been married to Carlo for a couple of years.'

'You see, you don't need a silly old AI like me.'

'So this is goodbye, my friend.'

'Yes, Johanna. Goodbye. May you all live happily ever after.'

# Glossary

**T**his novel is set on a world based on a ficticious psychopathic nut-job's vision of the European Middle Ages. To help paint a picture, the text has been peppered with words from that era. Their definitions can be found below.

Articles of clothing worn by a single gender is marked (F) or (M), otherwise marked (C). Architectural features are marked (A). Jewellery terms are marked (J).

| | |
|---|---|
| Aventurisation (J) | The concentration of metal particles within a gem that gives the appearance of liquid trapped within the crystal. |
| Bandeau (F) | A strip of cloth wound around the torso to support the breasts. |
| Barbette (F) | Narrow strip of cloth worn vertically around the face for attaching veils. |
| Braies (M) | Baggy knee-length underpants for attaching hose. |
| Bycocket (C) | Robin Hood's hat pointed at each end with a feather. Worn by men and women. |
| Cape (C) | An outdoor garment fastened by a pin or broach at the shoulders. Sometimes with a hood. |
| Chause (M) | Leggings attached to Braies with a garter at the knee to stop the garment sagging. |
| Chemise (F) | Full-length undergarment. |
| Cloak | An overcoat, with or without hood. |
| Codpiece (M) | A pouch to which Hose were attached at the crotch to accommodate male anatomy. |

| | |
|---|---|
| Coif (C) | Close-fitting, semi-circular hat. |
| Cotehardie (C) | A short tunic. |
| Crumhorn | An early woodwind instrument and musical abomination. |
| Fillet (F) | Narrow strip of cloth worn horizontally around the forehead for attaching veils. |
| Furlong | One-eighth of a mile. Literally a furrow long, as it was the length of the strips of land used in English agriculture in the Middle Ages. |
| Gambeson (M) | Quilted jacket worn as armour by archers. |
| Goffered (F) | Corrugated fringe on the front of a veil. |
| Gorgette (F) | Similar to a Wimple but looser and made of more lavish material. |
| Hood (C) | Large collar and hood. |
| Hose (C) | Thick woollen tights similar to leggings. |
| Jettying (A) | Constructing each story of a building to overhang the one below. |
| Kirtle (F) | Basic dress with detachable sleeves. Worn over Chemise and Bandeau but under Surcote, Cotehardie or Hood. |
| List/List Field | The arena for jousting competitions. |
| Machicolation (A) | The spaces in the overhanging battlements of castles to allow the defender to shoot at any attacker who reaches the castle wall. |
| Shiller (J) | The apparent luminescence of a gem caused by the refraction of light within it. |

| | |
|---|---|
| Steeple Hennin (F) | Clichéd woman's pointy medieval hat with veil. |
| Surcote (C) | Long tunic worn as a robe by men and over-dress by women. Sometimes they had open hems at the side from armpit to waist. |
| Templar (F) | A pair of tubular latticed baskets for dressing hair. Attached on either side of the face, to a crown or metal fillet. |
| Tocque (F) | Circular hat with inwardly sloping sides. |
| Wimple (F) | Oblong cloth covering the neck, chin and ears, leaving only the face visible. |

# Acknowlegements

The manuscript of this novel edited by Tina Williams from TWEditorial (http://www.tweditorial.co.uk), who gave it a professional shine. A sane man would have left it as it was. I am not a sane man, and apologise for any mess I have made since.

Without my wonderful family, none of this would be possible. My mother Patricia Rees was the first person to read the first draft of this novel, and along with my sisters, Janet Guy and Carolyn Davies have listened to my ideas and been ready to give useful advice. The whole family have been a constant source of encouragement and helped to maintain my sanity during the writing process.

I also want to thank everyone else who has read and commented on my latest project. This includes my good friends Timothy Farr and Kristian Barry. Also I would like to thank Lynda Carter for her assistance throughout.

The seed of this novel was the work of Joseph and Wilhelm Grimm, who wanted to preserve the folk tales of Europe. They were not the only people to do this, two centuries earlier Giambattiasta Basile collected Italian stories, they are the best known.

As a teenager, I discovered the genius of Arthur Rackham's painting "The Goose Girl", which shows the destitute princess talking to Falada's head in a gateway. In the foreground is the shadow, which seemed far to sinister too represent the character of Conrad. Then shortly after I had started writing my science fiction version of the story, I looked at the picture again. Ideas started fizzing like a piece of Sodium in water. The character of Kathyren Ellisford was born, a shadowy and supernatural figure who was the mother of all of Imogen's misfortunes.

I was debating how much background to give the character of Anita. For research I read Philip Pulman's retelling of "The Goose Girl" and its accompanying commentary, where he wonders about the duplicitous servants motivation. I thought, if an award winning author like Pulman wants more character background, it must be a good idea.

John Campbell Rees,
31st October, 2018